Eternity

By: Andréa Kohalmi

ISBN-10: 0615545092
EAN-13: 9780615545097
Library of Congress Control Number: 2011939784
Veritas in Lumenum, Novato, CA

For JG
with love & thanks

Preface

The cold spring breeze swept over my face freezing each tear in place. I lay on the freshly cut grass staring at the trees overhead as the sun peeked through the dense coverage of leaves and branches. My hopes and dreams were like the glimmer of sunlight—just a little too far out of reach from becoming a warm reality.

Sitting up slowly, I glanced around and shuddered. This wasn't the type of place where a girlfriend and boyfriend should be hanging out together.

"I miss you, Zach," I whispered as tears streamed down my face. The wind swirled around me, chilling my body to match the frigid emotions choking me. "I miss you so much," I cried. My body convulsed on each word. "I love you. I've always loved you. I will always love you...only you."

I turned to face him and kissed his headstone.

1 ~ Getting Over It

Oh my life is changing everyday
In every possible way
And oh my dreams
It's never quite as it seems
'cause you're a dream to me
Dream to me

The Cranberries, *Dreams*, <u>Everybody else is doing it, so why can't we?</u>
Written by: Noel Hogan, Dolores O'Riordan

"Mom, you've gotta let me go."

Her arms squeezed me tighter.

"Can't…breathe…"

"But I'm not going to see you for an eternity!"

"I'm just going away for a month. We have the phone, e-mail…"

"Final call for Flight 1443, boarding at gate E2, Boston to London. Flight 1443, boarding at gate E2, Boston to London…" the static sounding airport announcement faded into the white noise around us.

I didn't like the airport. No, that's not strong enough. I hated the airport. The rushing around, security checks, and waiting to board made my stomach sick. The repellent fluorescent lighting, generic grey walls and blue carpets were enough to induce a panic attack. To make matters worse, my mom trapped me in an embrace that was trying its darndest to squeeze out my breakfast, lunch, and dinner.

"I love you, Angie. I just want you to know how much I love you."

I sighed. Her insanity was just grounded in fear. After dad died almost a year ago, she kept us kids on a very tight leash. "I know Mom. I love you too. More than anything." I hugged her back and gave her a quick kiss on the cheek. "I really need to go now, k?"

I looked into her eyes and we didn't need to say anything else. It was obvious. We were both scared, for different reasons of course, but scared nonetheless. She was afraid of losing me. I was afraid of being alone and completely independent. This month-long trip to Great Britain was forcing me to face those fears, but I found it as exhilarating as it was scary. Besides, I was heading to college in the fall so this trip was both a test run and a getaway from the depression that had been plaguing me.

I handed my ticket to the woman at the gate. "Passport," she said in a very bored tone. "An-gel-ika Kiss?"

Wince. I hated my first name—no, not hate—*despised* it. "No," I snarled through clenched teeth.

"Ahn-gay-lĭ-ka," I obnoxiously exaggerated the pronunciation. To this day I swore my mom was high on pain killers when she named me. Angel Kiss. If she had a sweet tooth at the time, my middle name would probably have been Food Cake.

Looking at me like I was crazy, the attendant slowly handed the ticket stub and passport back to me. With a smug smirk, I glanced at my mom one last time and caught her shaking her head in embarrassment. I liked how my relatively shy side melted away over the past few months. The new edgier me liked to irritate people. Maybe it was a coping mechanism to help deal with the deaths of my dad and boyfriend or maybe I was growing up. Either way, it made me feel more mature.

I smiled and waved to my mom. She blew a kiss and waved back. Turning around, I walked eagerly down the gate toward the plane.

My uncurbed excitement helped me easily overcome my flight neighbor—a rather large man whose odor reeked of salami and bad beer. To my right was an empty seat. I hoped beyond hope it would stay that way. I wasn't in the mood to be sociable. I adjusted the head rest and wrapped myself in a pale blue fleece blanket covered in white fluffy clouds. The flight was scheduled for 11 p.m., but it felt much later. The preparations for the trip, my job, and the ride to the airport wore me out. I popped a sleeping pill and passed out before the plane backed out from the gate.

A recurring childhood nightmare plagued my uneasy dreams. My high school's boisterous basketball team and cheerleaders headed out on a class field trip to a mansion in the country. Our yellow school bus wound through a dark forest along a barely visible, single lane road toward an intimidating fortress, which sat regally atop a hill. We certainly weren't in Salem anymore.

As the sun set on this cold fall day, we hopped off the bus and walked through the expansive, exquisitely manicured green grounds toward the arched doorway of the prestigious home. While my friends wandered around the first floor, my feet were pulled—as if by an unseen force—up a majestic heart-shaped stairwell. Drawn to the top floor, I found myself wandering down a long, dimly lit corridor to a room in the corner tower. Curious, I walked across the dark room and out onto the balcony. To my surprised horror, I watched helplessly as the yellow bus drove away without me. My futile screams were absorbed by the frigid gusts of wind flapping against my red and white pleated cheerleading skirt.

Returning to the room, panic set in as I struggled to figure out how to get home. A soft scratching sound pulled my attention toward the room's door. Burning red eyes pierced the blackness. The creature's crimson gaze and brilliant white fangs glistened in a ray of moonlight shining across its face. Screaming like a horror-movie queen, I ran to the balcony's edge.

Knowing it trapped me, the wild, animal-like figure laughed menacingly and crept toward me on the white stone veranda...

The sound of the plane's engine humming and salami man's snoring roused me from the nightmare. It was a miracle that I felt so comfortable; there usually wasn't any room on planes. Disoriented, I opened my eyes one by one and realized my head had slipped from the pillow. It was resting heavily on the stranger beside me. I gasped and bolted upright when I noticed a keepsake of drool on his navy blue t-shirt's sleeve.

I couldn't look in his eyes. "Um, sorry," I managed to whisper virtually inaudibly. Obviously, that wouldn't suffice. This was going to be an excruciatingly long flight if I didn't apologize properly. My face burned in humiliation.

Working up enough courage, I glanced at his face. "Uhhh, uhhh, uhhh..." was all I could muster; my mind blanked. This twenty-something deity met my gaze with a knowing smirk and a twinge of playfulness in his eyes, which sparkled in a bright blue hue like the waters of the Caribbean. His eyes were complemented by perfectly coiffed light brown, wavy hair with golden highlights. The sides were trimmed a little shorter, but his hair teased me with a run-your-fingers-through-it-if-you-dare style. Carved by a master sculptor, his rugged, chiseled face wore a kind expression.

These thoughts raced through my head in a millisecond before I blurted, "Um, I'm sorry about using you as a pillow."

My cheeks felt like an inferno raged just under my skin.

His thoughtful stare hid an air of mischief, which lingered on his cheeks and mouth. *Mmmm, his mouth.* His full lips were luscious too. His face seemed to register my instant infatuation because his smirk turned into a widespread grin.

"And I'm sorry for drooling all over your shirt." It was best to get the entire awkward introduction out of the way. Then I could close my eyes, ignore him for the rest of the flight, and pretend it never happened.

"No worries. I've actually been waiting for you to wake up," his deep, melodic voice assured, luring me like a magnet. He had a beautiful British accent. I'm a sucker for accents. They sound so exotic and certainly better than anything spoken in a Massachusetts' dialect where R's are non-existent.

"The flight's been extremely boring and I can't sleep on planes."
His sincerity was endearing too.

"Me neither," I quipped. "Sleeping pills do it for me." *Great, now
he'll think I'm an addict.* I rushed to explain, "I'm not a druggie or
anything, but I get nervous when I fly." My gaze shifted to his damp
sleeve. On my face the burn smoldered deeper.

"*Really*, it's not a problem," he said so reassuringly I couldn't help but
believe him. "So, would you like to talk? I'll go mad waiting for another
two hours until they bring my complimentary peanuts and half can of coke."

"Soda and peanuts at night? Gross!" I blurted.

"Are you more a milk and cookies type of girl?" he teased with a
sly smile curling the right side of his lips.

"So?"

He raised his eyebrows. "Are you always this testy?"

"Sorry," I muttered, horrified that I was being so rude to the kind,
heart-stoppingly beautiful man.

"I'm just teasing. So, Angel, where are you going?"

"I'm traveling through...wait a second, how d'ya know my name?"

Even in the dimly lit cabin, I could see his cheeks blush in embarrassment. "Your boarding pass."

"You dug through my stuff?!" I accused. His sweet gaze defused
my anger and I immediately felt guilty for jumping to conclusions.

"No," he responded slowly, reproachfully. "You were already using
me as your pillow. I had very few options to keep myself occupied. I
counted the windows, overhead lights and compartments before I saw
your ticket sticking out of the bag. In case you're interested, there are
two hundred thirty-nine lights..."

"Not interested..." I was still peeved he read my name. "Why did
you call me 'Angel' though?" I turned toward him, propping one knee
on the seat so I could face him. Plane seats are not conducive to con-
venient conversations.

"I just figured a girl like you doesn't go by Angelika. That would
be like calling Heidi Klum, Brunhilda," his eyes twinkled playfully. I
couldn't help but laugh.

I felt so comfortable beside this god-like creature. I sat next to lots of cute, even hot-looking guys in high school but none ever paid this much attention to me. This one was different. I'd never seen a man so strikingly handsome in my entire life. His close shaven, flawless skin radiated a pale, pearlescent hue. His face literally glowed as the moonlight illuminated it.

"Angel is a perfect name for you," he stated emphatically.

"And why's that?" I asked, sensing a pick-up line was about to follow.

"Your auburn hair glows with golden highlights. It smells heavenly by the way, like coconut…I love coconut," he admitted nervously as his eyes met mine. The soft overhead lights accentuated the soft pink blush of his cheeks. "And your eyes—they sparkle like emeralds and…"

Shaking my head vigorously, I held up my palm to interrupt him. I hated being complimented even if it sounded like poetry spoken from the lips of a god. I was no angel. I was more like one of God's prototypes before the creation of the supermodels—an accident that got tossed into humanity's 'oops' pile.

"It's easy to be an angel with the help of lots of makeup," I said flippantly.

"Let me guess, you don't like compliments?" he asked sardonically.

"No. I don't like meaningless pick-up lines," I hissed much more harshly than I intended. Smelly man grunted in his sleep and turned to the window.

"Don't you think it's a bit presumptuous to assume I was 'picking you up,'" he said for the first time sounding a bit angry in response to my grouchy attitude.

Could I get away with swiftly pressing my lips against his? Just a taste. God, I beg of you. I won't ask you for anything else, if I can just see what it's like to kiss the lips of such a perfect work of human art.

This uncharacteristically intense, animal-like thought made my cheeks flush again. I hated being so self-conscious. "Sorry, I'm not used to having guys compliment me," I muttered, staring at the seat in front of me.

"Don't tell me that a gorgeous *angel* like you doesn't have a boyfriend to shower you with compliments?"

Ouch...very touchy subject. Feeling guilty immediately for the lustful thoughts that preoccupied me seconds ago, I didn't want to delve into a conversation about my dead boyfriend. "No."

His happy demeanor quickly became smug. He seemed satisfied knowing I wasn't dating anyone. Regardless of his feelings on the matter, I had only recently dammed the pain from Zach's death and didn't want to open the floodgates. This was going to be an uncomfortable ride if I didn't change the subject.

"Let's talk about something else. Religion, politics," I paused, "sex?" I added nonchalantly. Maybe it was because he was gorgeous or just friendly, but this overly extroverted remark didn't make me feel awkward in the least bit.

"What?!" He was clearly taken aback by my forwardness. My ruse was working.

"Or women's lingerie? I find a good talk about four for five dollar bargain granny panties always keeps a conversation interesting," I said completely matter-of-factly.

The left corner of his lips curled upwards. "We can talk about lingerie," he said in an impish tone, looking at me slyly through the corner of his eyes, "if it's about *yours*." His voice carried the word "yours" as if it was a wonderfully dirty word.

A lustful chill shot down my spine.

"Funny," I said deadpan. I thought for a moment and felt a crack in the dam. "You know, an old boyfriend said that to me once too."

"Old boyfriend, huh?" his eyes glimmered.

I sighed, recalling everything about Zach in a split second. "He was perfect. We had a connection," I looked him straight in his eyes. "You know—something beyond hormones and infatuation." I paused. I hadn't talked to anyone about my feelings in a very long time yet I was completely comfortable pouring them out to this stranger.

"What happened?" he asked cautiously.

"He…he…he d…" tears choked the rest of the words. I looked away as one escaped my eyelashes and crawled down my cheek.

Without hesitation he wiped the tear away, his hand lingering on my face tenderly for just a moment. A calming warmth radiated through his touch.

Closing my eyes, I turned away from him. My insides burned from the torturous pain to which I had only recently grown immune. A few months ago, I could've sworn my guts had been yanked from my body, stomped on, and then put back with everyone expecting me to operate functionally. I bottled everything then, every memory, every feeling, every word we ever spoke so I could just grow numb to the pain.

I couldn't hold onto them anymore. My hands covered my eyes as if they could somehow block the rushing river. Tears streamed onto my white cotton blouse making it look like it got caught in a rainstorm.

In a flash, the handsome stranger wrapped his arms around me and pulled me against his chest. Stroking my hair gently with one hand, he held me close with the other—my big pillow letting me cry and blubber all over him.

"Shhhh, shhhh," he said soothingly, sincerely. "I know what you mean. I've been there too. Quite recently actually."

While I didn't think he realized how tragic my situation really was, the tone of his voice convinced me that he knew exactly how I felt. His tenderness felt like heaven on earth.

"Shhhh, Angel." I could've sworn he whispered, 'Shhh, *my* Angel…' Maybe that was just wishful thinking on my part.

Eventually the tears subsided. "I'm sure you think I'm totally nuts. Who would break down like that in front of a stranger?" I asked rhetorically, wiping the dampness away with my sleeves.

Salami man interjected gruffly, "Will you shut up already?"

I was stunned. First, by the fact that he woke up. Second, by my comforter's reaction. He reached across me blindingly fast and grabbed the corpulent man by the collar, snarling, "Why don't you mind your own business?"

Draining any trace of blood, the man's petrified expression matched the pale white light of the moon which shone across his face. Like a wild animal, my champion backed down slowly still glaring at the man, who wisely broke the stare-down and turned to face the window.

I couldn't make up my mind. Was my new found friend a psycho or was I a psycho for feeling flattered? Somehow, he seemed more like a protector than psychopath. Besides, now I was doubly awestruck; he was handsome *and* chivalrous. Impressive.

The muscles in his face released their tension while he moved slowly past me and settled back into his seat. He hesitated for a moment, inches from my lips, and asked gingerly, "You okay?" The citrus-sandalwood fragrance of his aftershave immediately captivated my senses and my eyes closed automatically to soak in every bit of him. I nodded slowly, dazed by his very presence.

His friendly expression returned with a big toothy grin. "I almost forgot," he said, reaching into the pocket of the seat in front of him. "Weren't you saying something about nuts?" he winked and tossed a bag of airplane peanuts at me.

I broke out in a pathetic girly giggle. Salami man shifted in his seat and I pictured him rolling his eyes. I was never the giggling type of girl, especially not in front of a guy. I also rarely dressed in pretty clothes, wore makeup, or pretended to be someone I wasn't. This guy just made everything disappear, all my cares, all my self-awareness. Well, almost. A girl like me could never have a shot with a guy like him. That would be like one of Cinderella's ugly step sisters landing Prince Charming. It didn't happen in fairy tales, and it definitely never happened in reality.

As we settled back into our seats, he asked, "so where are you going?"

"Around England."

"By yourself?"

I nodded.

"It's a dangerous world out there for someone like you."

"What do you mean 'someone like *me*'?" I demanded petulantly.

"You're young, alone, and gorgeous. There are plenty of places you wouldn't want to be by yourself."

I glared at him shocked that I was being lectured about my carelessness…and that he thought I was gorgeous.

He paused pensively. I felt myself getting mad but not at him. I was annoyed with myself for losing control. He was just being kind. I needed to be more sensitive and less stupid.

"Life is made up of choices. Each of us has the power to decide which path we take. I just don't want you to get hurt," he spoke as if he'd known me my whole life. "Promise you'll be careful?" His brutally-honest genuineness was intoxicating. Although, I couldn't make sense out of why he cared about what happened to me.

He reached for my hand. I met his gaze and replied softly, "I promise." Oddly enough, I meant it too.

The minute our hands touched, wildfire ignited my body in the most wonderful way. More than an attraction, it felt like a drug pulsated from his fingertips through every inch of me.

My hand jumped from his gentle grasp. I turned gasping for air, shocked by the weird sensation. He looked at me tenderly. *Why is he so interested in me? Seriously! I'm freakin' frumpy Cinderella minus the magic wardrobe change and happy ending.*

"Sorry." It was the only word I could speak at the moment. My mind was incapacitated with thoughts of confusion, bliss, and longing. My thoughts drifted to a hypothetical future with this stranger—love, marriage, children, and grandchildren. I wanted to be grown up so badly and in many ways I already was.

The ordeals of the past year made me feel like I was forty. In losing my father, I switched roles with my mom. Combined with the horrific ending to my first and only love, I couldn't bear the pain. Shutting off the outside world was necessary to survive, to be responsible, to care. We were all mourning, but my family didn't understand the torture that rendered me useless every day.

This trip saved me. I needed the distraction. I needed to get away and they needed my depression to go away.

Handsome guy's gaze tried to decipher my thoughts. I feigned a smile and leaned back.

Reality just set in.

Father...dead

Boyfriend...dead

Me...all alone in an unfamiliar country...

"Excuse me, miss." Somewhere in the middle of a very deep, empty dream my body lurched back into the present.

"What?" I asked groggily.

"The plane has landed. It's time to leave," the flight attendant's voice urged. "May we assist you?"

"No...No. I'll be ok." I pulled my long hair back into a low ponytail and grabbed my bag. Only as I got up to leave did I realize that *he* was gone. Feeling an immediate twinge of sadness, I sighed. It all seemed like a vivid dream. Who knows, maybe it was. My grasp on reality wasn't too tight these days.

Happy to be on solid ground, I mindlessly merged with the sea of people teeming in the terminal.

A flurry of anxious people crowded the newsstands. A handsome man's face was plastered over the front page of every newspaper. He looked to be about forty-five with rugged, tanned facial features and dark curly hair. His exotic light brown eyes shone with a greenish-gold tint. The TVs hanging over an airport pub broadcast his face on every screen.

"*...police are looking for the perpetrators of this heinous crime. Sir William Endymion the tenth was a prominent figure in our country. His long, distinguished lineage has come to an end. Investigators are trying to determine who will inherit his fortune and amassed real estate acquisitions worth a reported total of 100 million pounds...*"

Flashes of the murder popped into my mind. Blood trailed down a mansion's red carpeted stairs through a massive entry. I shuddered trying to squelch the macabre thoughts. A vivid imagination got in the way of my reality fairly frequently.

Walking toward the exit, I looked for the local bus which would drop me off near my youth hostel in London.

"Excuse me, miss?"

My first reaction—fear—froze my feet to the ground. Who would stop me in the airport?

"Miss?" The voice came from a short man trying desperately to keep up with my swift pace. "Miss, are you Angelika?"

I sized him up from head-to-toe trying to figure out whether or not I should trust him. I cautiously replied, "Yes."

He smiled, relieved. "Miss, there's a private car waiting to take you to your accommodations."

"For me? Yeah, right." Who would've sent a car? Ignoring him, I walked toward the line of buses.

The man's voice became frantic. "Miss! Miss! There *is* a car waiting for you from a Mrs. Katherine Kiss."

Mom. I should've known better. Sighing, I followed the man, who was wearing a neat black suit with a pair of shiny black wingtips that matched the sheen on his bald head.

'Promise that you'll be careful.' The plane stranger's words echoed in my head. I was trying to rationalize this situation, but in the pit of my stomach something told me this ride was not right.

Gut feeling versus rational thinking waged their never-ending war in my thoughts as I climbed into the sedan's backseat.

2 ~ First Impressions

The drive to the hostel was uneventful. The music from my life-line—my overused, need-it-to-live iPod—drowned out the city noise. Along the Thames, historic buildings contrasted the rushing people and cars, instantly reminding me of home. For the rest of the ride my thoughts floated between London and Salem.

The youth hostel was a plain rectangular building with a yellowed stucco finish. Salmon colored Foxgloves and dainty white daisies brightened its faded façade in window boxes. Three windows lined either side of the front door while another six graced the second floor. Between the second-story windows hung a weathered plaque stating: *Aeterna Flamma Inn c. 1757.* A second more modern sign was fastened to the front door, *Welcome, Youth Hostel.*

After a petite, frazzled, orange-haired woman by the name of Mrs. McGinley checked me in, I grabbed my key and dragged the suitcases upstairs. Thankfully my roommate was away, so I could get settled without an awkward meeting.

Light, white bedspreads covered the two twin beds, which looked so inviting to my jet-lagged body. Assessing the thin coverlet, I was extremely glad that my overprotective mom sent the fleece blanket with me. London's late spring was 20 degrees cooler than Salem's.

Abundant sunshine brightened our corner room through two windows. Pulling back the white gossamer curtain, I opened the side window to let in some fresh air. The inn smelled like it was over two hundred years old, a bit musty with a tinge of damp wood.

Located on the outskirts of London, the hostel was close to the countryside. Its well-manicured grounds were austere yet massive. A dense forest surrounded the property. In the distance, about a dozen chimneys dotted the green carpet of tree tops.

Plopping my suitcase on the floor, I unpacked into the only dresser that was still available. Apparently my roommate needed three dressers and three quarters of the closet. I should've given her the benefit of doubt, since she might not have known about my arrival. Still, this was irritating.

Designer clothes hung neatly in the closet organized alphabetically by brand and in subcategories by color and design. About thirty pairs of shoes lined the closet floor. Prada, Gucci, Blahnik. *Great!* I thought sarcastically rolling my eyes. What was she going to think of my jeans, wrinkled t-shirts, and all-purpose sneakers?

Ignoring the unpleasant assumptions, I focused on unpacking my toiletries and pictures of my parents, siblings, and Zach. I flipped his picture over and traced 'Te Quiero' in his handwriting. A smile crept through my sadness at the memory of the first time he spoke these words to me. Worried that I might reject him if he said 'I

love you', he opted for 'Te Quiero' and let me ponder its meaning. Studying Latin I was at a slight disadvantage when it came to Spanish translations.

My heart squeezed sickeningly at the thought of his body lying cold and decaying underground. His death happened so suddenly. Every time the phone rang these days, I still reached for it instinctively, thinking it was him.

Sighing hopelessly, I glanced at the full length mirror's reflection of a nightmare: tousled hair, dark circles under my eyes, and a generally gaunt, sad expression.

A hot shower brought me back from the brink of the living dead. Hearing voices gathering downstairs, I quickly pulled on my favorite pair of jeans and a light, white cotton sweater. Lastly, I put on my happy face—small talk with strangers was not high on my list of fun things to do. Just thinking about meeting new people was making me break out in a sweat.

I sauntered downstairs reluctantly. The crowd was gathered in the bright parlor to the right of the staircase; jovial laughter and loud conversations echoed up the stairwell. Sheepishly, I peered around the doorway.

"All I'm sayin' is the Red Sox are hot. They'll do it again this year!" exclaimed a lanky guy. His spiky, reddish-blonde hair and freckles made him appear about fourteen, but his body was that of a man in his twenties.

"You're crazy man! The Yankees are gonna go all the way—All. The. Way," shouted the Yankees' fan emphatically. He sported a muscular build that made him seem more like a football linebacker than a baseball fan while his short, brown, messy hair looked like he just rolled out of bed.

Red Sox or Yankees, I didn't care. I was just happy there were two other Americans here with me.

"Shut up already, you idiots!" shrieked a very petite girl with smooth, dark skin and fierce, black eyes. "I can't take another minute of your lame ass sports talk!"

A pale faced, slender blonde sitting by the window sighed very loudly, contemptuously, but didn't lift her eyes from "Shakespeare's Complete Works." If I were a gambling woman, I'd put money on the fact that she was my roomie.

Their collective gaze shifted from the beauty queen to my awkward presence near the room's entrance. The guys broke out into laughter that reverberated throughout the inn. My cheeks flushed instantly. I shifted my weight toward the stairs.

Yankee guy jumped up from his seat on the coffee table and in two steps leapt over everyone. "No, we're not laughing at you. It just looked like you saw us crazies and were gonna run away. Come in."

He wrapped his arm around my shoulders loosely and dragged me into the room.

"That's Matt," he said pointing to Red Sox fan; "Rachel," pointing to the girl who nearly bit his head off; "Lilly," glancing toward my roommate, who didn't bother to look up from her book; "and Jack and Steve are the geeks in the back of the room trying to play chess."

"Heard that," Steve said without moving his eyes from the chessboard.

"I'm Mark," he said, extending his hand to greet me, his golden brown eyes reflected a kind and happy attitude.

"I'm Angel," I replied, shaking his hand and feeling a little relieved about the meet and greet.

Rachel turned toward me. "Well, Angel, before the idiots here started arguing about sports crap, we were planning tomorrow's agenda."

The coffee table was strewn with maps, bus schedules, visitor guides, loose leaf paper, markers, and pens. Rachel appeared to be the group's self-appointed leader. I knelt next to her and examined their sightseeing list.

Big Ben
Hyde Park
Buckingham Palace
St. Paul's
Westminster Abbey
Tower of London
Endymion Manor
The Tate Modern
Tower Bridge
Trafalgar Square

"What's Endymion Manor?" Considering I read just about every book, magazine, and travel guide about the country, I was intrigued by the anonymity of this place.

"We are NOT going there," Lilly stated emphatically without looking up from her book.

Rachel rolled her eyes. "The jocks want to go there because it's supposedly haunted but it's all the way out in Wales by Bristol Channel."

"Yeah, but a chance to visit a real haunted castle—come on, it'll be so much fun," Matt coaxed.

"Guys," Rachel seriously eyed the rowdy duo. "We'd probably have to spend the night there. Besides, I don't have a clue about which bus routes to take."

"Renting a car for a day won't kill us, Rach," Mark interjected. "And we can just sleep in the car on the side of the road if it gets late."

Her face contorted with disgust. "*No one* is sleeping in a car with you two morons."

"Well, we're going and any of you can come with us if you want. We'll get a car first thing tomorrow and we'll head out by ten," Mark offered to the room's inattentive audience.

"Other than the ghosts, what else is at Endymion Manor?" The guys piqued my curiosity; I had to know.

"It's a historical home that was owned by the Endymion family since the early 1500s through, well just a few days ago actually. Did you hear about the murder?"

So that's what all the commotion was about at the news stands. I nodded.

"Sir William's blood was found trailing from his bedroom to the front entryway where he tried to set off the home's alarm system. The police didn't find his body though, so the whole country is being turned upside down trying to locate him. The lawyers are having a field day trying to find any heirs. He was the last of the family's line."

"So he was just another rich guy. Why is everyone so upset?"

Lilly bolted out of her seat, rage burning in her cool, blue eyes.

Her caustic English accent burned my ears, "because he happened to be a very prominent man around the world. He owned numerous businesses and supported hundreds of charity cases," she paused, scrutinizing me distastefully, "like you."

Deep breaths, Angel. Deep breaths. I did NOT want to get into a ridiculous fight with my pretentious, stupid roomie. I sat on the couch and turned my attention back to Rachel. Realizing she wasn't going to get a response from me, Lilly stomped from the room.

Ignoring Lilly's outburst, Rachel continued, "The Endymion family has long history of studying and living abroad, but they always returned to Wales and supported its people. Even Sir William didn't live at the manor until about twenty years ago. The family has roots throughout Europe, so they're spread all over making this a nightmare for lawyers trying to track down distant relatives.

"The real story comes from the nearby towns and locals. They say that people used to be tortured there and the victims' screams can still be heard at night. Cults apparently roam the nearby countryside. Animal carcasses and human bones are found there all the time."

Sir William Endymion. Unwillingly yet vividly, my distracted thoughts envisioned the murderer hunting him with a blood-dripping dagger by his side. I shuddered.

"Didn't the authorities close the place down to investigate?" I asked.

"They did, but profits from estate tours support his charities. They're keeping some of the manor off limits, but the main areas are still open to visitors. You're not actually thinking of going with the jackass twins are you?"

"Hmmm, I don't know yet." It certainly seemed like an ideal distraction. Plus, I didn't really want to wander around London by myself.

She raised her eyebrows suspiciously. Matt and Mark jumped over the back of the couch to sit on either side of me.

"So, Ang, what do you think? Wanna go on an adventure tomorrow? Everyone else around here is boring." Mark's friendliness was contagious.

"We'll even let you have the whole back seat to sleep on," goaded Matt.

I didn't have to think about this. I wanted to go, but I didn't want to seem too eager. Of course, as was typical of my nature, I paused and caved, "Sure, why not?" Even though they were strangers, they felt like life-long friends.

"Excellent!" Mark and Matt exclaimed in unison. They began plotting the trip as if I wasn't sitting between them.

"Yo bro," Mark said. "Let's get our iPods and…"

"Did you just call me 'bro'? Seriously, do I look like a 'bro' to you?"

I stared at Matt with his dark brown eyes, reddish hair and freckles and burst out laughing. "See, Angel, agrees!" he shouted, slapping Mark, who punched him back. Caught in the middle of their fight, it was time for me to make a break for it. I managed to creep beneath their arms between hits.

"Dude that hurt!" Mark shouted.

"Did you just squeal? You're such a *girl*," Matt yelled back, their voices escalating.

"K, dudes," I mocked. "It's time for me to go. See ya tomorrow."

"Look bro," Mark shouted over the punches. "You scared her away!"

"Did you just call me 'bro' again?" Matt asked incredulously, punching Mark harder in the shoulder.

Rachel followed me to the dining room where I stole an apple and a couple dinner rolls. We walked upstairs. "Are you sure you want to go with them?" she worried. "Considering they're almost college seniors, they're so immature."

"Yeah, I like mysteries and weird stuff. The manor is mysterious and the guys are weird. It's a good combination," I smiled and bit into the shiny red fruit.

She shrugged her shoulders and we plodded off to our respective rooms upstairs. I was dying to find out more about Endymion Manor. Flipping through the first few pages of the "Guide to Great Britain," a piece of paper fell from the book.

On a neatly folded plane napkin was written:

Remember, you promised. Be careful.
~ Your pillow

How the hell did that get in here? A surge of emotions overcame me. Fear: was he a stalker? Joy: did he really like me enough to do this? Embarrassment: did I really appear to be such an idiot that I needed a reminder? Primal Lust: what a hottie—if only we could meet again.

I glanced at Zach's picture and guilt washed over me. *But he's not here anymore. I need to move on.*

The stranger slowly worked his way back into my thoughts. His face, his touch, his words swirled around in my head and he carried me off to sleep.

3 ~ Day Trip

I awoke extra early to dress and send emails to my mom and one of my best friends, Kelly. A lone computer stood in the corner of the parlor facing the backyard. I opened the internet and wrote a quick email to my mom thanking her for the ride from the airport.

Kelly and I had been friends since kindergarten. While we argued all the time, we ultimately always had each other's best interests at heart. We understood and supported each other through everything. Our drama du jour revolved around our other best friend who had been avoiding me like the plague for the past few months. I didn't want to think about him today.

My message to Kelly was a bit more in depth than my mom's. I mentioned the sweet stranger on the plane, my roommate, and my adventure today with the jocks. She'd surely love that. The mousy, self-conscious bookworm from Bishop Fenwick High was spending the day with twenty-something college seniors!

Thinking about the day ahead, I stared absentmindedly through the window behind the computer.

My breath caught. I jumped up, knocking my chair over. It crashed to the ground and echoed in the room, but I couldn't take my eyes off of the young guy staring at me through the window. He didn't seem real. He was more like a ghostly apparition. His extremely pale face was silhouetted in the hood of his black pullover with a little tuft of blonde hair sticking out from under it. In the brief millisecond that we gaped at each other, his deep black eyes burned through my face. A thin, ice blue rim encircled his huge black pupils which had crimson red rays piercing through them. In a flash he was gone.

I stumbled over the fallen chair and ran from the room right into Yankee and Red Sox by the front door.

"Ready, Ang?" Mark asked enthusiastically, opening the front door revealing a shiny red convertible glistening in the bright sun.

"Yup," I muttered as I grabbed my jacket from the chair by the door and ran to the car without looking back. As much as I loved adventures, the ghost freaked me out. I couldn't get away fast enough. Pretending that it didn't happen, I focused on our destination. "Now, I did tell people who I was with today in case anything should happen. So, no funny ideas, k?"

"Angel, you're like my little sister. What are you, eighteen?" Matt asked.

"Yeah."

"Exactly. I've got a seventeen-year-old sister at home. If she went away, I'd want someone to look out for her too. There's nothing to worry about. We're gonna have fun," he reassured, although I couldn't help but think that the jocks' idea of fun might not match mine.

Mark felt very comfortable behind the wheel. He drove it like a race car speeding through the gently rolling hills of the country-side, which was covered in multiple hues of green and gold. Taken with the beauty of my unfamiliar surroundings, we drove through Buckinghamshire, Oxfordshire, and Gloucestershire counties in no time at all.

In a couple of hours, we reached our destination in southern Wales. The convertible sped beyond a giant wrought iron gate and wound along a forested driveway that inched several miles toward the hilltop. Mark screeched to a stop beside two police cars in a parking lot hidden within a grove of trees.

"Angel, it doesn't bother you that some old dude was killed here a few days ago?" Matt asked curiously.

"Nope."

"You are a strange, strange person," Mark taunted.

With what I'd been through this past year, things like this no longer bothered me. The only comfort I found was in knowing that fate decides what's meant to be. It was one of the few things I couldn't control. Whenever my time was up, I'd have to go.

Besides, death haunted my thoughts daily. My mom forced me to go to therapy after Zach's death. *'What did you expect—standing at the edge of a bridge hypnotized by the water passing two hundred feet below? You're lucky someone stopped and pulled you back before you fell.'*

No one understood the pain I felt. It was like fate shoved its hand in my chest and yanked out my heart. A dull constant ache was all that was left. Instead of healing over time, the pain spread, so now I hurt physically over the perpetual and agonizing reminder of his loss. Zach wasn't just a boyfriend. He knew me, knew every facet of my soul. Without him, part of me was missing. How could I go on as half of a soul lingering between life and death?

"K, Ang?" Mark asked, realizing I seemed a bit preoccupied.

"Yeah, just thinking."

"Wow!" Matt exclaimed as we reached the end of the path through the trees. The guys began debating football after allowing the atmosphere to sink in for less than a nanosecond.

The forest opened up to reveal the imposing manor, its perfectly manicured grass, massive water fountain and gardens in the front yard. I trailed behind the jocks, staring at the landscape. The lawn was thick and soft. Red petunias and white babies' breath encircled the fountain in the center of which stood a statuesque carving of two angels wrapped in a loving embrace and staring adoringly into each other's eyes. They stood on a globe, snakes wrapped around their feet. Water danced around them at random intervals and pooled in the enormous basin below.

I wasn't feeling very loving these days. Quite frankly, the romantic sculpture made me want to puke.

My gaze shifted from the statue toward the imposing home. Intricate wrought iron handrails lined either side of the limestone steps leading up to the front doors. Three stone-covered arched gables covered the entryway, one main one over the double wooden front door and two others sitting off to either side of it. Stained glass windows colorfully contrasted the manor's gray stone exterior. The windows were bigger and more detailed than any of the ones I'd seen at churches back at home.

Grave in appearance, the immense Gothic-styled fortress featured little decorative architecture other than laced stonework along the rooftop and two turrets with spires on either side of the front facing.

I couldn't pry my eyes from the manor. It was intimidating, scary in a way. Despite its beauty, its presence radiated negativity. I could almost feel its history. A bronze plaque engraved with the family's crest was affixed to each arched front door. Its coat of arms featured a stripe across the top containing an intricate pattern of interwoven oak leaves while the center of the shield displayed a howling wolf with a crescent moon and star behind it.

Matt skipped up the stairs and held the door for me. The entryway opened into an enormous three-story foyer with a crystal chandelier hanging over an antique cherry table on which sat an extravagant, red, white, and pink floral arrangement. Carved, dark wood paneling covered the walls from floor to ceiling in the main entry, which was easily six times as big as my entire house. Crimson carpeting continued across the room and up the staircase which split in opposite directions when it met the wall at the second floor. From there both staircases met again on the third floor shaping the stairwell into a heart.

Behind the stairs, an incredibly detailed stained-glass window spanned the entire two-story wall. The two angels from the fountain held each other in this depiction, a tear glistening on the face of the golden-haired female. The sun streamed through their holy white, yellow, and gold features. In the background, however, an army of fearsome, dark angels brandished swords and daggers.

"Creepy," I whispered completely awestruck by the lavish architecture and dumbfounded by the threatening imagery.

"Pompous," Matt muttered.

"Bring on the ghosts," Mark added exuberantly.

We rejoined the tour group gathering on the eclectically-designed first floor. Like France's Versailles, grand halls extended infinitely on either side of the main entry. The halls' Greco-Roman architecture of white marble flooring and marble columns was contrasted by floor-to-ceiling gilded mirrors that reflected the windows and front landscape overlooking the forest. Crystal and gold chandeliers, smaller copies of the one in the entry, lined the length of both halls.

I drifted from room to room barely hearing the guide or realizing that other people were near me. The surroundings were strange yet familiar, eerie yet comfortable. The longer I spent in each room, the more at ease I felt in the manor. There was something about the place that demanded my conscious and unconscious attention.

At the end of the tour, the guide released us onto a limestone patio that wrapped itself around the back of the estate. To the left, a hillside of heather coated the ground in deep pink carpeting beyond which a dense forest led to the black-blue ocean. To the right, a hillside covered in lavender fragranced the air. An endless field directly behind the mansion led to a red brick labyrinth covered in green ivy and bushes.

I took a deep breath inhaling the sweet aroma of the lavender. The damp, fresh sea air carried a bite with it.

As the guys ran enthusiastically into the labyrinth, I promised to meet them in twenty minutes and headed back inside.

Captivated by the strange stained-glass window, I walked slowly up the stairs, my hand gliding along the mahogany banister. I couldn't peel my gaze away from the horrific image. The closer I got to it, the more nauseous I felt. And yet I didn't want to leave.

At the top of the stairs, the hallways were cordoned off by red velvet roping. All alone, I decided to investigate. The left hall didn't feel *right*, so I slipped past the roping and down the other hall instead.

The fifteen foot ceilings were covered in plaster carvings and lined with intricately detailed crown molding. Portraits of the Endymion family hung along both sides of the hall. Looking like a royalty, each glamorous and extremely wealthy family member was depicted in spectacular clothes and jewels.

About fifty feet down the corridor, the right wall opened into another stairwell that led downstairs to the second floor where a haggard man washed the black and white marble floor. Although numerous family portraits clung to the intricate wood paneling, this room was very bare in comparison to the rest of the home. Deep crimson drapes adorned the two-story-high windows. A lone gold chandelier with crystal accents hung over the middle of the room suspended from a ceiling medallion featuring cherub faces.

Emerging from the hall's shadows, I tiptoed halfway down the staircase to get a closer look at the room. The floor washer let out a horrified gasp. He stared at me, white as a ghost, and shook in terror.

"A...A...Artemis," he whispered, pointing at me with a quivering finger.

Clearly my trespassing startled him. I stepped toward him to apologize. "No, sor..."

"Don't come any closer," his trembling voice interjected. He brandished his mop at me.

"But..."

His gaze shifted behind me and his eyes grew wider with fear. Dropping the mop, he sprinted from the room screaming. I turned to run up the stairs and make my escape, but as I spun around I noticed what had grabbed the man's attention.

The ten foot tall portrait behind me featured a beautiful, slender woman with gold upswept curls and fair skin. A dark haired man with angled features knelt at her feet, kissing her right hand, a tear streaming down his cheek. Her left hand extended backwards into the shadows of the trees behind her. She reached toward an evil-looking, dark angel heavily washed in black and burgundy.

A plaque at the bottom of the painting contained the inscription:

Cenweard Endymion - 1503 - 1526 AD
"Artemis"

I wondered what Cenweard did to anger the Greek goddess so badly that he was forever captured so sorrowful and contrite. My eyes drifted around the painting absorbing its scenery. The woman's face was so unique and somehow familiar. Suddenly, I realized what horrified the man.

She was me.

Hurried footsteps rushed toward the room. I jumped up the stairs two or three at a time, bolted down the hallway, flew down the heart stairwell and through the front door glancing behind me all the way to make sure I wasn't being followed.

And then I hit a wall or it felt like it anyway. I ricocheted off of Mark's back. Falling backwards, I banged my head on the stone stairs outside of the front door.

"Spooked?" Mark laughed.

"Knock it off," Matt chided. "You ok, Angel?"

All I could do was groan. Matt helped me sit up. I rubbed the back of my head.

"Let me look," Matt suggested. He examined the tender spot gently. "You'll live. Think you can walk?"

I nodded. My head throbbed with a dull, radiating pain.

"Don't worry, Ang, Matt's had enough concussions to be an expert doctor on how to make the pain go away. You're in good hands," Mark stated matter-of-factly. "What happened? Did you see a ghost?" he paused, hoping ecstatically that he could go ghost hunting no doubt. "If you did, we're going back."

I shook my head. I wasn't ready to tell them *I* was the ghost.

4 ~ Detour

The sun sank slowly toward the horizon as we began our trip back to the hostel. Unfortunately, we got about a mile down the winding driveway before I had to throw up. Mark skidded to a stop. Matt pulled me from the back seat and ran into the woods with me. Poor guy. But he insisted on helping.

We repeated the scene two more times. Was it a concussion or my overactive imagination reacting to the weird house?

"Ang, we're not going back tonight," Mark said carefully, slowing the car to a near crawl as we entered the main road of the village at the base of Endymion Manor's hill.

He pointed to a little Tudor-style tavern. "Let's stop there and ask if there's a place to stay nearby."

"I thought you guys were all about sleeping in the car."

"No offense, but I don't want you hurling in my rental," Mark snapped as he parked the car on the side of the ancient, one-story building.

I really didn't want to go to a rowdy pub but didn't have much of a choice. Matt helped me out of the car and wrapped his arm around my shoulder supportively. Mark approached the bartender while Matt and I slid into a booth near the entrance.

In stark contrast to Endymion Manor, the tavern was closer in size to one of the mansion's bathrooms. Eight booths lined the front wall while eight tables were placed evenly across the floor between the booths and the bar. Everything—the walls, the booths, the chairs—was carved from wood. The place looked old and smelled like the damp trees of a forest.

Mark rejoined us, "Can you believe this shithole of a town doesn't even have an inn?" Coming from New York, I could only imagine how big a change this must've been for him.

"The dude said there's a vicarage down the road and we can ask for a room there. The vicar won't be back until after ten though. The next town over is at least thirty minutes away."

"Think you can hold out that long?" Matt asked.

"Yeah," I replied, my strength coming back. "I'll be ok. I'm feeling better already."

Mark roared with laughter. "Well yeah, Ang, you should feel better. You left a six mile trail of meals along the road."

"Funny," I glowered.

The guys decided I couldn't possibly have a concussion, so they let me rest in the booth. Surprisingly, the tavern was empty. I placed my purse against the window and propped my head against it. *Where's a good looking pillow when you need one?* Pulling my legs onto the bench, I curled into a ball and fell asleep before I could even close my eyes.

The smell of smoke and sound of boisterous laughter jarred me from my empty dreams. The locals had filtered in while I napped.

One of the middle-aged, oversized male patrons noticed I was alert and bellowed, "Look, Sleeping Beauty's awake!"

I blushed and wiped the drool from the corner of my lips while everyone in the bar raised their glasses and drank to my being awake. I was still caught in a cloud of grogginess when Matt slid into the seat beside me.

"Feeling better?" he asked.

My eyes blinked a few times as my hand slid across my head. The right side of my hair was tousled looking more like Medusa's mane than mine. Matt smirked and ran his fingers through my messy do.

A petite blonde barmaid brought over a pitcher of beer, "From the chap at the bar."

Mark raised his glass to us and then cheerfully encouraged a lively rendition of 'Beer, Beer, Beer' with the other barflies. He was having a grand time as the life of the party.

"Wanna try some?" Matt asked, caressing the pitcher.

"Why not?" I sighed half-heartedly. I didn't like beer. My dad let me have a few sips over the years, but I didn't care for it. I never partied in high school, so this was unfamiliar territory. College would surely change that this autumn.

Matt filled our glasses.

"What is this?" I asked warily.

"Magic Lagyr. You can't come to Wales and not taste an award-winning local brew."

I sipped it cautiously. The froth covered my nose and mouth. Matt laughed so hard I thought he was going to fall off the bench.

"Napkin," I demanded embarrassed, covering my mouth with one hand. He grabbed one from the far side of the table and passed it to me. "Would you allow your sister to drink?"

"Nope."

"Then why are you letting me? I thought you were looking out for me?"

"One, it's legal here. If we were in the U.S., I'd kick your ass out of the bar. Two, you need a good British drinking experience. What's more authentic than sitting in a bar drinking with the people who live here? You don't get this kind of atmosphere back at home." He laughed. "And three, something scared the hell out of you at the manor. You need to relax."

I took another sip of beer and avoided the froth this time.

"Ya gonna tell me about it, Angel, or do I need to drag it out of you?" He cocked an eyebrow. His expression was filled with intense curiosity.

"Matt, really, I don't want to talk about it." Honestly though, I just didn't want the only people I trusted in the UK to think I was nuts. Besides, the ghost at the hostel and the picture at the manor didn't make any sense. I needed to be alone to figure this stuff out.

The tavern was packed—standing room only and barely even that. I couldn't hear myself think.

"Are you ok?" he asked, sensing my antisocial vibe.

Mark appeared out of thin air at the end of the table. "What's wrong with you guys? This party is awesome!"

He flagged down the barmaid, wrapped his arm around her shoulders, and stuffed several pounds into the tip cup on her serving platter, "One more round, Beautiful. Taffy Apples this time."

"Excuse me, guys." I stood up.

"Where are you going?" Matt asked concernedly.

"Need some fresh air. There's too much of a smoke-beer-and-sweaty-man smell in here," I said, scrunching my nose. Matt's eyes twinkled in amusement.

"But you haven't even touched your beer," Mark begged. "Besides, the cider is on its way. I'm sure you'll like it. It's sweeter."

I stared straight at him, expressionless, reached out to pick up my glass and lifted it over his head. He closed his eyes expecting to get a beer bath. Instead I chugged half of it and slammed the glass back on the table. The nearby patrons gave me a standing ovation.

Suitably impressed, my jocks allowed me to leave.

Damn, that was gross! I wiped the froth from my mouth with the back of my hand and vowed never to pull a stunt like that again.

"I'll be back soon," I shouted over my shoulder, pushing past the jovial drunks. As soon as I made it outside, the fresh air hit me like a ton of bricks.

Across from the parking lot I found a few boulders that I turned into a makeshift seat. I stared out into the black nothingness before me. Here and there a flicker of light escaped the dense forest as the breeze swayed the foliage.

My mind began compiling a list of my trip so far:

1. *Hottie on plane*
2. *Scary ghost guy in the hostel's backyard*
3. *Hottie on plane…no, no, said that already*
4. *Endymion Manor*

5. *Maintenance guy who was terrified of me*
6. *Painting that looked like me*
7. *Hottie…oh, why did it have to be so hard to keep him out of my mind?*

Guess I got my day of mysteries and weirdness after all.

A loud crash inside the tavern grabbed my attention. I caught Matt staring at me through the window. He quickly looked away when my eyes met his.

It was comforting knowing someone was looking out for me. Being the oldest of four, I always had to be the responsible one. I liked the idea of having a big brother making sure I was safe.

Smiling, I thought about my list. The hottie on the plane topped it. He was a welcome distraction. Of course, I immediately felt guilty for feeling attracted to him. I should still be in mourning.

My thoughts drifted to my dead love. A montage played through my head: the time he brought flowers for me after my ballet recital; playing catch in the park; stealing a kiss under the mistletoe when my parents weren't watching; picking me up in his old sea-foam green Buick Skylark to take me to prom; throwing a three-pointer in his surprised face on the basketball court; our first kiss which started out so hesitantly, cautiously, and exploded completely unexpectedly with fiery passion. These happy memories faded into the call—

"Angel, is that you?"

"Yeah, hi Mr. Edwards. What's up?"

"Angel, is your mom there? I need to talk to both of you." I signaled to my mom to come over.

"She's listening. What's wrong Mr. Edwards?"

He sounded choked up. *"Zach was in an accident…Angel, he's dead…"*

I sank to the floor as the phone slipped from my hand—too distraught to cry, too shocked to move.

"Hopelessly, I'll love you endlessly[1]..." Looking at the round moon and twinkling stars, I whispered the lyrics to our song hoping that Zach could hear me wherever he was. Desperately wishing I could be with him, I angrily brushed away the tears which raced down my cheeks.

Life was unfair. I firmly believed that Zach was my soul mate. If this was true though, was I destined for a life without love? Or at most a sub-par love? What if fate intervened before true love could be realized? How many people go through life without meeting the "right one?" Is it because accidental circumstances prevented their love or that their lives were destined to be loveless?

I felt so guilty thinking about the handsome stranger, but I sensed a connection with him. He really didn't seem like a stranger at all. His warmth, his kindness, his electric touch were calming. Maybe I was imagining all of this to fill Zach's void. Or, maybe the stranger and I actually had a connection, but what good would that be since I had no idea who he was or, even better, where he was.

I glanced at the pub's window again and saw Mark staring this time. He winked and gave me the thumbs up sign. I nodded. Yeah, I was physically ok at this moment—mentally and emotionally, not so much.

From the corner of my eye I caught a strange glow illuminating the forest at the bottom of the hillside. I glanced back; neither Mark nor Matt was looking. *I'll be back before they notice,* I promised myself.

Fear didn't enter my mind. Two parts of me battled internally at my decision to investigate. On the one hand I was understandably wary. On the other, I was drawn to this light like a magnet. I couldn't justify the feeling. I just knew I had to see it.

The nearly full moon lit the winding path along the hillside fairly well. I rummaged through my purse to find the pepper spray and mini flashlight my mom insisted I bring. I kept the flashlight off—no need to draw attention to myself as I wandered through the English

---

1   Muse, *Endlessly*, <u>Absolution</u>, Written by: Matthew Bellamy

countryside…alone…at night. I realized the irony of the moment considering the promise I made to my plane god, but I felt secure and my finger was poised and ready to fire the pepper spray—just in case.

Jumping and weaving to avoid branches and brush, a little laugh escaped my lips at the thought of me leaping and twirling over the bushes and through the trees in the moonlight. I wondered who would be more frightened: me, if I happened upon unsuspecting forest dwellers or unsuspecting forest dwellers happening upon a crazy girl dancing toward them.

The intense smell of burning wood and incense constricted my throat and irritated my eyes. I followed the smell and glow until I heard voices in a clearing.

Hiding behind an old tree that could've easily concealed me, Matt and Mark, I listened to the group and spied them around the side of the trunk. Shrouded in long hooded robes, about twenty people stood in a circle around a bonfire. The fire light danced on the dark velvet sheen of their cloaks, which were outlined in crimson satin. The dark figures chanted in a constant low beat.

Then a strong, female voice rose over the rest:

> "…*Bring us strength, bring us power,*
> *Unveil fragile human fright*
> *We won't bend, we won't cower.*
> *Slither through the night*
> *Earth's serpent, 'til the right hour.*
> *Strike your bite at dawn's first light*
> *Reclaim our place atop the tower.*"

Too suddenly for me to scream, hands clasped over my mouth and carried me toward the fire.

5 ~ Legends

*F*ear gripped every part of me, but survival mode kicked in. I wriggled until I freed my right hand, which happened to be the *right* hand. Pushing the little button on the canister, I waved my arm releasing a widespread spray. Screaming, my captors dropped me to the ground knocking the wind out of me.

I rolled onto my back gasping for air. Someone kicked the pepper spray out of my hand and into the fire. The can exploded sending a wave of heat washing over us. Shards of firewood crackled and shot through the air. The crowd dispersed quickly to avoid the blast's aftermath.

Several of the cloaked figures hovered nearby. The voices were somewhat drowned out by the angry bonfire.

"What should we do with her?" asked a deep male voice.

"Where did you find her?" growled an edgy sounding female.

"Behind that oak," replied a younger male.

"Who is she? Was she alone?" retorted the woman not expecting an answer.

"I don't know," answered the younger, frustrated male.

"You men are useless, absolutely useless!"

The woman knelt next to my head. Her face and body were completely shrouded. She pulled out a jewel encrusted, silver dagger from her cloak pocket and lifted it toward the light of the fire allowing the reddish-orange hues to flicker across the shiny blade.

I still couldn't breathe enough to talk. I tried to inch away from her but a man was standing with one black-booted foot on my right arm.

The woman turned her attention from the dagger to me. In one swift motion, she spun the small knife in her hand and thrust it under my chin.

Droplets of blood slid down my throat.

"Who are you?" she demanded.

Frozen in panic, I opened my mouth, but no sound came out.

"Who are you?" she shouted more forcefully.

A sharp pain shot through my body as she pushed the dagger further into my jaw line. *Drip, drop, drip, drop, drip, drop.* Blood streamed slowly down my throat.

"Morgan, stop!" commanded a strong male voice.

Her head spun around to face the person behind her, but the dagger's point remained firmly implanted beneath my chin.

"Morgan," he repeated the warning.

"But she could be one of their spies, Edwin. They've gotten through before," Morgan pleaded. "We need to make sure."

"Look in her eyes, Morgan. What do you see?"

The firelight illuminated her dark, fierce expression. Morgan's dead gray eyes peered deeply into mine searching for something. The dagger slipped from her hands. The realization that she really wanted to kill me was finally sinking in.

Her henchman released my arm and I rolled over gripping my throat. Sitting up, I used my jacket's sleeve to wipe away the dripping blood.

The man called Edwin approached and stared at me intently. "My dear, you have placed yourself in a precarious situation. What is your name, girl?"

"Angel," I said steadily. I felt my courage rebuilding as I stared back at him defiantly.

He smiled at me arching his eyebrows. "And what is your business here, Angel?"

"Curiosity." *What else?*

"Humph," Morgan grunted.

Ignoring her, Edwin continued, "For lack of a wittier sentiment, curiosity killed the cat, you know?" He extended his hand and helped me to my feet.

"I don't mean any harm, I swear," I pleaded. "I was at the pub and saw the fire. I just wanted to check it out."

"Did they send you?" he demanded suddenly, startling me with the furious tone of his words.

"I have no idea what you're talking about!" I yelled back.

Shocked by my sudden force of bravery, Edwin backed down a little. "Then why are you here?"

"I'm telling you. I saw the blaze and wondered why such a huge fire would be burning in the middle of nowhere. Bonfires usually signal parties. I just wanted to know what was going on."

A crowd gathered around us. Someone handed my purse to Edwin who sifted through it. He pulled out my cell phone and quickly searched through my list of phone numbers and recently made calls. Finding nothing other than my iPod, tampons, lipstick, and a hair brush, he handed the purse to me.

"We apologize for the unpleasant welcome. May we escort you back to the pub?"

"Yes, thank you," I added. "I'm sorry for interrupting," I mumbled, sincerely feeling like an idiot for venturing into the unknown. Not to mention, now regret was seeping into my consciousness too. I should've listened to the handsome stranger's warning.

"Quite all right. We understand what it's like to be drawn to strange activities," he sighed heavily. "Sam, Cynan, please ensure she returns to the tavern. Blessed be, Angel." With that, Edwin returned to his group and they resumed their chanting around the fire.

Sam and Cynan stepped toward me. As they came closer, both removed their hoods revealing themselves. I didn't know what I expected to see. They all seemed so mysterious; I didn't imagine them to be human.

Sam was tall or at least a couple of inches taller than my petite stature. Her raven black hair was cut in a cute, ultra-modern bob that framed her super pale, thin, heart-shaped face. She appeared to be about my age. Cynan stood at least a head taller than me and was very massive. He could've easily played football against Mark and Matt and beaten them simultaneously. His straight black hair, cropped short on the sides but left long on top, flowed wildly as the wind licked it from all directions.

"I'm sorry for disturbing you tonight." Another apology was certainly needed.

"No worries, Angel," Sam said in a thin, sing-song voice. "My brother and I wanted to leave anyway."

"What were you doing back there?" I just had to know.

"We're preparing for the summer solstice in a few weeks," Sam explained.

Now I felt even worse, although I was still pretty pissed that the woman named Morgan attacked me. "Does that celebration have anything to do with witchcraft?" I asked intrigued. The sight reminded me of a few unexpected encounters I happened upon in Salem. Mark may not have gotten his ghost today, but I would've found both a ghost and witches.

"We're Wiccan," Sam corrected abruptly. "The locals bother us from time to time, which is why Morgan reacted so violently tonight," she explained lightly.

"But why would you purposely draw attention with a bonfire?"

"The locals who fear us usually stay away," she said, hopping over the trunk of a fallen tree.

"The ones who understand, don't care," Cynan added, squelching a smirk as he caught me fumble over the same tree trunk.

I turned to Sam quoting one of my favorite movie lines, "So, are you a good witch or a bad witch?"

Cynan rolled his eyes. Sam giggled and completed my "Wizard of Oz" quote, "Why, I'm not a witch at all!"

Cynan sighed, "If we were bad, you wouldn't be standing here right now." Instead of comforting me however, his statement sparked terror. How powerful were they?

"So, what was the meaning of the chanting? It sounded fairly evil."

Sam shook her head at my ignorance. "It was a spell of protection. We guard this area from the evil on top of that hill," she motioned at the manor, which the moonlight illuminated ominously in the distance. I shuddered at the memory of my encounter there. My experience was certainly out of the ordinary, but it wasn't evil. I stared sideways at the duo in front of me. What did they know about Endymion Manor? Was there something more to the imposing estate or was it a simple explanation such as the murder that just took place there?

We exited the forest and walked silently across the field toward the small hill beneath the pub.

"Angel, why is a *Yankee* strolling through the Welsh countryside all by her lonesome at night?" Sam asked. "Where're your mates?"

"At the pub," I explained.

"Are you staying in town tonight?"

"The bartender said something about inquiring at the vicarage."

Cynan and Sam exchanged knowing glances and exploded with laughter. Worry washed over me. "Shouldn't we stay there?"

"No, no," Cynan replied. "Don't misunderstand. The vicar is… hmmm, shall we say, interesting?" He paused, waiting for Sam's input. She doubled over in laughter.

"You'll be entirely safe there. It's just that the vicar is a unique sort of person—not your traditional man-of-the-cloth so to speak," Sam added, laughter still brightening her hazel eyes. "Come Cynan, let's hurry before Edwin worries."

"How about a quick pint first?" he pleaded, nodding to the pub.

"No." Sam may have been half her brother's size, but her demeanor demanded obedience. "It was a pleasure meeting you, Angel. Will you be in town for awhile?"

"Probably not. We weren't planning on staying tonight and I don't have any clothes," I said, glancing irately at my totally ruined, blood stained, light green babydoll top.

"Well, it was nice meeting you. Goodnight," she said.

"Try to get *some* sleep at the vicar's," Cynan added, bursting with laughter.

"Goodnight," I offered hesitantly to my escorts. What could the vicar possibly be like to warrant such a reaction?

They nodded and turned, disappearing into the shadows of the hillside. A soft mist crawled along the ground and enveloped them. My eyes strained in the moonlight to find the siblings but in an instant they were gone.

Weird, weird place. My gaze rested on the sleepy hilltop. The quiet countryside awakened an eerie sensation of inexplicable horror. Images of unfortunate villagers being tortured by wicked people clouded my thoughts.

Shaken, I started walking to the pub's front door. Movement along its far left corner caught my eye. Something shifted in the shadows under the tavern's sign which hung from the eaves. Fear battled courage in my mind.

I stared at the shapeless mass. Two red dots vividly pierced the darkness of night. The black figure stepped from the shadows. Its crimson glowing eyes leered at me.

My throat choked. I opened my mouth to scream, but fear trapped the sound. My feet were frozen to the ground as it started to creep closer.

The moon peeked out from behind the clouds illuminating the apparition from the hostel.

6 ~ The Vicar

"**A**ng, where the hell have you been?" Mark bellowed, rushing to me from the opposite side of the pub. "You scared the crap out of us. We can't help you if you don't freakin' help yourself."

Under other circumstances his statement would've hurt, but I was still frozen, locked in a stare with the red-eyed thing. I managed to raise my arm wordlessly to point at it.

Mark squinted in the direction of the pub. Dark clouds floated across the moon and the thing faded into the black night.

"You know, Ang, if I would've known a half a glass of beer would make you insane, I wouldn't've let you drink it," Mark said frustrated with my lost grip on reality. "You're psycho!"

"Jackass!" The word popped out like an unchecked reflex.

Breathing heavily and seething at each other, our angry interchange clouded over us palpably. Fury surged in my chest. I'd never experienced an anger so intense that I felt completely capable of ripping him apart.

I took several deep breaths to clear my mind. Shivering in the night air and at the thought of today's occurrences, I looked at Mark. "I'm sorry, but the bonfire out there caught my attention and I decided to investigate." I glanced toward the now nonexistent fire, which probably vanished into the night air along with Sam and Cynan.

"You've got to be kidding me!" he yelled. "Don't you have a safety switch in your head? Think about what you've been through today.

You were in a daze up at that freakin' house and you banged your head pretty damn hard.

"Matt and I are supposed to be watching out for you. We need to make sure you don't do anything stupid!"

Boisterous shouting and drunken singing echoed from the pub as someone opened the door and stumbled out. The other patrons were oblivious to our escalating argument.

"I am responsible for my life, not you!"

"Yeah, until the cops drag me and Matt off to jail because you disappeared on our watch," he fumed through clenched teeth.

Another pair of hands spun me around.

"What. Were. You. THINKING?!" Matt shouted rhetorically. His face contorted in a strange blend of anger and relief. Behind me, Mark's deep, angry breaths blew hot air against my neck.

"I didn't mean to scare you guys." Ashamed, my eyes dropped to the ground.

Mark growled.

"And I do have a safety switch. I can feel when something is dangerous. That," I said pointing toward the long-gone fire in the gloomy, mist-covered forest below, "did not feel dangerous."

"So, you're telling me that walking alone into the wilderness in the middle of nowhere wasn't dangerous?"

"Yeah."

"I think it's time to hire a new guardian angel for you 'cause apparently yours is on vacation," he scowled, our faces just inches from each others' again, snarling like wild animals not willing to back down.

Matt stepped between us facing me. He studied my face trying to figure out whether or not I was telling the truth. His eyes slipped from my face to my neck and blouse. Gasping, he dragged me beneath the street light. "Mark, get a damp towel. Now!" he demanded.

Taken aback by Matt's urgency, Mark ran into the pub without hesitation.

"What happened? And don't give me the silent treatment," he said forcefully. Furious though he may have been, the look in his eyes conveyed care and concern.

I lowered my eyes, embarrassed by my naïveté. "I met some people tonight who thought I was a threat. One of them got a little carried away."

"A *little* carried away!" his eyes burned with rage. In the dim moonlight his freckles disappeared behind the furious flush in his cheeks. "You've got blood all over you!" He tilted my face up to the sky to examine the puncture wound.

"How could they think that a little girl..."

Insulted, my eyes snapped back to glare at him.

"Woman," he corrected. "How could they think that a lone young *woman* might have been dangerous?"

"They said they've been attacked before and were being careful."

"Careful? Did you walk into a Satanic sacrifice? Why would they need to be careful?"

"They're Wiccans."

Mark burst through the pub's door and handed the damp towel to Matt. He dabbed the wound gently until he could see its extent. "It's not that bad," he muttered, "but it needs to be cleaned so it doesn't get infected. Let's go to the vicarage."

The vicar's cottage was less than a five minute walk from the pub. Matt rapped on the aged, wooden, front door. Silence. Impatient, Mark pounded on it.

A light flickered through the upstairs' window. Loud footsteps bounded on a stairwell followed by a tumble down the last few steps. "Bugger, bugger, bugger!" exclaimed an angry voice inside.

Not knowing what to expect, we looked at each other curiously as the door swung open to reveal a short, frail woman. Her plain brown hair was completely disheveled and a furry magenta robe was wrapped tightly around her solid, petite frame.

"What is it?" she asked gruffly.

Mark and Matt's mouths hung open, too shocked at the sight of the unbecoming woman to say anything. They struggled to talk but their mouths couldn't form coherent words.

"Um," I began. "We're very sorry to bother you, but we're looking for the vicar."

She raised one eyebrow suspiciously, "Why?"

"We're stuck in town tonight. We're hoping that he can tell us where to find a room for the evening."

She grimaced. "*I* am the vicar."

"Oh," I said surprised. I could almost hear Mark and Matt's jaws dropping further toward the ground.

Assessing us and guessing we were harmless, she smiled sweetly. "Welcome to Endymion. If you don't mind my meager accommodations, you're more than welcome to stay the night."

The vicar busied herself with preparations for our makeshift beds. Rummaging through her closet, she tossed several blankets and pillows over her head at Mark and Matt.

On our way into the living room, a loud voice bellowed from upstairs. "Are you coming back to me, sugarplum?"

The vicar blushed, matching the shade of her housecoat. "Yes, well, in a moment, dear," she stumbled over her words. *Explains the hair*, I thought amused by the idea of a woman of the cloth living in sin.

As soon as she completed a quick tour of the main floor, she excused herself and dashed upstairs.

Matt fumbled through the bathroom's cabinets and cleaned my wound with an array of ointments.

"Nice job, Dr. Matthew," Mark joked. "Ever think of being a doctor, dude? You've got a great bedside manner, not taking advantage of your helpless victim."

Matt rolled his eyes. "Knock it off, *dude*. And I already take care of enough people. I don't need any additional responsibilities." Turning his attention to me, he asked, "How does that feel?"

"Perfect!" I said, giving him a quick peck on the cheek. "Thanks."

His soft round cheeks blushed beet red.

A thunderous freight train roared through the silence of dawn. As the sunshine streamed through the window, it illuminated the engine...Mark.

Lying on the floor, Matt's blank stare gazed at me morosely.

"Get any sleep last night?" I yawned, sitting up on the couch to face him. I crossed my legs under me and stretched my arms trying to rouse the parts of my body which still wanted to sleep. The dagger wound throbbed dully, just enough to be bothersome.

"Are you kidding me?" he asked incredulously. "The monster in the corner snored all night. The hard, cold bed didn't help either."

"Come up here," I ordered, patting the couch. "There's no need to complain."

He climbed up and stretched across its length. "That feels *so* good," he sighed with pleasure. Matt truly felt like one of my brothers. I didn't even mind that he propped his feet on my lap. Glancing at my bloodstained top, he frowned. "Your shirt looks horrible."

"Hopefully there's a store nearby. Would you mind a little shopping before we head back?"

"Sure. Rachel would totally freak if we returned you in bloody clothes," he laughed.

Yawning, Mark uncurled from his cocoon and opened his eyes. "Mmmm, bacon." The tempting smell of bacon and fried eggs made my stomach to rumble. I hadn't eaten anything since yesterday's breakfast.

"Hungry?" Matt laughed. I blushed embarrassed.

"Me too," he smirked and leaned farther back on the couch.

Heavy footsteps sauntered into the room. The vicar, looking much happier and more put together, smiled broadly. "Well now, how are you this morning?"

"Great," we lied happily in unison.

"Wonderful," she said. After an awkward silence, she shook her head. "How terribly rude of me, I didn't introduce myself properly yesterday. My name is Bera and I'm the vicar of St. William's parish in Endymion Village."

"Nice to meet you, vicar," I replied, tossing Matt's feet to the floor and jumping up from my seat. "My name is Angel and these are my friends, Mark and Matt. Thank you so much for allowing us to stay here." I shook her hand.

"Is that bacon I smell?" Mark interjected, yawning.

"Mark!" Matt admonished.

"What? It smells great!" he exclaimed, completely oblivious to his rudeness.

Bera chuckled. "No problem at all. There's plenty for everyone."

The kitchen table was set with a white lace table cloth and simple white china. The pretty place settings stood in stark contrast to the faded orange cabinetry and yellow-brown linoleum.

Mark scooped several spoonfuls of eggs into his mouth and didn't wait to swallow before shoving in a strip of bacon.

"What's wrong with you?" I asked disgusted.

"Hungry," was the only word he managed to say without losing a crumb.

A knock at the front door distracted us from the let's-see-how-much-Mark-can-shove-in-his-mouth show. The vicar rushed to greet her visitor.

"Well, hello, Sam. What brings you here this morning?" she asked rather astounded. Considering Sam's evening exploits, she wasn't exactly the typical member of St. William's.

"Hello, vicar," she replied gaily. "Is Angel still here?"

"Come in. She's finishing breakfast."

"Hi, Sam," I greeted her eagerly, curiously. "These are my friends, Mark and Matt." The guys nodded toward her.

It was amazing how different Sam looked in the daylight. Her black bob glistened with a faint purple-blue hue which offset her sheer pale face. Her lips were a deep crimson. She was the living incarnation of Snow White. Dressed in dark jeans with a fitted, pale pink angora sweater, she looked mysterious and beautiful. From their undeniably infatuated expressions Matt and Mark clearly agreed.

Sam shoved a purple floral tote into my shocked hands. "I figured you may want fresh clothes." She glanced at my top.

"Thanks," I said completely taken aback by her generosity.

Smiling genuinely she turned to Yankee and Red Sox, who struggled to wash the plates without getting the watery mess all over the counters and floor.

Sam sighed, pushed both men aside, slid her thin body between them, and began directing their actions.

After cleaning up our beds, I rushed to the bathroom. Opening Sam's bag, I pulled out a knee-length denim skirt. Below the skirt was a neatly folded white cotton long-sleeved sweater. As I lifted the sweater, a note fluttered to the ground.

Tell your friends we're going shopping.
We need to talk.
S.

Intrigued, I got ready as quickly as possible while trying to avoid touching the disgusting scabby puncture wounds under my chin.

On my way to the kitchen, I overheard Sam debating the guys on the importance of soccer versus football in the world of global athletic influence.

"Where did you find her, Ang? I've never met a girl who can keep up with sports like this one," Mark thumbed toward Sam.

"I have an older brother," Sam explained with a sigh.

Knowing I needed to make my escape, I asked, "So, Sam, can you take me shopping?"

Matt and Mark exchanged nervous glances. "Angel, we need to leave," Matt offered calmly, but his expression betrayed his thoughts. He was reliving last night's disappearance.

"Yeah, but I won't be long, maybe a couple of hours." Neither man made a move.

"Come on, I need to get some *girl* things." I overemphasized the word "girl" hoping that they wouldn't want to know any more.

"Gross, Ang, 'nuff said," Mark blurted.

"I'll meet you at the pub by two, ok?"

Reluctantly, Matt agreed but the suspicious look on his face told me he knew I was up to something. I hugged Mark quickly and then Matt, whispering in his ear, "I know what I'm doing. I'll be fine."

The crease between his eyebrows furrowed deeply. He was far more worried than last night. Perhaps I should've been too.

7 ~ Journey

Sam rambled on about the weather until we were out of hearing range. She glanced nervously over her shoulder and quickened her pace across the cobblestone path to the pub.

"What's going on?" I demanded. I thought for sure she was just going to scold me again for last night's intrusion.

"I can't explain yet," she responded simply.

For some stupid reason I trusted Sam blindly and it didn't occur to me to push the issue with the cute stranger by my side. I was up for a little adventure. Since Zach's death, I gave up worrying about safety. Life's too short.

We walked silently past the pub and continued into the quaint little town. The pale tan and white cobblestone street was decorated cheerfully with a colorful array of potted plants and iron post top lanterns. The sun played hide and seek behind the heavy cloud cover and the smell of pending rain lingered on the breeze.

"Oh, before I forget," Sam paused. She opened her hot pink purse and pulled out a little purple plastic bag. "The coven wanted you to have this."

Opening the bag curiously, I found my flashlight and a new can of pepper spray inside. Her mood turned serious again as we rounded the corner at the end of the main street's shops. She sprinted confidently across the street and up a steep set of stairs leading to a lonely stone cottage. The pink, wooden sign suspended beside the steps stated: "Flora's Dress Shoppe."

"So, we *are* going shopping?" I asked confused.

"Sort of."

The store was neatly organized with exquisite dresses in every color and style imaginable. Hats, gloves, shoes, and purses filled every corner of the front room. The satin and lace was enough to suffocate anyone in a sea of girly frills.

"Good morning, Flora," Sam greeted the frazzled, plainly dressed owner cheerfully. Flora's short, light brown hair stood in a mass of frizzy, large curls haloing her head.

"Why hello, Sam," Flora answered startled. She was engrossed in a tabloid covering the latest royal scandal. "Haven't seen you in a fortnight. What can I do for you today?"

"My friend and I would like to look at the dresses in the basement. Do you mind?"

Flora eyed me suspiciously over her bifocals, but trusting Sam she nodded in agreement.

"Thanks," Sam shouted excitedly while pulling my arm after her toward the basement door.

"Call if you need anything." Flora adjusted her glasses and sunk into the magazine again.

Sam yanked me down the stairs slamming the door behind us in the process.

"What's in the cellar, Sam?"

"Last season's dresses."

"So you're going to dress me up on the way to the guillotine?"

"We don't have time, Angel. We must hurry."

I sighed anxiously and somewhat petulantly. Where was she taking me? And better yet, why hadn't she told me? I wanted to kick my own butt for wandering into the unknown last night. Now I had to deal with the consequences.

The basement mimicked the upstairs collection of designer gowns except we were squished between rows of a pastel spring garden instead of bright summer colors. Sam glanced around the room making sure no one could see us. We slipped through a door in the back of the room and entered a very cold, damp, dark storage space. The unfinished walls were made of the grey stone that lined the store's exterior.

"Turn on your torch," Sam commanded. She eyed every corner of the room warily, then rushed to the back and reached for a stack of shelves. The rack opened the wall behind it and we peered into a black hole. I pointed the flashlight into the opening which was covered in cobwebs.

"Oh, Sam, do we have to go that way?" I whined. "I hate spiders."

"Angel, there are far worse things in the world," she scoffed. "Please step into the tunnel." It wasn't a request; it was an order. She glimpsed back into the storage space before swiftly locking the door behind us.

The tunnel smelled musty, tainted by the odor of moist dirt and stale water. Tree roots crept along its earthen walls through which large rocks protruded randomly. Water dripped in the distance.

We interlocked our arms and tiptoed forward cautiously. Every sound stopped us dead in our tracks. The pounding of my heart sounded loudly in my ears.

"Are you going to kill me whenever we get to wherever you're taking me?" I asked, really not wanting to hear the answer.

Sam chuckled. "No," she whispered emphatically.

"Then why orchestrate this elaborate escape?"

"For your safety."

"What happens if Flora discovers we're gone?"

"She'll think we slipped through the back door to the hills behind her store. We do it all the time."

An ear-piercing howl echoed in the tunnel and raced toward us. In an instant, Sam flipped up a wand and zapped a barely noticeable orb of purple light ahead of us. It illuminated a gargantuan black wolf just before striking it down.

Petrified, my feet took permanent root. Sam was a witch with a wand. A wand that actually worked. A wand that just knocked an animal out cold.

"Come on, Angel," she coaxed. "We need to keep moving."

"B...b...but what if it follows us?" I worried, eyeing the beast carefully.

"It won't."

"How do you know?"

"I killed it," she said simply.

My immediate relief at not being mauled to death was quickly replaced by terror of the waif next to me capable of killing living things by a quick flick of her wrist. Witches, witchcraft, and folklore were part of my upbringing in Massachusetts. Sam's stunt was not normal for Wiccans of any sort.

I inched back to the tunnel door. "Where are you going?" Sam cried in a whisper.

"You...killed...it?" my terrified voice managed to squeak.

She took a deep breath and stepped slowly toward me locking my eyes in her gaze.

"I thought you were a good witch?"

"Angel, I'm a good *Wiccan*," Sam said calmly. "I was sent to protect you. Others are searching for you as we speak. This was our only option."

"Who're they? Why is anyone looking for *me*? What the hell is happening?!" I was freaking out. I couldn't help it.

"I can't tell you until we're out of here."

"Was that thing one of 'theirs'?"

Sam nodded.

My heart slowed its frenetic pace while my mind sped up trying to decipher who or what was after me and why.

"We need to keep moving. It's not safe for us to be here," she added sincerely.

I hesitated, took a deep breath, and began the march deeper into the tunnel's abyss.

"Just don't look down," she said flippantly, stepping over the dead animal as if it was a pile of laundry.

"Promise to tell me how you did that?" I asked still scared but rather intrigued.

"Sure," she said with a smile in her voice that made me doubt her sincerity.

We continued in silence for what seemed like hours. Water seeped through the tree roots and cascaded lightly down the walls creating an ankle-deep stream down the middle of the tunnel.

"This water won't get any deeper, will it?" I hoped.

"Shhhhhh," she whispered quickly. "Put out the light."

"Why?"

"Now!" she urged fiercely.

I pushed the off button and waited for her next direction. Despite the fact that I just witnessed Sam use a wand, project light from that wand, and kill an animal, I didn't think she'd hurt me.

"They're here," she whispered fearfully in my ear. "Three hundred meters ahead. Keep low and when I tell you to, press against the wall as far as you can and don't move."

Maybe I was still sleeping. This certainly rivaled my worst night-mares. I had a long history of vivid dreams. Trying to wake myself up, I pinched my arm so hard I was sure to have a black and blue bruise. As we further immersed ourselves into the blinding darkness of the tunnel's winding paths, very real voices echoed closer.

"Now!" Sam shouted into my ear in a muted whisper.

I ducked and burrowed into the brittle dirt wall. Leaking water cascaded over my hair and face. My body became completely rigid while I waited for the intruders to pass.

"Shhhhhhh," a male voice whispered a few feet ahead of us in blinding darkness.

"Shut up," retorted a second gruff male voice.

"You'll pay for that," growled the first.

"Mmmmm. Mmmmm," the second man mumbled struggling to speak.

They paused beside us. I caught my breath.

One figure sniffed the air. Crouching over us, he ran his fingers along the contour of the wall and dug his fingers into random patches of dirt and stone. Dust and shards of rock ricocheted off of my back.

Slowly, he inched closer until he towered over my huddled frame. He slid his hands down the entire length of the wall and continued over my body. Without warning he sunk his dagger-like fingernails into my shoulder and waist. The pain was excruciating, but I was unable to utter a sound or move.

He darted upright and turned to walk away.

My body eased with relief.

The footsteps stopped. One of them turned back. Instinctively, I tightened my body wishing I was a rock.

He took two running hops forward and kicked me in the gut with all his might.

"Owwwwwwwwwwww," he howled in agony.

Growling, he rubbed his face along the length of my body, pausing at moments to smell and analyze my frame. Satisfied I wasn't what he thought I was, his limps echoed in the stream drifting away into the distance.

"You ok?" Sam asked eventually.

"Uh-uh," I shook my head. The pain in my shoulder and waist throbbed dully.

"Just a little farther."

We detached ourselves from the dirt wall and swiftly, silently crept along the passageway until a slight glimmer of light illuminated a corner of the tunnel. As we approached it, the little dot of light brightened the maze revealing giant roots which must have belonged to an enormous tree above ground. Sam slid between the roots and ran her fingers along the dirt wall until she found what she needed.

She threw her body against the wall and a door opened into the clearing from last night's bonfire. There were no remnants of the fire, but even in the dim sunlight the grove of trees was unmistakable.

She whistled like a bird and Edwin stepped into the clearing from behind an ancient oak tree. His short cropped black hair with silver streaks overemphasized his pale, gaunt face, which looked nearly translucent against his black jacket and trousers.

"Edwin," she hurried breathlessly, "they were there. They were in the tunnel!"

He gasped. "We have no other choice then. We'll have to find another way." He looked sadly at Sam before pointing his wand at the tunnel door.

The tree shook violently as its roots detached themselves from the ground and slithered like serpents along the forest floor for several hundred feet before shooting into the earth once more.

The clearing quivered with such a tremendous force that it knocked us off our feet. The earth beside the tree buckled and pushed itself up slightly creating a raised mound of dirt. Another tremor shot the mound along the ground, winding itself in and around the trees until it stretched beyond our sight. In an instant the ground collapsed and was flat again. Ivy, ferns and underbrush crept across the land hiding the transformation. A strong gust of wind blew leaves across the tunnel door making it disappear.

My mouth hung open in wide-eyed fascination. "Sam, there's so much you need to tell me."

"In time," she nodded, turning to Edwin urgently. "We have to get out of here." The wind tossed Sam's short raven bob around her face mimicking the urgency of the situation.

He nodded once and grabbed our hands. Closing his eyes, he whispered "Avolaremus!"

I must've been dreaming because in the blink of an eye we appeared in a cramped yellow kitchen. Various herb bundles hung from a string of twine over the sink. A dark purple clock hung above the door. All of its numbers were replaced with XII and in the middle of the clock was written *The Witching Hour*. Oak cabinets and a light oak finished floor completed the room's simple, ordinary décor.

"If you can travel instantly, why did we have to trudge through the tunnel?" I asked slightly irritated and completely strung out.

"I'm not strong enough to travel that way yet without help. I'm practicing though," she reassured, rummaging through the cabinets.

"Then why didn't Edwin just come get me?"

"Would you honestly have gone anywhere with Edwin?"

I glanced at Edwin who was intently assessing my reaction. "No, I guess not," I gave in reluctantly, looking around the room.

The kitchen table sat next to a partition wall that separated the kitchen from a comfortable living room with white plush furniture, a stone fireplace, and an enormous Palladian window that overlooked an expansive backyard with green grass and a dense forest.

"Where are we?" I whispered to Sam.

"Morgan's cottage."

"What?!" *Delivering me to the wolves...*

"Don't worry. The whole council will be here in a second."

"Council?! I need air," I muttered and spun around reaching for the door.

A shooting pain hit my back buckling my knees. I crumpled into the kitchen chair beside me. Dazed, the room twirled around and around.

"Samantha!" Edwin screeched.

"She can't leave!"

He closed his eyes and breathed deeply, obviously irritated by Sam's unexpected stunt. "We'll give you five minutes," he said. Glimpsing at my limp body hanging from the chair, he changed his mind, "make it fifteen. Give a basic explanation to calm her. You know the task at hand, Sam. Don't jeopardize it."

"I know," she said firmly through clenched teeth. "I'm as much a part of this as you."

He glared at her and then swept out of the room. Sam turned her attention to me, her expression softening. "Let's clean you up in the loo."

She escorted me to the bathroom which was a painfully bright white hue. The only dash of color came from a bundle of lavender hung delicately from a purple organza ribbon over the white lace window curtain. Sam and I stood before the white porcelain sink and stared at the strangers in the mirror.

These were not the same girls who left the vicarage less than an hour ago. We were caked in dirt from head to toe. Streaks of dirty water deposited muddy residue on our faces and matted our hair with moss, twigs, and random bugs. My white shirt and shoes were now mottled brown. Sam's whole look resembled something akin to the creature from the black lagoon.

Sighing at the extensive clean up job at hand, Sam said, "Cynan will leave fresh clothes for you. I'll use the loo upstairs." She turned to leave but stopped dead in her tracks and spun around.

"Did one of them touch you in the tunnel?"

"Yeah, actually, he dug his fingers into my shoulder and waist. Are you going to explain what happened?"

"Take off your jacket," she demanded.

I slipped it off. Sam gasped in horror covering her mouth with both hands.

"What? I can't see," I complained, trying to look over my shoulder like a dog chasing its tail.

"Doesn't that hurt?" she asked apprehensively.

"What?"

"Angel, your sweater is covered in blood."

I turned my right shoulder toward the mirror to see that deep red blood stains soaked my entire shoulder blade and extended to my waist. I gasped so loudly that Edwin was knocking on the door in the next instant.

"Girls?" he asked.

"Send Morgan," Sam beckoned.

Morgan appeared in the doorway, a grave expression hiding her emotions. Her scary features from the night before had softened as she stood before me in a billowing, deep purple satin muumuu with gold trim.

"Sam, Angel," she greeted us solemnly.

"Morgan," we answered in unison, our eyes and voices scared.

"Angel, remove your sweater, please," she requested calmly, almost kindly. I guess I caught her on an off-day yesterday.

Usually I was far more modest than this. Even at my dance recitals I'd wear an oversized t-shirt under which I'd change outfits. Now I was stripping in front of strangers.

"Sam, how long ago did this happen?" Morgan asked, examining me.

"About fifteen minutes ago—do you think there's enough time?"

"Enough time for what?" I barked.

"To get the poison out of your system," Morgan said casually.

"Poison? Poison! Sam, what was in the tunnel?"

"The men we're protecting you from."

"*This* is protecting?" I asked, glimpsing at my wounds.

Morgan interjected. "If it weren't for Sam, you would've died fifteen minutes ago, Angel. Now, please lay in the dry bathtub as you are. I need to fix you before it's too late. Sam, get my healer's kit."

"Will I be ok?"

"You'll survive. The question is what the poison will do. There is a chance that the attacker was just trying to determine what you were. The bigger concern is whether or not he will be able to identify your blood."

"What...How? Why?"

"He will know for sure that you're here and he'll have his hounds track you."

"Oh..." my mind drifted to the wolf that lay silenced in the tunnel. "What's happening?"

Morgan didn't answer. Considering I was beginning to feel woozy, I didn't push the issue; although, the thought churned in my mind.

Sam returned in a few seconds with an old fashioned doctor's kit. Morgan pulled out several scalpels, numerous bottles, and herbs. She stuffed a marble mortar with various leaves and set them aflame on top of the cabinet beside the tub.

"Close your eyes, Angel. It'll be easier that way," Morgan assured.

I squeezed them shut and concentrated on her hushed chanting as she plunged the scalpel into each wound and poured some sort of liquid into each one. Though the wounds burned, the smoke from the herbal incense dulled my senses.

"Sam, how did we make it out of there alive? How come the men walked by us and why didn't I feel pain when one of them kicked me?"

"It's mind over matter combined with a heavy dose of wishful thinking," she smiled.

"Magic?"

"Call it what you want. We both wanted to escape undetected. I was able to convert us into rocks. I don't have much experience with shape-shifting though, which is why he nearly caught us."

"He dug his fingers into me so deeply. How much blood do you think he had on his hands? Do you think he'll be able to find me?"

"I'd imagine he got a handful of dirt and rock stuck beneath his fingernails, not your blood."

"Then why am I bleeding?"

"Mind over matter. You really weren't transformed into a rock or the dirt wall. I just visualized our transformation. Actually, I think you visualized pretty well too otherwise his kick would have broken your ribs. Although he experienced us as rocks, we really weren't. So whatever injuries we sustained, stay with us afterwards."

"Whatever you say, Sam, whatever you say." None of this made sense. Maybe I was still stuck in my nightmare.

When Morgan completed her ritual, she helped me sit up.

"How are you feeling?" she asked.

"Dazed. But there's no pain. Thanks, Morgan." I inspected my injuries expecting to see numerous cut marks and congealing blood, but my skin had healed perfectly. "Wow! That's so cool!"

Leaving me alone in the bathroom to get ready, I stared at my naked reflection in the mirror. The external injuries were gone, but

I was still caked in dirt. My body rebounded from so many tortures over the past few months. Its resilience really shocked me as I thought how my outward strength balanced my extreme internal vulnerability. Zach's death compounded with my dad's gave me a new "who cares" attitude toward life. In reality though, I just wanted to sink into a long forgotten dark hole and cry endlessly.

The morning's events made no sense. Obviously magic was involved somehow. The weird thing was that I wasn't scared of Sam or the strange things she did. Two days ago my life was normal and now here I was acting as if these supernatural events weren't extraordinary.

Gotta tell Mom to bring the shrink with her to the airport when I arrive, I thought wryly. Maybe I really had lost my grip on reality.

Rubbing my eyes and face out of frustration, the hot shower eased my cares and concerns. Absorbing its warm, renewing energy, I tried to forget the past 24 hours.

I rubbed the area where my wounds had been—so deep, so strange. The sores tingled as if little spiders were crawling furiously beneath the skin.

Sighing deeply I groaned at the thought of what was waiting for me. *Council?* How many people made up this council? Who was a part of it? What did they want from me? Conversely, what would I want or need from them once I'd know their intentions? So many questions, only one way to find out.

8 ~ Alliances

"**I** trust you're feeling better, Angel?" Edwin asked. Though his tone seemed concerned, his commanding presence demanded respect and attention. His serious expression and distinguished appearance reminded me of suave politicians.

I nodded briskly taking in the nervous eyes of ten ordinary-looking Wiccans evaluating me. My cheeks blushed with the rush of embarrassment. I hate being the center of attention.

"Do you know why you're here?" Edwin began.

"Sam said it's to keep me safe," I replied shyly.

"True, but before we get started we need to identify you…"

"Edwin," Morgan interrupted, "is that necessary? It's obvious she's the one, why else would they have followed her?"

"We can't be too sure. So much depends on this."

"Yes, but she's terrified already."

From the back of the room a hefty man with Einstein-like hair and a wandering eye spoke up, "I feel her. I *know* she's the one."

"Enough," Edwin interjected. "We will verify her." Turning his attention to me, he placed his hand on my back lightly and led me to an empty seat at the kitchen table.

My mind blanked. *Verify me?*—as if two attempts on my life in the span of fifteen hours weren't enough proof? Edwin placed a manila envelope in front of me. Confused, I looked at him, glanced at the envelope, and back at him. "Is this all?"

"Yes." I breathed a sigh of relief. "I thought for sure some sort of torture was going to be involved like mind games or broken bones..." *Shut up,* my thoughts interrupted. *Don't give them any ideas.*

He smiled at my ignorant idiocy and motioned toward the envelope. I emptied the contents onto the table carefully. Trembling uncontrollably, my fingers sifted through my birth certificate, pictures of my mom and siblings, pictures of my dad and me at a baseball game, my prom picture with Zach, a key to my house, a report card, my passport and my plane ticket home.

"Enough, Edwin!" Morgan shouted, grabbing my things and stuffing them back into the envelope. "We need her to cooperate, not run away!"

My gaze lingered on the envelope dangling from Morgan's fingers. "Please, somebody, tell me what's going on," I begged feebly.

Edwin knelt beside me. "Angel, there are forces beyond our control—yours, mine, all of ours," he said, gesturing around the room. "They are preparing for a battle..."

"Edwin!" exclaimed a short, eccentric woman in the center of the crowd. Her large, furry, fuchsia hat nearly knocked over the men next to her as she leapt to her feet. "You've already said too much. She must not know."

"She needs to know why she's in danger, Moira," he explained.

"But she is not one of us," added a young, dark-skinned man with kind, deep mahogany eyes. Under normal circumstances, I would've been offended at being called an outcast. Today, I was glad. He continued, "If she knows too much, or remembers too much, she may leave, which will be detrimental to the entire plan."

"She doesn't know the things we know, Edwin. She doesn't believe the things we do, either," interjected an elderly woman wearing a violet hat that matched the lavender hue of her bluish eyes.

"But she might remember," Edwin spoke softly, his eyes downcast. "That's ultimately our only hope. She may find strength in her memories."

"Or she may do something drastic because of them," argued the handsome, dark-skinned man.

"The Bellatori Dei commanded it. We must stand unified by their decision," soothed Morgan.

"You know as well as I that we've been infiltrated. Not just our council, but the entire circle has been penetrated and the perpetrators have not been caught. For all we know, the mole could be here right now!" Edwin exclaimed.

The council dashed to its feet, each shouting member pointing accusatory fingers at the others. A gentle hand rested on my arm. I glanced up to see Sam beckoning me to follow her. We slipped upstairs unnoticed. The group's yelling shook the frame of the house as we sat on a bay window sill overlooking the herb gardens and forest in the front yard. From my vantage point, there were no other homes or people nearby for miles.

"How are you?" Sam asked, worry painting her face and voice.

I needed to think about that. My mind was spinning with so many thoughts and emotions I couldn't think straight.

"I...I really don't know." All of a sudden I envisioned Mark and Matt frantically searching for me. "I need to call my friends, Sam. They're probably worried."

"I can't let you do that."

"Why not?"

"We don't know whose side they're on."

"What?" I asked incredulously.

"You heard Edwin. Everyone is suspect."

"But they could've killed me tons of times on the trip to the manor yesterday or even last night when I was all alone with them."

"Timing is everything. Each side needs to be very careful. One wrong move on either's part and the battle will be lost."

"Aside from the fact that I have no clue what you're talking about, I don't feel like Mark and Matt would hurt me. Please let me call them," I pleaded. If Sam and her crew harmed me, I figured the guys would be able to trace the call somehow.

Sam eyed me cautiously. "On one condition," she bargained, "you can't tell them where you are."

"Fine."

Leaving a voicemail for Matt, I battled feeling security with the jocks and complete insanity with Sam. She was very sweet, but the situation was quickly escalating into something that was a bit too sci-fi weird for me.

She stared intently, seeming to pick up on the fact that I thought they were all nuts. "Do you want to know what's happened so far?"

I nodded eagerly.

"I can't tell you everything, but I can share a little more now that we're safe. Our ancestors built the underground tunnel a couple thousand years ago. We're all direct descendants of the Celts who lived in the Welsh countryside far before Roman rule entered our lands. This specific group of Celtic people chased our enemies from mainland Europe to this region.

"We've protected the people around here—and all over the world— for a very long time. Over the past several weeks the celestial calendar pointed toward great changes that are about to happen.

"Edwin's brother, who was our high priest, was killed by an intruder a few weeks ago. This is why Morgan attacked you last night. You see, some of the others can change their appearances and make us believe they're something they're not. While we predicted your arrival, we needed to make sure that you were in fact the one we've been waiting for. You are linked to the changes that have been foretold."

She took a deep breath and exhaled slowly. "For centuries the tunnel was a safe—well, until today anyway—avenue for us to travel between the village and our homes. The wolf and the things," she said with great disdain, "belong to the other side. They have also been expecting you and will do whatever it takes to get you.

"As for how I killed the wolf, we all have powers. It's nothing extraordinary."

"But how do you do it?" I asked in disbelief.

"Lots of practice and self confidence."

"But I thought you weren't allowed to kill anyone?"

"We are bound by one very strict rule, 'harm none.' However, I was charged with defending you today at all costs, so the council will look the other way in this instance because it was in self-defense."

"But why would you risk your life for me?"

"Because, Angel, all our lives—our very existence—depend on you."

9 ~ Staying for a Spell

I didn't know what to say. I pinched myself to make sure I wasn't stuck in some comatose nightmare. Staring blankly through the window, I faintly noticed my confused reflection staring back at me. My attention shifted to a family of deer that walked into the clearing near the front yard. They grazed on the grass peacefully while the birds chirped gaily overhead. Sunlight streamed through holes in the dense cloud cover highlighting sections of the lawn and herb beds below. In front of the house an English cottage garden with a rainbow of flowers swayed in the gentle breeze.

I rested my forehead against the window, vicariously enjoying the tranquility just beyond my fingertips. How much had my life changed in a few short days? From the comfort of my boring and depressed home life I was thrust into the brink of insanity in a strange country with very strange people.

Then again, who's to say that any of this was actually real? Perhaps the coven was insane and I was caught in the middle of its delusions. If I appeased them now, I'd be safe until I found Matt and Mark tomorrow. So, I figured I'd play along with the coven's hallucinations.

"Sam," I said softly, trying to sound convincing, "I'll help you however I can."

Morgan appeared out of thin air beside us. I flinched banging into the window. *Bizarre.*

"Is it true?" she asked. "You'll help us?"

I nodded.

"I knew it!" she exclaimed jubilantly. "I felt the winds change."

We walked arm-in-arm down the stairs as Morgan announced the "good" news to everyone. I prayed she didn't have a sixth sense that would uncover my lie.

Silence engulfed the room as each council member exchanged unspoken words and glances. Then they roared in excitement and happiness. Out of nowhere, champagne appeared on the table and Edwin passed crystal flutes to everyone in the room. Since the entire council was still convened, I assumed they all remained in Edwin's good graces as trustworthy coven members.

"My dear," he turned to me, "we are forever indebted to you. We will protect you with our own lives to the ends of the world just as you save ours now. To Angel!" He raised his glass and the overjoyed crowd toasted my bravery...*or stupidity*...

As the celebration calmed, Edwin took charge. "Right then, we know what must be done next. We have twenty five days to plan."

"Twenty five?" I asked.

"Yes, they must wait until the blue moon which happens to be the second full moon of the month and the first after the summer solstice. The earth's cycle will begin entering its dark, hibernating phase by moving toward the winter solstice. The ones who are after you live in the dark and are most powerful then. This will be their ideal moment to strike."

"So, I'm supposed to stay hidden for twenty five days?" I asked incredulously.

"Not quite," answered Edwin. "They can't touch you until then. It's too risky for them to imprison you because we can break the truce and attack early, which would be in our favor. They won't chance it. You're too important to their cause."

"And you still won't tell me who they are and why they need me and not one of the other seven billion people in the world?"

"Right," said Morgan.

"Humph," I grunted, crossing my arms.

Ignoring my tantrum, Edwin continued, "We need to determine which of their soldiers wander the village. Their numbers will divulge how prepared they are. If they're worried about their safety, they'll stay clear of the town. And if we find Anchises, we'll find the High One."

"Who's Anchises?" I interjected.

"Anchises is the second in command and close confidant of the High One. However, he is more dangerous in many ways than the leader." Edwin's voice dropped and his eyes looked at me filled with a hidden message I didn't understand.

"The best way for us to assess their numbers and strengths is to mingle in Endymion," he said, changing the topic on purpose. "Tomorrow is Saturday and tourists will filter into town. It will be easier for us to walk among them without being obvious."

I stared at Moira's purplish, hot pink feather hat and didn't really think that mingling inconspicuously would be possible.

"What will we do with Angel?" inquired Morgan.

"She'll accompany us."

"Have you gone mad?" Sam yelled at Edwin. "We can't risk that chance. They'll fight us in the open street!"

"The Bellatori Dei are relying on our evaluation," continued Edwin.

"Can I say something?" I interjected. "There's one problem with this plan."

Edwin shifted his impatient and frustrated gaze to me.

"My friends."

The entire room looked at me curiously, begging for an explanation.

"My friends have protected me since I arrived in London. I can't just disappear. They'll get the police involved."

Morgan faced Edwin, "Do you think they were the ones sent to her?"

Edwin turned to me, "Has anything strange happened while you've been in their care?"

"Nothing that they caused. In fact they've been more worried about my well-being than you," I glared at the council. "No offense,

Morgan, but my friends haven't tried to kill me and, Sam, they haven't put me in harm's way."

"Well, perhaps they can meet us in town tomorrow. We'll judge them ourselves. Can you convince them that you want to stay here tonight?" he gestured toward my phone, which I had shoved into my skirt pocket.

I dialed Matt's number hoping he wouldn't answer. Of course, I wasn't that lucky. He picked up on the first ring.

"Uh, hi," I said as cheerfully as possible.

"Where are you? Are you ok?" he asked frantically.

"I'm fine," I said in the most soothing voice I could muster. "Listen, I want to stay with Sam tonight..."

"Absolutely not!" he roared so loudly the entire council jumped backwards.

"Listen to me," I tried to say convincingly. "I'm ok...no broken bones, no hurt feelings, no scary monsters." *Well, maybe...*

"Where are you? We're coming to get you."

This was going to be more difficult than I thought.

"I'm nearby. It doesn't matter anyway; I'm staying with Sam tonight. Just meet me in town tomorrow around ten, ok?"

His anxiety-ridden voice whispered, "Be honest. Do you feel really safe?"

I looked apprehensively at the eclectic, anxious group of Wiccans encircling me. "Yup," I lied.

Matt sighed. "You're not coming back tonight no matter what we say, are you?"

"You're getting to know me so well, Matt," I laughed.

"Ten a.m. tomorrow by the pub. If you're not there, we're calling the police, the FBI, the..."

"Understood," I rolled my eyes. "See you then." I hung up before he could persuade me otherwise.

"We need a strategy," Morgan ordered.

"Let her walk through town by herself," Edwin said casually.

"What?" the council yelled in unison.

"Hear me," he continued calmly. "If she wanders the town on her own, they will reveal themselves thinking she's defenseless."

"They know we're not that stupid, Edwin," Cynan said impatiently.

"Yes, but they'll be tempted by the situation. They'll keep her in sight. We'll be able to determine their numbers by observing their reactions."

"And Anchises?" inquired Moira.

"Hmmm," Morgan pursed her lips thoughtfully. "He's the tricky one."

"How so?" I asked.

"He can change his appearance and manipulate others' vision and thoughts. Thousands have lost their lives to his cruelty, viciousness, and murderous greed. He is stronger than all of us combined."

I swallowed hard, choking on air. "And you want me to wander by myself with this Anchises guy randomly looking for me? How does that make sense?"

Edwin interjected, "Anchises wouldn't be searching for you. He's too important to their organization for such a job."

"This will also give us a chance to observe your friends, Angel," Morgan added.

I considered the plan. "Where will you be?"

"Out of sight," Edwin added, "for you and them anyway."

"We'll be positioned throughout the town. You won't be harmed," Edwin reassured.

"The only recommendation the council makes," said the cool, pleasant, dark-skinned man, "is that you stay in plain sight, Angel. Do not hide. Do not disappear..."

I shuddered at that thought.

"...do not enter any places where you can be separated from the crowds."

I nodded completely unconvinced this was going to work. My mind was already imagining one of the bad guys catching me. If I was lucky, maybe they'd kill me quickly. If I wasn't lucky, what would I face? Torture?

Perhaps I was just overreacting. While the coven's warnings were urgent, part of me couldn't shake the thought that they were just a group of psychotic inmates who escaped the local mental health ward.

"Come, let's prepare you," Morgan said as she encircled me with her arms and led me outside to her garden picking up a light wicker basket on the way.

The exterior of the home looked like it had been plucked straight from a Thomas Kinkade painting. The large grey stone cottage was situated in a little glen surrounded by ancient, massive oak trees. A small, round garden filled with snapdragons, lilies, and roses adorned the middle of the front yard. The dirt driveway wrapped around the garden island and wound beyond the house through the tree groves and over a little hill before disappearing into the forest.

The council followed us solemnly into the endless sea of herb beds.

"Is this going to hurt?" I whispered to Sam.

She giggled, "No. Haven't you figured out yet that we won't hurt you?"

"Yeah, but Morgan did try to kill me last night."

"Yes, and she saved you today," she murmured.

I sighed resigned. It was obvious I had no control over the situation.

"Friends, hold hands," Morgan commanded, leading me to the center of the coven's circle. She exited it and walked clockwise around the group chanting a hushed incantation while pouring salt along the group's circular perimeter.

Perusing the garden and pulling a pocket-sized dagger from her belt, Morgan cut a variety of flowers and herbs. The aroma of fresh lavender, basil, lily of the valley, verbena, and thyme lingered on the gentle breeze. I inhaled deeply. It smelled so refreshing, so soothing.

Using her dagger, she cut an imaginary door into the salt circle and closed it once she was inside. She returned to me and opened her basket. At my feet she laid a small, circular, white marble altar, which was engraved with a silver pentacle. She wound the herbs together in turquoise, white, and silver gossamer ribbons. In the center of the bundle, she placed a single white rose.

Morgan set the herb bundle atop of the altar and then lit five silver tea-light candles at each point of the pentacle. After placing the lit match into the herbs, she raised her arms to the sky.

"Father sun and Mother moon,
We thank your infinite boon.
Protect Angel by day,
Keep her safe, out of harm's way.
Accept our offering now
In humble prayer we bow,
Accepting your bid to do right
Guard us purely in your light.
Earth, wind, water, fire
Protect us from evil's ire.
Goddess Spirit we ask in love
That you protect us from far above.
Blessed be."
"Blessed be," repeated the coven.

Morgan ended the spell by opening the invisible door through the salt circle. Each council member exited slowly, except for Sam. She walked over to me as I sat down behind the burning embers of the fragrant herbs, watching the candles' flames dance in the scant breeze.

Smiling, she settled lightly onto the soft grass opposite of me and extended both her hands over the altar offering. I placed my hands in hers. She closed her eyes, lowered her head and spoke softly, "Mother Goddess, guide us right as we fly through twenty five nights. Give me strength, give Angel courage, and give us the gifts we need to flourish. No matter the conclusion we thank your blessings, come what may. Bind us together as sisters today to fight side-by-side in our own way. Blessed be."

Sam hugged me tightly. "I won't let anything happen to you," she whispered into my ear.

I stared at her not knowing what to make of this statement. She clearly knew me better than I knew her. *But how?*

The quaint cottage brightened the black woods as the sun slipped into sleep. Most of the council had departed; only Morgan, Edwin, Cynan, and Sam remained.

"Sam, aren't you going to have to get home soon?" I asked. "It's getting dark. You don't want to be out in the woods by yourself."

"You're right. I don't want to be out in the woods by myself. But I'm not going anywhere. This is my home," she grinned and popped a green grape in her mouth.

"You live here with Morgan?" I asked.

"Yes, and Edwin and Cynan too."

A curious "Oh" escaped my lips.

Sam flashed her perfect teeth in a white toothy grin. "Morgan and Edwin are our parents," she clarified.

"Really?"

She nodded, smiling at my stupidity. I should've seen the resemblance.

I sighed lost in thought. The day's events were catching up to me physically and emotionally. I needed to think. "I'd like a few minutes by myself. Do you mind?"

"Sure. Just don't go outside alone."

I reassured Sam, thanked her family for dinner, and trudged upstairs to the hallway that overlooked the forest in front of the cottage. Sitting in the bay window, I pressed my forehead against the cold glass and stared at the soft golden glow of the cottage's lights cascading onto the grass. A strong breeze blew across the trees and shrubs creating the illusion of shadows jumping across the yard. A bright flash of cool blue light struck the center of the forest and illuminated a path right to the cottage's door. The waning moon peered through the heavy clouds casting itself across the yard.

The next twenty-five days were a death sentence of sort. Survival was out of the question. How could I, Angelika Kiss from Salem, Massachusetts, survive some sort of battle? How could I make a difference? I didn't even know what the battle was about. Better yet, what did I possess that the "other side" wanted or needed so badly? If supernatural powers were so common in the coven, what could a human girl with no skills, talents, or preparation possibly do?

Only a couple of months ago I welcomed death. I could fathom dying on my own terms if I wished it, but having someone kill me was another story. What would death feel like? Would it be quick and painless or slow and excruciating? Who would be the one to kill me? Would I be brave enough to defend myself or would fear freeze me? Would my dad be waiting for me on the other side? Would I see Zach again? *Zach...*

I opened my phone and scrolled through old pictures of my family in happier times: siblings playing, dad kissing mom, my fat black and orange cats. I lingered longer on Zach's pictures. Imagined visions of his death still tormented me. Did he feel any pain? What was the last thing he thought of? Did he know I loved him more than life itself? Was he hurting now because I couldn't move past his death? Would he be jealous if I found someone else?

I should have been thinking about starting college in the fall, not worrying about life and death and a weird war between people who clearly lost their minds! I zapped myself back into reality—well the reality by which most people live—and remembered my mom and Kelly would be worried about me.

Checking my messages, I found one from Kelly:

Moms freakin. Didn't send car... Wuz up?

Well that was a slightly disturbing discovery—although compared to the things I lived through today, it didn't shock me. If the good guys and the bad guys knew I was coming, one of them probably sent it. At least I didn't die. I should've trusted my gut feelings and taken the bus instead.

Sending a quick reply, I turned my attention back to the window and the pitch blackness just a few inches from my face. Placing my forehead against the window its cold touch eased my nerves. I opened my eyes slowly and raised my face toward the moon. It was missing from the night sky. At first my eyes didn't comprehend what they saw. Was I imagining it? I blinked again and realized that a mere two inches from my face were the red eyes from the hostel and the pub.

I fell off of the window sill as my screams echoed throughout the house. In an instant, Sam and Cynan were by my side. All I could do was point my shaky finger toward the window. "F...f...f...face!" I struggled to remember how to breathe. Cynan blocked me protectively from the windows while he strained his neck to look through them. Sam and Edwin ran outside to investigate.

Sam returned with a white rose. "This was on the front step," she explained, twirling the long, thorny stem curiously.

The family took turns guarding the home overnight in case the scary stranger returned. As I drifted off into a sea of rest-deprived tranquility on the floor beside Sam's bed, Morgan asked Edwin, "Do you really think we'll be able to protect her without losing our lives?"

Edwin paused, "I don't know, Morgan. I just don't know..." his words hung heavily with despair.

10 ~ Test

Although dawn birthed a new day, it still remained greatly impregnated by the prior night's fear.

Thoughts of my stalker, the wolf, and Anchises plagued me on the drive into the village. *What the hell is happening?* Perhaps I was in an accident; I was now in a coma; and all this was just a horrible nightmare. It couldn't be real, could it?

Shoving the iPod's earbuds in place, I turned the music up as loud as I could tolerate without going deaf to drown out the scary thoughts screaming at me. Instead I thought of my angel. He was always a bright light shining in my pessimistic darkness.

It seemed like it was just yesterday that Zach gave me the iPod and set up this song list for me. He loved making mixes. Speaking his feelings through music, he'd search through thousands of songs from various decades just to pick the perfect tunes. His obsession rubbed off on me. Music became an easy way to express my own thoughts and emotions. This playlist was perfect right now. It contained just the right mix of angry, placating, and pulsating beats.

I always told him I didn't need expensive gifts. I loved the little things—like this mix. And now, I'm grateful for the memories these songs conjured and for the peace they provided. My trusty iPod had been glued to my ears 24/7 since Zach died.

Edwin eased into a parking spot along a side road several blocks from Endymion Village's short main street.

"So, you seriously want me to wander around by myself?" I asked for the tenth time, feeling more terrified of this mission now than last night.

"Yes," the family replied in frustrated unison.

"But what if I need you?"

"You will not leave our sight," Morgan assured.

"What am I supposed to do? You'll be hunting bad guys and I'm supposed to stop and smell the roses?"

"Yes," Morgan insisted. "Blend in, fit in. Shop. Eat lunch. Have fun!"

My nerves were giving way. I felt completely unprepared. "Tell me again why Sam, Cynan, and I can't walk together?"

Closing his eyes, Edwin tried to maintain his composure before replying. "If they see a group of us together with you, they may very well risk an open attack. Now hurry, before they see us! "

"Angel, calm yourself," Morgan reassured. "You will not be in harm's way. They are too weak and there are too many witnesses."

Scared stiff, I stared at four sets of encouraging eyes. Drawing a deep breath, I stepped out of the car hesitantly and wandered into town alone, my eyes jumping toward the slightest of sounds and movements.

The village was packed with tourists. How on earth was I going to find Mark and Matt?

I should've known better. In no time at all, they were barreling through innocent bystanders, running toward me.

"Angel," they said coolly but embraced me, relieved to see I was okay.

"I told you I'd be fine," I scolded. I wanted to tell them everything, but they'd be put in harm's way with the coven. So I kept the weird happenings of the past 24 hours to myself.

"Yeah, but you're prone to finding yourself in situations that aren't good for you," Matt chided as he placed his hands on either side of my face to search my eyes for the truth and then inspect the scabs under my chin.

"Wanna get breakfast?" Mark suggested, diffusing the tension.

"Is food all you ever think about?" I asked in disbelief.

He pondered for a moment, before shrugging his shoulders. "Yeah. Pretty much."

I turned toward Edwin and Morgan, who kept a safe distance from me to be less conspicuous, and pointed subtly to my jocks. They nodded politely. Mark and Matt assessed them from head-to-toe before focusing their skeptical attention on me again.

"Ready to go back to London?" Mark asked curiously.

"Actually, I'm gonna go shopping for a little bit."

"You shopped all day yesterday. How much time do you need? There're like four stores in this whole town!" he exclaimed.

"I'd like to be on my own for awhile. I'm not saying that we can't be together. I just prefer you following me instead of shopping with me."

Mark and Matt raised their eyebrows and exchanged suspicious looks.

"So let me get this straight," Matt began, "you want us to keep you safe from a distance because you don't want to be seen with us?"

I thought for a moment and nodded. I didn't want to hurt their feelings, but Edwin and Morgan's warnings still sounded in my ears. Who could I trust?

Glancing around, Morgan and Sam shifted their weight fretfully. It was time to disperse before anyone noticed us.

I turned my attention back to Yankee and Red Sox. "Just do what I ask. A lot depends on this, k?"

Their perplexed looks were filled with mistrust, but they nodded anyway.

"Thanks. I'll explain later." Right as I said this, I wondered why I didn't just run away with them—run far away from the insanity. Then I remembered the wolf, the rock transformation, and my stalker's scary red eyes. Maybe something really was happening.

I walked with false confidence onto the cobblestone main street and began window shopping. The quaint town was no more than two blocks long and another two wide. The antiquated Tudor-style buildings brought its history to life. I was a sucker for historical stuff—the older the better.

Ordinary-looking, camera toting tourists meandered about the town. I blended into the aimlessly wandering crowds.

Matt trailed about fifteen feet behind me pretending to be interested in the potted plants lining the street. I smirked at the thought of this huge, athletic, macho guy caring about the assortment of dainty pastel flowers. Mark on the other hand wasn't as good of an actor and just glared stalker-like at my every move.

Cynan and Sam caught up to the jocks and from the looks of things they were explaining what was happening. I figured I'd play along; I didn't mind shopping anyway.

Mark was right. There were very few stores. In the distance Endymion Manor loomed atop of the hill that overlooked the tiny village. A handful of little shops and cottages lined both sides of the main street and ended with the pub on the left, which backed to the local cemetery.

A flock of girls bouncing up and down in front of the pub grabbed my attention. They crowded around a handsome, young guy who seemed to enjoy his audience.

His messy, loose, dark brown curls, smooth pale skin, and chiseled features belonged in Hollywood. He was tall and muscular, not built like Mark or Matt, but it was clear he worked out. He was rather attractive in a brooding James Dean or young Elvis sort of way, but he seemed far too arrogant. From the smile plastered on his face, it was obvious he loved the attention showered on him by the bevy of teenage girls trying to get at him.

His eyes glanced up and met my stare. Something about his magnetic gaze caught me off guard. I shook my head to get him out of my thoughts and returned to my shopping trip.

A shadowy, narrow alley stretched between the bakery and the shoemaker. The passage led toward the hillside and country fields I wandered through a couple of nights ago. Half-way down the cobblestone lane, a little stone porch jutted from the wall behind the bakery. Decorated with a myriad of potted flowers, it looked like a miniature oasis in the middle of a stark, barren desert of stucco and brick. Intrigued, I wandered toward it. A faded white wooden plaque hanging on the door claimed, "Ye Olde Book Shoppe."

Amused by this chance finding, I hopped into the store. Books covered every wall, every shelf, every available space. The front room had a four sided wooden shelving unit blocking its center. There was only enough space for one person to navigate his or her way through the sea of literature. The smell of old paper, faded blue drapes, pale blue wallpaper with gold imprinted fleur-de-lis, and a dusty mustiness caricatured the shop as a relic of Victorian England. As I examined the store's extensive collections arranged neatly on floor-to-ceiling shelves, a faint ray of sunlight streamed through the front window illuminating dust particles swirling through the place and landing on a row of mythology books set along the right wall.

For the first time since I entered the store, I realized I was the only one in there. I could've heard a pin drop. Anxiety washed over me until a man with short, white hair popped his head up from behind the check-out counter. He pushed his spectacles onto the bridge of his nose, which looked more like the ocean's continental shelf than a sensory organ.

His disheveled appearance did nothing to dissuade me from the fact that I knew I liked him instantly. His soft, round, clean shaven face appeared to be very kind. He wore a sky blue button down cardigan over a striped dress shirt and pair of khaki corduroy pants. I couldn't have imagined a more eccentric, or perfect, book shopkeeper.

"Hello, miss, may I help you find something?" he asked graciously.

"Thank you, but I'm just looking."

"Well, if you should need any assistance, simply ring this bell." He gently tapped the bell on his desk and its faint ring echoed in the vacant room.

"Thanks," I smiled, knowing that ringing the bell would be a completely unnecessary exercise considering the deathly still silence engulfing us.

I turned to face a stack of history books that resembled the Leaning Tower of Pisa and plucked out three: "History of Wales," "Occult Folklore," and "Ancient Mythology." Considering my current situation, I figured these might provide some insight. There was just one other book I needed.

"Excuse me, sir? Do you happen to have any books about Endymion Village?"

His eyes opened wide in surprise. He hesitated, "I'm not quite sure actually. I haven't had anyone request one about the history of the village before."

"Really?" I asked astonished. "Wouldn't tourists be interested in the town's history?"

"Well, we have books about the Manor," he corrected quickly. "However, the village…" he furrowed his eyebrows. "Let me see…"

His voice trailed off as he disappeared into the back of the store. In less than a couple of minutes he returned and handed two books to me. One was the tourist-focused story of the Manor. The second was an ancient leather-bound volume entitled "Endymion" with faded yellow pages.

Noticing my interest in the older book, he explained excitedly, "The 'Endymion' book has been here for generations. It's the only one we have. I'm afraid it's a bit outdated, but it should provide an acceptable overview of the village."

"Thanks!" A little insight on the crazies who lived here might help me better understand the place. I peered around the stacks and racks of books and found exactly what I needed. In the front, right corner of the store was an out-of-place bean bag chair and crude reading area.

Sinking squeakily into the navy vinyl chair, I hid behind the book. My quiet moment of solitude was quickly interrupted by a curious meow. A beautiful and quite plump black tabby sauntered over and hopped into my lap. I stroked her head lovingly; she purred contentedly.

"I've never seen Mrs. Cuddly-buggy take to a stranger like that before," the bespectacled bookshop owner remarked peculiarly.

"I love cats." Black as midnight, her thick coat felt like velvet beneath my fingers. The corpulent ball of fur stretched happily across my lap.

Screams and squeals sounded in the alleyway rushing toward the store.

My thoughts flew to Sam, Cynan, Mark, and Matt. *What's happening?* I sprung up violently from my seat knocking poor Mrs. Cuddly-buggy to the floor.

The shopkeeper rushed to the door. Lifting the end of the curtain hanging from the front window, I peered from the corner hoping I wouldn't be seen.

"Humph!" I growled vehemently. The local celebrity and his scantily clad entourage had arrived. Rolling my eyes, I settled back into the reading corner hoping they'd leave sooner rather than later.

"Shhh, shhh, ladies!" a smooth voice attempted futilely to calm the teenage groupies.

"Put a bloody sock in it!" a thin, high-pitched voice shouted. "He's trying to speak," she cooed.

Silence befell the crowd. I could just imagine his infatuated followers hanging on his every word and breath. I shook my head in disbelief that any girl or woman could act like a little puppy following its master everywhere.

"Ladies, wait here. I'll be back in a minute," the voice assured his cult in a sexy Londoner's accent.

"But I want to be with you!" shouted one voice.

"Please let us come with you," begged another.

"Ladies, I promise to return to your *beautiful* arms in less than five minutes." With that, the front door opened followed by a chorus of frustrated grumbling.

Pushing the door completely shut behind him, he sighed in relief and leaned against it.

"Must be nice having a legion of adoring fans," the level-headed shopkeeper observed.

"Sometimes," the celebrity muttered displeased.

"What can I do for you, young man?"

"I'm in need of reading material for my trip. I was thinking a nice, thick book on ancient mythology would do the trick."

Weird coincidence, I thought diving into my book and failing horribly at ignoring his egomaniacal personality.

"Let's see, what can we find in the history section?" the shopkeeper mumbled to himself.

""Asian Mythology," "Celtic Myths & Legends," "Greek Pantheons," "Medieval Faith," "Native American Belief Systems," "Paganism Now & Then," "Religious Freedom in Africa," "Roman Mythology,"" he paused. "Do any of these sound appealing?"

Running his fingers absentmindedly through his thick messy locks, Narcissus replied, "Do you have a compilation?"

I glanced at my copy of "Ancient Mythology" and, using my foot, slid it quietly to the other side of the bean bag chair and out of view.

Narcissus continued, "Well, do you have any books about the history of Endymion?"

"Yes, we have a nice assortment of guides and history books about the manor on that shelf behind you," the shopkeeper motioned to the books against the store's back wall.

"Do you have something specific about the history of the village?"

Looking puzzled, the shopkeeper glanced at me sideways. "I'm sorry, but that young lady has our only copy."

The celebrity turned his attention toward me. "Ah, thank you, sir," he said emphatically.

I needed an escape plan. *Should I pretend to be deaf? Maybe dumb? Maybe I'll pretend to get sick and I'll run out of the store. But I need to pay for my books first.* Unfortunately by the time I decided to pretend to get sick, he was in front of me. *Darn.*

Smiling in the most charming and disarming way, he squatted beside me and waited until I emerged from the safe confines of the book.

"Can I help you?" I asked in a cool and controlled manner, my eyes glaring at him.

"Why, yes, I hope *you* can help me," he said with a hint of mischief in his eyes.

I could see why the girls liked him. A mess of dark brown and golden highlighted curls stood in a rumpled mess on top of his head. It must have taken a couple of hours to get this hairstyle to look like perfect chaos. His clear green eyes gave him an air of handsome mysteriousness while they flickered with flecks of gold that matched the gleam in his hair. His thin straight nose balanced out his chiseled jaw line and pallid features making him look like the gods carved him from a piece of flawless, white marble.

To the best of my abilities I resisted his charm, but his good looks melted my frigidity. *No, no, no!* my inner voice commanded.

"My name is Rick."

"I'm Angel," I offered reluctantly.

"Well, yes you are," he said seductively.

"Oh, please," I snapped highly irritated. "What do you want?"

Taken aback by my unexpected rudeness, he raised his eyebrows. "Well then, you have two books which I happen to want. Are you planning on purchasing those?" he asked, pointing toward my mythology and Endymion books.

"Yes, actually."

"I'll give you twice what they're worth, if you'll let me have them."

"Don't think so."

His body stiffened. Apparently, he was used to getting his way. I didn't think he liked the idea of having to beg.

"Three times as much," he suggested.

"Nope."

"You're being entirely unreasonable," he grumbled.

"Really, if you have nothing else to say, please leave me alone. I'd like to read."

He narrowed his eyes and scowled. "Why do you want those so much?"

"Why do you?"

"You're unbelievable!" he exclaimed exasperated.

"I was here first!" I shouted in his face, completely aware that my argument made me sound like I was four.

Mrs. Cuddly-buggy jumped in my lap and hissed furiously at Rick. She swatted his face scratching his chin. I smiled at him caustically.

Glowering, he dabbed the scratch carefully with his fingers. Jumping up in silence, he glared at me and spun around to leave. He swung the front door open so hard that it banged into the wall before slamming shut. The gleeful squeals of his adoring fans faded down the alley.

"Well now, that was interesting wasn't it, Mrs. Cuddly-buggy?" I muttered, lovingly petting my new found friend and defender.

"Interesting indeed!" the shopkeeper exclaimed. "I've worked here for over forty years and never witnessed two people fighting over the same books."

I placed my selections on the waist-high checkout counter, which was an antique buffet table intricately carved from dark oak. Mrs. Cuddly-buggy twirled in and around my legs, purring like the engine of a Mack truck.

I fingered the pages of "Endymion." "May I borrow this one?"

"Absolutely," the shopkeeper replied without hesitance. "I feel safer knowing it's in your hands than his," he said flatly, motioning to the front door.

I couldn't have agreed more; though, my reasoning was a bit more spiteful than distrustful. "Thank you...er...what's your name?"

"Albert," he replied, smiling at my effort to be cordial.

"Well, Albert, I'm Angel. I'll come back soon. Thank you so much for your help."

I gathered my things and opened the front door cautiously, peering around the corner in case Rick was waiting to ambush me. Relieved that he was nowhere in sight, I thanked Albert again and stepped into the shadowy alleyway.

I knew that Mark, Matt, and the entire council were looking out for me but not seeing them felt rather unsettling. I hurried back to the main street and continued past the shoemaker's storefront.

Distracted by the altercation, all my enthusiasm for shopping evaporated. I walked to the end of the apparel store building, which sat diagonally across from the pub. I stood next to the waist high, grey stone wall which served as a fence from the main street to the rolling hills of the lush, green countryside.

Before I could regret my decision, I dialed my mom. I crossed my fingers hoping she wouldn't pick up. Ring one…Ring two…Ring three…*Yes! Almost into voicemail…*Ring four…

"Angelika?" my mom's weary voice asked.

"Yeah, hi mom," I tried to sound happy for her.

"Angelika Kiss, you are in serious trouble! Second-hand messages from Kelly do not count as keeping in touch with your family!"

"Mom, everything is fine. I'm obviously alive and well. I've just been really busy."

"Yes, apparently," she shouted. "Kelly mentioned something about a day trip with two boys you just met. Have you lost your mind? I taught you not to trust strangers when you were three. Do we need to have that conversation again?"

"Mom," I whined. "Come on. Mark and Matt are really nice and actually they've…"

"You know better!" she shouted.

"Don't you trust me, mom?"

"Angie, I trust you," she said, trying to regain her composure. "It's other people I don't trust; especially people I don't know."

"Mom, I'm old enough to make my own decisions."

"Yes, sweetheart, you are, but I'm not old enough to lose a child yet."

A lump in my throat choked my words.

"Mom," I sniffed as my eyes clouded over with an impending storm of tears, "Give me some credit. Besides, I've got a once in a lifetime chance to see a beautiful country now."

"Is it beautiful there?" she asked, her tone more tempered.

"More than you know. I'm looking at the rolling emerald hills right now which are right next to an enormous forest. And guess what?"

"What?" she asked intrigued.

"It's just like the movies. A couple nights ago a mist crept onto the field swallowing everything in its path. It's so cool in a very creepy kind of way," I laughed nervously. *Or just plain creepy...*

She forced a laugh. "Sweetheart, be safe. No matter what you do, remember to be careful."

"I swear, Mom, I will." *No need to tell her that a wild witch and wolf nearly killed me or that I'm being hunted by bad guys.*

"I love you, Angie."

"Love you too, Mom. Kiss the kids for me, k?"

"Sure will, sweetie. Call again soon."

Guilt-ridden anxiety hit me like a brick wall. Although I needed the break from my mom, siblings, and responsibilities, I truly missed her. I didn't even ask about what was happening at home.

Inhaling deeply, the tingle of crisp air refreshed my guilty conscience and body. I walked over to the wall of boulders across from the pub. Perching on top of one, I memorized the beauty of the hillside and forest. Chirping birds flitted over the treetops and across the fields. The green grass stood tall with yellow and orange wildflowers dotting the landscape. About a hundred yards beyond the base of the hill a narrow field stretched along the forest's natural border. The silence of the dense, dark forest exuded contentment.

The constant hum of people walking and talking on Endymion's main street became a numbing source of white noise. Opening my bookstore bag, I pulled out the "Ancient Mythology" book and began flipping through the pages. *Celts, Druids, Norway, Rome, Greece, England...*

I opened the chapter on the Arthurian legends. *Lancelot and Guinevere, how romantic...*I always felt badly for King Arthur, but how could he expect such a beautiful young wife not to fall madly in love with the most courageous and handsome Lancelot.

Scanning the countryside, my thoughts imagined Lancelot and Guinevere meeting in the forest's clearing to steal a passionate kiss. *Mmmmm...*

"You really hate me that much?" asked an irritatingly seductive voice, rousing me from my fairytale reverie.

"Why won't you leave me alone?" I exclaimed thoroughly exasperated, slamming the book shut. Where was Mrs. Cuddly-buggy when I needed her?

His train of mindless followers remained parked in front of the pub tapping their feet angrily, yelling at each other, glaring at me. *If looks could kill...*truer words were never spoken.

Suavely, Rick leaned against the boulder propping his hand next to mine. He wore a casual, but expensive looking jacket over a worn T-shirt and dark, dressy blue jeans.

"Because I can't believe you won't let me buy those books from you," he retorted persuasively. "And because I've never been more captivated by anyone."

Something's wrong with this man...why would he talk to ME this way? I was utterly ordinary. He had beautiful girls throwing themselves at him and he was talking to *me*. My brain might not have been functioning properly, but his was worse off.

I stared into his cool green eyes and turned my face so that our lips were in dangerously close proximity. "You want something you can't have and I'm not gonna give it to you." I smiled at the double meaning of my words for he wasn't about to get my books or me.

Our eyes locked. Finally, and somewhat reluctantly, I broke the spell by pulling away and turning to face the countryside.

"You're fascinating," he muttered.

"And you're obnoxious."

He laughed sarcastically. "And that's why I want to know you better. I've never met a girl like you before," he said innocently, dropping his debonair façade momentarily.

Cracks broke through my frozen lake of protection. *No...No...No!*

"Ang, why don't you introduce us to your friend?" Mark demanded out of nowhere. He broke Rick's trance over me before I could do something I'd seriously regret.

"'Ang'? Are you serious?" Rick jumped up, confronting Mark. "You call this exquisite goddess, 'Ang'? She is most definitely an angel," he said in a loathsomely, delicious way.

Mark's speechlessness was quickly counteracted by Matt. "Problem here, *Angel*?" he overemphasized my name while glaring at Rick scathingly.

"It's time for me to go." Rick leaned into me nearly touching his nose against mine. "Until we meet again, *Angel*."

With that he spun around and jogged back to the eager arms of his doll collection and I instantly remembered why I hated him. Matt and Mark wrapped their arms around me so that I couldn't get away while we weaved our way through the crowds back toward Edwin's car.

Edwin flew at Mark.

"You jeopardized our entire mission! Why did you interfere?"

"You could have had her killed because of your entire mission. We will not allow you to use her like that," Matt interjected, growling at Edwin. Until this very moment, I hadn't realized Matt and Mark's intense protectiveness.

"Enough!" Morgan assuaged. "We will continue this conversation at the cottage. Boys, follow us home."

The palpable tension mounted as Matt and Mark muttered on the way to their car and Edwin climbed into his.

I glanced back toward the main street and froze.

The face from the hostel, the pub, Sam's house—he was hiding behind his black hoodie on the other side of the street staring at me.

Probably due to the fact that I was surrounded by people I trusted, my fear vanished and I dashed across the road.

As he saw me approach, he literally vanished into thin air. There was no sign of him anywhere.

A spark of color caught my attention. Something lay on the ground where he had been standing. I sprinted to it.

A single white rose rested at my feet.

11 ~ Assessment

"That's gross," Sam said, creasing her cute button nose. "Why?"

"Perhaps because a mysterious stalker dropped it on the ground?"

"True, but you have to admit it's a perfect rose," I said, twirling the stem. Each petal opened just slightly releasing the most fragrant aroma.

"You've come a long way from being so worried about everything just a few hours ago," Edwin commented.

"What's the point in worrying about it?" I shrugged. "Whatever will be, will be, right?"

"So what did toerag want with you?" Cynan interjected, plopping himself in the kitchen chair beside me.

"Rick?" I verified. I barely understood American slang let alone British.

Cynan nodded.

"I don't know. He wanted to get to know me, I guess."

"I'll wager he did," Cynan laughed.

"We were taking bets on whether or not you'd snog," Sam added.

I pursed my lips, upset I was the source of their bet.

"He was cute. Don't you think so, Sam?" I asked.

"Cute? He's gorgeous! I saw how he wanted to get to know you."

"Yeah…he was weird." And it *was* weird. Why would he be interested in me? I'm utterly average. He's indisputably gorgeous and popular.

"Weird? What's weird about Rick Kingston?"

"Rick who?"

"Kingston. He's one of the UK's hottest new movie stars. Don't tell me you don't know who he is?"

"Sorry," I shrugged. "No idea."

Sam shook her head in frustration. "You are *so* lucky," she sighed, her eyes glazing over.

Morgan laid the table with a delicious spread of veggies, wraps, and summer fruit. We filled our plates and made ourselves comfortable on the living room's hardwood floor. Sam popped in a CD of classical music to calm our nerves.

Edwin and Morgan brought their conversation into the room as they sat beside us.

"It's apparent our little experiment today added more confusion to the situation. Since we couldn't complete our investigation," he shot a dark look at Mark and Matt, "let's try again tomorrow."

"What?" Morgan snapped. "Endangering her—or us for that matter—any more than is absolutely necessary is out of the question!"

"Then what do you suggest, Morgan? What are we going to report to the Bellatori Dei? Besides, there was nothing out of the ordinary in town today. We could all use some time to relax before we have to avoid the town altogether."

Clearly disagreeing with Edwin's sentiment, Morgan reluctantly asked me, "Would you mind visiting the town again?"

"I guess not. I actually didn't mind it so much today."

"As a precaution, I'd prefer you and Sam walk together," Morgan continued.

"But Morgan, that…" Edwin began to argue.

"Not another word, Edwin," she spoke fiercely, her thin frame shaking. In a flash she flew up from her seat, her hazel eyes burning ferociously. Strawberry blonde curls fell from the loose bun on the back of her head as she trembled.

Our eyes were glued to the fuming fearsome looks on their faces. Edwin hesitated just long enough for Morgan to sweep out of the room in a huff. He frowned at us and followed her swiftly.

We exchanged confused glances. Sam and Cynan looked worried but distracted themselves with their dinners. Afterwards, the guys relaxed watching a soccer game, Sam began a sketch, and I paged through my new books.

Snuggling into an oversized, soft, white chair which sat beneath the Palladian window, I spread the books across my lap. I paused for a moment considering the excitement the "Endymion" book had caused today. "Rick…"

"Rick what?" Cynan asked, turning toward me. His eyes studied me carefully.

"Nothing." I didn't want to speculate about why Rick would've wanted this book. Was it just a conversation piece? Did he really want it?

Cynan glowered. He knew I was holding back. "Well, we'll keep a close eye on that wanker tomorrow if he's in town."

I carefully lifted the ancient leather cover of "Endymion" and scanned the book until I found an attention-grabbing chapter entitled "The Endymion Family."

> …Endymion Manor, built by Sir William Endymion in 1495 for his lovely wife, the first cousin of Queen Isabella of Castile and Aragon, sits high atop the Welsh countryside overlooking Endymion village and the Bristol Channel.
>
> Sir William and his powerful wife ruled the region strictly. The devout Catholic family built a chapel at the foot of the hill upon which the manor stood. They attended mass every Sunday with the villagers. Although they were generous benefactors of the

arts and the local commoners, gossip of the couple's unhappiness and strange practices consumed the townspeople.

Sir William's close friendship with the Duke of Cornwall furthered gossip of the Endymions' deteriorating relationship.

However, in the year 1503, Lady Endymion bore an heir for Sir William naming him, Cenweard (pronounced Kēn * ward).

No one knows why, but the father and son's relationship broke apart as Cenweard neared his twenty-second birthday. According to our sources, some speculated it was due to his father's desire that Cenweard enter into an arranged marriage with the Duke of Cornwall's beautiful daughter, Lilith.

Shortly afterwards, Sir William was murdered and Cenweard assumed control of Endymion Manor as well as all of his father's properties and obligations. While the murderer was never apprehended, locals conjectured of Cenweard's role in his father's death.

Tragically, Cenweard committed suicide at the age of 23. After his death, Lilith revealed she was pregnant with his child.

The fatherless son inherited all of the Endymion family's assets...

While the Endymion line has continued through the centuries, the family's tragic beginnings in Wales have marred its history. Stories of ghosts and supernatural murders haunt this affluent and influential family's name and home to this day...

Interesting, very interesting.

"Sam?" I asked, startling her from an ink sketch of Rick. She was in the process of shadowing the edges of his face when my interruption caused her to draw a thick black line across the page. The picture's likeness to Rick was eerily identical. His eyes captivated me straight from the paper.

"Yes," she said annoyed.

"Would you mind if we went to the bookstore tomorrow?"

"Of course not. I haven't paid a visit to Mrs. Cuddly-buggy in awhile," she smiled.

"Mrs. Cuddly what?" asked Matt, raising his left eyebrow.

"The book shopkeeper's cat," I clarified.

"Man, I'm in serious need of sports," complained Mark, flipping quickly through the TV channels. "All this girly crap is killing me!"

We stayed up half the night, each of us obsessed with our own distractions. I awoke in the morning to find that we all passed out in the living room. Sam's face was glued to her sketch on the coffee table. Mark was outstretched on the floor, snoring loudly. If it weren't for his deep breathing, I would have sworn that Cynan was dead lying face down in the pillows on the couch.

Matt was missing.

I sat up craning my neck to look into the kitchen and around the corner to the bathroom. *Empty...*

Turning my attention toward the dawning sun, I caught Matt sprinting across the lawn, springing over the picnic table. His shirtless, muscular body glistened in the gold rays of the sunrise. He stopped suddenly and spun around to face me. I gasped, taken aback by his blank, black gape.

Embarrassed, I waved and quickly focused my attention on Sam who was slowly waking from her coma. She opened her eyes one at a time assessing her surroundings. When she realized all of us were now staring at her, she darted upright, the drawing clinging to her cheek.

"Oh, no!" she exclaimed, wiping drool from her mouth and peeling the dampened sketch from her face. The ink drawing of Rick's eyes, nose and mouth tattooed itself to her right cheek.

"Gives new meaning to drooling over a guy, doesn't it?" Mark laughed heartily.

"This will be useful. If you don't remember what he looks like, all you have to do is look at Sam's face!" Cynan laughed, bumping his fist into Mark's.

"Come on, Sam, let's see what we can do with that," I offered, walking her to the bathroom.

After a half hour of scrubbing, exfoliating, and covering up, we dulled the image so only the outline was visible.

I walked into the kitchen to find Morgan and Edwin making breakfast for the boys. My single white rose sat in a bud vase in the middle of the table. Morgan must have placed it there. I hadn't forgotten the night at the bonfire; she still scared me, but her caring, nicer side balanced out the insane fury that nearly ended my life.

Cynan leant casual clothes to Yankee and Red Socks. Matt showered and dressed and joined the smorgasbord affable as ever. I couldn't get over his workout. His caring kindness made him feel like a big teddy bear. Yet there was something supernatural about him this morning—animalistic in a way. The empty, black look in his eyes conveyed a power I hadn't noticed before.

Sam returned a few minutes later in red Capri pants, black ballet flats, and a white hoodie sweatshirt pulled over her head with black Jackie O sunglasses that hid most of her face.

"Samantha," Morgan chided. "There's no need to hide."

"If you had a picture of the most gorgeous guy in the world tattooed to your face, you'd hide too!" she exclaimed morosely.

The men roared with laughter. Sam's malevolent glare silenced them in an instant.

"It can't be that bad," Morgan said, examining Sam's face before agreeing. "Well, let's hope it'll be gone by tomorrow. Girls, would you like breakfast?" Morgan asked, changing the subject seeing that Sam was still visibly upset about her condition.

"No, thank you," I replied. "I think I'll try the pastry shop in town."

"Oooh, that sounds delicious. I'll eat there too," Sam agreed.

"Fine then. I guess we're ready to go," Edwin said. "Same responsibilities as yesterday—look for anything that seems out of place and keep your eyes on the girls."

Everyone nodded.

"Will the council be there too?" I asked.

"Yes," Morgan said carefully. "If any of the *others* are there, we'll need all of the help we can get."

12 ~ Take Two

"I guess this makes up for the shopping day when we were nearly killed, huh?" I joked with Sam.

She smiled, hooking her arm through mine. "Where to first?" she asked as we rounded the corner onto the main street.

Our eyes rested on the bakery. Beckoning us, the aroma of fresh coffee, tea, and cakes was too hard to resist. We ran across the cobblestones, giggling all the way. I ordered vanilla cappuccinos, a buttery croissant and a currant scone for Sam.

As we made ourselves comfortable at a small, round oak table, Sam opened her purse and pulled out a copy of Teen Hollywood.

"Seriously?" I asked condescendingly.

"I just thought you'd like to know more about Rick."

I couldn't help it—I rolled my eyes. Ignoring my reaction, she flipped to Rick's centerfold and shoved the magazine into my unwilling hands.

- Name: Rick Kingston
- Born: Waltham Forest, England
- Age: 21
- Hair: Brown
- Eyes: Green
- Likes: Interesting conversations
- Dislikes: Boring people
- Favorite movie: "Braveheart" & anything historical

- Favorite book: "The Plague" by Albert Camus
- Fantasy: Whisking away a special someone to a private castle for a romantic weekend
- First memory: Sitting in the countryside playing peek-a-boo with my mother in the tall grass and wildflowers
- Favorite accomplishment: Playing Romeo in the Royal Shakespeare Company's adaptation of "Romeo and Juliet"
- Relationship status: Single
- Idol: King Edward VIII—he gave up all of his power for love
- Favorite fictional characters: James Bond
- What do you look for in a girlfriend: Mystery
- Movie endings—happy or real: Depends on the characters
- Love or lust: A little of both
- Favorite car: The Aston Martin DB9 Volante convertible—actually any Aston Martin
- Favorite vacation hot spot: Peloponnese Peninsula, Greece
- Favorite part of the day: The quiet night as I fall asleep alone

"Thanks, Sam, but what happened yesterday was extraordinary. What's the likelihood of our running into him again?"

She shrugged. "He's filming a movie here and Endymion is rather small." She sighed, staring at his picture. "Isn't he beautiful?"

Caught in a moment of complete teenage normalcy, Sam was a complex contradiction. On one hand, she was just like all girls our age and on the other, she possessed powers that could kill. Yet her storybook face was impossible to resist. Her eyes conveyed wisdom well beyond her years, and her broad smile was filled with confidence and pure joy.

"Sure, Sam," I replied uninterested. "Are you ready to go to the bookshop?"

Albert was just where I left him yesterday, still situated behind the counter reading a novel.

"Well hello, Angel," he greeted enthusiastically. "I didn't expect to see you again so soon! Hello, Sam."

"Hi, Albert," Sam replied pleasantly.

"I couldn't wait to come back. I'm actually looking for more information about Endymion. May I look at your archives?" I asked.

"Certainly," he said eagerly, waving us into the backroom.

Dark, dusty, and musty, the room's eclectic character was topped with gothic shaped, stained glass windows, a leather chair reading corner, and a grey stone fireplace. A Tiffany table lamp sat upon a small, round, dark cherry finished table beside the chair.

Cherry bookshelves lined every free space of wall. Albert pointed to a section of ancient looking books with leather bindings and frayed ends.

"Are these yours, Albert?" I asked. Sam busied herself with Mrs. Cuddly-buggy, who purred contentedly in her arms.

"Yes. They've been in my family for generations. We trace our history back to the beginning of Endymion village."

"Really?" I asked, my interest piqued.

"My family once farmed the fields behind this bookshop. Over time, many travelers visited Endymion Manor so my family created this shop. Of course at that time we sold goods for traveling.

"Anyway, many of these are priceless, old texts," he added.

"May I look at them?"

"Why certainly. I trust you, Angel. And if something happens, I know where to find Sam's parents," he winked at Sam, who ignored him as she was thoroughly taken with the plump feline.

The tiny ting of a bell sounded. Albert excused himself to tend to a new patron.

"Sam, look at these!" I exclaimed in disbelief. "I can't believe they're just sitting out in the open."

"Albert takes great pride in his store. I'm not surprised."

My gaze skipped across the various titles. "There's a hand-written version of the bible here! That's got to be at least six hundred years old. Wow!"

"Uh-huh," she replied completely distracted by the cat, which pawed her face while she cradled it like a baby. Clearly, Sam was not going to be any help.

Numerous volumes about the country's history, the royals, and the battles fought in Wales littered the collection. Shoved between volumes one and two of the "History of Great Britain" was a book inserted backwards so the spine was hidden against the bookcase. *What's Albert hiding?*

I gently tugged the book from its prison. Gold calligraphy on the faded brown leather-bound cover simply stated, *Endymion*.

I didn't know what I expected to find today, but this discovery felt like the Holy Grail. With great care, I lifted the cover. The stiff, yellowed parchment seemed so fragile that it could crackle and disintegrate at the mere touch of my fingers.

The handwritten book resembled a diary. The table of contents laid out the chapters:

Endymion Family
The Manor
Missing
The Dark Hills
Mysteries

I flipped the pages quickly to read the *Missing*.

Missing
1497
Livestock

1498
Blacksmith's baby boy
Cows

1499
All children under the age of four

1500
Shoemaker and his wife

1501
Two travelers
Priest

1502
Five travelers

1503
Butcher's baby daughter

1504
Foreign dignitaries

The list continued through the centuries to the last inscription:

Sir William Endymion X

A shiver convulsed my body. Almost every year since the manor's creation, people or things had disappeared mysteriously. This must have been a coincidence. After all, people disappear everyday. But what was the probability of so many disasters striking a small village?

Flipping forward, I immersed myself in the *Mysteries* chapter and picked out the most interesting events from each year.

Mysteries

(1498) Duke of Cornwall visits the Manor frequently. Every time he arrives, demons possess Lady Endymion and escape through her fits of hysterics.

(1503) Town rejoices at birth of Cenweard Endymion. Sir William leaves the manor with more frequency.

(1505) Lady Endymion overlooks Sir William's infidelities.

(1510) Young Master Endymion is a saint. His parents' behavior speaks of Satan's influence.

(1525) Sir Cenweard Endymion spends much time with one of his household's servants. Girl died.

"It's fascinating, isn't it?" Albert startled me.

Trying to recover my breath, I panted, "Yes, yes it is. May I borrow this book?"

"Unfortunately not, I'm afraid. These are my family's private writings. You are more than welcome to return to read it again though," he suggested.

"Thank you," I replied a little downcast. The medieval soap opera surrounding the Endymion clan captivated me. Disappointed, I stared through the windows at the countryside. The gently rolling knolls and lush forest seemed so peaceful.

"Beautiful, isn't it?" asked Albert.

I nodded hoping I'd always remember its simple yet breathtaking beauty.

"It's a strange land. I wish we could unlock its secrets," he confided, his voice drifting away in thought.

I don't think you want to know what's going on right under your nose. How would he react—or anyone from the village, for that matter—if he found out that bizarre paranormal forces were battling in his backyard?

Glancing around the room again, an odd image at the top of the arched windows caught my attention.

"What's that?" I asked, pointing to the stained glass circle that looked like a cat's eye.

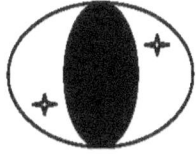

"That is the symbol of Artemis," he said with a twinkle in his eyes.

"Artemis?" I asked suspiciously, immediately recalling my encounter in the manor.

"Yes, Artemis was the Greek goddess of the moon and the hunt."

"What does the symbol mean?"

"It represents the moon in its four phases—new, waning, waxing, and full. The eye in the center symbolizes Artemis as the goddess of the hunt. The stars represent Artemis and her twin brother, Apollo."

"Why is that symbol here though? It's a bit out of place for a Welsh Renaissance building."

"Cenweard Endymion built many of these buildings and had the image added to as many places as possible."

Cenweard? Now that is *very interesting.* "Why?"

"Well, that's a mystery for all of us to figure out."

Sam looked up at me for the first time since we arrived. "We should leave. We don't want to be late."

"You need to leave already?" Albert asked sadly. With the lack of patrons and a street front entrance to his shop, it was no wonder he was desperate for company.

"Yes, we're meeting friends," Sam said innocently still stroking the fat cat.

"I see. Well, be sure to visit again," he answered kindly.

"We will," we said in unison and walked toward the front door. Sam slid her huge sunglasses back in place.

"What was that about?" I asked when we stepped into the alley.

"I just had a feeling that we needed to be somewhere else."

I raised my eyebrows at her skeptically. "Fine, but I want to go to the church."

"Why?" she asked, her eyes furrowed in confusion.

"I want to look through their records. There's a mystery surrounding Cenweard Endymion that needs to be figured out."

"What's the mystery?"

"There's a picture hanging in Endymion Manor depicting Cenweard crying while he's kissing the hand of the goddess Artemis."

"You lost me, Angel. What's the point?"

"Connecting the dots. What did he do to offend the goddess? Why would a devout Christian family dabble so heavily in a pagan deity? Why did he choose Artemis in particular, why not Hera or Aphrodite? Did you see the markings on the stained glass in the bookshop?"

Sam nodded and her eyes opened wide as she comprehended the task ahead. "So you want to read the church's records from five centuries ago?"

"Precisely."

We reached the end of the cobblestone alley and turned toward the pub.

"Traveling incognito today, are we?" asked an irritating yet sexy voice over my shoulder.

Sam gasped in fanatic delight. I spun around to find Rick's charming smile a few inches from my face. Glaring at Sam, I mouthed, "This is why we left?" She shrugged her shoulders and grinned impishly.

"Well, aren't you going to introduce me to your friend, Angel?"

"No," I quipped, walking briskly toward the chapel.

Keeping pace, he extended his hand to Sam. "Hi, my name is Rick," his buttery voice crooned.

Sam opened her mouth, but no sound came out. I smirked at the physical manifestation of her obsession. He beamed, clearly enjoying the fact that his presence made her speechless.

Finally she blurted, "I...I...I'm Sam."

"Well it's lovely to meet you, Sam. Or should I call you Samantha? 'Sam' doesn't do your beauty justice."

I rolled my eyes and, much to my chagrin, his lips curled coyly at my harsh reaction. Cocking an eyebrow and smiling slyly, his charm chipped away at my icy shield.

I just couldn't win with this guy. He wouldn't leave me alone if I was mean, and I'm sure he wouldn't leave if I was even remotely nice.

"So to what do we owe this," my hand waved flippantly at his presence from head-to-toe, "the *un*pleasantness of your company?" I asked icily.

"Didn't your mother teach you manners?" he retorted.

"Why yes she did," I replied sarcastically. "And she also taught me to be wary of strangers."

Stopping near the pub, I glanced around him. "So, where's your Barbie army?"

Rick grinned widely with a knowing look in his eyes. "I thought that's what bothered you yesterday, so I'm traveling incognito today too," he said, nudging Sam. A baseball cap and glasses dangled from his hands.

Sam giggled nervously and pulled her hood lower over her right cheek lest he notice her work of art.

Relieved that the dolls weren't shooting daggers at me today, a small weight of fear and anxiety lifted from my shoulders.

"Samantha, do you think you can convince you friend here to go on a date with me?" he asked with a voice as smooth as melted milk chocolate.

Sam giggled like a ditzy, smitten bimbo. I envisioned her as one of his doting minions, but shook the morbid thought from my head.

"Why should I go out with you?" I demanded.

"We're both passing through here and I thought dinner couldn't possibly kill you."

You have no idea.

His crystal clear green eyes sparkled at me as he continued, "I thought we might be able to find some common ground to pass the time while we're stuck in this God forsaken space of country."

"Uh…no."

"Why not?" he demanded impatiently.

"Because I don't know you!" I shouted.

"What's there to know? I'm twenty one. I'm a Cancer. I'm film-ing a movie in town over the next month. I've never had a lot of friends because apparently my celebrity is intimidating and hordes of gorgeous, shallow, boring girls follow me around all day. How's that?"

"Better," I paused, "but the answer is still no."

"Why?" he whined. His emerald eyes pierced me. "Do you have a boyfriend?"

"No," I said too honestly before I realized it would've been a perfect excuse. *Why couldn't I lie just this once?*

"Are you a lesbian?"

"No!" I shouted. *Again, that would've been a good excuse.*

"Then why not?"

Because evil monsters are after me. "Just because."

"You're so difficult!" Exasperated, he paused before flashing his ice-melting toothy grin. "I'm not giving up on you so easily, Angel."

He turned to Sam. "It was a pleasure meeting you, Samantha," his voice dripped with sweetness. "Oh, and I love your tattoo. I see you have good taste," he winked and motioned to her cheek.

Sam's pale, ghost-white face blushed to a deep Bing-cherry red in an instant. She was still too stunned and now too embarrassed to say anything.

Turning his debonair magnetism on me, Rick reached for my hand and caressed it lightly. Closing his eyes, he gasped quietly apparently pleased by the feeling of shooting electricity between our hands. His cold, light grasp cooled the boiling blood racing through my palms. Interestingly enough, I didn't pull my hand away from him even though my gut instinct told me not to fall for him.

He kissed my hand lightly staring captivatingly into my eyes all the while and said, "Until we meet again."

In place of my rock hard ice shield now laid a burning fire as I swooned from his chivalry. Having completed his spell casting, he smiled lusciously, bowed his head slightly, pushed his glasses and cap back in place, and navigated adeptly through the sea of tourists.

Equally mesmerized, Sam and I watched him in silence as he made his way across the square and back up the street toward the bakery.

Sam sighed. "I guess now that you've read his bio you really don't have an excuse not to go out with him," she added smugly.

"You and I both know it's not going to happen."

"Why not? He's beautiful. He's a star. And, he likes you! I wish I was that lucky," she muttered jealously.

"Yeah, but I'm not used to that kind of attention—especially from a guy like Rick. It makes me uncomfortable."

"You are so strange," Sam paused. "Maybe, we could go on a double date. Do you think he could bring a friend for me? Ooooh, I wonder how many cute actors he knows?"

"And I'm the strange one here? You don't know him any better than me! Besides, isn't there something greater going on beyond our fantasies right now?" I asked sarcastically, though I still didn't really believe it myself. "Maybe when all this is over—if we're still alive—then I'll consider going out with him."

"So there's a chance?" she asked hopefully.

"Provided I overcome the one in a million chance of surviving past the end of the month," I replied wryly.

Silence enveloped our soft steps along the cobblestone path toward the vicarage and chapel. Very few people made it this far along the road. Most of the commotion centered around the town square near the pub.

An elderly woman and her husband meandered arm-in-arm back toward town leaving Sam and me alone on the road. The chapel sat on a little mound about one block up from the vicarage. Like the other buildings in Endymion village, it had a faded white stucco finish. Four, gothic-style stained glass windows lined its side. A little bell tower adorned the front steeple with a spire reaching toward the heavens.

We knocked on the vicar's door. Bera opened it and, abundantly surprised by our visit, cocked her head to the side like a confused cocker spaniel.

"Well, hello there Sam, Angel," she said, still wearing her Sunday alb. "How can I help you?"

"We were wondering if we might be able to look through the church's records?" I asked innocently.

"Financial records?" she asked perplexed.

"No, sorry, records of Endymion's villagers, like their births and baptisms," I clarified.

"That's an interesting request," Bera stated, blinking deep in thought. "No one's ever asked for those."

"May we?" I urged gently.

"Why?" she asked suspiciously.

Sam jumped into the conversation, "It's for a wager Cynan and I have about our ancestors. He insists they didn't arrive in Endymion before 1604 and I know they were here at least seventy five years before then."

I stared at Sam admiring her boldness, sincerity, and ability to lie to a woman of the cloth. Even I believed her.

"Are you gaining something good from this bet, Sam?" Bera semi-heartedly scolded.

"Actually, yes. Cynan will do the dishes for one month."

Relieved at the innocence of the gamble, the vicar agreed with a smirk. "Well then a quick glimpse at the records seems justifiable. Follow me, ladies."

She wrestled with the keys beneath her robe as we crossed the grass to the chapel. She unlocked the heavy mahogany doors and, exerting great effort, pulled them open. Their hinges screeched in rusted pain. We stepped cautiously onto the slate stone floor of the plain ivory vestibule. A small metal stand stood next to the front door holding pamphlets on *This Summer's Endymion Chapel Events*.

"Wait here," Bera directed.

She strolled into a room off to the right. The heavy wooden door slammed behind her and echoed around us.

We opened the main doors of the chapel.

The one drawback to living in Salem was that few historical buildings still stood in their original forms. Many had been renovated to some extent throughout the centuries. The only additions to this ancient building were the coat of paint and electrical cords stapled to the walls and ceiling to light the austere chandeliers and sconces lining the room. While all of the other walls were bare, an alcove in the front of the chapel was covered in intricately carved wooden panels.

My gaze shifted from the walls to the massive stained glass window over the altar. I froze in place as sunlight streamed through the depiction's central figure.

Sam followed my stare. "What's wrong? Haven't you ever seen the Virgin Mary before?"

"That's not Mary," I whispered solemnly.

"Who would it be then? We're in a Church of England chapel. The angel armies of darkness and light are standing behind her going into battle. That's Mary in the middle, standing on the world and conquering evil—see the snake under her feet?"

"That's not Mary," I insisted. "She's standing on the moon, not earth, Sam. That's Artemis..." The face in the window was identical to the one hanging in Endymion Manor, which was identical to mine.

Sam scoffed but wandered closer. Her already pale face drained of any remaining color as she turned and pointed at me. She squelched a gasp with her hands. Running to me, her footsteps echoed on the slate floor. She grabbed my hands and pulled me into a pew.

"It's just a weird coincidence, Angel," she assured quietly. "It's impossible to think you're the only person who ever lived looking like that," she nodded toward the window.

"Yeah, but what are the odds?"

"I agree it's strange, but that doesn't mean anything."

"Doesn't mean anything?" I quoted in a raised whisper bordering on hysterics. "I think it's slightly ironic that I'm supposedly caught in a war between good and evil and my likeness happens to be captured in the middle of some weird Endymion family scandal."

Just then the vicar returned with four large volumes of leather bound books.

"Sam, if you win this bet, I believe that since I'm helping you I'm also entitled to some slavery from Cynan," Bera smiled. "Well, girls, I need to run back to the vicarage to ring my mum. I'll lock the chapel in about a half hour; you have until then. Please be very careful with these books. They're ancient!"

"Sure thing, vicar," I said still a little dazed from my discovery.

Sam took the first book and I took volume two as Bera looked over our shoulders briefly. I avoided looking directly at her, although she may have already noticed my uncanny resemblance to the face overlooking her in the chapel daily.

When the doors slammed, Sam and I exchanged glances and she whipped open volume one.

Taking great care to only touch the bottom corner of each page, I turned them gently until I found 1525 A.D. On every sheet were five columns:

Nomen	Propositum	Tempus	Adnotatio	Astrologia

The first four represented name, purpose, date, and notes. The last column contained strange markings with circles and dots.

"Sam, what are these pictures in the last column?"

"They seem to be astrological signs."

"Why would Christians need to keep track of that?"

"The people were simple and superstitious. Many held onto ancient pagan practices. They tied the ongoings in the sky to events that happened here."

My finger traced over the delicate parchment and the seven entries from 1525.

Nomen	Propositum	Tempus	Adnotatio	Astrologia
Patrick Bertran	Natus	9 Ianiarius	Filius de John Bertran	⊘
Patrick Bertran	Baptisma	23 Ianiarius	Filius de John Bertran	●
Margarete Pendragon	Natus	4 Julius	Filia de Christopher Pendragon	⊘
APCE	Matrimonium	2 December		○
Artemis Pendragon	Mors	29 December	Filia de Christopher Pendragon	⊗
Sir William Endymion	Parricidium	31 December		⊃
Justin Bysshop	Absens	31 December		⊂

I translated the description column deducing the meaning of each event.

> *Birth*
> *Baptism*
> *Birth*
> *Marriage*
> *Death*
> *Murder*
> *Missing*

"Look, Sam," I pointed excitedly at the entry for death. "It's the only woman who died in 1525 and her name was Artemis," I shouted in a hushed whisper. My puzzle was coming together. "What's the moon sign mean?"

"I think that means there was a full lunar eclipse that day."

I could barely control my excitement. "Her name was Artemis and she died the day of a full moon's eclipse! Do you know what this means?"

"No."

Suddenly I felt dejected. Everything was clear and simultaneously incredibly confusing. "I don't really know either except that Artemis was the Goddess of the moon and Cenweard's Artemis died during a full lunar eclipse."

"Yes, but mythology and reality are two separate things."

"Are they, Sam?" I asked incredulously. "You *are* living mythology."

Sam stared into my eyes; her own were filled with a worry I didn't understand. She turned away quickly and picked up another book.

"Hold on. I want to see what happened to Cenweard." Flipping to the entries from 1526, I easily found the only one that mattered.

Nomen	Propositum	Tempus	Adnotatio	Astrologia
Cenweard Endymion	Mortem Sibi Consciscere	24 Iunius	Filium de Sir William Endymion	⊗

"I thought there would be more," I said disappointed. "It just says that he committed suicide. The interesting thing is that he died just like Artemis on a day with a full lunar eclipse."

"You know Latin?" Sam questioned suspiciously.

"High school language requirement," I replied nonchalantly.

"Who would've thought something you learned in school would be so helpful now, eh?" We laughed.

Sam pulled the book out of my hands and flipped back to the page with the entries from 1525. Looking around and seeing no witnesses, she ripped out the page along with the one noting Cenweard's death.

"What are you doing?!" I exclaimed.

"We need them more than the church," she folded the pages carefully and stuffed them into her shirt under her hoodie.

I shook my head. "Destruction and possession of stolen property—I really don't want to be shipped back to the U.S. because I was your accomplice."

"Oh, calm down. We'll return it when we're finished. I swear the book hasn't been read in centuries. Did you hear the way it cracked when you opened it?"

Her rationale made sense, although a nagging pang of guilt knocked on my conscience's door. We were stealing, pilfering from God's house no less. Then again, it wasn't likely that Bera would let us look at the records again without arousing more suspicion.

Shame-free, Sam opened the other books and paged through the entries while I looked around.

Two sets of ten pews filled the tiny chapel. The stark white walls were washed with color from the mid-day sun shining through the stained glass windows, which portrayed biblical events. However, set into the top third of every gothic window panel was Artemis' symbol. It was also engraved all along the top edge of the white marble altar and on the back of the vicar's chair. Hidden in the details of the alcove's paneling were numerous depictions of celestial bodies, gods and goddesses, angels, demons, and the goddess's symbol. Interestingly enough, the carvings were nearly void of Christian markings.

A large billowing tapestry covered most of the wall directly behind the vicar's chair. All of the windows and doors were closed. Where was the breeze coming from?

The chair was fastened to the floor making it difficult to access the space behind the wall hanging. Pulling it out of the way, I extended my arm behind the chair and ran my hands up and down the wall when I touched something circular. *A doorknob?*

I turned the cold knob and, with a loud creak, the door opened into a black hole beneath the floor.

"Sam! You've gotta see this," I yelled.

No response.

"Sam?" I pulled my head from behind the tapestry to look into the pews.

She was gone!

"Sam?" I whispered, fear tightening my vocal chords.

A loud crash echoed from behind the tapestry and, as I glanced toward it, a sharp pain pierced my neck. Limp and powerless, I fell into the black abyss.

13 ~ We Meet Again

The pain. The unbearable pain. Kill me now…

Smoke? Smoke! Where am I? Why can't I move? Why can't I speak? Open eyes, damn it, open! Good, my head can move side-to-side. Why won't my eyes open?

'Sam! Where are you?' Warm tears streamed down my face, but I couldn't see anything, say anything, or feel anything.

Help me! Someone help me, pleeeease! I cried to the inattentive audience in my mind.

Deep voices were getting louder and more intense.

"Oh, oh silver moon

Our lady in white

We feel your magic power

Grow stronger each night

Magic all around

We hear her call

She casts her spell

Enchanting us all."[2]

Sam's ear-piercing shrieks cut through the methodical chanting of deep male voices.

---

2   "Silver Moon" chant from Celtic Steel, http://www.wicca-chat.com/chants htm

'Sam!' I tried to yell desperately. *Damn it, Angel. Open your freakin' eyes!*

Suddenly, a strong hand held something soft, cold and wet over my nose and mouth. I choked on the bitter smell and taste as it burned my nose and mouth. Although it was anchored, my body felt like it was floating.

"Angel!" Sam's screams grew louder, penetrating my daze. A loud smack halted the chanting; something heavy fell to the ground.

'Sam!' my brain cried. My throat and eyes burned with the heat of a thousand fires biting my insides. *I'm going to die. This is how I'm going to die. What happened to the council? Where're Matt, Mark, and Cynan?*

Like a stiff board sinking slowly into the sea, my senses faded into awareness. I was lying on something very hard and ice cold.

Tingling sensations crept through my feet gripping into my legs like a million tiny daggers climbing my body. I tried to kick my legs free but something locked them together.

Hurried footsteps crackled over leaves and branches nearby. Smoke choked me.

Open eyes, open! My eyes rolled around in their sockets unable to focus. Pitch blackness swirled overhead. The faint outline of leaves and tree branches twirled inside the spinning black blanket of the night sky.

The deep consistent thud of chanting began again with more urgency:

"We bind and we bind you
From harming yourself and us.
We bind and we bind you
From working any deeds.
We bind and we bind you
From joining any forces but ours.
We bind you to remain bound
Until the moon lies full over ground
And we unbind you to do our will."

My heavy head rolled lethargically to the left. I willed my eyes open only to see Mark and Matt tied to trees, dangling unconsciously.

No!

I forced my head to fall to the right. As my eyes tried to focus on the blurry images I saw Cynan tied to a tree lifelessly. The black figures shuffled around something on the ground.

Sam! 'Get your hands off of her!'

One of the figures threw her limp body over its shoulder and propped her against a tree trunk while another tied her to it. Bright red blood stained her pale angelic face as she hung helplessly, unconsciously.

Burning rage matched the piercing pain inching its way up my limbs. My eyes tried desperately to discern the objects around me. Countless candelabra illuminated the clearing in the woods. Black candles burned with red flames in complete stillness, not one flickered.

Fighting the urge to fall into a deep sleep, I rested my head on its side again and peered through the tiniest slits of my eyelids. With fearful realization I discovered that my cold, hard bed was actually an ebony granite altar.

Countless black cloaked, inhuman figures knelt, encircling my pyre. Standing like statues, two were positioned on either side of me, their arms folded.

Ironically, my suicidal tendencies from the past few months gave way to survival mode. My head and eyes rolled uncontrollably as all of my senses burst to life. A shooting pain seared through my chest.

"Owww," I screamed, my voice echoing in the forest.

"Gentlemen, our guest of honor will grace us with her presence after all," a deep, sinister voice spoke from behind me.

"Ass—," I muttered.

My tormentor laughed menacingly. In a flash, his frigid hand choked my throat.

"Young lady, you will learn your place," his frozen breath seethed each word into my face. The figure's tan rugged features were accentuated most evilly with deep black eyes marked by vivid red rays.

With all of the strength I could muster, I spit into his demonic face.

In a millisecond he slapped me so hard that my head smacked the other side of the platform. A dull pain throbbed through my temple as he gripped my hair and thrust my head to the side. Slowly pulling a dagger from his cloak, he calculatingly drew it closer to my jugular.

I saw nothing and felt nothing except the anticipation of my short life ending.

A hand appeared out of nowhere gripping my torturer's wrist tightly. The voice belonging to the hand spoke calmly yet forcefully, "Not yet. That will do us no good."

Reluctantly, my tormentor released me.

My mind and body lingered in a dense fog. However, I was able to move my head now. I glanced over my body to see that I was bound tightly by white satin ribbons. My clothes were replaced by a gold opalescent, airy feeling gown which left me feeling cold and naked.

My stomach churned at the disturbing thoughts conjured by my imagination of one of these evil people violating me.

Before I could throw up, my torturer yanked my right arm from its binds and hissed, "Let us continue brothers." The chanting started again more viciously than before.

He held my arm in such a tight grasp that if I moved, it would have been ripped from my shoulder socket.

"We seal this binding with her blood," he said, thrusting the dagger-shaped nail of his index finger into the inside of my forearm.

"By the light of the moon and the stars above…"

Blood poured from the burning wound as he carved a crescent moon into my skin.

"Owww! You bastard!" I screamed with all of my might. "Get your hands off of me!"

Ignoring my plea, he completed the spell, "The High One's will be done."

At this proclamation, four guards, who had been holding torches, crouched beside each of my friends and lit piles of twigs and leaves beneath their feet. The two figures at my side shifted their bodies exchanging hidden glances.

"No!" I screamed with every ounce of energy my voice could gather.

A cold mist crept up the sides of the altar and covered me like a ghostly blanket. Convulsing from the abuses it had to endure, my body shivered uncontrollably.

A gust of wind broke the intensity of the ritual and wafted the hoods of the men standing on either side of me. I gasped in horror as the profile to my right belonged to my red-eyed, unnamed stalker. My horror turned to panic-fueled terror as I glanced to the face at my left.

The handsome stranger from the plane!

Ear-splitting thunder shattered the deafening silence surrounding us. In an instant, my body was swept off of the altar and was flying through the dense forest.

Barely able to hold my head up, I glanced at the clearing to see gleams of light shattering the dark night, reflecting off of silver blades. Flying tight on my trail however was the nameless stalker. My thoughts drifted anxiously to the identity of my kidnapper.

Unable to hold on, my mind and its worries slipped into a numb coma.

14 ~ The Dream

I awoke from a deep abyss to find myself on a cloud-like four poster bed covered on four sides by a white, gossamer curtain. Sleep felt so good, so refreshing. I didn't want to wake up. I rolled onto my side clutching the soft pillows close to my body.

I had no cares. My blissful existence was too perfect to ruin with thoughts of responsibilities and other harsh ideas. I stretched, yawning widely.

Candlelight glimmered from a silver candelabrum beside my bed. Flickering gold luminosity glowed throughout the room's shadowy blackness.

I slipped quietly from the bed to the cold, wooden floor. A delicate white robe hung carelessly from a solid oak emperor chair next to a matching side board. Slipping my arms through the robe's sleeves, I adjusted my white chemise with wide, embroidered bell sleeves.

Never in a million years did I think I'd find myself in a situation like this. I squealed ecstatically.

The glow of candlelight highlighted an enormous collection of books. I picked a random story and stared at it enthralled by its colorful hand-painted pictures. Replacing the book, I glanced around the room awestruck.

An enormous cross hung over the stone fireplace. Although the walls weren't decorated, extensive oak bookcases and shelves lined all of the spare walls. Priceless vases, carvings, decorations made from china and jade, and an endless library of books adorned every inch of the shelves. *I must have died. This is what heaven looks like, feels like.*

I couldn't believe I was here. After so much time, I had finally come home—home to him.

Raising my left hand, I twirled the dainty gold band around my third finger, mesmerized by the candlelight dancing off of its shiny finish.

A flicker of light illuminated a pale box set upon a small round table next to the balcony door. Excited at the thought of my endless adventure within the confines of this room, I skipped over to it and whisked it up into the palm of my left hand. A waxing moon, full moon, and waning moon were carved into its top.

I unraveled the scrolled note beside the box:

Mi Love,

May wre love be entwined forever, ceasing never.

Thy devoted husband

How was I worthy of such a perfect man? He treated me far better than I deserved. I reread the note and smiled at the handwritten word 'husband.' *He's my husband! All mine, forever.* I couldn't imagine a better, more magical life than this.

I cautiously opened the hinged box top. "*Semper Te Amo*" was carved into the inside of the top, while deep blue velvet lined the bottom. Inside laid a thin gold link chain from which an exquisitely detailed crucifix dangled. It was breathtaking. I had never seen jewelry like this before. Christ's figure was so intricate in its engraving.

I slipped the crucifix around my neck. The cold metal swung low brushing lightly against my chest. If only it was my husband's lips brushing lightly there instead. I couldn't wait for him to join me.

Excited at the thought of finally being with him, I needed to cool my thoughts. Gliding over to the balcony, I fastened the deep red velvet curtains to the doorframe and unlatched the double glass doors. Blowing briskly, the icy cold breeze bit my body.

The full moon glistened brightly over the fresh layer of snow coating the gardens below. I felt like a princess looking out over her kingdom.

An inexplicable and eerie darkness began to creep over the moonlight, extinguishing it. A frigid shiver shot down my spine at the sight of this creepy, supernatural phenomenon.

Rushing back into the room, I locked the doors securely. Fascinated by the strange sight, I chanced a glance and caught the full moon slip into oblivion. Alarming gloom befell the room. The candles cast ominous shadows scampering across the walls.

A floorboard creaked near the bed. *He came back,* I thought eagerly.

I felt myself saying the words, but the voice was not mine. "My dearest love, I've been waiting for you."

The gossamer robe slipped to the floor and I loosened the gown to reveal my left shoulder hoping to entice him. From the corner of the room closest to the doorway, a pair of red eyes flashed.

My terrified scream echoed in the tiny sanctuary.

In a blindingly fast instant, the intruder's hand covered my mouth with a painful grip. He threw me onto the bed.

"You've ruined everything, you filthy, worthless peasant," the angry voice growled, his figure obscured by the sheer curtain.

Petrified, I crouched against the headboard praying my husband would save me.

"You do not belong here," the voice fumed.

He climbed onto my wedding bed; his fierce blood-red eyes glared murderously at my very existence.

"No!" I screamed at my beloved's father.

In an instant he pounced upon my body and pulled me straight onto the bed. I struggled to free my legs which he pinned between his own. His vast body felt like a boulder against my twig-like frame.

"Please, no, I'll do anything. Just leave me be," I pleaded.

Saying nothing else, he smacked my flailing arms out of the way. The sound of my right arm cracking sent a wave of excruciating pain through my torso.

"Stop! Please!" I begged.

He slapped me so hard that several of my teeth fell out.

"Aaaaaaaah, Aaaaaaaah, Aaaaaaaah," my unanswered cries reverberated around us.

With my legs solidly squeezed between his thick thighs, he ripped my gown. His hungry eyes assessed every inch of me. My free arm covered my chest as he crept closer. With the strength of a hundred bears, he angrily swatted my other arm out of the way breaking it at the elbow.

"Please, oh, please stop! I'll do anything!" I cried as blood streamed from the corners of my mouth.

"There's only one thing you can do."

"Anything!"

"Die," he growled furiously.

My eyes opened wide with fear and the knowledge I would never see my husband again.

He slid his thighs between mine. Freeing my legs, I kicked him in the chest so hard that he fell off the back of the bed. Rolling off of the funeral pyre, my dead arms dangled uselessly at my side. I ran to the balcony door thrusting it open with my body and screamed into the still night air, "Help! Help!"

Silence replied as the moon slowly emerged from her queer sleep. His fingers squeezed my neck, making my body succumb to his strength.

Tears rushed forth like an angry river at the thought of my beloved husband discovering my lifeless body. I prayed he would find a way to get past the horror about to happen.

Sounds could no longer escape my lips. The dry, ache in my throat knew that no matter what I yelled or how loud, I had no savior tonight.

Hoisting me by my neck, the red-eyed monster glared at me with a passionate loathing. "If I can't have you, no one will," he scowled scathingly, staring covetously at my broken body.

He walked slowly, deliberately to the edge of the balcony. The crimson-stained gown hung loosely from my shoulders as the icy air congealed the blood dripping along my snow-white skin. The metal crucifix froze in place.

Mysteriously emerging from the midnight sky, the full moon illuminated my bloodied white nightgown billowing in the frigid breeze.

"Until we meet again," he scoffed haughtily, his red eyes livid with contempt.

One-by-one the boney fingers released their fierce, stony grip.

The wind embraced me as I plummeted into the void of the cold winter night.

15 ~ Salvation

Convulsing in hysterics, uncontrollable tears streamed down my face.

Strong arms encircled me tightly, cradling me in their warm grip. I fought against them uselessly; they only squeezed me tighter.

"Shhhh, Angel, it's ok. Everything's all right," a soothing, familiar voice comforted, while a hand stroked my head gently.

The flickering dim light of a small flashlight cast a dark shadow over the face belonging to the voice.

I wasn't sitting on a couch but on a lap. Squinting, my eyes tried to distinguish his face. A glimmer of light danced off of his wavy, light brown hair and god-like good looks.

"You!" I squealed ecstatically, throwing my arms around the neck of my handsome plane stranger.

His arms held me securely against his warm frame. "Everything is ok now. You're safe."

The night's events resurfaced in my consciousness. I pulled away from him distrustfully wondering what role he played in the evening's festivities.

"How did you get here? Where did you come from? Who are you? Why did you take me?" I blurted fearfully. After all, he was with the others. Was he one of them or was he on my side? Was he trying to trick me?

"Nice to see you again, too," he smiled sincerely.

Although my instincts told me he was safe, my mind didn't allow me to trust him. I waited.

"You've been through quite a bit since the last time I saw you," he continued.

"My questions, please," I asked as sweetly as I could tolerate considering that I just escaped certain death.

"I can't answer the first two. Regarding the third, I'm a close friend of yours. As for the fourth, I thought you might want to be rescued from the grasp of evil. Does that help?"

He could've been lying, but my heart believed him. I threw my arms around his neck again and cried wildly. "I'm so scared. I don't know what's going on, and I'm so afraid of being alone in...in," I debated the right word to describe it, "in this...insanity."

He smiled sincerely. "You made friends though. You're obviously not alone," he said calmly, stroking my hair.

"They're not like you though," I stared into his bottomless ocean eyes. I dropped my arms and looked away quickly realizing that I might be rejected. "I'm sorry, I shouldn't have said that." *Stupid me*, I didn't even know him. I was obsessed with a complete stranger.

"You're going to have to stop apologizing every time you see me," he laughed.

Embarrassed, blood rushed to my cheeks. "It's just that I feel so comfortable around you—no one else makes me feel that way."

I gazed into his eyes, but his expression concentrated on something a million miles away.

"You ok?" I asked.

"Yeah, just thinking about..." he replied distractedly.

His beautiful eyes refocused on the present. Even in the darkness, their piercing deep blue hue glimmered in the faint light. "How are you feeling?" he redirected.

"Um, fine, I guess."

"Fine?" he asked incredulously. "How much do you remember?"

My eyes opened wide in horror as the night's events flooded my memory. I looked down at my body and saw he had covered me in his black cloak. Underneath, however, I still wore the light, gold shimmery, barely-there gown. I gasped at the realization that my handsome stranger and nameless stalker had been positioned over me throughout the ordeal.

I pulled the cloak around me tightly. Excruciating pain shot through my arm. Pulling up the cloak's sleeve, I found it bandaged tightly in a black shirt.

Glancing at my savior, I realized that his bulging biceps and firm pecs were only covered by a short sleeved, white undershirt.

I unraveled the improvised bandage to see the crescent moon carving. Considering it was a fresh wound, it looked like it had been healing for nearly a week. Its bloody, scabbing appearance made my stomach flip. I quickly hid it beneath the shirt again.

"How long have we been here?"

"A few hours."

"And where is *here* exactly?"

"Tunnel Cave."

That explained the damp, dark coldness enveloping us.

"What did they do to me?" I whispered, afraid of the answer.

"They tried to keep you from hurting them by performing a superstitious binding ritual that's supposed to render you powerless."

"Is that all?" I asked, peering at the cloak and my gown underneath.

"Their women prepared you," he reassured, understanding my subtle insinuation.

I sighed. Relief lifted a heavy, disgusted weight from my shoulders. It still grossed me out, but at least I wasn't violated. Even Zach hadn't seen me naked and we dated for two years.

"Did you…did…uh…did you…," I couldn't ask him this. My cheeks burned in awkward humiliation at the mere thought.

"The clearing was very dark, no one saw anything. My only goal was to get you out of there alive."

I gasped, "What about my friends?"

"I'm sure they're fine by now too," he said confidently.

"How do you know?"

"The coven's council showed up when I made my escape with you. Unfortunately, they arrived late. None of you should've endured what happened tonight."

A fiery sting throbbed through my arm again. Instinctively, my hand lurched at it squeezing it tightly.

His face grew wary with concern. "Let me see," he requested tenderly.

Extremely carefully, he unwrapped his shirt to reveal the unwanted tattoo. Visibly percolating, burning blood boiled beneath the skin's surface.

Placing my forearm cautiously between his hands, he took a deep breath, stared intently at it, and muttered something inaudibly. All of a sudden, ice-cold energy radiated from his hands and cooled the wildfire engulfing the lesion.

Dumbfounded, I gawked at him trying to figure out what he was. Could he be a part of the coven's delusion? But how did he find me on the plane? Was that a mere coincidence?

"How are you doing that?" I asked quietly.

"Magic," he said slyly, looking at me through the corner of his eyes.

"Magic?" I retorted in sarcastic disbelief.

"It depends on your definition of magic. For the purpose of our conversation, magic is the easiest way to explain it. Is that better?" he asked, releasing my arm.

I wiggled my fingers and stretched; the pain had subsided completely. "Yes, thank you. Why did that burn far worse than any cut I've ever had and why did it look like it was coming to life?" I resisted the urge to throw up at the thought.

He paused, looked at the injury, and slowly lifted his head to meet my curious gaze. His furrowed eyebrows creased his forehead in thoughtful hesitance.

"Please tell me," I begged desperately. "I really want to know."

Concentrating on the wound, he took a deep breath and muttered, "A vampire cut you."

"Vampire?!" I shrieked, not entirely certain I heard him correctly. "Are you kidding me? It's not enough that some weird battle is about to take place, but now we need to add vampires to the mix too? Am I on a twisted reality show?"

He chuckled sullenly, "No show. All of this is real."

"I can understand the whole thing between good and evil and even witches with unexplainable powers, but vampires? Everyone knows they're not real."

"That depends on your definition of a vampire."

"Do they run around sucking people's blood?"

"Depends on which ones you're talking about."

"There's more than one kind!" I screamed horrified.

He nodded serenely. Oddly, as the idea of my life and death hung in the balance, my feelings for the stranger surged in my chest. *Is it wrong to feel turned on when I nearly died tonight? What's wrong with me?*

"So, how exactly did that vampire make this hurt so badly?"

"It's a chemical reaction of sorts."

"Chemical reaction? You mean, the vampires aren't just supernatural blood suckers, they're also scientists?" I grumbled angrily.

He smirked at my ignorance. Irritated, my eyes narrowed coolly. "Well, how should I know? Apparently, nothing is impossible anymore!"

"True. I'm just amused by your stamina."

"Stamina?" I quipped testily.

He laughed. "You nearly died tonight and, right now, you're worried about the chemical composition of vampires."

"I'm worried about things I don't know," I corrected.

"I get that," he continued. "You just amaze me."

I amaze him? Are you kidding me? Plain Jane little me, amazes this god? No way! My heart leapt with joy and beat faster at the thought that he might like me. Though he was a stranger, I felt like I'd known him for years.

"The chemical reaction comes from their make up. They're dead; you're not. If they penetrate your skin, some of the chemicals from their body get into you. You, being very much alive, do not react well."

"Will it turn me into one of them?" I asked fearfully.

"No," he paused, continuing in a whisper, "it just deadens the skin where they penetrated it."

"What?!" I exclaimed clearly unhappy at the thought of my forearm's skin decaying.

"You'll be fine, I swear," he assured.

"But what about the carving?" I asked, risking a glance at my arm while he re-bandaged it.

"That, unfortunately, will be an unpleasant memento from this evening."

I sat in silence on the cold, rock-hard cave floor, when a realization occurred to me. I looked at the stranger inquisitively. "Who are you really?"

He frowned apparently hurt by my blunt statement.

"I mean, I don't even know your name. You never told me," I corrected.

The lines on his face smoothed and he smiled sweetly. "It's CJ."

"So, can I ask some questions, CJ?"

"Depends on what they are," he replied guardedly, raising an eyebrow.

"Oh, not you too," I whined in frustration. "I'm apparently going to die in a few weeks, yet no one will tell me what's going on. If I'm going to die, I want to know why."

He leaned toward me quickly and very seriously said, "You're *not* going to die."

"How do you know? The odds of me surviving are pretty marginal. I mean, look at me. Do I look like a soldier?" As much as I wanted to believe that everyone was delusional, after tonight's events the proof of their convictions was all too real.

"As long as I'm with you, I guarantee you won't die."

I nodded happily at the thought that he'd be with me for a while, but the thought that his presence was only temporary wrenched my heart painfully and irrationally.

"What's wrong?" he asked, seeing my pathetically depressed expression. "Is the bandage too tight?" he asked quietly.

I shook my head.

"Are you cold?"

I shook my head. Although, I suddenly realized I was shaking. CJ pulled me into his lap and cradled me as he leaned against the cave's wall.

"You might not be cold, but I'm freezing," he chuckled, pulling me close to his chest.

Shivering under the black velvet cloak, I adjusted myself so I could wrap it around his shoulders.

Resting against his arm, I stared at his profile trying to absorb his features. He was more beautiful than I remembered. He was peace. He was perfection. I couldn't believe he was here, let alone holding me in his arms. This was like a mini dream come true. Trembling from our frigid surroundings, I cuddled deeper into his warm, safe grasp.

Thinking of safety, my thoughts drifted to the evening's dangers and the memory of my nightmare. An uncontrollable shudder shook me.

"What is it?" he asked. His left hand caressed my waist.

"The dream I had..." I took a deep breath unsure of how much I should divulge. Then again, I knew from past experience that keeping it bottled inside would only make the nightmare return with more disturbing details.

"I was happily locked in a tower waiting for my husband to get me. But a red-eyed man attacked me and broke my arms. Then he..."

"Stop!" he demanded, turning his head away from me.

Completely taken aback by his reaction, I lurched backwards. CJ closed his eyes, a peculiar look of anger and agony tormented his kind face.

"I'm sorry," I said quietly, my eyes downcast.

"I didn't mean to scare you. It's just that it reminded me of what could've happened if we were a few minutes too late tonight."

"It was just a dream," I reminded him cautiously.

He paused contemplating my words. "Yes, you're right...just a dream," he repeated, sounding like he was trying to convince himself in the process. He glanced briefly at me before lowering his eyes. His chiseled features softened in the shadows.

"As long as I'm with you, you *will* be safe," he promised solemnly. "I'm sorry I've failed you so far."

"I'm still trying to figure out why you're helping me in the first place," I said, hoping to placate him.

His kind and honest eyes stared deeply into mine.

My heart fluttered. I'd known him for a total of a few hours and yet my body reacted as if I loved him. It didn't feel like the excitement of infatuation. This was a deep, strong urge to care for him, be with him. Even my rational side couldn't outweigh the surge of emotions twisting my heart and insides most pleasantly.

Despite the fuzzy, warmth tingling within me the cave's icy temperature chilled me to the bone. I snuggled into his chest and he wound his arms around me tightly.

"Can I ask something else?"

"Sure," he said quietly, his mind clearly distracted by our prior topic.

"What are you?"

"That's not important."

"It is to me!" I shouted emphatically. "If you're risking your life for me, I'd like to know who you are exactly and why you're bothering."

"I can't tell you."

"Why not?"

"Because," he said with a smile in his voice.

"What if I guess? Then will you tell me?"

"Sure," he agreed too quickly, making me doubt the sincerity of his easy reply.

"Scotland Yard?"

"No."

"British Secret Service?"

"No."

"FBI?"

"No."

"C.I.A."

"No, are you finished with the assumptions?"

I paused, smiling flirtatiously. "No...Why can't you tell me?"

"It's not safe for you to know any more than is necessary. If I tell you, it'll jeopardize my job to protect you."

"But how do I know I'm safe with you if I don't know who you are?"

"Because you can feel it," he said certainly.

I processed his words. It was absolutely true. From the moment I first saw him I knew I trusted him. "How did you know that?"

He laughed once, "I know you better than you know yourself."

"That's what I'm talking about. What are you? Mind reader, fortune teller, superhero, what?"

"Hmmm," he paused. "I like the superhero analogy. Let's say I'm like Batman. I'm your handsome, debonair friend by day and caped crusader at night."

His words sank slowly into my understanding of the situation. "What's happening?"

He drew a deep, solemn breath. "Don't you see that everything you've been through so far has been connected? What do you think is going on?"

"I don't know," I said frustrated. "I think I'm trapped in an episode of the Twilight Zone as a pawn between two psychotic groups of people."

He smirked, probably at my quick-tempered absurdity. "You're right on one point."

"And that is?" I asked impatiently.

"You are caught between two groups. Although, I'm offended you think we're all insane." *So, he is one of them.*

"What would you call it then?"

"Two groups of people fighting for what they believe is right."

"Like terrorists?"

He pondered the idea for a moment. "Yeah, I guess you can say that. One group is similar to terrorists in that they want to destroy life as we know it."

Could my reality be so surreal? "Look, are you ever going to tell me who you are and what exactly is going on? Because if you don't, I really don't see any point in cooperating with you—any of you."

"Look at me, Angel," he said dangerously close to my lips, which at the moment had a mind of their own. "I promise, *promise,* that you'll know everything when it's safe for everyone involved."

"A decade from now?" I jumped backwards enraged. "That's not good enough. Stick yourself in my shoes for a minute. Imagine being yanked from a life of blissful ignorance less than a few days ago and thrust into a supernatural web of lunacy. I can't take it!"

"Don't for one minute think you're the only one who feels confused, hurt, and yearning for more!" His forehead wrinkled and his eyes flashed angrily. Closing his eyes, he took another deep breath. Composing himself, he continued, "I want to tell you everything, but I can't. I'm following orders. The stakes are too high. We can't afford to jeopardize our position. If I tell you everything now and they capture you, they'll have enough time to find out our plans, defeat us, and hurt you."

"Humph," I grunted.

He pulled my chin up to meet his gaze. "Please trust me. I will tell you everything as soon as I can."

The sincerity of his deep blue eyes shot through my soul. Being that close to his face, I just wanted to melt into his lips. He could've told me that he was an evil vampire and I would've agreed in that instant for him to bite me.

His hand slid down my back and his body shivered. I pulled the cloak around us again and wrapped my arms around him.

CJ didn't feel like a stranger. He felt like my favorite pair of jeans that hugged every part of me. In this moment I didn't need anyone else. I didn't want anyone else. In his arms I felt like I returned home.

16 ~ Protection

A faint glimmer of daylight brightened the entrance to the cave. CJ slept peacefully against the hard, cold, damp wall. His wavy golden brown locks looked so inviting; I just wanted to run my fingers through them.

Stop it, psycho! That's so not right. I don't even know him! I hated my rational side.

Disgusted with myself, I slid from his lap carefully. He muttered something unintelligible while I tucked him in with the cloak.

Tiptoeing toward the cave's mouth, sharp and slippery rocks dug into my bare feet. Undeterred, the dawning sunshine beckoned me and, as I reached its healing glory, the light melted yesterday's dark fears. I stepped into the grassy field just beyond the entrance and closed my eyes. *Inhale. Exhale. Inhale. Exhale.* It felt good to be so far away from the anxiety and terror of the night before. Contentment replaced worry.

Dainty purple flowers dotted the lush brush and grass of the empty moors. Jade fields and knolls reached endlessly into the distance meeting the blue horizon. It was obvious why CJ brought me here. We were far away from everything.

A light breeze kissed my face. I leaned into Mother Nature's welcoming gesture. The wind's invisible fingers stroked my hair while my diaphanous gown fluttered in the wind. The sun reflected a golden glow off of its iridescent texture. Never before had I felt so in harmony with the environment. I belonged here, existing somewhere between reality and nature's mysticism.

"You're beautiful," CJ remarked quietly a few steps behind me.

I spun around to face him. The sun gleamed blindingly off of my dress while the zephyr whipped around it. Instant embarrassment washed over me as CJ's perfection and supernatural superiority shot me back to reality. Resentment replaced my newfound contentment.

"What's wrong?" he worried.

"Nothing," I muttered, turning to face the moors whose emptiness echoed my own. My ludicrous attraction toward CJ had to end. He belonged somewhere on Mount Olympus, while I fit best lost in a sea of mediocrity.

He wrapped the cloak around my shoulders encircling me in the process. His arms lingered loosely around my body and his heart thumped loudly against my back. Its rhythm hypnotized me.

He rested his chin on my head. "I wish we could stay here forever, just like this," he whispered.

I sighed reluctantly.

"Don't be sad," he said, turning my body to face his. He lifted my chin to meet the deep blue ocean of his eyes. "We need to go back and prepare for what's coming."

"I'm scared," I spoke softly, closing my eyes afraid and embarrassed to admit this weakness. Before Zach died, I had the fearless courage of Teddy Roosevelt. Now, a stuffed teddy bear could shame me. "Can't I just run away?"

"Sure," he said realistically. "But without our protection, they'll capture you and our lives—mine, the coven's, your guardians'—will be lost."

"That sounds so far beyond me, so unreal."

"I know," he said calmly, still holding me. "But just because you don't understand what's going on, doesn't mean you can't choose to do the right thing."

"How do I know what's right when I don't understand what's happening?"

"You can feel it, Angel."

I rolled my eyes but nodded. I knew I had to stay. I knew my friends' lives, my siblings' lives, and my mom's life depended on the outcome of this stupid war—whatever it was.

"Are you ready to go?"

"In a sec." Spinning away from his safe, warm grasp, I stepped onto the moors taking a mental picture of its serenity. The wind enveloped me while the sun tried to thaw its cold bite.

CJ extended his hand, "Come." Wrapping his arms around me protectively, he whispered, "Avolaremus."

In the blink of an eye, we were outside of Sam's cottage. Dizzy and nauseous, my stomach nearly leapt out of me from this terrifyingly exhilarating way of traveling.

I steadied myself and stepped toward the house.

"Stop!" CJ shouted.

"What?!" I exclaimed frightened.

"You can't go inside like that," he said, pointing to my tight fitting, nearly-translucent gown. He tucked me into the cloak and buttoned the entire front from my neck to the ground. "We don't need to share your perfection with anyone else, huh?"

I blushed. Certainly my deity was flattering me just to make me feel better. I looked away shyly, pushing stray strands of hair from my eyes while trying to ignore the compliment.

Observing my uncomfortable reaction, CJ grinned and placed his arm around my waist. "Let's go."

The air inside the cottage hung heavy with tension.

Sam flew from her seat and hugged me, "I just knew you were ok. I knew it!"

"You're alive!" I cried relieved, squeezing the air out of her. I didn't want to let her go. We both came so close to the end.

I pried her from my embrace to look at her.

"Holy crap!" I screamed horrified. "What did they do to you?"

Sam's sweet, angelic face was contorted in a mess of swollen black-and-blue bruises. A deep red gash sliced her right cheek.

My eyes welled with furious, guilty tears. "Why? Why would they do this to you? They wanted me. They had me. Why would they hurt you?"

My gaze shifted from Sam to the sobering sight of the battered faces filling the kitchen.

Matt's somber, guilt-ridden expression met mine and he looked away shaking his head, "I failed you, Angel. I failed to protect you."

Mark, looking surprisingly solemn, didn't even lift his eyes from the kitchen table. Cynan sat like a statue, his eyes glued to the floor. My worry shifted to Edwin and Morgan.

Morgan sat beside Cynan, mindlessly twirling a spoon in a cup of tea. Her wavy, strawberry blonde hair starkly contrasted the ghost white hue of her face. Standing behind her, Edwin rested his hand on her shoulder. His expression wavered between sadness and fear. Both parents looked tired and worn, but they did not bear the marks of their children.

"I'm so sorry," I muttered to the silent audience. "I'm so sorry you had to endure this...because of me."

Cynan shook his head. Covered in black and purple welts, his caring eyes narrowed in concern and rested sadly on my face.

"Angel, we knew what could happen," Sam said.

"That doesn't make it right!" My lips trembled as my imagination spewed speculative images of pain and torture from the looming battle.

CJ placed his hand lightly on my shoulder. "Sam, Cynan, please take Angel for a walk."

Edwin's eyes opened wide with fear. Morgan whimpered. Mark and Matt shifted uncomfortably in their seats.

Silently, Sam and Cynan escorted me through the back door. Noticing my bare feet, Cynan grabbed a pair of flip-flops set near the door and placed them in front of me. As we reached about twenty-five feet from the home, the verbal floodgates of hell were unleashed.

"We had no idea, CJ. None. We never intended this to happen..." a contrite Edwin rushed to apologize.

"ENOUGH!" CJ's roar echoed through the forest startling the three of us. Picking up our pace, we ran into the woods.

CJ continued to bellow, "You used her, Edwin. You used her as bait. Bait! Do you have any idea how you jeopardized the entire operation?"

"CJ you must understand…"

"I had to reveal my position last night. They'll change their plan, which puts us at a serious disadvantage. You had one job to do and that was to keep her safe. No one asked you to dangle her like a fresh piece of meat in the lion's den!"

Edwin screamed, "My children nearly died because of her…"

"Don't you dare blame this bloody mess on her! Had you kept her out of harm's way, you wouldn't have risked your children's lives either. Our existence depends on her survival!"

By this point we were about 500 feet from the cottage but could still hear the entire argument as if we were sitting beside them.

"How much farther should we go?" Cynan asked Sam.

"Until we can't hear them anymore," she replied.

"I don't feel like going to France today," he scoffed.

Edwin continued defensively, "…gave the council a job to do and we executed that responsibility. We needed to assess the danger in the area."

"And you don't think you could've accomplished that any other way? You know better than anyone else no one can be trusted. Your leadership skills are in serious question right now. The Concilius Patri will reevaluate your role," CJ yelled ferociously.

"No!" Morgan gasped.

"Morgan," CJ lowered his voice. "This doesn't concern you. The council recognizes your work and the sacrifices you've made so far."

A door slammed and a car sped away. Edwin must've escaped CJ's wrath.

"Mark, Matt," CJ started. "You are her appointed guardians…" his voice trailed off.

We reached a little stream seemingly painted amid a myriad of browns and greens. Sam sat on a large rock overlooking the babbling brook rushing beneath her fingertips. Dangling her feet, the water danced between her hot pink polished toes.

I knelt in a patch of soft moss by the side of the brook and dipped my fingers in the cold, fresh water. Cynan leaned against a massive oak tree and watched us in silence, his long black mop top waving in the gentle breeze.

The light wind lifted CJ's scent from his cloak. The man not only looked delicious but smelled delicious too. The aroma of citrus, lavender, and sandalwood transported me back to the memory of lying in his arms.

Chirping birds yanked me from my sweet daydream, reminding me why we were banished to the woods.

"I'm so sorry," I said, glancing from Sam to Cynan. "You're my friends. Just as you're looking out for me, I can't allow anything to happen to you."

Sam's feet hung limply in the flowing water, her eyes hypnotized by its constant undulations. Cynan gazed at the sun peering through the tree tops.

"I want to learn what I can to prepare myself. I know you can't tell me anything, but if I can learn to defend myself and you, I'd..."

Sam shook her head. "It's too dangerous."

"Sam?" Cynan winced as she turned her battered face toward him. "We can teach her the way, can't we?"

"That takes years. We have three weeks."

"But the basics might help her in the very least be more confident, maybe more."

Sam considered his suggestion. A conniving grin brightened her face. "You're right, Cynan. We could teach her the *basics*," her voice rose enthusiastically. "Morgan and Edwin mustn't know. They'll worry we're breaching the Bellatori's edicts."

"When can we start?" I asked eagerly. This had to be better than watching the grass grow from the living room's confines.

"It'll take a couple of days to gather everything and plan the lessons. Cynan, can you find a safe place to practice?"

He nodded readily.

"What do we do in the meantime?" I asked.

"Well, I'm sure the townspeople heard the screams last night. We should go into town to show everyone we're fine," Sam said.

"Ahem," Cynan coughed. "Have you looked in a mirror lately? You can't go anywhere looking like that."

Sam touched her face suddenly remembering that she more closely resembled the Phantom of the Opera than Snow White.

"Well, I can go incognito again. It won't look that out of place considering they saw me like that yesterday," she said.

"And the rest of us?" Cynan asked.

"We can just say that you got into a fight with Mark and Matt while debating sports. Who wouldn't believe that three testosterone-charged blokes got carried away?"

"Well, I'm going to need a fresh change of clothes," I added.

"What's wrong with your clothes?" Sam asked sarcastically. "You don't want to show up in an evil henchman's robes?"

"Nah, I don't think that would be a good idea. Plus, I'm feeling fairly naked in the gown they gave me."

"No, don't take that off," Cynan interjected suddenly.

"Pervert," Sam scolded.

"Not for me," Cynan clarified. "We may get free lager at the pub!" he laughed.

Sam shook her head in disgust. "We better head back. It's going to take awhile to make us presentable."

"At least Angel will be ready before all of us. She doesn't have a mark on her!" Cynan exclaimed.

"Not quite," I corrected. I pulled my hair back to reveal the bruise on my forehead and temple. Then I pulled up my right sleeve and removed CJ's t-shirt bandage.

Sam and Cynan gasped in horror.

The wound had continued to scab. However, the skin in and around the crescent moon became a dull grey hue and felt hard and gritty to the touch—kind of like dry coral or sandpaper.

The siblings exchanged worried glances. Sam shuddered. "Morgan should look at that before it spreads and ends up killing your arm."

17 ~ A Night Out

CJ and Morgan were speaking to each other at the kitchen table. Both were smiling, so I figured that was a good sign.

"Where's Edwin?" Cynan asked.

"He stepped out for some fresh air," Morgan said simply.

"Morgan, please look at Angel's arm," Sam requested, wasting no time.

I handed CJ's shirt back to him and extended my right arm to Morgan.

"Oh, dear," she exclaimed surprised. "Does it hurt?"

"Not anymore," I smiled gratefully at CJ, who was concentrating sullenly on the wound.

"Come with me. Sam, please cut several branches of St. John's Wort from the garden. Cynan, fetch my matches and white gauze."

Morgan led me to the stark white bathroom. CJ followed close behind, the muscles of his jaw clenched tightly with distress.

"CJ, hold her arm steady," Morgan directed, examining the injury.

"I thought I stopped it," he said, his voice pained with regret.

"You cleaned it well. This is just an extra step. My mother spoke of its use for certain vampire attacks," Morgan stated simply as if vampiric wounds were commonplace topics of conversation.

Sam and Cynan arrived simultaneously with their supplies. Morgan lit the branches of St. John's Wort and extinguished the flames allowing the smoke to fill the air around us. Using the blackened branches she traced a pentagram on the crescent moon. The wound began to burn immediately. Now I knew why she asked CJ to hold my arm. It twitched involuntarily from the invisible fire consuming my skin.

CJ's nauseous split-pea green expression stared at me apologetically. I smiled and shrugged. With everything that had happened to me lately, this was very low on my list of painful and scary things. Though his eyes were still narrowed in worry, he smirked at my nonchalance and shook his head in disbelief.

Morgan placed several smoldering St. John's Wort branches against the dead skin taking great care not to touch the healthy parts. I flinched worrying the branches might seer my arm, but the skin in and immediately around the crescent moon must have really been dead. I felt nothing.

She fastened the remaining flowers tightly against my forearm with gauze and completed her incantation as CJ and I watched with dumbstruck admiration.

"All right, so what are we doing this evening?" Morgan asked, releasing me.

"We're going to the pub," Sam blurted. Considering Morgan's cool, skeptical look, perhaps Sam should've built up to the announcement instead of proclaiming it.

She peered questioningly at her daughter. "Do you remember what happened in town yesterday?"

"Come on," Sam whined. "That was at the chapel and I'm not suggesting we go there alone again. The pub is probably the safest place for us other than here. Besides, with the screams echoing from the forest last night, the people in town need to be reassured. This will show them that we're alive and well."

"Yes, Sam, but you're not well and have you seen the boys?"

Sam glared indignantly at her mother.

Morgan glanced at CJ. "What do you think?"

CJ's eyes drifted over each of us, debating the question. "It'll be fine as long as we stay together and only go for a short time."

"Sam?" Morgan asked.

She grunted unhappily, "Fine. Agreed."

"Well then, get ready. None of you can go out looking like a beaten horde of street rats," Morgan added.

Sam and Cynan bounded upstairs.

Morgan turned to me, "Angel, you may only give yourself a sponge bath. Do not get that wound wet until morning, understand?"

I nodded. Morgan followed her children upstairs.

CJ looked at me slyly, "Sponge bath, huh?"

"I hate sponge baths," I growled.

He looked at me coyly wanting to say something else, but his face blushed and he reconsidered his thoughts. I smiled at him seductively and walked through the bathroom door closing it on his rather disappointed face.

Adding some of Morgan's leftover St. John's Wort flowers to the bath, I filled the tub and slipped the cloak from my shoulders. The mirror's reflection of the gossamer gown's shimmer caught my eye. Aside from my wild hair which had gotten a wind-swept style from my travels, I couldn't believe how pretty I looked. Frumpy, plain me was no more. I gawked at the attractive woman gawking back at me.

The iridescent gown had a wide cowl neck line that draped lightly across my chest. Its shirred waist gathered at my hips with a long ribbon belt of the same material. If the gown hadn't been used for such despicable purposes, I may very well have kept it.

Instead, I ripped it off and tossed it like a dirty rag into the trash can, shuddering at the thought of vampires touching me while I was unconscious.

Stepping cautiously into the shallow basin of burning hot water, I sank into its welcoming sanctuary. Glancing at my forearm I thought of how delicately CJ held it while Morgan completed her work. The memory of his being upset at my pain made my heart skip a beat. *He's sensitive, protective, kind, gentlemanly, and gorgeous—could it be that I found the perfect man? Of course he'd be perfect, he's not normal.*

I toweled off and looked at my reflection. My face aged at least five years over the past five days. I looked less like me with each passing hour. These creepy new circumstances were propelling my body, awareness, and emotions into unexpected changes.

Distracted, I pulled on Sam's white pencil skirt and pale pink, loose fitting, long-sleeved blouse. I hastily styled my hair to hide the bruise along my left temple. Rummaging through the cabinet beneath the sink, I found some of Sam's makeup and brightened my eyes with mascara and added a light brush of pale pink lip gloss to accentuate my lips.

Satisfied with my transformation, I reached for the door knob. Pausing, I glanced back at the mirror. *What am I doing?* I never dressed up for anyone...until now.

Breathing deeply, I opened the bathroom door to find CJ leaning against the couch waiting for me, holding a single daisy. He wore a casual suit jacket over a button down, navy, satiny shirt which complemented his eyes. Once I met his kind gaze, I fell right back into the hopeless insanity.

"Wow," I uttered before realizing I had turned off my inner monologue.

CJ flashed a dashing smile and handed the flower to me.

"You look beautiful," he said simply and extended his arm so we could walk together. My blushed face probably matched my shirt.

I twirled the daisy in my fingers happily, ignoring the fact that Sam and Cynan were staring at us mischievously from the kitchen.

"Ready?" Morgan asked, walking into the room.

CJ and I followed the crowd. Actually, floated would be a more accurate description. I was in heaven. As I tucked the daisy behind my right ear, I nearly collided into a frozen wall of my shocked friends.

"You like it?" CJ asked at the sight of the platinum convertible.

"Whoa, man, that's a Mercedes SLR McLaren Roadster!" Mark shouted.

Thrilled that I was speechless, CJ pulled me to the car running his fingers along its sleek body.

"What do you think?" he asked enthusiastically.

"Uh, wow!" I wasn't an aficionado, but I knew what a Mercedes was and I could appreciate its sleek beauty.

"Perfect, isn't it?" CJ was very proud of his new toy.

"How did you get it?"

"Job perk," he said flippantly.

"Dude, this is freakin' awesome!" Mark exclaimed drooling all over the car as he examined it from every angle explaining each detail to Matt and Cynan, his captive audience.

Bored, Morgan and Sam climbed into Mark's convertible, waiting for them to return.

CJ put his arm around me and dragged my stunned presence to the passenger side. Swinging the door open vertically, he held my hand while I lowered myself into its smooth leather contoured seat.

"Excuse us, gentleman," he said proudly, pushing past Mark, Matt, and Cynan. "We'll meet you at the pub."

He jumped into his seat and revved the purring engine. Flooring the accelerator, we lurched forward at the speed of light.

"Let me guess, you haven't played with any toys in awhile?"

"You don't like it?" he asked dejected.

"It's not that I don't like it," I rushed to explain. I didn't want to hurt his feelings. "It's just...well...it's too much for me. I like simple things. This is unnecessarily extravagant."

His expression looked contemplative and slightly upset.

"I'm sorry," I continued. "I do think it's awesome, but I'd much rather travel the other way."

"Which way is that?" he muttered.

"Flying through space and time instantly while you hold me close."

A large smile beamed across his handsome, gloomy face. "Well, that's good to know for future trips. In the meantime, can you enjoy this pumpkin carriage, Cinderella?"

I giggled. Hanging on his every breath, I couldn't deny it—I was falling in love.

The car flew through the countryside at magnificent speed, my hair blowing wildly in the wind. I hated to admit it, but the car *was* phenomenal.

CJ's deep, reverberating voice interrupted my reverie. "Open the glove compartment."

I reached forward and a small, lavender colored box wrapped with a white ribbon popped into my hands.

"What's this?" I asked completely shocked and surprised.

"A little something I found for you."

Curious, I slipped the lid off of the box. Inside laid my iPod.

"How did you find it? I thought I lost everything yesterday."

"I have my ways," he glanced at me. Noticing that I was getting choked up, he immediately asked, "What's wrong?"

I fought back the torrent of tears. "CJ, this means so much to me. It's the only thing I have left that connects me to my boyfriend in a living way. It's priceless," I said quietly. The physical reminder of Zach unleashed a tsunami of guilt which washed away my feelings toward CJ instantly.

"Well, if you're happy, then I'm happy," he grinned.

We arrived at the pub in what seemed like a matter of minutes— too fast for me, I wished the drive could've lasted infinitely. A perfect gentleman, CJ rushed to the passenger's side, opened the car door, and offered his hand to me before I even had a chance to unlock the seat-belt. His mere touch sent a wave of electricity jolting through my body causing an uncontrollable, yet perfectly pleasant shiver.

"Are you ok?" he asked, his eyes wide with alarm.

No, not really. Every time you touch me I feel like lightning runs through my veins. "Yes," I lied. "Just a little cold."

He tore off his jacket and placed it carefully around my shoulders. His scent engulfed my senses causing me to nearly trip over my own feet. *I'm so pathetic.*

Thankfully he didn't draw any attention to my lack of coordination. Without saying a word, he put his arm around my waist to balance me. His touch set another round of butterflies loose in my stomach.

My attention was fully focused on walking straight and not looking like an enamored idiot. As I walked through the door, I looked up from the floor for a millisecond—just long enough to see Rick sitting at the bar, brooding over a pint. When his eyes met mine, he instantly beamed, that is, until he saw CJ.

I waved to him. He acknowledged me with a curt nod before abruptly turning back to his beer.

"Know that guy?" CJ asked curiously, sliding next to me on the bench of the large corner booth.

"Yeah, apparently he's some sort of celebrity. He's got an *amazing* group of fans." Caustic sarcasm.

"How so?"

"About twenty faultless girls in a variety of colors and sizes wearing skimpy outfits fight over him every day. Isn't that every guy's dream come true?" Thinking about his entourage, it looked like Rick flipped through a magazine and ordered them as human accessories.

"That's not really my cup of tea."

"Why? Are you gay?" I blurted before thinking. *Please, God, please don't let him be gay. Of course with my luck, the only guy I find incredibly attractive and nice would be, wouldn't he?* "There's nothing wrong with that, if you are," I added quickly and sincerely, just in case.

CJ smirked, "You really think I'm gay? I'm going to have to reevaluate what kind of mixed signals I'm sending."

"If you're not, then why wouldn't you find a bunch of dim-witted, model-like girls throwing themselves at you attractive?"

"Because my type is more of the demure, smart, and courageous variety," he gazed deeply into my eyes.

My mind blanked. I sighed audibly realizing too late I was acting like a love-struck zombie. Around CJ, I was no better than Rick's Barbies.

I shook my head trying to clear my thoughts, "Uh, so what should we talk about?"

"What would you like to discuss?"

"You." *Again, editing my thoughts before speaking would've been a good idea.*

"Well, I'll do my best to answer then."

Good. Maybe I can figure you out.

"Favorite color?"

"Midnight blue." *Deep. Dark. Mystifying.*

"Favorite season?"

"Autumn." *Mine too!*

"Least favorite season?"

"Winter." *Yeah, the dead coldness is a turn off for me too.*

"Favorite story?"

"Shakespeare's Romeo and Juliet."

"That's a bit macabre, don't you think?"

"Depends on your point of view."

"But…"

He interrupted, "I thought you were asking questions to get to know me better, not evaluating my answers."

"Well, that depends on your answers," I replied smugly. "Favorite music?"

"Josquin des Prez."

I arched my eyebrow. "That's a name you don't hear every day."

He smirked, "Continue please." *He really likes playing the mysterious guy.*

"Fate or Chance?"

"Hmmm…both." *How? Maybe he's just indecisive.*

"Books: fact or fiction?"

"Both." *Levelheaded or really indecisive?*

"Nighttime or daytime?"

"Night." *Interesting. There're lots of things to do at night.* Damn it. *Stop it, Angel!*

"Miracles?"

"Absolutely." *Spiritual?*

Just then, the entire gang arrived and plowed their way toward our table.

"Damn," I said, frustrated at the interruption. CJ winked at me enjoying the fact that he was off the hook.

Sam nearly sprinted into the pub looking around hopefully. A blindingly beautiful and rapturous grin spread across her face the minute she caught a glimpse of Rick. She waved enthusiastically at him. He smiled sweetly before scowling in my direction.

Morgan practically dragged Sam to the booth by her elbow. Every few steps, Sam would glance over her shoulder to see if Rick was still looking.

"How was the ride?" Sam asked sarcastically.

"Leave her alone," Cynan barked at his sister. "She's just jealous," he directed to me.

"I promise to take you for a ride, Sam," CJ offered. "If you want to, that is."

Sam looked like someone knocked the wind out of her as her jaw dropped to the ground and her eyes nearly popped out of her head. Apparently CJ's power extended beyond me. "Uh, yeah, I'd love to go for a ride with you," she drooled.

A sudden pang of jealousy twisted in my stomach. I didn't want to share CJ.

A jovial waiter set appetizers on the table and greeted Sam, Cynan, and Morgan. Looking at Sam, he said, "That young man has been waiting here all day for you and your friend."

Sam blushed. "Really?" she asked excitedly.

"He sent all the pretty girls away hoping you'd come," the waiter continued as he cleared the table next to ours.

Before I could warn the others, Rick hopped off of his barstool and made his way toward us. Sam's eyes fixated dreamily on the object of her affection. He wore a very relaxed fit of dark trousers with a snug, long sleeved multi-colored shirt that hugged his body in all the right places. His tousled dark brown hair shimmered under the fluorescent lights. But what really grabbed my attention was the perfect smoothness of his flawless face, which was complemented by cherry-red lips. He was hotter than his Barbies.

"Angel, Samantha," he greeted us with his velvety sweet voice. He extended his hand to Morgan, "Hi, ma'am, my name is Rick."

"Hello. I'm Morgan," she said coolly, studying his face. "Sam told me a lot about you."

"I had the pleasure of making your daughter's acquaintance yesterday. She's beautiful and incredibly sweet and polite." He cast a dirty look at me.

Sam swooned; Morgan grabbed her hand to steady her. Enjoying Sam's reaction, Rick smiled dashingly. Slowly his joyful gaze morphed into a concerned squint as he really noticed Sam.

"Samantha, what happened to you?" he exclaimed, truly upset by her appearance.

Sam had tried her best to cover up the gash but the scab brightened under her blushing cheeks. Thankfully, the Jackie-O glasses hid the black and blues around her eyes and nose.

"Oh nothing," she dismissed flippantly. "I just got caught in the middle of the boys fighting over football."

Rick glared at the bruised bunch of Mark, Matt, and Cynan. His murderous stare sent a shiver down my spine. He seemed to run on a high voltage of passion 24/7. Whether it was love, hate, or concern, he didn't express emotions half-heartedly.

"You need to find better company, Samantha—friends that won't send you to a hospital."

Rick's chivalry captivated Sam. She was completely speechless and, from the looks of it, completely incapable of thinking or moving. Across the table, Matt was restraining Mark while Cynan extended his arm in front of him in case he decided to jump at Rick.

Rick's gaze shifted to me and he smiled with added effort. "Angel, I was hoping you've reconsidered my invitation?"

Surprised, CJ snapped up his head, his eyes accusing me of something that hadn't happened.

"Sorry, Rick," I replied before all of the men would beat him senseless. "Don't think so."

"I don't give up easily," he said suavely, ignoring CJ and the murderous glares from the rest of the table.

Staring into Rick's eyes everyone disappeared. He reached over CJ's dinner to lift my hand. He shuddered slightly as his lips brushed it with a light kiss, which sent the charge of a lightning bolt through me. "Until tomorrow then," he promised with a glimmer of hope in his eyes.

By now, Matt and Cynan were leaning against Mark with all of their might. CJ's eyes flashed furiously from Rick to me.

Ignoring the guys, Rick turned to Sam and Morgan, "Good evening, ladies." Satisfied with the damage he caused, he swept through the pub slamming the front doors behind him.

Shaking, Mark was about to snap.

"Didn't we tell you he was a tool?" Matt exclaimed to CJ.

CJ simply shook his head staring intently at Mark. When Mark met his gaze, he relaxed.

"You ok, Mark?" CJ asked.

"Fine," he seethed. "I just hate that dude. Hate him more than…"

"Football?" Sam interjected lightly. Her comedic timing lightened the atmosphere instantly. The rest of the evening proceeded pleasantly without incident, but I kept looking at CJ wondering what he was thinking. His otherwise pleasant demeanor had been replaced with a scowling seriousness.

We finished our dinners and accomplished our goal of letting the locals know we were all alive and well—for the most part anyway. The sun slipped beneath the nearby hillsides as CJ's car crawled along the country roads; its driver clearly preoccupied.

"CJ?"

"Hmmm?" he replied completely distracted.

"What are you thinking about?"

"I can't tell you."

My body tensed in anxious anticipation. "Are you mad at me?"

"Mad at you?" he sneered.

"Are you?" I pressed.

He paused and drew a long, deep breath. Avoiding my fearful gaze he concentrated on the road. "It's not about you. It's about me wanting to rip Rick's head off without feeling an ounce of remorse."

"Oh, is that all?" I sighed relieved.

"Is that all?" he echoed skeptically. "You're not terrified by a rage so powerful I could kill someone?"

"Not particularly."

"Why not?" he asked in disbelief.

"Because I trust you. You wouldn't hurt me or anyone unnecessarily. And I think that Rick could use a lesson or two in humility."

"Angel, you don't even know me," he said exasperated. His tone left me second guessing the blind trust I placed in him. Was he really that dangerous?

But he was right. I didn't know him. Embarrassed, I stared out the window. I didn't want to end our night on this sour note. We needed a distraction.

"Can you tell me more about the vampires?"

"You *want* to know more about them? I thought after your last encounter you'd prefer never to think about them again."

"I'm absolutely, positively sure. Please," I pleaded. Other than desperately wanting to hear his melodic voice, I hoped this would finally give me a better idea of what was coming.

"It's a long story. Are you sure you want to hear it? You have enough nightmares as it is." He was delaying.

"I'm sure."

He paused reluctantly and sighed. "Before God made the earth, he—or she," he corrected, glancing at me apologetically, "made many other beings and entities to fill the universe, but the angels were the pride of his creation.

"Eventually, he made the earth, plants, animals, and people who lived blissfully in perfection. They didn't know suffering and pain because the Creator provided them with everything.

"A dissenting group of angels was jealous of the people on earth because they thought the Creator liked their simplicity more than in the angels' glory. They organized an uprising. Of course, they were easily defeated and the Creator, refusing to destroy them, banished them to earth.

"Are you all right, Angel?"

My face was frozen in suspense. "I thought these were old Sunday school stories?"

CJ laughed. "Well they're similar, but the details have been lost."

"Are you serious? The fallen angels? All this really happened?"

"Yes," CJ said patiently. "Do you want me to continue or have you had enough?"

"Please go on," I begged.

Assessing my expression and words to make sure I honestly wanted to hear more, he continued, "So in an act of vengeance, the earth-bound group turned its attention to people. Their goal was simple—destroy humanity, end the world..."

"What? Like the apocalypse?"

CJ's eyes creased suddenly, staring at me in speechless bewilderment. I thought my question was fairly straightforward. Then again, maybe he was just taken aback by my overly eager, ignorant assumptions.

"Um, yes, actually," he stammered eventually. "But at first they figured they'd turn humanity on itself. They seduced women creating half-human, half-divine offspring, who had unique powers and sometimes looked like a cross between animals and people. Mythological stories come from these half-breeds.

"People revered the angels' power and considered them gods. As humankind became corrupt, it lost its connection to the Creator. The angels no longer needed to interfere in the mayhem. Humanity turned on itself inflicting pain, war, and suffering. They decimated God's design for life outside of heaven.

"He sent his faithful archangels, seraphim, and cherubim to protect the people and convince the fallen to return. He still cared for them and was willing to accept them back into his good graces if they'd ask for forgiveness.

"Self-righteous and proud, they refused. The holy ranks prepared for battle.

"Now, angels can't be destroyed easily. The archangels made a silver dagger that they blessed in earth's wind, water, ground, and fire. While the lightning-like energy of these weapons could damage the angels, having the weapon thrust through their hearts is what actually killed them. Once an angel was vanquished, its body instantly burned in a pillar of fire leaving behind a pile of dust. These ashes were collected and scattered in the ocean.

"Both sides continued the war—each winning and losing over the past quarter million years or so. One day the fallen angels realized they needed help. Arrogantly proud and self-confident, they never considered assistance of any kind before.

"They assessed their progeny's talents and determined the most powerful to be the demi-god son of Gaap, a fallen angel with bat wings, amazing hearing, and taste for blood. As the son matured he developed a taste for *human wine*," CJ sneered sarcastically. "Eventually the diet killed his body, but, as a half-immortal, his soul continued to inhabit it. He discovered the secret to eternal life."

"Vampire?" I asked hesitantly.

CJ nodded, parking the car in front of the cottage. Sprinting to my side before I had a chance to open the door, he offered his hand and helped me from the seat. Since I was clearly lost in thought, he held my hand lightly and guided me to the porch. As I reached for the doorknob, he pulled me back into his arms.

I stared into his eyes unsure of what to do, knowing what I wanted to do. Gazing deeply, caringly into my eyes, he playfully fingered the daisy behind my ear. His hand slipped from the flower and caressed my cheek setting off sparks that could've started a raging wildfire.

"Oh, Angel," he said softly, leaning his forehead against mine.

An overwhelming electrical charge pulsated between our bodies, lighting my heart ablaze and flip-flopping my stomach. My eager eyes met his adoring gaze, but his expression transformed from one of love to worry.

I pulled away shocked at his sudden emotional change. He shook his head and opened the front door, allowing me to step through. As I climbed the stairs to Sam's room I looked back at him confused, but he disappeared into the kitchen.

I wanted nothing more than to comfort CJ from whatever worries plagued him. Unfortunately, my own worries prevented me from taking any action. *What if he doesn't really like me? What if I'm reading all of the signs wrong?*

More importantly, what about Zach?

18 ~ Puzzle Pieces

The full moon illuminated my limp body as my nightgown billowed in the frigid winter breeze.

"Until we meet again," he said haughtily, his red eyes peering furiously through mine.

Screams pierced the still night air, but the screams weren't mine. The torturous shrieks came from inside the manor. My husband! He saw what was happening. He was in pain.

The monster released me slowly from his fierce grip. I plummeted into the blackness of the cold winter night. My soul wrenching shriek, "Noooooooooooooooo," echoed infinitely.

"Angel, Angel, wake up! It's just a nightmare," the distant sound of CJ's voice faintly penetrated my dreams. His hands gripped my arms tightly and shook me awake.

One-by-one, my eyes opened, squinting to see him through the bright sunlight streaming through the windows.

I bolted upright trying to remember where I was. Gradually, my eyes focused on Sam's pale pink walls and white furniture. I peered at what had been my bed. The blankets were strewn across the floor—a physical manifestation of the nightmare's deadly struggle. Sam's lavender PJ top hung loosely from my shoulder, which I quickly readjusted more modestly.

CJ tenderly wiped away the rivers cascading down my cheeks. "Was it the same dream?"

I nodded unable to form words yet. He furrowed his eyebrows, sadness seeping from his gaze. Dropping his hands from my face, he sat silently upon Sam's bed staring emptily through the window.

CJ's complexity bothered me. He was definitely deeper than his earth shattering good looks. The question was how deep? Could I tread through his waters or would I find myself drowning at sea?

I managed to find my voice and croaked, "What time is it?"

"Noon."

"What?!" I shouted. "Why didn't anyone wake me up?"

"You were zonked out. No one wanted to bother you."

"Where's Sam?" I asked, still slightly disoriented.

"She went to the market with Mark."

"She went willingly with Mark?" I asked in disbelief.

CJ nodded, smiling weakly, "It helped that he was driving my car."

"You let Mark borrow your car?" I asked in disbelief. "That's like giving a baby candy. You're never going to get it back!"

"It's just a thing, Angel. It doesn't matter," he said lightly. I really never met a guy like this. I knew guys who treated their cars better than their girlfriends. They'd never let another guy borrow their girlfriend or car. "Everyone else went to the council meeting."

He swept away a strand of hair hanging in front of my face. "Do you want to go for a walk, get some fresh air?"

"Sure," I said eagerly. I needed to get out of this room. "I'll meet you downstairs in about thirty minutes."

He smiled happily and started for the door. He paused at the entry and turned to say something but thought better of it and hopped down the stairs.

While I strolled over to Sam's closet looking for an outfit, I tried to make sense of every minute detail of CJ's actions and my neurotic attraction to him. He probably just thought I was some sort of nut case and was being nice to me because his job required it.

Distracted, I sat at Sam's white computer desk and ripped a piece of paper from her school tablet. I needed to jot down some thoughts from the past few days:

Good battling evil
Vampires & witches?
Religion vs. mythology
What or who do I believe?
Trust in CJ, Sam, Cynan, Mark, Matt, council
Do I trust others or myself?
How does Endymion Manor fit into the battle?
Murders at the home...why?
Cenweard & Artemis
How is she involved?
What does this have to do with me?
Miscellaneous: who sent car to airport? Who
is my red-eyed stalker? Magic tunnel?
Transformation into rock?
Artemis' symbol

Writing helped me feel better even if the contents were ridiculous. I shoved the paper under a book and rushed to the bathroom to get ready.

When I stepped into the shower, the makeshift bandage with the St. John's Wort flowers caught my eye. I was truly afraid of what ugly sight might meet me beneath the dressing.

Holding my breath, I quickly unwound the gauze and delicately lifted the flowers off of the wound. The outline of the crescent moon burned bright red against the stark white skin inside of the scar and surrounding its perimeter. *Not bad,* I thought examining it from different angles allowing the light to illuminate every aspect of it.

The idea of a vampire's fingernail slicing my skin and forcing it to decay still made me queasy. Luckily, I found a bandage which covered about seventy-five percent of the area.

Staring intently through the kitchen window, CJ was oblivious to my approach. A long sleeved white linen shirt hung loosely on his perfect form while his khaki pants clung to a rear so perfect that Michelangelo's David would've been jealous.

"I'm ready," I announced, shoving the lust-filled thoughts into the far corner of my brain. I wondered why these thoughts were surfacing now. It's not like Zach and I went past second base. We vehemently agreed to protect our virginity until we were ready to handle it—even though it was rather difficult to remember this agreement on more than one occasion. As soon as CJ walked into my life, this promise to myself disappeared. Unfortunately, my passionate thoughts of CJ were married to a ton of guilt. One couldn't exist without the other. I still loved Zach. I still felt bound to him, but he was gone.

CJ spun around and flashed his gorgeous smile, melting me instantly.

The bandage caught his attention. I frowned in dismay as I was hoping not to think about it again.

"How's that looking today?" he asked deeply concerned.

"Fine. The grayish-green fleshy decay is gone. The only problem is that the scar area is whiter than the rest of the skin."

"At least it's on the inside of your arm," he suggested thoughtfully.

"Yeah," I said my lips curling into a smile, "and I always wanted a tattoo, so this will serve two purposes for me."

"Two?"

"Yup, I got a tattoo and permanent souvenir from my trip."

CJ shook his head in exasperation at my lightheartedness.

He was so beautiful I just wanted to—well, I'm ashamed to admit what I 'just wanted to' do.

"Instead of a walk, would you mind if we go shopping," I suggested. Considering my obvious lack of self control, this would be better than staying at the house alone with him. "As long as we avoid the chapel, we should be ok. Right?"

"Sure," he agreed eagerly.

He popped a disc into Mark's car's CD player. A complicated, yet sweet melody filled the air.

"What's this?"

"Josquin des Prez. I thought you might like to hear a little bit of my favorite music."

We drove in silence the rest of the way into town. It wasn't awkward; still I didn't know what to make of CJ. A strange push-pull dynamic tethered us. It seemed like he wanted me to get closer to him, but then he'd push me away again.

He parked next to the pub and walked a couple of steps behind me as we made our way to the store. I have to give him credit. He didn't wait outside like I expected. His cheeks were flushed with excitement and his amused eyes followed my every move.

I picked up a white lacy top and held it against my chest, "What do you think?"

"No."

"Why not?"

"It's see-through!" he exclaimed.

"You wear a camisole under it," I explained.

"No."

"Why not?"

"Because guys will just imagine you without it."

"Fine." I shoved the shirt back onto the rack. At least he was talking to me and didn't seem bothered or depressed. The complications from last night disappeared, which was a very good thing.

"What about this one?" I asked, showcasing a pink babydoll satin top.

"Hmmm, yes," he paused, looking around the rack. "But I like it better in dark purple. It complements your eyes."

I blushed. *He noticed my eyes!*

"And actually, what about these?" In two seconds, he picked out five pretty tops for me in an array of colors and styles.

"They're perfect!" I exclaimed incredulously. "Were you a personal shopper before?"

"Nope," he said proudly, laughing at my sarcastic assumption. "I just know what looks good on you." I glanced at him in time to catch his knee-weakening smile and a twinkle in his eyes. My insides tried to jump out of my body in ecstatic glee.

He abruptly diverted my attention by selecting several pairs of pants, skirts, and shorts. He even found a pair of black ballet flats, white kitten heel sandals, and a pair of sneakers.

"I think that's it. Thanks! We finished in record time. I thought we'd be here all afternoon." I was really hoping it would've taken longer. I didn't want to go back just yet.

"Wait, don't you need some...uh...foundation garments?"

"What?" His question caught me by surprise.

"You know—granny panties," he laughed, recalling our first conversation. Was this the reason for his amused expression when we entered the store?

Blood rushed to my cheeks, blushing them with a deep, smoldering burn. "When I mentioned that on the plane, I never thought I'd actually be shopping for underwear with you."

"Well?"

"Well, what?"

"Don't you need them?"

"Yes, but aren't you going to pick them out for me? You did such a great job with the rest of the clothes." I couldn't resist the flirtatious invitation.

"I don't think that's such a good idea."

"Why not? You've got great taste."

"True," he smiled sarcastically. "Except that when it comes to that I might pick them more for what they do to me than for your comfort," he muttered shyly, quickly turning away from my view.

I cocked my left eyebrow at him. The angel and devil sitting on my shoulders were heatedly debating how wrong it would be for me to seduce him. I sighed as the good angel won and I picked out a few items to go with the new clothes.

As I walked into the lingerie section, my eyes lingered on a row of bridal gowns. I ran my fingers along the low neckline of one that was covered in French lace with tiny beads and sequins.

CJ strolled over to me, noticing my preoccupation.

"It's beautiful, isn't it?" I asked, wondering why I wasn't immediately embarrassed that he caught me staring at the display.

"Yes, it is…" his voice trailed off. "But I thought you liked simple things, nothing fancy."

"I'll make an exception when it comes to this. I've always imagined what being married would be like."

Before I could stop myself, an image of CJ jumped into my mind with us lying on a very large, soft, white bed surrounded by roses and candles. He kissed me and softly caressed my body as we…

"Imagining being married right now?" CJ interrupted my uncontrolled stream of consciousness with a soft whisper into my hair.

His proximity sent a shiver through my body.

"You ok?" he asked, quickly stepping back.

"More than you know…" I whispered in response to his curious stare.

"You know, it's not just a girl thing. I think about it too…"

Standing next to each other, we stared at the clothes in silence, lost in our private thoughts. It wasn't awkward. It should've been because I'd known him for less than a day, but it wasn't.

"Speaking of things you wear to bed, I figured you might want something to sleep in too," he handed a few PJs to me. One was a black satin pajama set with short sleeves and pants decorated with little red hearts. The second was a soft cotton jersey tank top and boxer short set in hot pink. The last one, a plain white sleeveless nightgown, had buttons down the front and an eyelet overlay across the chest.

"What do you think?" he asked apprehensively.

"They're perfect!" I was sincerely amazed by him.

CJ smiled rather contentedly with his accomplishment. He insisted on carrying everything too, so the pile of clothes sat just below his nose. After maneuvering his way to the sales desk, he set them down carefully.

"That will be 657 Euros," the clerk said.

While I fumbled reaching into my back pocket to pull out a credit card, CJ flipped his wallet open and paid for the purchase in cash.

"What are you doing?" I asked irritated and mortified. "That cost a fortune!"

"I'll just expense it as part of my job," he grinned.

"That's not right, CJ."

"It is when you are my job," he retorted, glaring obstinately.

The sales clerk watched our interchange inquisitively not knowing what to make of it. I ignored her eavesdropping. "But CJ..."

"Not another word," he said firmly. "I wanted to do something for you—something 'little' as you put it. You needed these, I wanted to help. Case closed. Besides I picked out most of it."

Very reluctantly, but graciously, I mumbled, "Thank you" at CJ's smug, triumphant face.

He carried four large bags only allowing me to hold the smaller bag of lingerie. Stepping into the plaza side-by-side, I giggled.

"What is it?" he asked curiously.

"Oh, CJ, I've never had so much fun shopping before! I'm still mad at you for buying all of this, but thank you!" I exclaimed and hopped up to give him a peck on the cheek.

He touched his cheek as I pulled my lips away from him. Realizing my forwardness a little too late, I blushed and looked away shyly.

"Angel?" a voice cried from across the street, stirring me from my embarrassing faux pas that left me yearning for more.

"Oh no," I mumbled, closing my eyes, wishing he'd disappear.

"How are you today?" Rick asked enthusiastically, sprinting toward me.

"I'm fine. Shopping." I dangled the little black bag from my fingertips in case he doubted the statement.

Rick nodded at CJ. At least he acknowledged him today.

"Aren't you supposed to be filming a movie? Why is it that you never work?" I asked irritated. *Just leave—you're ruining my moment here!*

"Actually, that's what I wanted to talk to you about. Would you like to come to the shoot tomorrow?"

"Me? You want *me* to watch you film the movie?" I asked incredulously.

"Yeah. And you can bring your friends," he added cordially.

"I'll think about it," I offered in a very non-committal, flippant tone.

"Great!" he said, ignoring the hint that my appearance wouldn't be likely. "We start shooting at dusk in the old cemetery."

Rick backed away from us toward his car.

"Wait, what's the movie about?" I asked.

"It's an action film with vampires and werewolves. Terrifying!" he said with a sparkle in his green eyes that matched the enormous grin exposing his perfect teeth. "See you tomorrow," he added excitedly. Spinning on his heels, he turned and hopped into a sleek, deep red sports car and sped away.

"If Mark likes my car, wait until he sees Rick's."

"Why?"

"It's a Lotus Evora sports-GT—that model is in limited production. You don't drive something like that for its looks. It's all about speed." CJ paused his envious stare after the car to glance at me. "What's wrong?"

"I didn't even tell him I'd go," I complained. I didn't care about the car. I was more worried about the unofficial date Rick tricked me into right in front of CJ.

Glaring intently after the car and its driver, CJ's expression vacillated between curiosity, anger, disbelief, and general displeasure. His wary gaze shifted to Endymion Manor.

"What's wrong?"

"That place," he said motioning to the manor, "has a horrific history. I'm not looking forward to going back there."

"Is that where the battle takes place?"

He nodded.

I quivered at the thought of having to go there, let alone having to fight. It still felt like a surreal joke.

"Let's not think about that and ruin the fun we're having, eh?" he said, replacing his mood dramatically with a more light-hearted tone. "Do you want a cup of tea or coffee?"

A mini-date, maybe? I thought hopefully. "Sure!" I said a little too enthusiastically.

He ran into the bakery and returned with two cups of coffee and a bag of goodies. "You haven't eaten anything yet. So, in case you're hungry..." he offered the bag to me. "You need to eat eventually."

What a god! Sensitive...thoughtful...perfect. Sigh.

"Thanks." I looked around at the benches facing the town. "Do you mind if we sit there instead?" I pointed to the boulders across from the pub. "I don't feel like people watching today."

We climbed onto the enormous stones and sipped the scalding coffee with cream and lots of sugar. Spending so much alone time with CJ literally made me ecstatic. A smirk escaped my lips.

"You're very happy today," he remarked joyfully, concentrating on his drink. "I like seeing you smile."

"I am happy. I had a great afternoon." Afraid to look at him, I added, "with you."

I felt his gaze resting on my face and purposely didn't look at him in case his expression rebuffed my overly honest comment. Blushing for the nine hundredth time today, I turned my attention to the hills and forest. Dense clouds cast a dark shadow over the land making it look more sinister than usual.

"It's hard to believe everything started right here just a few days ago." My pensive attitude matched my deep-in-thought stare at the lush, green hill and field in front of me. "My old life seems a world away..."

"Have you wondered what your life would be like without any of us in it right now?" he asked slowly, choosing each word carefully.

"Yeah, peaceful!" I quipped sarcastically.

His crestfallen expression was more than I could bear. I quickly added, "...and boring."

CJ perked up. "Where would you be right now, if it wasn't for this mess that's keeping you here with us?"

"Honestly?" I asked, taking a very deep breath knowing my answer, knowing CJ wouldn't want to hear it, and knowing I was incapable of lying to him.

"Yeah, honestly," he mocked.

"Buried..." I whispered. A shiver shot down my spine at the sound of my own voice uttering the words out loud.

His eyes opened wide and his ashen face suddenly looked old and worn with deep concern. "What do you mean?" he asked cautiously. A subtle anger boiled just beneath the surface of his question.

"Well," I paused, trying to gather my thoughts so I wouldn't upset him further. "As you know, my boyfriend, Zach, died."

I stopped again hoping the rivers of my eyes would remain dammed. As I dropped my head to focus on the cup, CJ inched closer and placed his arm around my waist. His warmth and a jolt of passionate desire within me cleared my head.

I continued softly, "...living without him has been unbearable. When I came here, I was ready to leave this world and move onto whatever punishment would await me on the other side. I just kept hoping that wherever I'd end up, I'd be closer to him. If we would have broken up, I could've moved on, but I'm trapped in a world I don't want to be in. Life flies by at lightning speed and I'm stuck crawling through each day in slow motion."

"Is your life really worth sacrificing for him? Wouldn't he want you to move on and be happy?" CJ asked guardedly.

"Of course he'd want me to be happy. But without him my life isn't happy—or whole. I'm fine on my own, but he was my other half, my soul mate."

"How do you know that though? There are billions of people in this world. Maybe he was a very special part of your life, but you're meant to be with someone else," he offered kindly.

"I know I can probably fall in love with someone else, but I think that's a coping mechanism. In my heart, deep inside, I know Zach was my true love. I don't want to live without him..." I paused, glancing bashfully at CJ, "well, at least I didn't until I met you."

His arm tightened around my waist. His gaze dropped sorrowfully into his coffee.

"I know what you mean," he said softly, fiddling with the white disposable cup. His worried, saddened expression was being tortured by some unexplainable force.

"I didn't mean to upset you," I regretted, trying to comfort him in an odd role reversal.

"You just reminded me of my own life. I've been so caught up in my mission here that I nearly forgot what it was like to really feel everything."

"What do you mean?"

"I have to block out my past in order to concentrate on the job ahead. If I allow emotions to control me, I won't survive what's coming," he said solemnly. "My other life seems like it happened centuries ago when it really hasn't been that long," he paused, dropping his hand from my waist. "Death separated me and my girlfriend too. She was perfect. She loved me more than anything in the entire world, certainly more than I deserved. And I loved her more than she could ever know," his voice broke. He avoided my gaze. I wanted him to see that I could be compassionate too and not just the self-absorbed monster I'd become. I wanted to hold him, make his pain go away.

"I never had a chance to say goodbye to her. You'd think time would make things easier, but moving on has been more painful than I ever imagined. Being near you reminds me so much of her and the life we had together. I miss her."

"So, you accepted this job as a suicide mission?"

He chortled, "Not quite. I have a more positive outlook than you. I accepted it because it would allow me to protect someone—you—in a way that I can no longer protect her. Maybe I can make a difference for you and then you can go on living a normal life after this."

"Normal? I don't think there will ever be anything normal about my life again, CJ. There's no way I'll ever be able to go back to my regular life."

"Not even to your family?"

I bowed my head, mortified that I had so easily forgotten about them. "I want to see them, but I can never be the daughter or sister they knew. I can't go back and pretend like none of this happened. Plus, I'd miss Sam, Cynan, Matt, Mark…and you…too much."

"Sam, Cynan, Matt, and Mark will always be a part of your life." He hesitated, looking deeply into my eyes with heart-wrenching, palpable agony, "but I have to leave as soon as my work here is finished. It's part of the deal for this job."

"Oh," I said simply, feeling my insides tear apart as if a monster was clawing my guts to shreds. "I see…" I turned to concentrate on the fields, my mind drifting far, far away hoping to find a place where the pain couldn't reach me. I didn't want to break down in front of him. I didn't want to allow myself to be more vulnerable than I already was with him. I was treading in dangerous, emotionally-charged territory.

CJ reached for my hand, slowly, tenderly taking it into his own. He lightly traced his thumb over its trembling surface. I didn't want to feel his warmth. I didn't want to feel drawn to him. I didn't want to fall in love with him any more than I stupidly already allowed myself. I pulled my hand from his grasp more harshly than I intended.

From the corner of my eye I saw his face fall disheartened.

"Promise me you won't give up?" he asked quietly. "I couldn't live with myself if something happened to you."

"Why?"

"What do you mean 'why?'" he asked confused. "I don't want you to die."

"No, I get that. I mean 'you don't even know me,'" I quoted him. "We only met five days ago. Why do you care about what happens to me?"

He stared into my soul. He didn't need to say a single word. I could see his tortured heart bleeding and twisting in an anguish so intense I was incapable of understanding it.

Tears welled in my eyes—tears crying not for me, but for the excruciating ache that tormented his thoughts, a pain I exacerbated when he was only trying to comfort me.

The sound of thunder rumbled in the distance. An unnatural darkness overhead suddenly enveloped the village casting dark shadows on the ancient buildings' pale walls. The handful of townspeople strolling along the square ducked into stores taking cover. A loud silence sounded in my ears broken by earth-shaking thunder. In an instant, a fork-like flash of lightning struck into the middle of the forest followed by another at the foot of the hillside beneath us.

"It's time to go," CJ said calmly, although his actions betrayed the ease of his words. As he hopped off of the boulder, he managed to gather all of the bags into one hand and scoop me up with the other.

A torrent of rain rushed through the skies over the manor and raced toward us.

I wrapped myself around his neck and waist so tightly that he didn't need to hold onto me. Within a few bounds from the boulder, we were at the car.

Unlike his typically chivalrous tendencies, he tossed me into the car like a rag doll and threw the bags onto my lap. The rain soaked us while it transformed the car into a bathtub.

CJ didn't even bother opening his door; he just leapt into his seat and started the ignition so quickly I didn't even see him insert the key.

The convertible's rooftop rose automatically as the car spun around in the square. The tires squealed in pain. Flooring the gas pedal, we sped toward the main road.

"Put your seatbelt on, NOW!" he yelled as the car's top snapped into place. Water dripped from his nose and chin. The dampness glistened in his blondish locks.

Despite his angelic handsomeness, the ferocity of his voice scared me. Shrinking away from him, I sat as close to the door as possible. He glanced nervously through the windows and the rearview mirror. What happened to the sensitive man who poured his heart out to me not two minutes ago?

Barely clinging to the road's curves, the car skidded along the cobblestone streets' soaked surfaces. The storm altered our surroundings so drastically that it looked more like midnight not four o'clock on a summer afternoon.

The trees and bushes, usually cheerful in their green hues and flowery accents, appeared black as night. The road was barely visible through the sheets of rain.

With my back plastered against the door I stared at CJ's determined face afraid to lose eye contact.

A movement in the bushes beyond him distracted my gaze. Red eyes pierced the black velvet world outside our speeding bubble.

Then another pair of blood-red dots appeared floating beside the others. My nauseous stomach sank. The eyes weren't floating; they were keeping pace.

Guessing these eyes might not be restricted to CJ's side, I spun around to look through my window. A set of silver gems locked on mine just a few feet from my face.

"AAAAAAAAAAAH! Go faster! Oh my God, CJ. Oh my God!"

I glanced at the speedometer, sickeningly realizing we were already speeding over one hundred fifty kilometers per hour. A sea of red and silver eyes trailed our car in the coal blackness surrounding us.

"What are those things?" I yelled, my voice trembling.

"Vampires," he paused, "and werewolves," he replied, gritting his teeth, trying to concentrate on the sharp turns, which twisted through the dense forest.

"Oh, is that all," I said sardonically. "Can't you go any faster?" I screamed.

"I'm trying," he retorted scornfully.

The convertible tossed us from side-to-side while CJ weaved through the trees trying to maintain tire contact with the road. The eyes behind us were gaining distance.

"We can't escape. They're everywhere!"

"Do me a favor. Think positively!" he shouted.

I did not care for his new attitude.

"What good will that do? At least if I think about what will happen, I'll be prepared for the worst," I argued heatedly.

"It'll make all the difference in the world," he said, his eyes burning into mine. "Please?" he pleaded intensely.

I looked through all of the windows. We were surrounded. Some of the eyes were waiting in the road not far ahead.

"Angel, listen to me, close your eyes," he waited for me to shut my eyelids. "Picture us speeding past them. In your mind, make a wish and picture us arriving safely at Sam's house."

I tried to replace the idea that we were going to get caught, tortured, and killed with CJ's less dramatic imagery. I kept replaying the sequence in my imagination. Slowly, I felt stronger and more content. The fear began to subside.

"Can I open my eyes now?"

"Yes, but only if you keep thinking positive thoughts."

"Fine." Giving our surroundings a quick 360° assessment, the fearsome red and silver eyes were fading into the dark background.

The convertible flew through the fields and over several hills before screeching to a halt outside of Sam's cottage. Grabbing my bags, he hurriedly jumped out of the car locking the doors behind him. Nervously looking around to make sure the area was safe, he quickly unlocked my door and tossed me over his shoulder. As we reached the front step, Edwin yanked the door open and pulled us into the cottage.

"Good heavens! Are you ok?" he asked fearfully.

"I'm fine," I replied, hanging upside down from CJ's back. "You can put me down now," I commanded impatiently.

CJ's taut muscles softened against my body as his tension melted away. Calming himself, he threw my clothes onto the parlor's light oak floor and set me on my feet. Ignoring our audience's curiously frightened stares he grabbed my arms almost painfully and drew me into his face. "Angel, *are* you ok?"

I nodded slowly not knowing what he wanted me to say after we were chased and nearly caught by a supposed army of supernatural beasts.

"What happened?" Morgan cried.

"They almost got her. We were so close—too close," CJ uttered, collapsing into one of the parlor's country blue demi chairs.

"Who almost caught her?" Edwin asked softly.

I was scared to look at CJ. His composed countenance usually exuded tremendous confidence. Now, he pressed his lips together tightly and his somber expression conveyed primal fear. Morgan knelt by his feet and placed her right hand over his clasped fists.

"Sam, chamomile tea! Cynan, the lavender candles," Morgan barked. Sam and Cynan rushed from the room.

"Deep breaths, CJ," Morgan calmed, "deep breaths."

Sam returned silently handing cups of tea to us. I sat in the matching blue chair and sipped the tea quietly waiting for CJ to come out of his waking coma.

"Morgan," Sam whispered, staring sideways at me, "why isn't she reacting like CJ?"

"She's in shock. It'll come, just sit by her." Sam scooted over to me silently and sat by my feet.

"I see you bought clothes. Why didn't you wait for me?" she muttered upset. I grunted a tiny laugh in reply. Near-death experiences clearly took a back seat to shopping for Sam.

"They were everywhere," CJ started, still staring at the floor. "Everywhere..." his voice trailed off.

"Who was?" Mark asked in an unusually caring tone.

"Vampires..." CJ muttered.

Morgan gasped. Edwin teetered on his feet before grabbing his temples with his hands. Matt and Mark exchanged worried glances.

"But we made it back," I added optimistically, hoping I could pleasantly affect the dark mood hanging over us. I was starting to enjoy this positive thinking bit.

Sam glared at me, "But you almost didn't, Angel."

"What were they doing out in hordes in the middle of the afternoon?" Cynan interjected while lighting a never ending supply of candles placed strategically across the floor, on the window sills, and on the coffee table across from our chairs.

"That's certainly strange," Edwin commented. "The waning moon is moving into the phase of the new moon. This is when they're the weakest. Why would they attempt something so bold in the middle of the day?"

Unaware of the speculating going on around him CJ added, "Werewolves too."

Sam and Morgan gasped.

"Man, we miss all the action," Mark complained in typical fashion before catching Morgan's glare. "I'm just sayin,'" he corrected poorly, shrugging his shoulders.

"Why would they attack so openly, so obviously?" Edwin wondered aloud.

"There's only one reason," CJ glanced toward him. "They're stronger than we anticipated...far, far stronger..."

19 ~ Numb

Edwin drew a very deep, slow breath. His heavy gaze rested on the grounds outside of the parlor's bay window. Morgan tapped CJ's hands urging him to drink the tea.

My thoughts immersed themselves in the terror of our drive through blackness, the red and silver eyes trying to overpower us—lurching forward, jumping at us, running faster than the car. I lightly placed my tea cup beside the Tiffany lamp on the table between our chairs.

"Sam," I began quietly, "I think I'm going to have my breakdown now." My body shook violently, my eyes wide with the knowledge and delayed understanding that my life very nearly ended today.

"Sam, get the compresses," Morgan demanded.

"I'm...s...s...sorry," I tried to explain, "it j...j...just caught up to me."

CJ's face looked pained at my reaction, but he stayed in his seat shaking his head at the floor.

Worried expressions preoccupying their faces, Cynan, Matt, and Mark stood like silent statues propped against the parlor's cream colored wall.

"They caught me off guard. I can't believe I put you in such great risk," CJ apologized.

"You couldn't have known," Edwin comforted him. "They must be incredibly confident to expose themselves so carelessly."

"It doesn't make it right, Edwin," CJ continued morosely.

"You're right. It does not," Edwin suddenly snapped coldly. "But nothing good will come of castigating yourself over something that didn't happen."

CJ sighed in frustration and relaxed slightly against the back of the chair. Although he was turned toward the windows, his reflection and thoughts seemed a million miles away.

Morgan tended to my compresses. The cold, damp cloths combined with the fragrance of the lavender candles instantly soothed my nerves.

"Cynan, Matt, Mark, we have research to do," Edwin ordered the silent trifecta, which followed him upstairs.

"Angel, will you be all right in here for a minute if we make some preparations in the kitchen?" Morgan asked maternally. The tenderness of her words sounded incredibly uncharacteristic, but I enjoyed the thought of having a "mom" take care of me for the moment.

"Yeah," I replied gratefully. My shuddering was beginning to subside.

As soon as Sam and Morgan stepped out of the room, CJ jumped from his chair and knelt at my feet taking both of my hands into his.

"I owe you an apology," he began suppliantly. "I got so involved in my emotions and the moment in town today that I let my guard down."

"We were having a serious conversation. That doesn't mean you let your guard down. Isn't it better that you talked about your feelings? Maybe now you'll be able to focus on your job," I suggested.

"You don't understand. I *must* put my emotions aside completely in order to keep you safe."

"But why? Emotions, feelings—these things are a part of all of us."

"But they hinder me. I can't let them get in the way of making sure you're protected."

"So, you're supposed to be a robot?" I asked slightly irritated. He was ruining our tender bonding over our joint experiences of love lost.

"Yes, actually," he said simply. "It's just that…" his voice drifted, "…nevermind."

"What?" I asked tenderly, squeezing his hands to encourage him.

He slowly raised his head and met my gaze; his honest eyes were filled with hope. He began again slowly, forcing each word from his mouth with tremendous effort. "It's just that…well, it's just that I find it so easy to forget myself and my responsibilities around you."

"What?" I asked incredulously.

"Angel, you draw me to you with an unexplainable force. Ever since I saw you on the plane, I knew my mission would be virtually impossible if I had to spend even a minute around you. Every word you speak melts my heart. Every touch ignites a fire in my soul. Your pure passion and kindness are more than I can take. I feel myself wanting to abandon my entire task for just one kiss from your lips." He closed his eyes and rubbed his cheek against my hand.

Surely I was imagining this. I blinked thinking I might wake up. But CJ's touch was real. His words were real. His authenticity and vulnerability were real.

Blushing in a daze of ecstasy, I glanced through the front window. The chaotic turmoil battling within raged like a wildfire. I hadn't imagined his interest in me. This god somehow found me as intriguing as I did him. "Is it wrong of me to feel the same way?"

Darkness clouded his eyes. He kissed my hands tenderly, his breath and lips sending an urgent rush of volcanic heat coursing through my veins.

"Despite that, from now on I promise to keep my distance from you. I can't jeopardize your safety or your emotions because of my selfishness."

I stared at him in disbelief. The fire in my chest froze. I didn't know what to say. Was it possible to shut off such strong feelings so simply?

He continued, "I know it doesn't make sense to you, but I can't allow my guard to fail again. And I don't want you to need me the way

I need you, because my presence in your life is—regrettably—very temporary."

One-by-one, the pieces of my heart crumbled into the violent storm raging in my stomach. I jumped to my feet and ran upstairs to Sam's room. Glancing back just once, I saw CJ's head collapse into my seat. I slammed Sam's door and fell onto her plush pink bed, my body trembling with uncontainable sobs. Why couldn't her room be black? I needed surroundings that matched my mood.

A soft knock resonated on the door and a faint voice asked, "May I come in?"

"Sure," I managed to blurt amidst my heartbroken blubbering.

To my absolute surprise, Morgan walked through the door somewhat hesitantly carrying a tray that had a handle-less white tea cup in the middle surrounded by lit red, pink, blue, white, and black tea lights. She had something up her magical sleeve. Nudging the table lamp on Sam's night stand, she slid the tray onto the extra space.

"May I speak with you?" Morgan's expression was marked with serious concern.

I scooted over on Sam's pink cloud to make room for her. Picking absentmindedly at a decorative pillow's lace fringe, I glanced at Morgan. Her solemn appearance hadn't changed as she rubbed her forehead and smoothed her eyebrow with one hand.

She took a deep breath and looked at me expectantly. "Angel, I'm not very good at discussions like this, but your mum isn't here and I don't expect you'd tell her any of this anyway."

She paused, waiting for me to reply. Unfortunately, my thoughts were solely fixed on the harsh let down that CJ delivered just moments ago. My fingers felt separate from my body as I watched them flick the pillow's ruffles.

"I can't imagine the fear you endured tonight. I can't even begin to understand it. The one thing I can tell you is that you mean a lot to all of us. And, while you may not understand or maybe even care about the situation that is consuming all of our worries, you still have a choice in the upcoming...event."

"I do?" That was news to me; I thought I was being guilted into it. Wasn't the whole of humanity depending on me?

"You can either choose to accept what is happening and learn from the experience as it opens your eyes and life in ways you never knew possible. Or..."

I knew there was an "Or" hiding in the speech.

"Or, you can choose to reject everything that's happening, hope you survive the turmoil, and go back to living your life as if all of this was just a bad dream."

"Clearly, there's no choice for me," I barked sarcastically. The CJ topic was eating away all of my patience.

"Clearly there is," she contradicted. "Why do you feel that you don't have a choice?"

"Because if I choose to ignore this situation, all of you will suffer, my family will suffer, and somehow mankind will suffer."

She smiled an irritatingly omniscient smile. I played right into her trap. She was good.

"It's still a viable choice. You don't have to do anything you don't want to do. Your conscience and heart are driving your decision, aren't they?" she asked somewhat rhetorically.

I nodded still annoyed she had manipulated me so easily.

"Then your choice is already made. You're just reluctant and angry that it's not the easier of the two options." She paused to think about our conversation so far. Contemplatively, she began again. "Is it your choice in the matter or fear which bothers you the most?"

"Put yourself in my shoes. Wouldn't you be terrified too?"

She smirked and nodded. "Courage isn't learned or found. It lies within. Whether you believe it or not, you were born with it. You can do this."

Her eyes softened and my body relaxed, releasing the tension which gripped my muscles during her lecture.

"Angel, I hate clichés..."

Join the club...

"But, what doesn't kill you makes you stronger, no?"

"Except in my case it may actually kill me." I caught her off guard. *Yes!* Morgan intimidated me with her extensive knowledge of everything. I needed this childish victory.

She smiled at me maternally. "It depends on your perspective."

I furrowed my eyebrows unsure of what that meant, but before I could ask, she continued.

"Secondly, there's CJ."

Oh no! I did not want to open Pandora's Box with my friends' mother. I looked at her worried about where this conversation was heading. 'He's too old for you. You're too young. You live in another country.' The list of potential issues raced through my thoughts.

"Angel, CJ is...unique, shall we say?"

Yes, he's a god and I'm a lowly, pathetic human.

"He cares for you in a way you can't possibly know."

Before I could interject she held up her palm and cut me off. "It's very complicated. Under any other circumstances, you could be together, but your safety depends on him right now. I know it seems very cold of me to say this. It's clear you are both very fond of each other, but please respect his wishes."

I was stunned. It was bad enough being dumped before we even started dating. It was worse being forbidden from him. The rebel in me wanted to run downstairs, throw myself onto him, and tell everyone else to go to hell.

"You have every right to be angry with me," Morgan added gently patting my knee. "But I do care about you, Angel. I would give Sam or Cynan the same advice."

Morgan walked over to the tray, picked up the small white cup, and handed it to me. I looked in it and glanced at her hesitantly.

She understood my cautiousness immediately. "It will help you heal."

"Heal? Is that all? Not forget everything and live like a zombie for the next few weeks?"

Morgan laughed. She was a beautiful woman when her face didn't wear her cares. Her curly, strawberry blonde hair bounced with her laugh which smoothed out the lines on her face. She must have been gorgeous when she was younger, back when her fears didn't include a stranger who had the potential to ruin her life and family.

Despite Morgan's aggressive strength, her kindness and concern tempered my one-sided view of her. Her presence felt warm and positive. She was not only a tough woman, but someone who truly, purely wanted to do good.

"I wouldn't hurt you," she assured, chuckling. "This will help you feel less like a bus just hit you."

"What's in it?"

"Warm apple juice with a dash of vanilla, ginger, cinnamon and a few strawberries for good measure."

I looked at her carefully. She didn't appear to be lying and the stuff certainly smelled like hot apple cider. The strawberries sat at the bottom of the white cup. What did I have to lose at this point?

I closed my eyes breathing in its sweet aroma and drank the potion.

Morgan's eyes flashed with happiness. "You know, Angel, I'm rather proud of you. Most non-Wiccans aren't as accepting of our practices as you have been."

"Once I got beyond the odd notion you were all trying to kill me, I felt pretty comfortable around you," I admitted honestly.

She laughed. "Are you ready to come downstairs?"

"In a few minutes. Thanks...for everything, Morgan," I added politely.

She smiled, carefully lifted the white tray and exited the room, nodding to me with a tight smile on the way out.

I swirled the concoction in my hand wondering what it was going to do to me. I already felt warm and fuzzy inside so it obviously had an effect. I swallowed the rest in one gulp and then picked out a strawberry and sucked on it mindlessly.

Then POP! CJ was back in my mind. His kindness, deified perfection, and thoughtfulness tightened a vise around my bleeding heart.

I laid down on the pink nightmare beneath me and stared at the white ceiling. I was going to have to make an appearance downstairs eventually. How was I going to act around CJ? Clearly, any and all flirting had to end.

CJ was so sweet, and I didn't want to hurt him. However, I couldn't ignore the sparks which flew between us. What was the biblical passage about casting off the hand that gives you a problem?

I'd have to pretend he didn't exist. It was the only way I could separate myself from him. Anguish boiled inside of my chest. I rolled onto my side hugging Sam's pillow wishing I was five again—a time in my life when my family was still intact, I had no responsibilities, and everything was normal.

20 ~ The Lessons Begin

The next morning I tried to block out every CJ-related thought by concentrating on song lyrics. That cheered me up a little bit. Humming, I dressed in the pair of jeans CJ got for me as well as a fitted black tank top which had an angel's halo and wings bejeweled on the front of it. I tried my best to forget that all of my clothes were from him. I knew it was a bad idea to let him buy them.

Pulling my wet hair into a ponytail, I noticed the bruise on my left temple was turning a unique shade of blue, purple, and green. *Whatever*, there was no need to impress anyone anyway.

Tiptoeing down the stairs I held my breath as I walked into the kitchen. Mark, Matt, and Cynan were scarfing their breakfasts in typical fashion. Edwin was drying the dishes that Morgan handed to him over the sink. Sam leaned against the kitchen counter staring into the living room watching TV. Thankfully, CJ was nowhere to be found.

"Good morning," I said sheepishly, afraid of what they thought about my disappearance last night.

A chorus of "heys" and "mornins" hung in the air without so much as a glance in my direction.

Sam pointed over her shoulder to a cup of tea behind her. "I made that for you in case you're thirsty. Oh, and Cynan and I convinced Edwin and Morgan that you have to learn some sort of self-defense. We'd like to work on lessons with you."

"Thanks," I said curiously. Everyone avoided my gaze. Did they blame me for CJ's reaction last night?

"Uh…speaking of drinks…Morgan, what did you put into that juice last night?"

"Why?"

"Because it knocked me out cold."

"That's an unusual reaction to have to something so simple. I think your body just needed rest."

I supposed she was right. Other than the hole that gouged itself through the center of my heart, I felt refreshed. I plopped myself down in the oak chair beside Matt. He adjusted himself to make more room for me between the three brawny men.

"I can't take this crap anymore," Mark roared, jumping from his seat.

Five pairs of mortified eyes stared at him along with my confused set.

"We should've talked to her last night. She's obviously in denial," he ranted at his dumbstruck audience. "Look at her, she's clearly not normal." Peering mischievously through the corner of his eyes at me, he added, "but we knew that already."

Mark's expression abruptly turned serious again. "Angel, do you have any idea what happened last night? Don't you have any reaction to it? What's wrong with you?" he pleaded.

Edwin glared at him, anger flickering behind his grey eyes. "Mark!" he bellowed.

Mark flashed an alarmingly violent glower at Edwin. Reluctant and fuming, Mark dropped into his seat against the living room partition. Staring at me expectantly, everyone waited for my reaction.

"So CJ and I got into an argument. Can't I have some time to myself?" My anger at their intrusion flushed my face.

Mark scoffed, rolling his eyes. The rest of them gaped at me bewildered.

Leaning into me, Matt whispered in my ear, "We're not talking about CJ."

"Then what?" CJ was the only topic from yesterday I cared about.

Edwin turned quizzically toward Morgan, who stopped washing dishes to join the attack on me. "What did you give her?"

"It was supposed to dull the pain, Edwin, and help her move on."

"Clearly she's moved on from the wrong issue," he raised his voice.

"My intent is one thing. The outcome depends on her mind and body. You know that." Her scathing tone sounded nothing like the maternal reassurance from last night.

"Why? What should I be consumed with right now?" I demanded.

"Uh, the fact that a very large group of vampires and werewolves nearly devoured you," Mark suggested caustically.

The vague memory slithered into my consciousness. "Oh, that..."

"Yeah, *that*, Angel!" Mark's exasperation bit through my thoughts.

My eyes dropped to the floor attempting to comprehend how the horrifying experience escaped my thoughts. Every time I imagined the red and silver eyes jumping at the car, my mind immediately drifted to CJ's determination to save us, to save me.

"I don't know. It's just not as important."

"Not important?" Mark exclaimed aghast at my indifference.

Matt turned to Mark so abruptly it startled all of us. "Get out!" he yelled. "Can't you see you're making this worse? Just get the hell out of here and come back when you've calmed down!"

For the second time this morning, several pairs of eyes stared in disbelief at the unfamiliar situation unfolding in the quaint kitchen. Mark jumped from his seat and shoved the table away as he stormed through the front door.

"Angel, what are you thinking?" Morgan asked carefully.

"I don't know. I'm worried about CJ. I really don't care about the whole vampire-werewolf thing."

"But why don't you care about them? The chase must have been incredibly traumatic."

With all of my might I tried to focus on the hungry eyes hunting me. CJ's face kept interrupting the memory.

"It's CJ," I muttered.

"What do you mean?" Edwin asked.

"I felt completely safe with him. I knew he wouldn't let anything happen to me."

Morgan and Edwin exchanged pained glances. Rubbing her forehead and shaking her head, Morgan returned to her dishes. Edwin mumbled, "Well, that complicates matters."

"How?" I asked naïvely.

"We—us and CJ—agreed last night it was best for him to stay away from you as much as possible," Cynan clarified.

My eyes welled up. No more alone time with CJ. No more of his magnetic energy that lured me inexplicably. Matt put his arm around my shoulders in a failed attempt to comfort me. The dampness clouding my vision soon spilled over their dam. I took a deep breath and haphazardly wiped away the tears. I needed to toughen up, close this chapter. CJ obviously wasn't meant to be a part of my life the way I wanted him to be. So what if he was my first breath of fresh air since Zach?

Decidedly, I focused on Sam. I needed a distraction. "When can we start the lessons?"

Her suspicious glance worried about my sudden change of topic. "Now, if you're ready."

"Let's go."

"Wait," Edwin cautioned. "You may no longer go anywhere unprotected. At least two people must be with you at all times, Angel. Matt, please go with them."

Matt shoved the last piece of bacon into his mouth, hopped from his seat, and swung the kitchen door open, allowing us to pass through.

"Until Morgan and Edwin finish protecting the forest, we have to stay within the yard," Sam explained on our way to the picnic table in the backyard's lush grass.

The table was covered with a red gingham cloth and had an array of materials on it including candles, herbs, and ribbons. The thing that caught my attention was the large black leather book with the silver inscription that read, *Book of Shadows*. The foreboding volume had a large silver and black leather buckle that secured its side.

"What's that, Sam?" I asked hesitantly.

"Wiccan lessons—and more," she added slyly. "Everything I've learned so far is documented in it. I'm going to use it to teach you. Ok, first thing's first," she pulled me onto the bench beside her while Matt pretended to play an invisible game of catch a few feet from us. "Close your eyes," she commanded. "What do you feel?"

I slouched in my seat and tilted my head toward the sky. "You staring at me and it's making me uncomfortable."

"If this is going to work, you have to be serious," she reprimanded harshly. "Relax and feel."

I took a deep breath and committed myself to Sam's strict lesson. Sighing deeply, my senses slowly opened up to my surroundings even though I couldn't see them. "I feel a light breeze and the sun's rays are escaping through the tree tops. It's warming my skin."

The sun's rays did more than just warm me. They healed me, energized me. The anxious worry over my feelings for CJ melted away.

"I feel...good."

"Would you say that you're content, happy even?"

I thought about her suggestion. My heart still ached for CJ, but it felt miles away from the torment which ripped me apart last night. "Content."

"Ok. Now open your eyes and remember the chase from last night. What did you see?"

Staring intently at the grass, I considered her question. The answer was easy. Who could forget the excitement of the hunt so apparent in them? "Their eyes."

"What did you feel?"

"Fear."

"Fear of what?"

"Fear of getting caught, killed, eaten," my voice escalated with each word in heavy sarcasm.

"Can you feel some of that fear now or at least remember it?"

I closed my eyes again and imagined the terror mounting in me as the eyes charged toward us. My hands felt clammy and I broke out in a sweat.

"Now imagine the sunlight shining through the darkest part of that memory or feeling."

Opening my eyes I pursed my lips together in exasperation. "Sam, how am I supposed to interrupt such a disgusting memory with happy thoughts of sunshine? C'mon."

"Close your eyes and try please. The point here is to fight fate with positive resistance."

"English, please?"

"Positive thinking, Angel."

"How exactly?"

"Haven't you ever heard of cancer patients who go through chemo and all kinds of treatments or any patient for that matter who has a positive outlook on life? They tend to recuperate faster or at least feel better than patients who are stuck in a doom-and-gloom mentality. You can change things by thinking differently about them."

I sat up straight and looked closely at Sam's intense expression. She whole-heartedly believed this.

"Do you think I could've done this already without knowing it?" I wondered aloud.

Her eyes creased, "What do you mean?"

"Last night I kept thinking we were going to get caught by those… things." I shuddered. I couldn't bring myself to call them by name. "CJ asked me to think positively, so I envisioned us arriving here safely. When I opened my eyes, they were far away."

"It's possible you were able to affect the outcome."

"But they were everywhere—fifty maybe even a hundred of them and they kept pace with the car. Some of them even outran us and tried to cut us off."

Her eyes opened wide. "Yeah, I think you have a good grasp of lesson one then, but you should still practice. You never know how you'll react when you're in a panic." She took a deep breath and continued,

"Close your eyes again, imagine the vampires and werewolves chasing you, and remember your feelings. Focus on the worst thing that you see or feel and then in the middle of the darkness imagine light breaking through it. Force the light to get bigger and bigger until it shines over all of your feelings and the things you see. The trick is not just to see the light, but to believe in it so completely that you can feel it."

"Got it," I said impatiently. Last night proved I could do this. "I'll definitely keep practicing that. What's next?"

She grabbed my hands and made me stand. "Rub your hands together vigorously for a few seconds and then pull them apart about five centimeters. What do you feel?"

Not thinking I was capable of anything, I rubbed my hands together and pulled them apart slightly. It started slowly—a curious sensation—and began to spread. "Something warm is pulsating through my palms and fingers. It tingles."

"Good, now pull your hands apart a little further concentrating on that feeling and then push your hands closer together, but don't let them touch."

The feeling weakened and strengthened with the push-pull force of the imaginary binds between my hands.

"Do you feel it?"

I nodded, excited. "What is that?"

"Your energy," she smiled.

"My energy?"

"Yes." Noticing my confusion, she tapped her fingers against her forehead trying to figure out how to explain it to me. "I've got it. Have you ever seen Star Wars?"

"Yeah," I replied apprehensively. This was going to be interesting.

"Luke uses the 'force' to fight. Your energy is kind of like the 'force.' You need to tap into earth's collective unconscious, believe in it, and then you can use it to do things. Your energy is like a sixth sense and with practice you can use it to defend yourself or to attack. It helps you see, not with your eyes but with every part of your being."

"Sam, that's the weirdest thing I ever heard."

She rolled her eyes. "Just think about it ok? It'll make more sense as you keep practicing. Your energy can affect your surroundings. Remember the wolf in the tunnel?"

How could I forget? It nearly killed us. I nodded.

"Well, I used my energy combined with an awful lot of will. The main thing is to use your energy while thinking positively to keep you safe."

"So you're not going to teach me any spells or give me a magic wand or something? You're telling me that my best defense is in my head?"

She nodded with an ear-to-ear grin.

"Have you heard any of the conversations surrounding me lately? I'm evidently only playing with a half a deck up here." I tapped my right temple for added effect.

"Still that's your best defense and offense. A gun, a wand, these things don't work unless the brain tells them what to do. Every person and being on earth has energy. Most people just don't know they have it. Once you realize what you have and how powerful it can be, you'll see that you can naturally change almost anything."

"It still sounds like hocus-pocus."

"If I'm teaching you hocus-pocus, what do you call the other side's power?"

"Voodoo?" I offered with a smile.

She scoffed and shook her head in exasperation. "Ok, next lesson."

Grabbing my hand she pulled me into the middle of the backyard where the sun more easily shone through the trees illuminating the lush, soft green carpet beneath our feet.

"This lesson is a combination of two things: feelings and energy of other living things."

She kicked off her sandals and I followed suit throwing my flip flops at Matt. Someone needed to bring him back to reality during the bottom of the ninth.

Sam stood beside me. "Lie down, close your eyes, and turn your head to the sun."

"Lie in the grass? With the bugs?"

She arched her left eyebrow at me indignantly.

The grass poked through my clothes and tickled my neck, but its fragrance was heavenly. I always liked the smell of freshly mowed grass.

Once the tickling subsided, my body melted into our natural surroundings. Submitting to the welcoming arms of Mother Nature freed me from the worries plaguing my thoughts. With each breath of fresh air my own needs and desires seemed to fall into perspective.

"What do you feel?"

"Contentment." I didn't want to move. The soft grass bed was the perfect spot for staring at the clouds.

"What are you thinking?"

"The sun's warmth is like a medicine I didn't know I needed. It feels so good on my skin." Regret and sorrow filled my mind. I'd been wallowing in my situation so much lately that I missed life's pure and simple pleasures.

"Excellent. Make a memory of that feeling."

"How exactly?"

"Remember everything you're feeling right now—warmth, peace, and smell. Memorizing every element of this moment will make it stronger. When you need this memory later, it will easily resurface in your mind. The stronger the memory, the stronger your energy will be."

"Ok," I replied skeptically, inhaling deeply. The fragrance of damp leaves, underbrush, and dirt flooded my senses—not quite the pleasant aroma I had hoped to capture in a lasting memory. I took another deep breath, this time concentrating on the sweeter, faint smells that drifted on the breeze. Roses, lavender, rosemary, mint. I made a mental note to remember these scents along with the sunlight which enveloped me like a warm, fleece blanket.

"Ready?"

I nodded.

"Stare at the trees and focus on their perimeter. Do you see anything?"

"The trees, the sky. What am I supposed to see?"

"Every living thing has an aura, which is like a light that radiates from its energy. With practice you'll be able to see different colors."

"When you look at a person, how do you know what to look for?"

"Well, for me, I can see the aura around a person's head and shoulders most easily."

"What does it look like?" I was fascinated about seeing people in a whole new light—pun intended.

"Look at the trees again. The aura looks like a see-through light radiating just above the tree line. A person's aura reflects his life, health, and beliefs. For example, someone who is angry or passionate will have a lot of red in his aura. Someone who is wise and optimistic will have a yellow aura while those who are spiritually awakened have a gold aura much like the pictures of saints. White means purity; green is sensitivity or jealousy; purple is humility or spirituality; blue means calm."

"You know I'm never going to remember all that."

"It's all in my Book of Shadows. Besides I'm giving you a very basic explanation. You need to practice," she said sternly and then turned toward Matt.

"Matt, come here, please. I need you to model for us," Sam commanded.

"What?" Poor Matt's freckles disappeared beneath an embarrassed flush.

"Don't be self-conscious," Sam assured him. "We just want to stare at you for a little bit," she teased.

"That's not helping, Sam," he said shyly.

"Oh, come on, just stand by our feet."

Exhaling in defeat he stared at the cottage avoiding our gaze.

"Angel, do you see any colors around Matt?"

"Just the white. Should there be other colors?"

"Hmmm, I see gold, white, pink, and a little red, but I think that's because I pissed him off." Turning toward Matt, she quipped, "Pink? Really?"

Agitated, he clenched his fists until his knuckles looked like they'd pop through his skin. He burst angrily, "Are you finished?"

"Yeah," she whispered, her eyes wide in shock at his reaction.

Matt stormed off and leaned against one of the large oak trees, his back facing us. He was usually the most level-headed of all of us, but he was complicated; more complicated than I originally thought. I wasn't used to his assertiveness since I simply assumed he was the quiet one while Mark was the more outspoken one of the two.

I wanted to let him know he could confide in me, but I was afraid to bother him since he evidently wanted to be alone.

I turned to ask Sam about our next lesson, but she was already strolling across the lawn to Matt. She touched his back gently and peered around his arm staring at his face with the intoxicating innocence of her pale blue eyes.

He hung his head low and shook it in response to whatever she asked. They stared at each other for a moment and then unexpectedly burst into laughter.

Feeling like a third wheel, I crossed the lawn and entered the kitchen.

In the middle of the room in all his glorious, statuesque godliness, stood CJ.

21 ~ Confrontation

Giving into the temptation to run away, I reached for the doorknob. But remembering I wasn't five years old, I managed to find some courage rooted deep in the cobwebbed recesses of my mind.

"Hi," I said softly, distracting myself by opening the refrigerator. I really didn't want anything to drink or eat, but I needed to occupy myself. My only alternative was to stare at him and that had gotten me into enough trouble already.

He stood in silence behind me. The electricity from his eyes rushed wildly up and down my spine.

How long did I have to keep up this charade of sifting through the fridge before he'd talk to me? About ten seconds elapsed, but it seemed like hours.

Slamming the door, I spun around to face him. My cold guard melted at the sight of his troubled face. I closed my eyes so I could spill my thoughts before he could spellbind me again.

"Fine, don't say anything. Whatever," I said flippantly and rushed through the backdoor.

Storming through the backyard, I couldn't find Matt and Sam. Edwin's caution echoed in my ears. I needed two people with me. I wasn't going to stray from the house though. I just didn't want to be in it with CJ, and I wasn't about to go exploring in order to find Matt and Sam.

I decided this would be a great time to investigate Morgan's gardens just beyond the front yard. She had every herb imaginable in beds that extended about twenty feet. Taking a cue from Sam's lessons, I sat carefully in the middle of the gardens and breathed deeply trying to relax.

Sam's teachings surfaced above the painful thoughts and I tried to think positively. Unfortunately, the positives all involved making CJ mine somehow and not quite about me protecting myself from the emotional stress.

Silent tears brimmed over my eyelashes. I leaned over my knees holding my face in my hands as if that might prevent the tears from escaping. It only made it worse. At least I didn't wail like yesterday. I gave into my sadness figuring it would be better to get it out of my system and then maybe, hopefully move on from the pain.

A strong pair of hands embraced my arms from behind.

"Stop," I cried. I climbed out of the garden and ran back to the house rubbing my eyes.

He flew in front of me blocking my way.

"Leave...me...alone," I sobbed each syllable, sidestepping him.

He blocked me again.

"Get out of my way!" I shouted furiously. I couldn't see him anymore through the flood.

"Angel, please listen," he begged quietly.

"Why? What's left to say?" I wanted to wrap my arms around him and forget the world, but I couldn't give in. I needed to protect myself from the pain. The more distance we had between us, the easier it would be to forget him.

"Let's go for a walk."

"No."

"Very well then, have it your way. Morgan and Edwin will be home in a few minutes and then Morgan will give you another concoction to drink."

I glowered at him spitefully. "Speak," I ordered acerbically.

"Everything I said last night was true," he spoke to my back as I continued to walk quickly so I wouldn't have to look at him. "Please try to understand. I can't allow you to think there will ever be anything more to our relationship."

I quickened my pace. Why did I have to relive the torture from last night? An invisible dagger twisted through my heart. "This is supposed to make me feel better?" I shrieked. Rivers streamed down my face.

"In a few weeks, I'll have to leave and you'll never see me again. It's not fair to you to feel an unrealistic hope in thinking that will change and…Please stop running!" he grabbed my arms and spun me around to face him.

His sorrowful eyes spoke the truth. He didn't want this any more than I did.

"Don't you think the decision should be mine to make about how to cope when you leave?" I asked bitingly. "I didn't ask for any of this. I didn't want to be thrown to the wolves, so to speak, and have to fight for my life as well as the world's!"

"Your pain will be far more excruciating if I get close to you now and then leave," he suggested rationally.

I looked away as a tear escaped my eye, "I'd rather have three weeks with you than none at all."

Yanking my hands from his firm grasp, I skulked toward Morgan's endless rows of rose bushes. The picture-perfect flowers mocked me ironically. Their beautiful petals and heavenly scent were invitingly enticing while the sharp thorns guaranteed pain if someone dared touch their beauty.

CJ followed behind me silently. I didn't know what to say. A cosmic force bound us together. I could feel it. But how could a reasonable being explain that to someone she only just met without sounding insane?

A few paces behind me, CJ started again softly. "Angel, you don't know half of what I know and I know your future. It doesn't look good if you get too attached to me now."

"Don't I get a say in this?"

"You can say whatever you want and I promise to listen, but I can't promise to do what you ask."

The words blurted from my lips before I could think of a more tactful approach. "Don't you feel it, CJ? Am I really just that hormonal or nuts? Don't you feel our connection? It's like I'm shocked by a taser every time you touch me. The electricity flowing between us could light an entire town!

"Now I don't know about you, but that doesn't happen with anyone else I touch. It's only ever happened with one other person in my life and even then it was only a hundredth of the power you generate."

I stared into the sad, turbulent seas of his eyes. They managed to calm me slightly, at least enough to stop my screeching tirade.

"Don't you feel it, CJ? Can't you feel it?" I whispered sadly, staring at the grass.

He grasped my face between his hands and pulled me just inches from his eyes.

"My body, my mind, my soul aches every minute that I'm away from you, Angel. I don't want this space between us any more than you do."

The energy from his hands radiated through my body. His sweet breath and heavenly fragrance hypnotized my every thought.

"My very existence is meaningless without you. Your life is what matters to me most and I will—I must—protect you at all costs, even if I need to deny what I want most."

"CJ, I don't want you to sacrifice anything because of me."

"It's not a sacrifice, Angel. It's my duty."

"Yesterday, it felt like my world ended at the mere thought of your not being in it. Surviving the vampires and werewolves was a piece of cake compared to you."

"That's just it. Don't you see?"

I shook my head. Apparently I was too dense and irrational to understand any of this.

"Having to survive the vampires and werewolves should never have happened in the first place. Being so near to you, so vulnerable with you, I completely forgot my purpose, my duty to protect you. I should've seen them coming, not two seconds before they attacked, but miles away. I put your life in danger and that's unforgivable because it risks the battle's outcome, not to mention your safety."

His rationale slowly seeped into my cognizance. I hated it, but it made sense. He was only doing this because he cared about me.

"Why does it have to be like this?" I croaked, quelling a sob stuck in my throat.

"There's no other way." Bleak sadness tinged his words.

I held my head hoping to stop the spinning whirlwind of dizzying thoughts. From the corner of my eye, I saw CJ reach his hand out to comfort me. Thinking better of it, he resisted and dropped his hands to his sides.

I yearned for his hesitant touch, knowing it would be detrimental to both of us. Still, I wanted to feel him and I didn't want to deny the obvious attraction tethering us together.

"There's only one way I can get over you," I paused and looked at him. His patient eyes waited hopefully for my *brilliant* suggestion. "I'm going to be mean to you. I don't want to do it, but it's the only way I'll be able to rid my mind of you."

He laughed. His entire body rocked with laughter. An over-whelming urge to punch him overcame me. I spun around and stalked away. It was for his own good. I'm sure he didn't want his perfect, god-like nose broken.

He caught up to me easily and grabbed my left hand. I yanked it firmly from his grasp.

"Sorry, Angel. It's just that I thought it was going to be something much worse. You giving me the silent treatment—that I can deal with."

"What did you think I was going to say?"

"Uh-uh, I'm not giving you any ideas." His mood became serious again. "You know how I feel about you. And if we weren't bound by the world around us, I'd willingly give myself to you. I'll survive whatever you do to me now as long as I can keep you safe."

22 ~ Hurray for Hollywood

Morgan and Edwin were preparing an afternoon tea when we walked through the kitchen door. I didn't miss their exchanged glances over the fact that CJ and I were together.

Mark and Cynan lounged on the sofa in the living room, drinking beer and watching soccer. For some reason the sight shocked me. I thought only American guys liked to drink, belch, and watch sports while damning the referee to hell. I guess all guys are pretty much the same no matter where they live.

Matt burst through the back door with Sam punching and scratching his brawny back.

"Take it back, Matthew. Now!" she screamed as she beat his back with her tiny fists.

"Nope," he laughed heartily, enjoying her furious reaction.

Moving so quickly that he looked like a blur, in one fell swoop he grabbed her wrists, scooped her up, and tossed her into the white chair beneath the window.

"Aaaaah!" Sam screamed like a frustrated wildcat and leapt to her feet ready to attack.

"Samantha!" Morgan shouted, "mind your manners."

Out of Morgan's line of sight Matt smirked and winked at her. Mark and Cynan sat motionless on the couch not having moved a millimeter during this interesting exchange.

Sam huffed angrily and crossed her arms on her chest. Matt smiled and walked into the parlor apparently giving her enough space to cool off.

Squinting her eyes in Matt's direction, her jaw set determinedly, Sam didn't even glance at me as I approached.

"Uh, Sam, do you want to talk about it?" I asked timidly.

"He said he couldn't figure out whether I was a wicked witch or just a moody bitch!" she said through clenched teeth which clearly ached to bite Matt.

Cynan roared with laughter. "You have to admit he has a point." Eavesdropping, Matt's booming laughter echoed through the house.

Like the strike of an eagle, Sam flew from her chair, talons outstretched. She clawed Cynan without pause. Surprised by her ferocity, he couldn't fight back.

Mark scooted down on the couch to avoid spilling his beer.

"Samantha!" Edwin and Morgan shouted. "What has gotten into you?"

"Nothing," she muttered scathingly, dashing from the room and punching Matt in the gut as she flew past him on her way upstairs.

"So we were discussing plans for tonight." Morgan changed the subject ignoring Sam's tantrum.

"Last night CJ mentioned you wanted to go to Rick's movie set, Angel," Edwin said simply.

My glower could've killed CJ. I actually willed it for a second. He knew I didn't want to be near Rick. Was this a ploy to get me to hate him so he could push me away easily?

"I thought I should practice the lessons Sam taught me today," I argued.

"Nonsense, Angel. How often do you get invitations from a celebrity? We've already ruined your holiday. You might as well have *some* fun," Morgan added lightly.

"Have you forgotten yesterday's chase?" I demanded, frightened they actually failed to remember this miniscule, yet important detail.

"You won't be alone. Everyone is going with you," CJ added simply, ignoring my caustic glare.

"Everyone? I thought you were supposed to keep your distance from me," I quipped sarcastically.

"Almost everyone. I won't be anywhere near you."

"If I go without you, doesn't that defeat the purpose of your job to protect me?"

"I'll be there, you just won't know it. We wouldn't mind surprising the other side. It would be easier to defeat them now than waiting until they gain more strength. Besides Rick likes it better when I'm not around."

My fingers twitched with rage. I wanted to slap the smirk off of CJ's face. Maybe getting over him was going to be easier than I expected. I just needed to focus on his irritating qualities. Unfortunately, he had none. They were only a reflection of my wanting to be mad at him.

"But I really, really don't want to go," I complained, wishing someone would agree with me. Mark and Matt looked hopeful; they wanted nothing more than to stay as far away as possible from Rick.

"Angel, we're going," Morgan insisted. "We'll meet in the parlor in two hours."

I reluctantly followed the men upstairs and sauntered into Sam's room. With ears like a bat, Sam must've heard what was happening because she had about ten outfits placed strategically on her bed, hanging from her headboard, draped over her desk chair, and swinging from the curtain rods. The thought of seeing Rick again apparently helped her get over her fight with Matt.

Ignoring my gaping expression, she dressed in a black mini skirt with a tight, ruffled red satin sleeveless top that was more appropriate for someone who was thirty than eighteen.

Distracted by her transformation, I vaguely remembered needing a jacket. "Uh, Sam, may I borrow a coat or something?"

She eyed my outfit distastefully. "You're not going like that are you?"

"I honestly don't care about impressing Rick and I sure as hell won't change for him. Besides I'm comfortable."

"Fine," she mumbled testily. Searching through her closet, she pulled out a tight-fitting, quilted black jacket with silver zippers and tossed it at me. "At least that will match your top."

"Thanks," I muttered. "I'll meet you downstairs."

"Wait, aren't you going to brush your hair or put on makeup?"

"Sam, I don't even want to go."

"Stay here," she commanded, shoving me onto her bed.

Sam rushed to the bathroom and rummaged loudly through the drawers. Anxiety tied my stomach in knots at the thought of the makeover she was about to unleash on me.

"Absolutely not, Samantha!" Edwin bellowed from the hallway.

"But..."

"No. Change immediately!" It sounded like Edwin was going to have a heart attack; he could barely spit out the words.

Sam stormed back into her room and slammed the door.

"Sit still," she directed irritably. Remembering her violent outburst with Matt, I was afraid to do anything contrary to her orders. Part of me hoped this was just a bad episode of PMS. If her behavior was tied to the lunar cycle, I was acutely afraid of how she might transform as we approached the full moon.

Freeing my hair from its ponytail, Sam assaulted it violently with a brush. She primped it, parted it, adjusted it, and sprayed it.

"Good," she said pleased with her work.

Next she attacked my face with tweezers, brushes, and foreign colored powders and pencils. Adding a dash of mascara and lip gloss, she stepped back to examine her living palate.

"That'll do, I suppose," she sighed in disappointment before turning to her closet to search for a new outfit.

I avoided looking in the mirror on the back of her door, afraid that I'd see a beauty queen or clown—both equally scary.

She finally settled on a mid-thigh length black skirt and a flowing pale blue satin, capped sleeve, jacquard top. Grabbing a black jacket and my hands, she dragged me from the room.

Sam skipped lightly down the stairs. Edwin scowled at the compromise on the outfit. Matt blushed as he watched Sam float to the front door. Considering this an interesting development, I wondered how much I missed over the past few days being selfishly consumed in my own problems.

I followed awkwardly after Sam fully aware of my gracelessness compared to her pretty femininity. I felt like a servant following a princess. A wave of heat rushed through my chest when I caught CJ glancing at me. His cheeks flushed pink and he looked away embarrassed. My heart ripped a little bit further at the thought of our situation. It took every ounce of my weak self-control not to look at him again.

Suddenly, CJ vanished. My mind raced again trying to decipher what he was, but there wasn't time to dwell on it. Edwin ushered us into the cars.

Once we were on our way, fear gripped my thoughts.

"Edwin, why do you think we'll be safe? There were so many of them yesterday. They can easily overpower the eight of us."

"The council will be there along with reinforcements."

"Reinforcements?"

"You needn't worry. As CJ said, you won't see him or the others, but they'll closely guard all of us."

"Why are we going out there in the first place?"

"We aren't going to let them intimidate us into hiding until the battle. We can defeat them easily if they decide to engage us now. It's a strategic tactic for us to show them we're confident and prepared."

"Are we prepared?" I asked fearfully. *I* sure didn't feel prepared.

"Yes. I'm certain they won't attack tonight though because we'll outnumber them."

"How can we outnumber fifty to a hundred blood thirsty demons and their overgrown pets?"

"Our numbers will rank around five hundred. We'll be completely safe."

The thought of having five hundred protectors easily calmed me until another fear replaced it.

"Is there any way to identify a vampire or werewolf aside from its red or silver eyes?"

"Sometimes not even that," Edwin replied matter-of-factly.

"What?" I squealed. I was counting on that obvious indicator.

"Well, their eye color usually only changes when they're getting ready to fight."

"Remember our lesson about auras?" Sam prodded gently.

I nodded.

"Auras are indicators too. Vampires and werewolves usually have a lot of red in their auras because they're ruled by their passions. Vampires also have black holes in theirs. They've destroyed their lives and are technically dead so their auras are no longer whole. Werewolves' auras have a lot of grey. The grey represents secrets, which in the case of werewolves is their ability to change from human to wolf," Sam said with a sneer.

"Well if you can see their auras, won't it be easy to figure out who's who?"

"Not necessarily. They can conceal their identities," Morgan added.

"How?"

"They lie."

My face must have looked extremely puzzled because she immediately continued her explanation.

"It's mind over matter. If they can convince themselves to believe they're something else—namely a normal human—then their auras will reflect the type of person they imagine themselves to be."

I closed my mouth realizing it was still gaping from dumbstruck shock.

"Regardless, we'll all be with you tonight. They'll feel our combined energy in the air. I'm sure they'll keep their distance."

"But if they were willing to attack yesterday, will these precautions make a difference?"

"Yesterday you were alone with CJ. Today you have a small army. They won't attack, not when they're at their weakest."

My instincts were yelling a warning that something was going to happen tonight. Unfortunately, I couldn't see the future, so I blindly relied on my feelings, which were currently churning in my gut.

The forest sped by as we drove along the winding macadam. The black leaves of the trees and bushes rustled in the evening breeze. Purple twilight cast dark shadows against the foreground, illuminated dimly by the setting sun. Picturing the red and silver eyes from last night, I easily imagined them here watching, waiting.

If they caught me, what were they going to do with me? Or worse, what were they going to do *to* me? Edwin mentioned they needed me. Why? What could I possibly offer them that they didn't already have? I was no one of significance. Bridging the gap between childhood and adulthood was bad enough, why did I need to add an element of paranormal craziness to it? Wasn't my life complicated enough already? Love, loss, death—these were relatively normal human events which all of us experienced. I hadn't figured out how to cope with any of that yet and now I had to deal with this freaky crap.

Vampires. Werewolves. They were the stuff of my childhood nightmares, surreal figments of my imagination. They were supposed to be pretend. Evidently the stories came from somewhere. I just always thought there was a natural explanation like human werewolf syndrome, when bodies are completely covered in hair, or vampire disease—the sufferers of which are oversensitive to sunlight.

Never in a million years did I think I would become part of my nightmares. What other supernatural beasts wandered the earth? I shuddered at the possibilities. Vampires and werewolves were bad enough; I didn't want to imagine the other creatures too.

About a hundred of Rick's adoring dolls lined up at the bottom of the cemetery's hill behind a row of very large, very intimidating security guards. We walked between the girls and the wrought iron fence that kept the cemetery separate from the backs of the aged village buildings. The graveyard reached from the side street we parked on to the back of the chapel, which was about four blocks away. It didn't look like the whole knoll was used as a memorial. Sporadic benches lined a winding path that extended from the graveyard to the chapel suggesting the locals used this multipurpose dead zone as a walking path and park too.

Seeing that we came with parental supervision, the security guards didn't bother to stand in front of us at the far end of the fanatic herd. Instead they focused their attention on the screaming, wailing teenyboppers chanting, "Rick, Rick, Rick, Rick…"

This was going to be a long night. I pitied the guards who had probably been listening to the girls' high pitched screeching for hours. Hoping to get Rick's attention, the girls waved magazines and posters with sayings like 'I♥Rick' and 'Rick Kingston: Let me be your queen.' Even worse, their skimpy outfits barely covered the essentials. No wonder they were jumping up and down; they had to keep warm somehow.

Rows of decrepit tombstones and markers lined the lush green hillside. Trees grew haphazardly among the plots. Apparently, the early inhabitants of Endymion Village just worked around nature to plant their deceased.

The vegetation mimicked the forest near Sam's cottage. Tall, fat oak trees and evergreens blocked the sky from view while shrubbery crawled densely along the forest floor. If it weren't for all of the markers and dead bodies, it would've made a pretty park.

Sam was visibly floating on cloud nine. Endymion Village wasn't the type of place where the locals saw a lot of action. This must have been a once in a lifetime event for them. No wonder Edwin and Morgan insisted on coming tonight.

A voice bellowed in the distance, "Quiet on the set!"

The girls silenced themselves instantly, each face anxiously hoping to catch a glimpse of Rick. Sam grabbed onto my shoulder, standing on her tiptoes to get a better view.

Several grips were stationed strategically on either side of the knoll. A crane operator sat hidden at the very top of the hill while steadicam operators, the camera crew, and lighting technicians manned their posts. An extensive movie crew kept the actors in check and happy, offering drinks, adjusting their makeup, and picking at their costumes.

Hidden in the trees, someone cried, "Action!"

A loud explosion rocked the cemetery as fire and smoke billowed from the northwest corner of the land. The trees rustled in a gentle breeze.

Slicing through the air like whips, five furry gigantic wolves zoomed effortlessly over the tombstones. Instinctively, I jumped backwards right onto Morgan's toes. Hugging my arms, she whispered, "They're just actors."

How stupid of me? Ironically, this was a vampire-werewolf movie. My gut feelings still bothered me though. Red and silver eyes danced in my memory. I really expected to be mauled alive tonight. *Happy place, happy place...where the hell is my happy place?* I blanked on all of Sam's lessons. As I began hyperventilating, Sam wrapped her arm around me. Reading my mind, she suggested, "Remember the sunlight, the breeze, the fragrances?"

I nodded feebly.

"Think about them. Block everything else."

I closed my eyes and imagined the sunlight shooting the red eyes, then the silver. Automatically, my mind pictured a bubble of sunlight surrounding me. I walked through the darkness and the eyes shied away from me.

A loud BANG captured my attention just in time to see a huge black blob dart overhead and land on top of the knoll. Under the blue-purple sky it was too dark to distinguish the thing's features.

A lighting truss cast a reddish-orange glow on the figure illuminating its blood red eyes. I gasped. Morgan and Edwin embraced Sam and me protectively. The werewolves scampered wildly in different directions as the figure jumped about twenty feet into the air before landing promptly in front of one of the werewolves. The beast growled at the black, red-eyed figure who backhanded it and bit into its throat. Blood squirted through the gouges in its hairy neck. The vampire turned around slowly and sniffed the air menacingly to track its next victim.

"Cut!" a loud voice bellowed.

The dead werewolf stood up, ripped his head off, and shoved the vampire. "Next time don't bite so hard, man. Remember you're only *pretending* to be a freakin' vampire."

"I got carried away," the velvety vampire's voice replied glibly.

"Asshole," the werewolf shouted over his shoulder, skulking away.

Acting as if nothing happened, the vampire approached the man sitting in the director's chair.

"John, don't you think it would work better if the crane shot me from behind as I flew into the air landing in front of werewolf one. The dolly grips can easily get a better shot of me from both sides once the crane is out of the way and the steadicam can just shoot from the bottom. We'll cut the number of takes we need to do by at least half."

This vampire knew his stuff. I wondered if the director was going to respond or punch him. I wouldn't have minded a fight, so I thought the punching option would be most interesting.

The director mumbled something and the vampire shrugged and walked away. Suddenly, he stopped in his tracks, snapped his head up, and glared in our direction.

Ignoring his screaming fans, he glided up to me and his vivid crimson eyes locked mine into an enchanted trance.

Like steroid-fueled linebackers charging their opponents, a group of Barbies pushed their way toward us and tackled me. Rick caught me before I hit the ground and pulled me into his arms protecting me from the crazed girls.

He shouted irritably at the body guards prompting five walls to jump between us and the horde of angry dolls trying to trample me to death.

"I didn't think you'd make it tonight," his silky voice said surprised.

"I...I...I didn't want to come," I stammered honestly. Part of me didn't like him, but I couldn't seem to remember *why* I didn't like him.

"They made me," I pointed an accusatory finger at Edwin, Morgan, and Sam.

Releasing my waist from his firm grasp, Rick turned to Sam. "Lovely to see you again, Samantha. Looking breathtaking as always," he said, raising her delicate hand to his perfect, full lips.

"Morgan, it's a pleasure to see you again." Rick evidently had a special way with women. He then nodded in acknowledgement to a skeptically-faced Edwin, who was trying to decide whether or not he liked Rick.

Turning his full, intense attention on me, my knees felt like Jell-o. I couldn't even remember if I had knees let alone what they were supposed to do.

"I'll be finished in an hour. May I meet you at the pub?" he asked kindly. His gleaming eyes told me to accept his invitation.

Against all better judgment, my voice agreed weakly, "Sure."

His lips coiled into an enormous, beautiful grin. He was clearly pleased with himself and my inability to say 'No' tonight.

As Rick stepped away from me still locked into my eyes, I realized how cold I had become. My whole body shivered. Was it Rick's effect on me or just the cold night air? I glanced at Sam who was wearing far less than me and she stood perfectly still, happy, and content, dreaming about Rick kissing her hand no doubt.

In one smooth motion, Rick slipped off his black leather jacket and swung it around my shoulders. I stared blankly at it confused by his chivalry and glanced back at his wide smile. Considering his womanizing talents, I'd assumed he'd allow girls to die for him without another thought for their well-being.

"Thank you," I muttered, curiously staring like a dumbfounded idiot into his red hypnotic gaze. "Uh, don't you need this for your scene?"

"I've got extras. You can keep it."

I nodded because his eyes told me to nod.

"See you soon, Angel." His grin spread from ear-to-ear. He was getting his way and he liked it. A little voice buried deep inside me told me not to like it too, but I didn't want to listen.

The truss lights gleamed off his dark, loose curls as he strutted confidently back to the set.

I was speechless, dumbstruck, and completely infatuated. My surroundings swirled around me in slow motion. I vaguely became aware that four body guards were protecting me from the angry mob of girls screaming obscenities and trying to rip Rick's jacket off of me.

Realizing my incoherence, Sam wrapped her arms around me. "Are you ok?"

"Uh, not really," my voice quavered.

"He finally got to you, huh?"

"Yeah." I sounded like a complete idiot. I felt more like a celebrity stalker than a normal adult.

A shiver shot through me. Automatically, I pulled the jacket on a little tighter. His scent lingered on its collar. Instinctively—or more like animalistically—I lifted the collar to my nose and inhaled his completely intoxicating, exotic, and seductive scent. My body heat intensified the fragrance lingering on his jacket, which felt like Rick had completely enveloped me.

"I'm going to pass out. My head…" I swooned, grabbing my temples.

"Sit," Sam commanded as I began to hyperventilate.

"Hot…hot," I managed to say. A wave of fire poured over my body. I collapsed.

Sam ripped off Rick's jacket and the black quilted one beneath it. Morgan propped my head in her lap. The freezing air drifted over me and cooled the invisible fire burning my skin. I snuck a glance at my arms thinking they'd be bright red, but they were paler than ever.

Another shiver shot down my spine relieving the feeling that I had just walked through a blazing inferno.

Morgan glanced at Edwin who scanned the woods and people. Gasping for deep breaths, the cold air cleansed my lungs and I darted upright more alert than when I arrived.

"Do you feel better?" Morgan asked hesitantly.

"Yeah, much. I haven't felt this good in days. My body is alive. WOW!" I thought for sure if I jumped off of a building, I'd be able to fly. Exhilaration pulsed over my skin and through my body.

I sprung up from my seat. Sam stood warily by my side. "Are you sure you're ok? You look a little...strange."

"I feel great. I really haven't eaten in a couple of days. Maybe that caused it."

"Yeah, maybe." Sam didn't take her eyes off me as I scanned the knoll for Rick.

After the seventh take of the same scene, we decided to walk to the pub. The body guards escorted us the entire way because several of the groupies tried to attack us.

"Evenin', Edwin, Morgan," the bartender yelled, his voice echoing in the empty tavern. "Glad to see some familiar faces. The group from Hollywood bought the bar for the night. They're an odd lot. Have you seen them yet?"

Edwin laughed. "Ah, Jack, that's just because most of them are Americans!"

He turned to me realizing his gaffe. "Sorry, Angel, you're not included in that."

I glared at him skeptically, but he didn't seem to notice. Morgan, Sam, and I made ourselves comfortable in the large corner booth while Edwin bought beer and soda.

An eerie, soul-reverberating screech scratched along the window beside us.

Terrified, we lurched to our feet defensively only to catch Mark's hearty bellow. Matt and Cynan rolled their eyes and motioned for us to get them into the pub. The place was surrounded by the Barbie army, whose chants of "Rick, Rick, Rick," resonated throughout the tavern as our guys walked through the doors.

"How irritating!" I exclaimed.

"You know, you weren't that much different from those bimbo robots tonight," Mark commented.

"What?"

"Come on, Ang, you passed out after that asshole put his coat on you. Are you really that into him?"

"No," I lied guiltily.

"I thought you hated him?" Matt asked curiously.

"I do!" *I hate him for making me feel like an infatuated bimbo.*

"Then why did you faint?" Cynan added.

"When did we start playing twenty questions?" I demanded angrily.

A resounding echo of screams announced Rick's arrival along with the rest of the cast and crew. Rick made a beeline for our table and jovially greeted everyone including Mark, Matt, and Cynan. I looked at him cautiously. His face was still caked with white makeup and his dark brown hair stood wildly on end. At least his red contacts were gone.

"Are you enjoying yourselves tonight?" he asked everyone but stared at Sam.

"Yes," she said meekly. "Thanks for inviting us."

"Glad you came."

He turned his handsome face toward me and asked sweetly, "May I speak with you for a few minutes...alone?"

I glanced at Morgan and Edwin and they nodded in approval. Mark, Matt, and Cynan weren't as accepting while Sam appeared lividly jealous.

I mouthed "I'm sorry" to Sam as I picked up Rick's jacket and followed him to a table in the back corner of the room.

His eyes immediately captivated me. They sparkled like deep, bright emeralds. Mine were just a muted green with grey-blue rings around the irises.

"Oh, before I forget, here's your jacket," I said, handing it to him. "Thanks for letting me borrow it." My skin still smoldered from the unusual burn.

Flashing his dashing toothy grin, my knees began to wobble again. It was a good thing I happened to be sitting.

"Glad to be of service." Staring confidently into my gaze, he leaned forward mesmerizing me with an invisible vise which pulled me into him. The room and people around us disappeared.

"It meant a lot to me that you came tonight. I know I'm not your favorite person in the world," he dropped his eyes to the table. Was this gorgeous man actually shy or was he just acting—trying to lure me into his trap.

Rick lightly caressed my fingers as they drummed robotically on the table. His touch radiated a cold energy which shivered and slithered up my arm. He pulled his hands away.

"I'm sorry, was that too forward?" he asked worried.

"It just sent a chill through me." I was concerned. The more time I spent with Rick, the deeper I fell under his spell.

His deep stare locked on my face searching for something hidden behind my expression.

"What?" I asked curiously.

"You're driving me crazy."

"Me?" I asked in disbelief. I was utterly perplexed. Rick Kingston, Hollywood star, was into me?

"You're not like other girls. You're complicated," he smirked. "Let's see, you don't like compliments. You don't care that I'm rich or a celebrity. You don't allow me to get close to you and yet you don't push me away. You're an enigma, Angel, but I *will* figure you out." His goal sounded a little more like a threat than a game.

"Let me guess—an exotic trip or lavish gift wouldn't soften you toward me either?"

"Not a chance."

Fiddling with his jacket's zipper, he leaned back into his chair.

"You know, I'm not good at this whole relationship thing. I've never had to work at it. Girls have always thrown themselves at me."

"Isn't that every guy's dream?" I scoffed.

"No—well, yes—at first anyway. It just gets old fairly fast."

"Why me though? I'm not like your groupies and you'd have to work your butt off to get me to believe anything you say."

His emerald eyes flashed gloriously, twinkling in the light. "So there's hope?"

"I didn't say that," I corrected quickly, but it was too late. His mind was visibly scheming. "Stop!"

"What?" he asked mischievously.

"I can see you're up to something. Stop."

"Why?"

"Because I don't want you to get hurt or disappointed whenever I have to let you down."

His cool gaze jumped with happiness. He was undeterred. "I can take it."

"We'll see."

"So how much longer will you be staying in this pit of hell on earth?"

"A few weeks. What about you?"

"Same."

We sat still for a few seconds, awkward silence pounding in my ears.

"Oh, thanks for being nice to my friends tonight."

He creased his eyes and eyebrows in confusion.

"*All* of my friends I mean," I clarified, glancing at Mark, Matt, and Cynan, who were glaring at Rick murderously.

"Oh, that. Sorry, I've been on edge lately. I didn't mean to offend them," he half-heartedly apologized, casting his eyes momentarily on their table.

Behind Rick's confident exterior hid an uncertain boy. I found that part of him endearing. The cocky arrogance I could do without.

He raised his eyebrow and smiled crookedly.

"What?" I asked suspiciously.

"I love your shirt."

I glanced down realizing his focus centered on the middle of my chest. The crystal accents formed a halo over a little oval shape with wings behind it.

"Cute," he continued. "So, are you really an angel or a devil in disguise?"

"Funny," I said sarcastically.

His smile stretched into a mouthwatering grin. "Do you want to go for a walk?" he asked, suddenly changing the subject.

"Now?"

"No, ten years from now," he mocked. "Yeah, now."

"Sorry, I can't leave with strange men. You understand, right?" I teased.

Slightly disappointed, he rebounded quickly. "That's fine. Why don't you bring your friends?"

"Seriously?" I asked incredulously.

"Seriously."

"Where did you want to go?"

"I have to go back to the trailer, so why don't we go through the cemetery?"

"Are you kidding me? You want to walk through the dark cemetery at midnight."

"With your friends," he corrected. "So we won't be alone, since you're clearly afraid of me."

"Hardly," I lied.

"Then prove me wrong," he teased.

"I don't do bets, Rick."

"Fine. How about, please Angel, I'd really like to go for a walk with you," his round gem-like eyes begged, "...and your friends."

"Let me ask, ok?"

"Sure," he said excitedly, knowing he was going to get his way.

Morgan eyed him suspiciously, but Edwin thought it would be a great idea since we had to head back to the cars anyway. Rick motioned for us to follow him through the pub's kitchen. None of the cooks bothered to look up.

"Sneak out of here often, Rick?" Cynan asked.

"Yeah, they're used to it," he said, waving to the staff.

Outside, we followed Rick up a set of stone stairs to the path which stretched along the hillside toward the cemetery. Morgan, Cynan, and Edwin led the way while Rick and I trailed about a car's length behind. Mark and Matt teased poor Sam incessantly a few feet behind us, though from the sound of Sam smacking them every few seconds, she was standing her ground.

Walking along the edge of the black forest, the dimly lit path aided in our escape from Rick's fans. Thoroughly distracted and completely terrified, I kept glancing nervously past Rick waiting for red and silver eyes to pierce through the shrubs and trees.

The sweetness of summer flowers and the fresh fragrance of the trees and evergreens danced on the breeze. Revitalizing my senses, the scent alleviated my fears of what might be lurking in the woods.

The cool night air tingled in my throat and shot a chill down my spine making me shiver. In an instant, Rick's jacket was hanging on my shoulders. His left hand lingered on my back for a second until Matt coughed conspicuously.

"And you were worried about my fans. These guys are far scarier than the girls chasing me," he whispered sarcastically, shoving his hands in his pockets.

"Thanks for the jacket, again," I said appreciatively. I tried desperately to control myself by keeping my nose away from the jacket's collar. "Now what happens if you catch a cold or pneumonia because you were walking in the freezing cold night air?"

"I never get sick."

"Figures," I sighed caustically.

"How's that exactly?"

"You're already a celebrity plus you're nice and good looking. It's not quite fair that you never get sick too. Some people have all the luck." I said too much, too honestly. I always had a habit of speaking without thinking.

Rick smiled sheepishly staring at the path ahead. In no time at all, we reached the hillside. Crew members still lingered in the area, cleaning up the set and preparing for tomorrow's shoot.

"Do you want to see how they make me fly?" Rick asked enthusiastically.

"Sure, why not?"

Morgan and Edwin were engaged in a heated argument and the rest of the group was occupied with Sam's outfit and her idol worship of Rick. I knew the minute I'd start moving, they'd be close by.

Rick led me to the top of the hill and showed me a crane rigged with a special apparatus which hooked underneath his costume.

"...then a guy just pulls me up and down on the strings. It's really cool," he said proudly.

"Aren't you afraid of being tethered that high?"

"Things like that don't scare me. I wouldn't mind taking the stuntmen's jobs some days. They have a lot more fun."

I glanced at the remaining crew. Everyone was oblivious to Rick's presence, or they just didn't care. I wondered if Rick's newness would wear off if I got to know him better.

Regardless, after the CJ debacle I wasn't planning on finding a boyfriend. In a few weeks I'd either be dead or back in Salem trying to adjust to normal life. I really didn't want to get to know Rick, but he was a refreshing character after being locked up all day with everyone else.

I looked around the cemetery taking in the ancient tombstones.

"Aren't they great?" Rick asked, following my gaze. "This place was perfect for our movie. We didn't need many props."

My attention shifted to the monuments at the top of the knoll. A black shadow floated in front of a white marble angel statue standing on a formidable granite platform.

Eyes frozen on the shape, my breath caught. It turned toward me flashing his hungry crimson eyes.

I gasped.

Rick laughed. "It's just one of our extras. I know we're in a cemetery, Angel, but it's just a movie set. Nothing scary. Well, at least nothing scarier than your friends back there."

I turned back to the eyes, but they were gone. Curious, I walked toward the angel monument with Rick on my heels.

"Angel?" Mark bellowed, running up the hill after me. "We need to get home. Come on."

"In a minute."

"No. Now," he said firmly.

I stopped in front of the statue and saw everything I needed to know. Carved onto the middle of the platform's front facing was Artemis' symbol. At the angel's feet lay a single white rose.

The red eyes belonged to my stalker.

23 ~ Debate

Brilliant red eyes. Stalker. My thoughts raced, trying to decipher my creepy admirer's intent. He was definitely a vampire—the red eyes told me that much. I couldn't figure out why he hadn't attacked me yet. What if Rick was right and he was just an extra who took his costume home with him to scare other people for fun? Then again, how would he have known to find me at the hostel or Sam's house? The placement of the rose was interesting. Perhaps the rose he left for me the other day really wasn't intended for me. Maybe I startled him and he dropped it
by accident.

Whatever the reason, he didn't frighten me—well at least he didn't terrify me anymore. His presence scared me because he always popped up unexpectedly.

And Rick. Now that I was away from him, my head was clear and my skin no longer felt like it was baking in an oven. A flood of emotions unleashed themselves as my thoughts drifted to CJ. How could I have so easily forgotten the man I was willing to die for just yesterday?

A guilty part of me wondered when I'd see Rick again. Mark, the barbarian, grabbed me from the top of the knoll, threw me over his shoulder, and dragged me away. I waved goodbye to Rick who tried to squelch his laughter, highly amused by Mark's irritating antics.

Edwin pulled the car into the driveway and we hopped out. Sam turned the lights on in the parlor as I ran into the dark kitchen for a drink.

A black figure leaned against the sink in the darkness.

"AAAAAAAAAAAH!" I screamed.

Sam flipped on the lights to reveal the trespasser. "Angel, what's wrong with you?" she chided.

"Me? What's wrong with him?" Turning to CJ, "Why the hell were you hanging out in the dark?"

"Don't you think it would look a little odd if someone saw a stranger walking through the house with none of the family at home?"

"So you wanted to scare us to death?"

He rolled his eyes. "You know that's not true."

The rest of the family milled about the house getting ready for bed. Irritated by CJ and unsettled by Rick, I poured a glass of milk and sank into a kitchen chair needing to calm down.

Sitting across from me, CJ glared with his arms crossed on his chest.

"What's your problem?" My blunt tone was harsh, but I was too tired to play games.

"Did you have a good time tonight?" His tone was unpleasant.

"Yeah, it was fun. Seeing how they make a movie was pretty cool."

"Is that all?"

"Why?" I asked suspiciously.

"'So are you really an angel or a devil in disguise?'" CJ mockingly quoted Rick.

My mouth dropped open. How did he hear my conversation? Was he envious? "So what?"

"And what's with nearly passing out? Does his Hollywood manufactured perfection really make you so lightheaded?" he growled.

"I can't believe you!" I yelled in disbelief. "You're the one who said nothing can happen between us and now you're jealous?"

"I'm not jealous. I'm worried about your safety."

"My safety? I was surrounded by people. You're just jealous!" I snapped. "So if I can't be with you, I can't be with anyone at all? How dare you?!"

"You know I have a job to do. I'm only looking out for you," he argued calmly.

"Drop the pretense, CJ. Besides, it's not like anything happened tonight."

I waited for his reply, but the burgundy hue of his cheeks and throbbing vein in his temple suggested he was apparently too angry to form words.

"You chose this path, CJ. Even if I wanted something to happen with Rick—which I don't—but if I did, you'd have nothing to say about it. You're the one who said you're leaving in three weeks. I have to stay here and move on with my life. Well, part of moving on includes making friends. Don't you want me to be happy?"

The anger seething from his stormy eyes yielded to sadness and regret. His sorrowful gaze cracked through my anger.

Instant guilt. I wanted to take back my words, but it was too late.

Whatever I felt with Rick wasn't nearly as deep as the connection with CJ. I didn't want to be sucked back into my feelings for him though. He was a closed book in my mind. Sometimes life is just a fairy tale with a crappy ending.

He stared at me expectantly. Not knowing what else to say, I placed my glass in the sink and stormed out of the kitchen. Two seconds later, the front door slammed and an engine purred to life. Glancing through the second story windows, I hollowly watched the platinum Mercedes speed into the night.

My heavy heart already lay in broken pieces in the pit of my stomach. The dull ache of each miniscule part didn't hurt nearly as badly as when it broke apart yesterday.

I ripped a piece of paper from Sam's tablet. I wanted to write something, but what? My hand moved mindlessly across the paper while I stared out of the window into the black, moonless sky.

Glancing at the paper, Zach's eyes stared back at me. At least my subconscious could see my real problems. I was unrealistically hopeful with CJ because he seemed to fill Zach's void. And Rick, well, he didn't compare to either of them; he was just fun to be around.

Towel drying her black bob, Sam returned to the bedroom in a tight red tank top and black pajama pants with cherries on them. "Wasn't Rick amazing?"

"How specifically?"

"How?" she stared at me as if I was crazy. "He let you borrow his jacket. He wanted to go for a walk with you. He was nice to all of us tonight—including the boys. And he was more gorgeous than ever before. His hair is unbelievable and his chiseled nose and lips... ahhhh." She flopped backwards onto her bed reliving Rick's every movement, mannerism, and word.

Seeing Sam lost in her memories of Rick, he raced to the forefront of my thoughts again. As much as I wanted to forget about him and focus on CJ, I couldn't. Was I really becoming so shallow that a handsome celebrity could alter my deep feelings for CJ? Or were my feelings for CJ shallow? In which case, what kind of cruel, superficial demon was I? Did this conflict come solely from the lack of Zach and my friends in my life? Or was I a shallow bimbo stringing guys along because I selfishly craved the attention? Regardless of how I looked at it, I had serious personal issues which needed to be sorted out.

"Angel, did you hear me?" Sam roused me from my daydream.

"What? Sorry. What did you say?"

She sighed impatiently, her shoulders drooping in defeat at not being able to hold my attention. "Aren't you happy that he likes you?"

"Likes me?" I asked dazed. I liked the attention he showered on me, but it just dawned on me that he might really like me.

"Oh, come off it. You see how he looks at you and speaks to you." Jealousy dripped from her words.

"Perhaps you're right, but I'm not looking for a relationship."

"But he still wants to see you?"

"Yeah, he mentioned something about that."

Sam sighed happily, an infatuated smile creeping over her lips. Reading her thoughts, which were painted plainly on her expression, I reluctantly made an offer. "Do you want to go into town tomorrow to see him?"

"Can we?" she squealed ecstatically.

"On one condition."

Skepticism clouded her happiness. "And that would be?" she asked slowly.

"You need to convince Mark, Matt, and Cynan they need to come with us and we need to have the coven around too."

"No problem," she breathed excitedly and jumped off the bed. Her lithe body glided across the floor and down the hallway to Cynan's room.

Still sitting at the desk, I glanced back at my sketch of Zach, sighing at the sight of his eyes. A little part of my stomach churned at the thought of a life without him. Time certainly wasn't healing this pain.

I shoved my drawing to the side and pulled out my notes trapped beneath Sam's books. It was time to add a few more thoughts to the list.

Good battling evil Vampires & witches?
Religion vs. mythology auras
What or who do I believe?
Trust in CJ, Sam, Cynan, Mark, Matt, council
Do I trust others or myself?
How does Endymion Manor fit into the battle?
Murders at the home...why?
Cenweard & Artemis
How is she involved?

What does this have to do with me?
Positive thinking makes me feel better
Sunlight/smell protects me and changes things
Miscellaneous: who sent car to airport? Who is
my red-eyed
stalker? Magic tunnel? Transformation into rock?
Artemis' symbol
Red-eyes = vampires, Silver eyes = werewolves
Jealousy?

I wasn't sure how to add any of this up, but writing signified progress somehow. I shut off the desk lamp and climbed into my bed.

Hugging an extra pillow, my thoughts lingered on Zach: his crooked smile; the first time he traced my hand with his fingers before working up the courage to take my hand into his; leaning against his shoulder as we moved awkwardly in circles at our first dance; walking through the park as red and yellow falling leaves swirled around us.

Silent tears escaped my sleepy eyes. I didn't think it possible, but my heart's broken pieces shattered into a million smaller ones.

Zach held me tenderly against his chest beneath a green canopy of tall, leafy trees. Rays of sunlight illuminated his boyishly handsome features which radiated a golden glow. Staring deeply into my eyes, he leaned in apprehensively to kiss my anxious lips. He hesitated wanting to prolong the fleeting moment. I couldn't wait. Tiptoeing I threw my arms around his neck and hungrily pushed my mouth against his. Zach passionately, fiercely returned my affection in matched desperation. His hands tightly pulled my lower back even closer against his warm frame.

I couldn't remember why I was upset. My body felt whole. My soul felt complete. There was no pain only unaware, peaceful, blind bliss.

Slowly, he stepped away from me, tears glistening in his eyes. Sorrow and pain tinged his otherwise radiant expression. A stinging ache and fear pierced my happy moment.

Keeping me an arm's length away, his face faded from view.

'No!' I yelled.

Slowly, his eyes came into focus again only the face wasn't Zach's.

CJ stood before me, his deified sharp features softened by a loving kindness.

Confused, I called for Zach. The impish look of his grinning eyes and round face reappeared for a millisecond only to be replaced by CJ's again.

The golden aura around his body burned with the brightness of a nuclear explosion forcing me to close my eyes. As the light dulled, I peered through my eyelashes in time to see Zach and CJ split into two people, each holding one of my hands.

CJ stepped by my side placing his arm around my waist. We took a step backwards extending my arm still connected to Zach. I clutched onto it ferociously. Zach hung his head low, shaking it as a tear slipped down his cheek.

He released my hand from his warm grasp, mouthing, "Te Quiero...always."

Shouting and crying, I futilely begged him to stay, but his aura brightened into a blinding golden-white brilliance.

When I opened my eyes, Zach was gone. My hand remained outstretched grasping at the emptiness he left behind. Brown and green hues of foliage swayed in the breeze around us.

Tightening his hold on my hips, CJ turned me around and led me into the woods. A ray of sunlight illuminated our dark path. I kept glancing over my shoulder hoping Zach might reappear, but I knew he was gone forever. Walking side-by-side, CJ navigated me through the dense, unfamiliar forest.

24 ~ History

Still gripping to Zach's straight-jacket-like embrace and devouring kiss, I wished myself back into the dreams to keep from waking. Once I opened my eyes, I knew he'd truly be gone.

Dawn's prying light streamed through the windows. I growled at the unpleasant, unwelcome, silent alarm. The clock on Sam's night stand flashed 6:00 AM.

Frustrated I kicked off the bed covers and grabbed Sam's black quilted jacket punching my arms through the sleeves as I crept down the stairs. From the sound of things—or lack thereof—I was the only one awake. Tiptoeing through the kitchen, I pulled the back door open gently, hoping that it wouldn't give away my breakout.

The morning light greeted my face with a tender kiss as the dew-tinged breeze billowed through my hair. The damp grass tickled my bare feet. Climbing onto the wooden picnic table, I sat cross legged absorbing the silence of my peaceful surroundings.

I laid back on the table, propped my head against my arms, and closed my eyes. The tepid wind danced with the ruffles at the bottom of my gown.

Focusing on the leafy ceiling swaying about fifty feet overhead, the babbling brook and twittering birds sounded in the distance.

Why couldn't life be simple? I wasn't naïve enough to think my life wouldn't be filled with challenges, but hadn't I been dealt more than my share of obstacles lately? I was still trying to come to grips with my dad's and Zach's deaths. I hadn't lived the life of a normal teenager in about a year. Part of me wished I could rewind my life and tell myself from two years ago never to take any moment for granted. Now, I'd give anything for another moment with Zach or even just to get into a car on my own and go shopping with no chaperones.

"I thought you were under strict orders not to go anywhere without two people," a smooth voice rang sweetly into my ear.

"And I thought you were supposed to stay at least ten feet away me because I'm hazardous to your health."

He sat on the bench placing his arms next to my head clearly ignoring his orders.

I refused to open my eyes. Part of my body still lingered somewhere between consciousness and the dream world. I liked floating in the nothingness, hoping Zach could still reach me somehow.

"Good morning, Angel," CJ offered politely, starting over.

I still hadn't made up my mind as to whether or not I had forgiven him for yesterday's jealous outrage. Didn't I have every right to go on with my life?

Of course, the whole situation created conflict. I wanted to be with CJ, but I couldn't be with CJ. I needed to distance myself from CJ, but I didn't want that either. I found his over protectiveness endearing and his sensitivity attractive. His god-like appearance induced a panic of lustful thoughts.

I still figured being mean or silent was the best remedy to cure my broken heart, although I knew that was a losing battle. Considering we lived under the same roof, it was a bit difficult to get away and find a moment's peace alone.

"Still mad?" his aching tone broke my concentration. As much as I wanted to ignore him, I wasn't immune to the hurt in his words. I fought against the painful urge to respond.

"Fine, I'll talk," he paused, waiting for my reaction. Sighing at my scornful silent treatment, he continued reluctantly. "You are absolutely right. I do want you to be happy. That's what matters most. If Rick makes you happy, then I won't stand in your way."

Anger brimmed over my protective wall. I snapped my head toward his voice and opened my eyes. I didn't anticipate his nose only being an inch away from mine.

Caught off guard, my testy response slipped from my mind completely. His scent and proximity were mesmerizing.

Smiling slyly, he asked, "Yes?"

I forced my head to turn back to the sky and took a deep breath of fresh air to cleanse my system from his addictive drug-like presence.

"This has nothing to do with Rick." I intended to shout this, but he knocked all of the angry intent right out of my head.

"Humor me and say it is."

"Why?" I asked, concentrating desperately on the leaves dancing in the morning sunshine against the sky's bright blue blanket. With each word that CJ uttered, my heart beat stronger. Opening my mouth was a bad idea. I couldn't afford to hope.

"Because I might be able to get past all of this if I think that you're in love with someone else."

"I'm not going to lie to make you feel better."

CJ leaned into my ear whispering, "Please?" His breath slowly warmed the side of my neck creating a surge of hormone-induced frenzy that pulsed through my body.

"Don't do that," I commanded weakly, secretly wishing he wouldn't stop.

"Why?" Another wave of his breath tingled on my neck.

"Because a zap of lightning is nothing compared to the electrical charge that shocks me every time you're near."

"Now you know how I feel."

"What do you mean?"

"I feel you in every part of me, every thought, every dream."

This was everything I wanted to hear and everything I knew I shouldn't. The pieces of my heart danced wildly. Surely my chest would explode from happiness and hope.

"Aren't you supposed to be concentrating on your duties?"

At the cold reminder, he pulled away stiffly. His blue eyes screamed blankly in frustration.

"Angel, I can't do this every day," he motioned back-and-forth from himself to me. "Please make me feel like I'm not worthy of you."

I sat up to face him. "CJ, I'm the one who's not worthy, and it would kill me to have to hurt you. I'd rather die than see you in pain because of me."

He looked at me incredulously. Throwing his hands behind his head he leaned back to face the sky. The sun's rays glistened around him.

"Well, we need to figure something out. Neither of us can go on with all this tension."

I thought for a minute and a strangely simple solution jumped into my thoughts.

"This is so stupid, but I'm going to say it anyway."

"Nothing you say is stupid."

"Yeah, well, this will be pretty close, but maybe it'll bring closure."

He waited eagerly as I fought the emotions raging within begging me not to utter the words. This was most definitely not what either of us wanted.

Slowly and unwillingly the words slipped from my lips, "Let's just be friends."

His face darkened, eyes tightened. "You're right. That *is* bad."

We stared at each other in silence agonizing over a relationship that never was.

"I see the silver lining," he offered eventually, sighing reluctantly. "We still get to be near each other without the emotional complications."

My rebuilding heart stopped mid-beat. Suspended inside my chest, it remained a broken shell.

"I guess it's better than the struggling we've endured over the past week."

"It's been a week already?"

CJ nodded sadly. Our time was running out.

"We have three weeks left exactly."

Not even the intense sunlight could cheer my mood. I found it irksome, grating—a reminder of the brightness I once had or could have had in my life. And now, it was just a ticking time bomb counting down to a life without CJ—or, slightly less importantly, my death.

The morning passed slowly. Miraculously, Sam convinced the boys it was in their best interest to go into town today. After she changed into and out of about a dozen outfits—Edwin sent her back at least seven times, and she didn't like five of her own choices—we headed for the front door. CJ sat beneath the living room window reading my mythology book.

"Aren't you coming?" I asked him.

"No. Have fun," he replied uninterestedly, avoiding my inquisitive, suspicious glare.

"CJ, you should go," Morgan suggested, focusing on folding laundry and completely unaware of our awkward friends-only arrangement.

"The coven will be with them, Morgan."

I strongly suspected this reaction directly correlated to our new "just friends" status. I walked toward him nonchalantly and plopped onto the couch. "Well, if you're staying, then I'm staying."

He looked at me curiously. "I thought you wanted to go into town."

"Not particularly. I'm just going for Sam's sake."

"Then why would you stay here with me?"

"Because friends don't abandon each other." *Because I can't stand to be away from you for more than a second.*

"I'm fine, Angel," he assured, returning his attention to the book.

"Come on. Drive me in your car, please. You can go as fast as you want and I won't complain," I begged innocently.

For a split second a mischief-filled joy touched his eyes and he considered the possibility.

"In all seriousness though, I didn't have my daily lesson, so I was hoping to talk to you."

He searched my eyes looking for the hidden agenda. I'm sure he discovered it—I sucked at hiding things—but he caved anyway. "All right. I'll be outside in five minutes," he said grudgingly, trying to hide his enthusiasm.

Skipping happily to the driveway, I climbed into CJ's car, which irked him immensely because he wanted to open the door for me.

"Just because we're friends doesn't mean I can't be a gentleman," he chided.

"It doesn't matter to me," I said excitedly. I was beginning to like this new arrangement. Now I didn't have to worry about avoiding him. I only needed to curb my hormones to an acceptable friends-only level.

"So, what did you want to talk about?"

"Well, yesterday, Edwin and Morgan began explaining the vampires and werewolves to me. I was wondering if you could fill me in on the missing details and finish your story."

"You really want to hear more? I thought they scared you."

"They terrify me, but I'm curious," I shrugged.

He laughed for the first time in days. It was contagious; I had to smile too. "If you insist," he said. His amused, deep-blue eyes twinkled in the sunlight.

He slowed the car to a mere 120 kilometers per hour and continued the tale. "Ok, so remember, the demi-god son of a fallen angel became the first vampire," he waited for me recall the story. I nodded eagerly, and he continued, "He couldn't be killed because his body was already dead—frozen in time. Whenever he was injured, he would heal instantly returning to the condition he was in when his body died.

"Hadrianus, as he was called, developed amazing powers. Since his body was dead it couldn't process food, but it needed nourishment to be strong. Apparently blood was the only thing which strengthened his body. A vampire's body absorbs blood, which gives it amazing physical strength. Hadrianus became unstoppable.

"His craving for blood was endless. He had a difficult time adjusting to his new existence though. On the brink of madness he unleashed his anger on the angels. The head angel promised him an eternal kingdom if he would kill humans. Since he wasn't exactly mentally stable, he agreed and began to wipe out humanity—drained them to be exact.

"Hadrianus developed his talents. He was stronger than five hundred men, faster than lightning, and his hearing was so acute he could hear conversations from miles away.

"Am I boring you, Angel?"

"No, please ignore my expression. I'm totally engrossed. Keep going." I knew I'd fit into this story somewhere and without this knowledge I had no chance of surviving the impending battle. I ignored the fact that my stomach was tied up in anxious, nauseous knots at the mere potential of meeting Hadrianus myself.

CJ drew a deep breath and continued. "After a day of bloody gluttony, he left his final victim semi-drained and dragged him home to finish him later. For days the person convulsed with tremendous force. Hadrianus' curiosity saved the man's life, or doomed him depending on your perspective. He watched him waste away until the man's body died finally and was reborn as a vampire. Fascinated by the possibilities of creating clones of himself, Hadrianus produced a small army of hirudo, a.k.a. bloodsuckers."

"Weren't they worried about having too many vampires and not enough people to sustain the blood supply?"

"The angels weren't concerned with the vampires' existence. They simply used them to meet their goal of ruining the world." Glancing at me thoughtfully, he paused expecting another question.

"The fallen appointed Hadrianus as the High One, king of all the vampires and named his group Aeterna Flamma."

"What?!" I exclaimed horrified, nearly jumping out of my seat. "Aeterna Flamma?"

"That's the name of the hostel where I was staying!"

"I'm aware."

"Is that just a weird coincidence?"

"Didn't the council say that we've been expecting you for quite some time now?"

"Yes, but how close was I to danger?" Blood flooded my cheeks as my anxiety levels flew through the car's roof.

"You weren't."

"How can you be so confident? It was a lucky chance then that the day after I arrived, I came on the day trip from hell which has lasted seven days so far! What if Mark and Matt weren't there?"

"We've been keeping an eye on you too, not just the bad guys. In case you haven't fully realized this yet, Mark and Matt are one of us. They were on the plane with us too. You were never in any danger."

"I think I need to lie down." A wave of nausea swept over me like a flash of fire. How much of my life had been orchestrated by these people? How long had they been interfering? How much of my life was real? What *was* real?

CJ swerved to the side of the road. He grabbed my face with both of his hands. "Look in my eyes, Angel. What do you see?"

"I'm gonna throw up, CJ. Let me go!" I struggled uselessly against his grip.

"I'll take my chances. Look in my eyes," he insisted forcefully.

His deep blue irises undulated around the axis of his coal black pupils soothing the hurricane in my stomach. His strong hands radiated a cold, calming energy through my cheeks. My limp body slid lifelessly back into the seat.

A gentle rap on the window echoed distantly in my ears. I faintly heard Cynan's voice ask if I was ok.

"She'll be fine," CJ replied. "She got a little worked up."

"So you knocked her out? Why is she bloody knackered?"

"She'll be fine in a couple of minutes."

Mark's laughter yanked me back to reality, albeit dazed and slightly confused. Blinking wildly, my eyes tried to focus on the dashboard.

"Dude, if you just wanted to make out you should've told us, we would've kept driving."

CJ's knuckles turned white; the steering wheel cracked under their pressure. Before he could snap and kill Mark, I interjected feebly, "Shut up!"

Laughing, Mark and Cynan jogged back to their car.

"Are you ok?" CJ asked concerned.

"I'll be fine. How did you do that?"

"It's one of my many talents," he grinned mysteriously and arched an eyebrow.

"Am I ready to hear about your talents yet or do I need to wait?" I slurred.

"You most definitely need to wait," he laughed.

As the car slid back onto the road, he pulled the windows down. Gusts of wind slapped my face, bringing me back to life. After a few minutes, my head stopped spinning and I sat up straight.

"Feeling better?"

I nodded loosely.

"Don't worry, you'll be fine soon," he smirked.

Worry bothered my thoughts. "Will we all be fine in a few weeks?"

"We're better prepared than ever before," he replied confidently.

That barely soothed my fears. I felt like a little kid being thrown into the middle of World War III with no map, weapons, or directions.

CJ patted my thigh—blood boiled beneath his touch wanting more. "You *will* be ready. I promise."

I placed my hand over his long graceful fingers. "I don't know what I'd do without you," I whispered to his warm hand.

His lips curled into a weak smile, but a hint of pain lingered in his eyes. I hated this friend rule. We both did. He pulled his hand away from my grasp.

Sullenly I begged, "Please tell me more." If I couldn't feel him physically, the sound of his voice would at least keep him close.

"I think you've had enough scary stories for today."

"Pleeeeeeease," I pleaded. I didn't know when I'd get another chance alone with him. I needed as much information as possible.

He stared into my eyes trying to determine if I was truly ready for more. He shook his head and gave in. "Fine," he sighed. "Hadrianus and his followers became known as Aeterna Flamma. The fallen angels allowed the vampires to ransack earth so they could concentrate on their battles against the Creator's angels.

"Hadrianus knew his vampires couldn't exist if they killed all the people. They figured out they only needed blood to be super strong. Their undead bodies didn't require food of any kind to survive, but they craved blood like a drug. Some of the vampires fared well on their self-imposed diet restrictions. Many of them still kill people, either for the fun of it or because they want to maintain their powers. Some resorted to draining animals for their meals. One of these desperate vampires attacked a wolf one day, but—like Hadrianus—he didn't finish him. The wolf acquired the human qualities of the vampire.

"The werewolf was as strong and powerful as the vampire while being able to transform between both wolf and human forms."

"Are werewolves really just animals?"

"They used to be until the wolves started biting humans. Today they're a mixed breed. It's hard to tell vampires apart from regular people because they look like us and act like us. There are a few characteristics which point out their true identities, but it's very difficult to uncover them. The werewolves are like that too. In wolf form, most look like regular wolves, albeit they're more ferocious and ill-tempered. The ones who've been werewolves for a long time have gotten used to their human forms and easily fit in among people."

"Wow…" I couldn't find a word to describe my thoughts or feelings. This seemed horribly inadequate yet simple and to the point. "So, do werewolves only come out at night or during full moons?" I hoped.

CJ laughed. "No. They can come out whenever they want. People probably just saw them more often during full moons because they're easier to see in the light. The stigma stuck. And no, they can't die from silver bullets. The witches have an interesting way of handling them.

"And while we're debunking myths, vampires don't have fangs; garlic and crosses don't discourage them; and stakes through the heart only piss them off. They can come out during the day, but since they're technically dead, they can't be in hot sunlight for too long. It makes their skin decay. Although, once they're out of the sun they heal instantly.

"The mythic vampires are a strange lot. They look like us and act like us. The only real difference is their diet. Plus, they teeter between the living and the dead. They can mingle with humans because they once were human, but they have the benefits of being in spirit form too—their bodies don't really limit them. Despite their super strengths, they still have human needs and emotions much like you and me."

"What do you mean 'mythic vampires'? What about the other vampires you mentioned in the cave?"

"Mythic vampires are the ones people have exaggerated through movies and books—mindless bloodsuckers without a care for anything. The other vampires are far scarier than the ones we're going to face." His expression darkened. Wisdom burned vividly behind his eyes. Part of me wanted to know his thoughts; a slightly stronger part of me froze in horror.

The sound of the vampire's nail ripping through my arm's flesh echoed in my mind. Vampires. Crimson eyes. Malevolent, hissing voices. Carnivores that indiscriminately kill people for food, or blood anyway. I shuddered at the thought of what scarier creature may exist.

CJ clenched his jaw and pressed his lips into a tight line apparently concentrating on the road. I knew there was nothing I could say to convince him to tell me about the more terrifying species. At least they wouldn't be involved in the fight.

"What about the angels? Do they fly?"

He smirked. "Angels don't walk around with wings hanging off of their backs. They look like us too." He glanced at me through the corner of his eye, assessing my reaction. "And yes, they can fly."

As I contemplated the wealth of knowledge I'd just been given, I couldn't help but notice the sun glistening off of CJ's hair making his strong, pale features glow. An air of mystery surrounded him, yet he simultaneously felt extremely familiar.

"Wow…" I said again.

"It is a pretty good story."

"Um, yeah it is," I agreed, only I wasn't commenting on the story. "So, are these things still running around here?"

"Yes."

"Are they all involved in the event happening in three weeks?"

"Yes."

I gasped inaudibly. My mouth dropped open but was incapable of producing any sounds. CJ's hand reached for mine before my mouth opened the whole way.

"I'm just human. I don't have any special powers. I don't stand a chance against angels, vampires, and werewolves!"

Thankfully his hands radiated a soothing warmth through my trembling grasp.

"You're far more powerful as a simple human."

"How exactly does that make sense?" I asked sarcastically.

"You haven't tapped into your talents yet. It's your abilities they're after. With you on their side, they could conquer all that's good once and for all."

I had no idea what he meant by my "talents" because my mind was too preoccupied with the idea that they wanted to use me one way or another to destroy our side.

I became aware of my surroundings again when CJ handed me to Cynan. Apparently I wasn't quite over my wooziness yet. CJ disappeared down the street leaving us by the stone steps leading into the cemetery.

"Where's he going?" I managed to ask.

"He can't be near you, remember?" Cynan answered simply.

"Oh," I nodded feebly, angry that I had forgotten about the number one problem affecting our friends-only rule. We walked up the stone steps and looked into the graveyard.

There were two sites I tried my best to avoid from this vantage point. The first was Endymion Manor, which was visible on the hilltop behind me. The second was the chapel at the end of the path ahead of me. My experiences with both places still preyed heavily on my nightmares. In an eerie twist of fate, I felt most comfortable in the cemetery filled with hundreds of corpses. Knowing my luck, zombies were probably part of the undead army too.

The movie crew was in the process of dismantling and removing its equipment. An enormous security guard in a neon yellow jacket strolled over to us. "Can I help you kids?" he hollered in a husky, raspy voice.

"We just wanted to walk through here, if that's ok?" I asked, trying awkwardly to sound both authoritative and sweet.

"Sorry, until they're finished packing up, this area is off limits," he ordered, pushing us back to the stairs with his massive frame.

"Johnson," yelled a familiar, suave voice. "They're with me. It's ok." Johnson looked at us suspiciously but allowed us to pass.

Rick jogged down the knoll wrapping one arm around Sam and the other around me in a quick hug. "I didn't expect to see you here today," he said happily. His wild hair was a perfect mess and his black leather jacket hung open loosely giving him an attractive bad-boy appeal.

"We were in town and wanted to see if you'd like to hang out," I explained.

I had never seen Rick shocked. His pleasantly surprised expression froze in place. When he finally found his voice, he turned his charm on me. "I've been waiting for the day when you'd look for me instead of the other way around."

I smiled hoping he'd think it authentic.

"Well, while you're here, do you want to see my trailer? There're all kinds of interesting things in there like props, costumes, and equipment," he suggested optimistically.

"Sure," I agreed. His debonair grin spread widely across his flawless face. "Why don't you take Sam and Matt and we'll follow in just a few minutes?"

His smile melted into a mild frown. "You're not going to ditch me are you?"

"Rick, I don't ditch my friends," I assured, although I was positive Sam was hoping we'd leave her alone with him. "We need to take care of a couple things and then we'll be free to spend some time with you—that is, if you'd like to, of course," I offered innocently, knowing my coy expression would manipulate him in my favor.

My pathetic attempt at flirting worked marvelously. Rick agreed instantly; I felt guilty instantly. I wasn't comfortable manipulating him, but right at the moment I didn't want him to explore the cemetery with me either. It was bad enough knowing my current friends thought I was crazy. I didn't want the only normal person I knew to think that too.

Rick courteously offered his arm to Sam, who nearly fainted with excitement. Matt followed reluctantly, his jaw clenched tightly, clearly not enjoying being volunteered to go with Rick. They hopped down the stone steps to the cobblestone street where the trailers were stationed out of view.

"Ang, why are we here?" Mark asked suspiciously.

"I thought you wanted an adventure?"

He raised his left eyebrow, squinting his golden brown eyes at me skeptically.

"Before you dragged me away last night, I saw something."

"Ooooh, did you find some monsters?" he teased.

"Angel, lead the way before someone catches onto us and throws us out," Cynan interjected seriously.

Even more magnificent in the daylight, the white marble angel dominated the cemetery's landscape protecting its occupants from her eight-foot-high platform. Easily reaching about ten-feet-tall, the statue's long, flowing hair was frozen in an imaginary breeze. Her outstretched wings spanned another six feet in either direction poised and ready to fly away. In her delicate hands, she cradled two pieces of a heart. A single tear marked her cheek as her peaceful face gazed over the broken contents.

Tall, thorny white rose bushes guarded the granite base. My stalker's single rose offering lay in stillness at the angel's feet. The wind swept around us gently parting the tree canopy, allowing the sun's rays to illuminate sparkling crystals in the marble statue.

Mesmerized by the angel's magnificence, I forced my eyes to pry themselves from her eternally frozen, heartbroken expression. Walking up to the base, I ran my fingers over Artemis' symbol. What did this mean? Why was Artemis everywhere? Was this connected to the pagan goddess? If it was, why was she in a Christian cemetery? If it wasn't, why was there a monument to the village girl who lived five hundred years ago?

A hurricane-like gust of wind howled in my ear and knocked me into the thorny bushes.

"Damn it!" I screamed, bracing myself against the platform.

"Ang, you're a beacon beckoning for trouble. How the hell did you do this?" Mark asked bewildered.

"The wind pushed me," I defended, realizing too late how ridiculous this sounded.

"Sure it did."

"Just because you're as big as a house and can't feel anything doesn't mean it's not real!" I yelled.

"Chill out." Mark placed his hands on my shoulders and pried me away from my barbed attacker.

The thorns' death grip began to rip holes in my knit shirt and jeans. The rose bush had essentially become one with my outfit. If Mark kept pulling, we might very well have ripped out the entire bush.

Leaning against the platform, Cynan stared at the angel and her granite stand. "Wait!" he shouted. "Mark, pull her back a little further."

Mark tipped me closer to his chest. The thorns tore my top bit-by-bit.

"It's a grave," Cynan muttered.

"Grave? Whose?" I asked excitedly.

"It says:

Mea amor, Mea vita, Mea angela
1509 – 1525
Artemis Pendragon."

"What?!" I screamed in excitement.

"Shhhh," Mark reminded me. "What does the Latin gibberish mean?"

"My love, my life, my angel..." I translated in a solemn whisper. "Help me get out of this bush please."

Trying carefully not to prick himself or touch me inappropriately, Cynan pulled each thorny branch carefully from my shirt and freed me in a couple of minutes.

"Cynan, did the Endymion family use this cemetery too?"

"I'm not sure. The rest of the grave markers are pretty small and they look like they belong to the villagers, not a wealthy family. There's a path behind this statue which leads down the other side of the hill. Do you want to investigate?"

"Yes, finally some action!" Mark exclaimed exuberantly.

Dense trees and shrubbery covered the other side of the hill. Sunlight barely touched the forest floor obscuring our visibility.

"Do you guys hear that?" I asked.

"What? I don't hear anything," Mark said. The silence was deafening. No birds. No bugs. No forest creatures.

"Yeah, me either. It seems like we're the only living things here," I replied as Mark and Cynan shoved branches and vines from our path. The trail disappeared completely beneath the overgrown foliage.

"We *are* in a cemetery," Cynan laughed. "Hopefully we *are* the only living things here."

Despite the creepy surroundings, I felt remarkably calm. With the memory of the red and silver eyes buried deep, my instincts lacked any sense of an ominous ambush.

The path stretched to the bottom of the hillside leading to a small clearing. In the center stood a plain, square limestone crypt stretching at least twenty feet high and wide. Absent of embellishments, flowers, and bushes, the building more closely resembled a storage unit plopped in the middle of nowhere.

Double bronze doors carved with angels and saints guarded the entrance. Baring their sharp teeth, four menacing, winged granite gargoyles the size of Mark warded off unwelcome intruders from each of the crypt's top corners. *Endymion* was carved in elegant calligraphy over the top of the doorway.

"Scared, Ang?" Mark teased.

"No," I snapped defensively. I was in no mood for his antics. "It just feels weird. The dead belong underground, not accessible through a door."

We walked around the mausoleum examining both the site and its surroundings. The worn stone suggested the tomb had been standing here for centuries. From the amount of dirt and cobwebs covering the place, no one had visited it in centuries either.

"It's so far away from everything else. You'd think they didn't want anyone coming here."

"They clearly didn't want anyone here," Cynan trembled, glancing around. "Can't you feel it?"

"Feel what, dude?" Mark asked irritated. Although from the blank look on his face, his macho words masked a smidgen of fear.

"The energy is negatively charged," Cynan added deeply concerned.

"Great," Mark said warily. "Angel, let's go."

"One minute."

Mark rolled his eyes. Cynan stared apprehensively at the oak and evergreen tree ceiling, his stare darting to different shadows dancing above us in the sunlight. I walked around the building looking for any symbol or marking which might offer clues. The angels on the front doors looked like the holy kind, so I assumed the place didn't necessarily house evil occupants.

Startled by a breeze rustling the bushes behind me, I spun around to see the beginnings of another path.

"Guys! I found something," I yelled urgently and pointed to a two foot section of a dirt path. "It looks like another trail. Can we go?"

Mark drew a deep breath considering my question carefully.

"I thought you were Mr. Adventurer," I taunted. "Come on!"

Mark turned to Cynan who was still scanning the forest. "What do you think, Cynan, should we?"

Cynan's uneasiness made me nervous. "The coven would have warned us by now if there was trouble," he rationalized. "I think we can go, but let's be quick," he cautioned.

Mark kicked and pushed the brush and vines aside to clear the narrow path which was restricted by massive tree trunks lining both sides.

Turning around, Mark glanced beyond me. "Cynan, dude, you're leading the way out," Mark warned with a laugh as a tree branch smacked his face when he looked forward again.

I tried futilely to stifle my laughter, which echoed in the tree cavern around us.

"Maybe you want to lead the way, Ang," he spit spitefully.

"No thanks, I already fought with a rose bush today. It's Cynan's turn."

Cynan was too distracted by the woods and darkness to care about our conversation.

After a few minutes on the flat path, a smaller clearing came into view. The thick foliage overhead gave the false impression that the sun had set.

A foreboding object rested alone in the middle of the clearing. Guarded by a wrought iron fence nearly twice as tall as Mark or Cynan, a single, decrepit tombstone cried for company that never came. The top left corner of the tombstone crumbled away while ivy scaled its cracked frame. The bottom half was covered in dark green and brown moss.

A plaque on the fence's gate warned: *Unhallowed Ground.*

Unbothered by the sign—after all, my guardians were with me—I feebly attempted to open the gate, which was rusted shut.

"Mark, can you open it?" I asked sweetly.

"Did you read the sign?" Mark questioned in disbelief. "These places are reserved for *special* people. People who I'm sure you don't want to meet."

"Just do it. You can stay out here and keep Cynan company."

"I really wish you wouldn't, Ang."

"It's not like I can get lost. It's a ten-by-ten space with no other way out other than the gate you're going to open for me right NOW," I snarled.

Growling in response, Mark channeled his irritability and yanked the gate free from its corroded hinges. Hesitating, I inched closer to the worn headstone. It appeared as if no one had touched it since its occupant was interred. Brushing the ivy aside, I tried to scrape the moss away. I didn't know why I needed to know who was occupying the plot beneath my feet other than to satisfy my own morbid curiosity.

Slowly the engraving cleared, revealing:

1503 - 1526
Mors Voluntaria
Eternal Punishment
Cenweard Endymion

My hands froze over his name. My knees buckled. A torrent of sobs and screeches ripped through my chest. Shrieking hysterically, I collapsed against the tombstone. My brain registered the fact that this was an irrational reaction, but my body continued to convulse as if it was being tortured by unseen forces.

Before I realized what they were doing, Mark and Cynan dragged me to the perimeter of the fence. They propped my back against the wrought iron bars. I pulled my knees into my chest and rocked back-and-forth. My body and brain seemed to be two separate entities no longer tied together.

A pair of strong arms reached through the bars behind me and wrapped around my chest.

25 ~ Confused

"**A**ngel...Shhhhh. It's ok," the heavenly voice comforted tenderly. My body jerked around, reached through the bars, and wrapped its arms around CJ.

"I don't know what's happening," I sobbed. "I just saw his name and...suicide...so young..." I wasn't making any sense, but my stream of consciousness was uncontrollable.

Holding me tightly through the iron prison, CJ stroked my head and back until my sobbing ended. I pulled away from him thoroughly embarrassed. How would I explain momentary-lapse-of-sanity to my already wary friends? CJ wiped away my tears tenderly. A curious look of fear and sadness crossed his expression.

Mark and Cynan's eyes were locked on mine with wild fear. "I told you not to go in there," Mark muttered.

"Is she ok?" Cynan asked caringly.

"What happened?" CJ worried.

"I have no idea. I can't control myself," I answered, staring intently into his eyes hoping to find a sense of peace in them. "Maybe I'm remembering Zach subconsciously and this just set me off." My thoughts blurted through my blubbering and runny nose. Thank goodness I wasn't trying to impress any of these guys. They looked at me like I was their crazy little sister. Well, except for CJ who watched me in a loving, non-brotherly way.

The subtle distress on CJ's face masked violently churning seas within him.

"Why are you upset?" I whispered. "Is it because I can't keep it together for more than five minutes these days?"

"It's not just you," he replied solemnly. "This family has had a long history of senseless tragedy. It's hard not to be overcome by the residual energy surrounding this place."

Pulling me close again, the cold iron bars trapped either side of my face. CJ placed his forehead against mine; his healing touch melted the emotional pain away.

"Let's go," he suggested softly, casting a quick, rueful glance back at the lonely tombstone.

We made our way silently along the path toward the knoll, Mark and Cynan leading, CJ resting his hand on my back guiding me forward. I glanced back one last time. The sun glimmered through the trees momentarily illuminating the grave. It was just another day for us as we made our way through life. And it was just another day in eternal damnation for the contents of the abandoned tomb.

Suicide – Eternal Punishment - Cenweard Endymion

The words repeated themselves through my thoughts as we reached the top of the hill. Poor Cenweard Endymion. What would have driven him to this horrible end? How was Artemis involved? Did he kill her and then himself out of guilt?

"Will you be ok?" CJ whispered in my ear.

I nodded, distracted by the questions preying on my mind.

"I'll see you soon," CJ said as he vanished.

"Well, you got your adventure, Mark," I laughed weakly.

"Ang, I'd rather go into the dark woods alone at night knowing that vampires and werewolves are waiting for me," Mark scoffed. "I'd stand a better chance against them than having to protect you on an afternoon walk."

"I'll make a note of that," I replied dryly.

On our way down the hillside, I attempted to put on a happy face. Hopefully Rick wouldn't pick up on the depressed turmoil bubbling just below its surface.

Sam, Matt, and Rick were leaning against the cemetery's stone wall when we arrived. Leaning dangerously close to Sam, Rick charmed her so much I feared she may have stopped breathing. From the look of Matt's incensed eyes and brooding expression, he was ready to kill Rick.

Fortunately—or unfortunately from Sam's perspective—when Rick spotted us, he broke his trance over her.

"Angel!" he exclaimed exuberantly, walking over to me and reaching for my hand. His cold grasp sent shocks of fire through my system.

"So, do you want to go to the pub?" I suggested, pulling my hand from his.

"Uh, yeah," he hesitated, looking me up and down. "What happened to you?"

I peered at my blouse and pants suddenly remembering my unlucky altercation with Mother Nature.

"Oh, I fell."

"You fell?" he asked incredulously. "It looks like you were attacked by a wild animal," he glared at Mark and Cynan. Mark shook his head and silently mouthed an obscenity. Thankfully, Rick ignored him.

"I fell into a thorny bush that didn't want to let me go. Mark and Cynan freed me, but I destroyed my shirt in the process."

He grinned mischievously. "Well then, we need to get you out of those clothes."

Mark took a rash step toward Rick clearly intent on killing him in one punch.

"Chill," Rick told him dismissively. "She can't walk around town looking like she's been mauled. She can have one of my shirts, unless you want people staring at the holes in hers?"

As much as Mark wanted to hate Rick, he couldn't disagree with his logic. Rick pulled me into his trailer and flipped through a rack of dry cleaned clothes. "Here you go. I have lots of these."

He closed the door behind himself to give me privacy. His plain, tight black t-shirt fit perfectly. Luckily it smelled like fresh dry cleaning and not Rick. A vision of me growing feverish in the town square and ripping off my shirt was not appealing. I had caused enough headaches for the poor guys today.

The trailer had very little room. There were two racks of clothes along the side wall across from a lit vanity and makeup table with a black director's chair personalized with "Kingston" on its back. A mini fridge and plush two-person chair lined the back wall.

A stack of Rick's headshots sat organized on the right side of his desk with a silver pen lying on top. An expensive looking silver cell phone was placed on the left side of the desk engraved elegantly with A.E. on it. *The life of a celebrity,* I thought as I rushed through the trailer door.

"Sorry, Angel, but I can't go with you," Rick said sullenly. "The director changed our schedule, and I'm due on set in an hour."

"Oh, that's too bad." I tried to look disappointed, but relief washed over me. I had a lot to think about.

"Unless," he glanced at everyone, "you'd like to keep me company while I get ready?"

"Absolutely!" Sam squealed and dashed inside before any of us could stop her.

It was a tight squeeze with the six of us, but we managed. Sam didn't mind sitting on the vanity table so she was eye-to-eye with Rick and close enough that he brushed against her every time he turned around.

Rick explained the upcoming scene to Sam while the guys rummaged through his clothes, props, and costumes. Once Mark found the video games, the world could've ended and he wouldn't have noticed.

Before long the Barbie army's chorus of "Rick, Rick, Rick" neared the trailer.

"How do you put up with that?" Matt asked, gazing through the window at the crowd of girls.

Rick shrugged, "It's part of the job."

"It's more like a job hazard," Cynan corrected.

Rick smiled. "I'm used to it."

I pretended to be interested in their conversation, but I couldn't stop thinking about Rick. I wanted to hate him. I wanted to stay away from him, but something inexplicable about him made me crave more. Maybe it was his mysteriousness or the fact that he'd do anything for me. Or maybe I was just a fickle girl looking for love and fulfillment in all the wrong places.

If I loved Zach so much, how could I fall so easily for Rick or CJ? Was I so desperate? The one thing I knew for sure was that I missed Zach dreadfully. I missed the ease of our relationship and the innocence of first love—not to mention the lack of supernatural madness.

Nonchalantly, Rick pulled off his shirt and examined his torso in the vanity. Having a cartoon moment, Sam's eyes bugged out of her head and her tongue unraveled, rolling to the other side of the trailer.

"One of the werewolves rips off my shirt. I want to make sure I don't need any cover up." Glancing at Sam he misread her expression. "I'm sorry, Samantha. Does this bother you? I should have asked before I undressed."

Sam moved her mouth, but no words came out. Finally in a breathy whisper she managed to say, "No, it's ok."

Rick's muscular frame matched the strength of his chiseled jaw line and perfect, narrow, angular nose. I wondered how much time he had to work out everyday to maintain his amazing pecs and eight pack. He could rival Mark in a fight despite the fact that Mark towered over him by at least six inches.

I hated admitting this, but I couldn't stop staring at Rick either. His body was impressive. Adding to his bad boy persona, a red hourglass tattoo outlined in black was positioned perfectly between his massive back muscles a few inches below the base of his neck. Its crimson color starkly contrasted his pale skin. Red, orange, and yellow flames painted the length of his arms, reaching like fingers across his chest and along his back encircling the hourglass.

After what seemed like an eternity, Rick pulled on his black t-shirt, which hugged his body like a leather glove. Sam's face fell in undeniable disappointment. Rick pretended not to notice and turned around to face me. Placing his hands on my waist, heat rushed through me. My heart stuttered.

"Will I see you tomorrow?" he asked enticingly.

"I'm not sure. Sam's parents may have planned something."

Rick glanced at Sam to verify this. Thankfully, she maintained some control over herself and nodded.

"I don't know if I can go a day without seeing you, Angel. Promise you'll come," his cool green eyes begged.

Forcing myself not to fall under his spell again, with great difficulty I managed to say, "Sorry, I can't promise."

Dejected, he turned to Sam. "Samantha, please convince your stubborn friend to have some fun in town tomorrow."

Hypnotized by Rick's eyes no doubt, Sam nodded absentmindedly.

"Good, thanks," Rick said smugly. "Oh, before I forget, did you still want one of these pictures?"

Sam nodded eagerly.

He pulled a picture from his stack of 8-by-10s and sprawled silver ink over the black and white image: *To Samantha ~ You've bewitched me. ♥ Rick*

He handed the picture to Sam. "Is that ok?" he asked, worried because her face froze in a dazed grin.

"Thanks to you, we're going to have to carry her to the car," I said sardonically.

"Well since this is my fault, I can carry her," he offered sincerely.

Sam's petrified body literally tipped off the side of the table.

"I think you've caused enough damage today," I laughed.

Matt knelt over Sam and cradled her like a baby. "Can you walk?" he asked kindly.

"Uh-huh," she nodded, her eyes unfocused.

"Sure you can," Matt patronized, setting her down and protectively wrapping his arm around her waist.

"It's time to go guys," Matt suggested. "Good luck tonight, Rick," Matt said, guiding Sam down the trailer's steps.

"See you dude," Mark said civilly.

"Later," Cynan added, jumping through the trailer's door.

Before I could step outside, Rick grabbed my hand and tugged me back to him. Wrapping one arm around my waist, he pulled me into his chest. His intoxicating scent plunged me into a downward spiral of euphoria. "Even one day will be too long, Angel. I *need* to see you again," he begged in the low baritone which drove me mad.

I closed my eyes resisting the temptation to give in. "No promises, Rick." I peered through my narrowed, cautious eyes to gauge his reaction.

"Well then, until we meet again," he sighed in resignation and lifted my right hand to his lips, kissing it tenderly. Despite the soft sweetness of this chivalrous gesture, a shiver shot through my body followed by a fever, which radiated slowly through my veins.

"Till then," I said flippantly, hoping he wouldn't realize the control he had over me.

He smiled devilishly and led me through the trailer door. The Barbie army stampeded toward us. They were scarier than the vampires and werewolves who were actually hunting me. Ten body guards surrounded us until another twenty corralled the herd. Security swiftly whisked Rick to the set.

CJ was in his car when we got there, an angry scowl plastered across his otherwise angelic face.

"You wanna ride with us instead?" Matt asked apprehensively, guessing CJ's irritable mood was not going to make for a pleasant drive home.

"Nah, I'll take my chances." I knew the reason for the scowl. Me.

As I approached the passenger's side door, CJ jumped out of the car and opened it politely in silence. I climbed in and he slammed it much harder than usual. Revving the engine, he turned the music up and skidded in an instant turn from the parking spot. We missed the car in front of us by a millimeter.

His dead eyes stared straight ahead.

I had to break the silent treatment. "So, did you see anything weird today?" I asked hesitantly.

"No."

"Did you get a better sense of what might be going on in Endymion?"

He scoffed. "Depends on what you mean."

It took half a second for me to figure out that my question could be interpreted in two ways: battle or Rick.

"How Endymion fits into the battle?" I clarified.

"No."

I slouched into the soft leather seat, crossing my arms over my chest, staring straight ahead. "Are you going to talk to me again?"

Silence.

"Fine then," I paused. "Weren't you the one who told me to act convincingly with Rick?"

He burst. "I said to humor me and *say* it's because you liked him better. Say and do are two different things!"

"What?"

"Just tell me, do you really like Rick? Be honest."

"You know I don't."

"No, I don't know. From the look of things you're putty in his hands. Is that what you want?" He paused, "Is *he* who you want?" A tinge of remorse and jealousy cracked his irate expression.

"No!" I yelled emphatically.

"Then why did you let him hold you like that in the trailer or flirt with you or kiss you!"

CJ's words cut through my calm collectedness. Everything he said was true and I didn't like Rick. Or, at least, I didn't want to like Rick. I wanted CJ, but Rick was eagerly willing to dive into a relationship. Hating to admit it, I really missed love and everything that came with it.

"I don't know," I replied blankly.

"What do you mean you don't know? You either like him or you don't."

"It's not that simple. Something happens to me when I'm around him." A scary thought occurred to me. What if, subconsciously, I was using Rick to get revenge against CJ? I knew the Rick issue bothered him. I consciously never wanted to hurt him, but was this a deeper form of vindictiveness? Was I really that cruel?

Why did Rick evoke such strong and strange responses from me? Sure he was good looking, debonair, and head-over-heels for me, but was there something else? Was I really attracted to him despite his Barbie entourage and just denying my feelings? Or was I using Rick hoping CJ would change his mind?

"You like him," CJ whispered sadly.

"I don't know. I don't want to, but...maybe...there is something there. What's wrong with me? I feel like a basketball being bounced back-and-forth between the two of you."

CJ stared ahead blankly, refusing to look at me.

"I'm only human CJ. I'm not like you, whatever you are. I know what I want, but I can't have what I want. I know why my body surges with electricity every time you come near me, but I don't know why Rick's touch disarms me instantly."

Silence.

'Fine then,' my inner child was ready to scream. "How's this 'just friends' arrangement working for you?" I fumed sarcastically.

"It was easier trying to avoid you," he replied quietly.

His sincerity caught me off guard. "I'm sorry," I apologized. *I'm sorry for leading you on. I'm sorry for flirting with you. I'm sorry for making this more difficult than it needs to be...*I wish I could've said this, but I couldn't seem to get the words out without bursting into tears.

He sighed heavily, still staring blankly at the road ahead. "Don't be sorry. I'm like an addict and you're the perfect high."

26 ~ Preparing for Battle

Cenweard Endymion's grave and his family's mysteries haunted my thoughts all night. Did Cenweard harm Artemis? Did he kill his father to gain the family's wealth? Perhaps my sympathies were misdirected. Maybe it wasn't 'poor Cenweard' but 'predator Cenweard.'

Aside from the unanswered questions surrounding Cenweard, how was the Endymion family tied into this war between good and evil?

Plagued by a never-ending stream of questions, a night of restless sleep did nothing to ease my guilt in the morning. I was torn between two guys. Neither should be mine because in three weeks I'd either be dead or on a plane heading back to Massachusetts. Neither could be mine because one had obligations, the other a career and slew of girls who would kill for him.

I got ready and made my way to the kitchen. I wondered what wonderful piece of news awaited me today. Surely, it would be something which would confound me just like every new surprise.

Hanging from the precipice of reality by my fingertips, I slipped one centimeter closer into insanity with each passing day. I looked up from the kitchen table where I plopped myself to find CJ, Matt, and Cynan staring at me curiously. They knew I was nuts too. Then again, I couldn't remember entering the kitchen or sitting down so my certifiable insanity wasn't really in question. It was a fact.

Ignoring my obliviousness, Sam turned to me unleashing all of her beatific sweetness. "So, what do you want to do today?"

"Nothing," I said distastefully. *I want to curl into a ball in the darkest corner of the closet and become one with the dust bunnies.*

"I know just the thing that will get you out of this mood," Sam said enthusiastically.

I knew what was coming. "No, Sam."

Completely ignoring me, she continued, "A trip to the bookstore."

"Tempting, but no."

"Rick will get you out of this mood. You light up every time he's around."

I glanced at CJ whose expressionless face hid his thoughts. I didn't need to see them though, I could feel them. He was hurting.

I just wished she'd drop the pretense that any of this was for my benefit. "Sam, I really don't want to go anywhere."

I could have sworn that CJ smirked smugly as he stuck his head in the fridge rummaging for something.

Disappointed, she half-heartedly reminded me, "Don't forget you need to have lessons today."

"Can't that wait?"

"I promise we'll have fun," Cynan said enthusiastically with the most feeling I had ever heard from him. "*I'm* teaching you."

"What do you have planned?" I asked, suddenly not as depressed. His excitement was contagious.

"You'll have to wait and see," he said glibly, winking at me.

"When?" I was ready to get away from the memories surrounding me in the house.

"Two hours. This will give you time to get into the right frame of mind. I can't teach you if you're not going to be receptive."

I inhaled and exhaled deeply, resigning myself to

a day of learning when I really just wanted to sleep.

"I promise. You won't be disappointed," his flat brown eyes flickered with a sparkle of exhilaration just before he bounded upstairs.

I poured a glass of orange juice, wandered outside, and dropped onto the picnic table's bench. The morning sun peered through the trees playing tag with the shadows. Fluffy clouds dotted the sky looking like they were painted on the heavenly canvas. Why couldn't it rain? I needed a day to match my mood, something dark, gloomy, and utterly miserable.

When it came to love, a small part of me wanted what most girls wanted—marry the man of my dreams, have a family, and grow old together. Clearly fate's plans were a little more complex. My life, as I knew it, was erased a week ago. My life, as I hoped it would be, was about to be erased permanently in three weeks time.

Shadows danced along the silhouette of my arms. Apprehensively, I turned my right forearm to face the sun. In the sunlight the area in and immediately around the crescent moon reflected a transparent, porcelain paleness.

Working up the courage to run my left index finger along the blood-red scar, it felt cold to the touch and had the texture of sandpaper. A few seconds later the area felt enflamed. *Gross!* Not only did I have a visual reminder, but it manifested pain as well. *Damn vampires!*

Struggling with the intense physical changes and life-altering decisions from the past few days, I cradled my forehead in my hands. Mark jumped onto the seat next to me.

"Mind if I join you?"

"You don't need to sit with me. I'm having a cranky day."

"Ang, I'm not going to leave you alone while you're having a nervous breakdown."

I sighed. *He asked for it.* The verbal floodgates burst. "I'm so confused. Who should I believe? What should I believe? There's too much stress and pressure. And then as if I don't have enough to worry about, throw CJ and Rick into the mix."

"Ang, you're not alone, you know. We're all human, well, more or less, but we can still relate. Although, if you want to discuss CJ and Rick, talk to Sam. Killing bad guys—that's my area of expertise," he said proudly.

"Aren't you afraid?" I asked, alluding to the fact that certain death awaited us in the very near future.

"Nope."

"Not at all?"

"No."

"Not from dying, not from death?"

"No."

"Why not?"

"Why should I be? I'm fighting for what I know is right."

"But if you could pick another way of life, would you?"

"A life that's easier and less hazardous to my health?" he scoffed before his expression faded into concerned contemplation. "It's tempting, very tempting, but I can't abandon my responsibilities. This job isn't about me. It's about doing the right thing."

"I know what's right and wrong, but a part of me just doesn't care about the battle."

"Why?" he asked, furrowing his eyebrows.

"Screw the fight! I just want CJ. It's this weird draw to him. The only thing I know for sure is that whatever it is, it's strong enough to make me feel like part of me is missing when he's not around."

"Gag me," Mark rolled his eyes and pretended to vomit. Seeing the hurt look on my face, he rolled his eyes again and sighed in defeat. This girly conversation was definitely taking its toll on his manliness. "Maybe it's wishful thinking on your part," he offered. "You miss your boyfriend, don't you? CJ's nice and he likes you, so he may be a way for you to hold onto someone you loved and lost."

I spent the rest of the morning spinning Mark's words around and around like a washing machine until I had wrung them out so completely they didn't make sense anymore.

Unwilling to do anything but mope, my feet dragged me to Cynan's afternoon lessons. His twinkling, chestnut eyes were more alive now than this morning.

"Cynan, you're scaring me." His joyous bravado was balanced by a terrifying, warrior-like appearance. He pulled back his long black mane into a ponytail revealing the closely cropped sides of his head and a chain of skulls and cross bones tattooed around his neck.

He looked confused. "Why?"

"I've never seen you so enthusiastic about anything."

"That's because it took a great deal of planning to pull this lesson off, but you're going to *love* what I have in store for you."

Smiling broadly, he spun around and walked into the woods. He glanced back at me and taunted, "Aren't you coming?"

"Where're you going?" I worried. "Aren't we supposed to stay by the house?"

"Supposed to? Yes. Will we? No."

"But what about not going anywhere without two people?" my voice trembled anxiously.

"You're procrastinating. Let's go."

"No. You're scaring me," I insisted.

He exhaled a huge frustrated breath. "Matt and Mark are waiting for us. Come on. It's safe and beautiful," he added convincingly, extending his hand toward me in a gentlemanly gesture.

Assessing Cynan's intentions from his truly honest expression, I placed my hand in his and he led me just inside the coverage of the forest. Once we were out of sight from the house, he turned to face me and lifted my other hand in his. He closed his eyes and spoke quickly.

"Ancient lives and ancient wisdom

Take us to this ancient kingdom

History alight, there's nothing to fear

Take us now to Manorbier."

Not knowing what to expect, my hands latched onto Cynan's in a death grip. As if we were being sucked up by a giant vacuum, gravity stretched our bodies until we lurched forward into a bright white tunnel that sparkled with gold iridescence. Winding in every direction the passageway caused us to spin and spiral around each other. Ghost-like, Cynan's nearly transparent body tried to hold onto its shape but his face kept morphing farther away from its real form. Despite the painful looking distortions, he smiled playfully.

The roller coaster ride ended abruptly. We levitated in the white nothingness of the tunnel for two seconds. I looked at Cynan cautiously wondering what to expect next. He grinned knowingly just before we dropped several feet to the ground. Landing on my butt, I stared awestruck at the amazing sight before me.

Still holding onto my hands, Cynan lifted me to my feet. We stood at the edge of a tree grove, which surrounded the ruins of an immense grey stone gatehouse. A narrow passage cut through the gatehouse and was bordered on both sides by three-story-high fortress walls.

"Manorbier Castle," he stated proudly as if he was its king. "Sam and I found it when we were kids. We overheard a coven member say the spell and followed him here. Since then, this became our hideout from Morgan and Edwin," he smiled mischievously.

"Where are we?" I wondered aloud.

"Southwest Wales near the bay. It doesn't quite have the privacy that Endymion Manor's lands do, but it's beautiful. Unfortunately, the castle is a tourist attraction now."

"Aren't you worried about the people?"

"No one ventures past the main grounds. It's easy to get lost in the dense trees and shrubs."

Cynan tugged me into the woods gently. We weaved over and around crowded bramble, bushes, and moss and ivy covered tree trunks until we reached a small clearing where the sunlight barely escaped the branches overhead. Surrounded by tall trees in all shapes and sizes, thigh-high wild grass, ferns, and weeds crowded the space.

"I'm going to teach you self-defense," Cynan spoke eagerly.

"Isn't that what Sam taught me?"

"She taught you the Wiccan way. I'm teaching you the *vampire* way."

Horrified, I backed away. Is this what my instincts tried to warn me of?

He grinned at my fear. "I know a few more things about fighting physically than Sam. She relies on her instincts. I prefer hand-to-hand combat—just in case of course."

"Naturally," I quipped sarcastically. "So why did we have to come all the way out here to learn this?"

"Morgan and Edwin think it's too dangerous, but, after your experience in the cemetery, I have no doubt you need to know this. If you can't gather your energy or thoughts the way Sam taught you, you're going to have to know how to fight." Cynan hurried to a rectangular table covered in a black velvet overlay, which he pulled back to unveil an array of frightening weaponry.

A ray of sunlight glistened off of the shiny silver and bronze metals.

"How did you find these?" I asked awestruck.

"I took...borrowed...them from the coven's archives. You need them more than a dusty, old bookshelf."

About twenty gadgets lay on the table. They ranged from iron arm cuffs (in case hand cuffs weren't enough, I guessed), a face restraint mask (to prevent vampire teeth from biting you, no doubt), daggers, swords, sickles, scythes, and miscellaneous other weapons.

"Who uses these?" I ran my hands over their intricate details. Energies of triumph and failure radiated from the instruments. My hand lingered over a narrow, one and a half foot dagger. Elaborate engravings of good and evil angels decorated its isosceles blade through which a cross was carved near the handle. The sleek, pitch black wood grip had a silver knob at one end and two silver angels at the other attaching it to the blade.

"I wouldn't touch it if I were you," Cynan warned.

"Why not?"

"That is similar to a pirate plug bayonet. It's extremely sharp. You shouldn't touch it though because it doesn't belong to our side. It's a fallen angel's dagger. They leave a lot of residual energy on their belongings to ensure their weapons can't be used against them."

"Why would angels need daggers? Aren't they immortal?"

"Human attacks can't kill them, but these weapons are a different story. Aeterna Flamma needed an advantage over the Bellatori Dei so they created an arsenal to attack the others, who only had those silver daggers," he said, motioning to a similar pirate plug bayonet with a diamond encrusted silver handle. A carving of fire decorated the blade.

"Can I touch this one?" If it was from the good side, it was worth a shot.

Cynan shrugged, eyeing me carefully.

Timidly, I reached toward the handle and wrapped my fingers around it.

"Owwwwwwwwww!" A fiery, sharp jolt of energy electrocuted my hand. I dropped it instantly.

Cynan laughed so hard he clutched his sides.

"Why didn't you warn me?" I demanded angrily.

"This was more fun."

"Fu…"

"Oh, come on," he interjected before the obscenity slipped from my lips. "You wouldn't have believed me anyway and I just saved us the trouble of trying to find you later when you'd break into the coven's archives to touch it there."

My guardians knew me a little too well. Pretty soon I wouldn't be able to breathe without them knowing.

"Besides, I told you they have residual energy."

"Does it shock the angels when they hold them?"

"No, since they created them, they're immune to the feeling."

"But it's so strong."

"Yes, and so are they."

"But why electrical current? That felt like lightning."

"Remember Sam's lesson about energy?"

"Yeah."

"That electric shock is the angel's energy. They are like light: quick and very powerful, like electricity."

I thought about the equipment in front of me. "If the angels are immortal, then how can they be killed at all?"

"Technically, we're all immortal. Life here is temporary, but when we die our souls move on. The angels live infinitely as well. Unfortunately, when they came to earth their divinity merged with human forms and they became susceptible to death, even if it can only come at the hands of another divine being."

"Fascinating…" My eyes shifted to a strange hand-held instrument with crescent-shaped blades extending from either side of the grip. "What's this?"

Cynan shuddered; his face darkened. "They're double-bladed sickles that can be held in your fist. Those belong to the undead."

"Vampires?"

He nodded solemnly. "It takes a lot to kill them because they move so fast. Our bodies hold us back, while theirs don't because they're dead already. It's like trying to catch a ghost."

"But why do they need weapons? Aren't their teeth enough?"

"Well, sharp teeth are fine if you're attacking a human. They also work if the vampires are trying to stun another vampire, but to kill a vampire, they need these. The blades' edges are encrusted with diamonds—earth's purest and hardest stone and the only thing that's powerful enough to do serious harm to them."

"How does it work?"

"A vampire incapacitates another one, usually by several deep bites that make the victim look like he survived a shark attack. While the victim is stunned, the vampire chops off its head with the sickle."

"Isn't that overkill? Incapacitation by decapitation?"

He grinned. "No. Remember the undead can heal themselves. Only one thing can kill them. Their remains need to be disposed of properly by Wiccans," his eyes flashed animatedly. "We set fire to the bodies, which are usually still moving, and then we gather the ashes and scatter them in the ocean."

I should've been disgusted by his enthusiastic, text-book explanation, but was too caught up in the moment. "Why dump 'em in the ocean? As a precaution in case they come back miraculously from ash?" I said sarcastically.

"Unfortunately, their bodies can come back from the fire if one of their kind collects all of the pieces. Our way ensures that they're dead, but it's more like a cleansing ritual. They're unnatural and this rite connects them with nature again in death. All people and animals are born of Mother Nature. The fire burns them to ash returning them to the dust of the earth. The ashes are then scattered in the wind and purified by the water of the sea."

"The elements?"

"The best form of purification, don't you think? It's our way. We don't want to harm anyone, but if we have to in self-defense, the least we can do is cleanse them as they leave this life."

"What happens if you're not around to perform the ritual?"

"The vampires who vanquish their victims claim them as prisoners of war. They take them back to their headquarters and try to convert them to their respective sides. We try our best to collect as many as possible to minimize the vampire legions. Good or bad, vampires are not natural and shouldn't exist."

I nodded. While the idea that the undead armies followed battle protocol was disturbing, it seemed like an acceptable alternative to destroying the enemies.

"What are all of these?" I asked, staring at the tools of torture.

"Most of these are generic weapons used by both sides. That's a war spear; double edge battaxe; screamer axe; the coustille, hoplite, and gladiator swords; cumberjung; African throwing knives; and Indian bich-hwa," he said pointing to each item. "Many of the human guardians use more inventive weapons which have been passed down from their ancestors. The point is really to disarm a vampire or werewolf long enough to burn them."

"What's this?" I asked, pointing to a long wooden branch with two large pointed crystals embedded into its pronged ends.

"That's ours," he said proudly.

"A wand?" I asked curiously. "It looks so weak compared to the others."

"Perhaps, but it's the only one that can project energy. The rest of them are used in hand-to-hand combat."

"May I touch it?"

He nodded. Curiosity danced in the gleam of his eyes.

I ran my hand over the top of it expecting to feel energy but nothing happened. Lightly grasping the foot long branch, I picked it up gently staring at the perfect crystals.

"How does it work?"

"Glad you asked. Are you ready to begin?"

I nodded eagerly and placed the wand on the table.

"First, prepare yourself the way Sam taught you. Focus on the elements around you and find peace."

Dragging my fingertips over the top of the feathery ferns, I paced back about ten strides, just enough to feel like I was part of nature without any distractions. I breathed deeply filling my lungs with the fresh forest air and absorbed the sun's rays which danced through the tree canopy. I felt peaceful, but I didn't know about finding my energy. I still felt like me—simple, too human me.

"What am I supposed to feel, Cynan?"

"There's no way to describe it. You just need to try. Are you ready for a little game," his voice sounded oddly menacing.

Fear clouded my thoughts. What was about to happen? Cynan didn't look like the sweet big brother I was used to seeing. His otherwise soft round face tightened and his chestnut brown eyes turned black like a great white shark hunting its prey.

My heart pounded so hard I thought it would jump out and run away. Cynan grimaced, glaring at me like I was a seal he was about to devour.

"Mark, Matt," he beckoned with his finger not moving his gaze from mine.

My jocks wandered into the clearing next to each other completely unaware of what was about to happen. Catching Cynan's locked gaze on me, they stopped dead in their tracks trying to make sense of the situation. I couldn't break my stare with Cynan worrying he'd do something the minute I lost my concentration.

Slowly, deliberately, Cynan raised his wand holding the red crystal side and pointing the clear quartz end at Mark. I gasped, guessing his intention. The gasp broke my focus and Cynan shot Mark with a thin, white light that zoomed like a faint dot from the end of his wand.

Still facing me, Cynan didn't even notice that Mark's eyes rolled to the back of his head as he froze in place and fell backwards, straight as a plank.

Was Cynan one of the others? Did he call us out here to finish us off? Why did I come? I should have listened to my gut feelings.

My body swayed side-to-side trying to anticipate his next move. Cynan raised his arm toward Matt.

I shook my head, but words escaped me.

Terrified, Matt blurted, "Dude, this isn't what we talked about. What are you..."

A jolt of electricity cut off his words as his knees buckled and he fell forward into the shrubs.

"CYNAN!" I screamed.

Cynan smiled—a slow, curling, evil grin that matched the black death in his eyes. Walking over to the table, he paced back-and-forth before the tools of torture.

I debated my move. I couldn't run; I'd just get lost in the woods and he'd find me anyway. I couldn't just stand here; he'd kill me quicker than Mark and Matt. I glanced sorrowfully at my guardians' lifeless bodies.

I leaned over my knees breathing deeply to avoid passing out or throwing up. The sun peeked through the clouds and touched my back warming the frozen horror gripping me.

A weird sensation of terror and anger mixed with peace inside my chest. It jerked me upright. I glared at Cynan who was debating whether he should use an African throwing knife or black handled pirate plug bayonet next.

I only had one fighting chance at this and I wanted to win or, in the very least, survive. How could I turn the emotions raging within into an energy which protected me?

I glanced around. The green leaves overhead swayed lightly in the delicate breeze.

Stretching my palms toward the shrubs, I imagined my energy radiating to them and theirs into me. I couldn't feel anything, but I kept thinking that it was there regardless. Maybe I just needed to believe in it. Maybe I just needed to believe in me.

Cynan pulled two tan leather gloves onto his right hand and a black rubber one on top of them. He picked up the black-handled dagger and wound his arm as if he was going to launch a fast ball at my head.

My hands outstretched, I cringed and waited for the assault.

Suddenly, Cynan was distracted. His eyes darted to the side before focusing on me again. He paused a moment, the dagger's blade held in a launching position over his head. A malicious grin spread across his face.

Allowing myself a miniscule glimpse in the direction of Cynan's gaze, I watched in panic as CJ walked unknowingly into the clearing. Cynan's smile broadened malevolently. His arm twitched and I knew the dagger would be in me in a second.

He brandished the shiny metal—the sun gleaming off of its evil carvings. His arm lurched forward, but his body changed direction. The dagger hurtled straight toward CJ.

"Nooooooo!" I shrieked, throwing my hands in front of me reaching uselessly toward CJ, who was fifty feet away.

My mind recorded the events in slow motion as the dagger maintained a straight course right through CJ's heart.

27 ~ Reality

My world ended.

Hyperventilating, I collapsed to the forest floor fighting to find a reason to stay alive.

Lying in the dense, dark green ferns and tall grass, the cold dirt floor cooled the angry and scared adrenaline pulsing through me. This couldn't be happening.

I rolled to the side. My body began convulsing as it had in the cemetery.

"CJ," I whispered through silent, breathless sobs. "CJ…"

"Damn it, CJ, why did you interfere?" Cynan's bellow pierced the desperate numbness swallowing me.

"What do you mean 'interfere'? I thought you were finished."

Paralyzed on the ground, confusion clouded my thoughts. Could that be CJ's voice? Didn't he die? But I saw the knife reach his chest.

"You broke our concentration," normal Cynan's voice complained.

"Bull shit. You nearly killed me."

"You wouldn't have gotten hurt. You didn't let the blade touch you anyway."

"I wasn't prepared, Cynan. Thanks for stopping it."

"I thought you did that."

"It wasn't me."

"Angel?" the voices asked in unison.

Suddenly, their tones turned frantic. "Angel? Angel! Where are you?"

Was their conversation part of a hazy hallucination? My mouth moved, but my voice was frozen in shock. My body still trembled from the look of Cynan's dead black eyes and CJ's lifeless body being absorbed into the earth because I was too weak—too human—to help him.

"Cynan, if you scared her to death, I'm going to kill you," CJ's tense voice threatened. I never heard CJ's voice quaver with such urgency and viciousness.

I couldn't make a sound. My body lay limply on a bed of ferns hidden by the tall grass.

CJ scooped me up and hugged me tightly in his arms.

"Angel," he whispered ecstatically relieved, pushing his cheek against my forehead. "You're ok!"

My catatonic state briefly released me so I could utter, "Matt? Mark?"

"Cynan's taking care of them right now."

My body flopped against CJ's chest as he sat down in the ferns, cradling me in his arms. I closed my eyes, allowing him to caress my face, my hair, my back. His arms were heaven in my personal hell on earth.

"Cynan wasn't going to hurt you," he assured.

"Not me," I whispered. "You."

"What?"

"He killed you."

"What?"

"The dagger flew into your heart."

"It didn't though. I'm here aren't I?"

I nodded weakly unconvinced that the vision before me was real.

"Angel, I'm here. You're here. Mark and Matt...well, they'll be all right in a few minutes. We're fine," he said simply, stroking my arm.

I shook my head, feeling like I just went to a funeral and the corpse popped up yelling, 'Surprise!'

"Hold me," I begged. Every time he loosened his grip, my body shuddered. His body heat radiated a peaceful energy through me while I rested my head against his neck.

"You didn't really think Cynan would hurt you, did you?"

I nodded, feeling stupid immediately for thinking my friends would've put me in mortal danger. Slowly tilting my head backwards, I gazed into CJ's eyes. The fear of losing him was more than I could bear.

He glanced at me curiously trying to read my expression.

I hated just being friends. I wanted so much more. I wanted to feel him emotionally, spiritually, intellectually, and physically. I nestled my face into the crook of his neck again, hugging him tightly, letting his energy calm my nerves. I never wanted to let him go again. They'd have to surgically remove me.

"Do you think you can walk?"

I still couldn't feel my limbs, so I shook my head.

As if I weighed no more than a feather, CJ jumped up and carried me back to the others. He leaned against a massive oak tree, holding me to his sculpted torso.

"Dude, if you ever do that again, we'll kill you!" Mark fumed at Cynan.

"That was uncool, Cynan, seriously uncool," Matt added irritated.

"You agreed to help," Cynan reminded them gently, while mixing a pitcher of steaming purple goo.

"Yeah, but you didn't tell us you'd be in full attack mode. Man, you're scary!" Mark shouted, his voice breaking and sounding off.

"Drink that. You'll feel better in about an hour." Cynan handed each of them a glass of bubbling slime.

CJ set me down beside a huge rock. Leaning my back against it, the sun's game of peek-a-boo overhead mesmerized me. Rays of light sparkled through the swaying treetops illuminating tiny butterflies and other insects dancing on the breeze.

With one arm still wrapped around my waist, CJ said, "I wish there was another way to teach you."

"Me too," I scoffed. "Cynan scared me."

Cynan's booming laughter bounced off the ancient trees around us. CJ's killer glare silenced him immediately, but, undeterred, he walked over to us. "You did very well."

"How? I was so afraid I couldn't even move," I muttered, still furious with myself for nearly letting my friends die.

"You stopped the dagger from hitting CJ." His matter-of-fact tone was tainted with enthusiasm.

"What?" I asked confused. "How?"

"We don't know," he continued, "but CJ didn't stop it and neither did I. Considering that Mark and Matt were down and there was no one else around, it had to be you."

"But I didn't *do* anything."

"When CJ walked into the clearing, what were you thinking?"

"I didn't want you to hurt him," I blushed, knowing that the full truth would embarrass all of us. If I could've thrown myself in front of the dagger, I would have died for CJ.

Cynan turned to CJ, barely able to contain himself. "Do you know what this means?"

CJ nodded proudly and smiled at me. His eyes laughed with joy.

"You mind explaining it?" I asked, frustrated by their silent interchange and my cluelessness.

"You projected energy. That usually takes years of practice, Angel. Well done!"

"But I don't know how I did it. How will I be able to do it again?"

"You must've gathered enough energy to combine with your anger. The stimulus—me—triggered the reaction and you threw everything you had at CJ."

"Oh..." They could've been speaking Greek, because I didn't understand it at all.

"We're just amazed you were able to do it at all," Cynan said surprised.

Mark and Matt walked over to us. Mark glared at me while Matt looked slightly dazed and confused.

"You know, Ang, I don't know how to feel about you right now," Mark said in a pained tone.

My forehead creased in concern and my lips slowly melted into a frown. "Why?"

"I thought you liked me at least a little bit. Matt and I have only saved your ass a bunch of times but, apparently, we don't compare to your affection—or affliction—for CJ."

"If I would've known what to do, I would've saved you too," I paused. "Well, maybe not you, but Matt definitely."

Matt grinned triumphantly while Mark skulked wordlessly to the weapons' table.

I took a deep breath and tried to digest what Cynan said about projecting my energy. "Do you really think that's possible, Cynan?"

"No one else intervened. Fortunately for CJ, your reaction saved him from a lot of pain." Cynan smiled victoriously, "I can't wait to tell Sam I'm a better teacher than her!" He jumped up and rushed over to the table where Mark began play fighting with the black daggers. The shocks visibly electrocuting his arms did nothing to dissuade him.

"Are you ready to go back now?" CJ asked softly.

"More lessons with Cynan?" My eyes grew wide with fear. My psyche already struggled with the fact that I nearly allowed my friends to die. I couldn't endure another lesson. What was Cynan going to do next? Strap Sam to a table and try to decapitate her hoping I could save her in time?

The right corner of CJ's lip edged upwards into an amused smirk. "Have you had enough for today?"

"I think so. Being responsible for the near deaths of three of my friends is a huge lesson."

We sat in silence for a minute staring into each other's eyes—our unspoken thoughts shifting obviously to our more personal issues. We both knew what the other was thinking, but we couldn't break our friendship pact. Life was hard enough.

I wished I could muster enough courage to tell CJ that I loved him—loved him so much that I would sacrifice my life for him. I was completely aware my feelings were ludicrous considering I'd known him a little over a week.

In one of our previous encounters, he mentioned that my involvement in this battle was expected, that people on both sides had been waiting for me. Perhaps that's why he felt so strongly for me.

"CJ?" I asked, watching his undulating oceans carefully for a reaction. "Um, I was wondering. How long have you been keeping an eye on me?"

His eyes narrowed the tiniest bit. "I can always see you, Angel." Embarrassed, he shifted his gaze toward the guys, "Even when you can't see me."

"That's...um, pretty creepy," I hesitated. His answer should've bothered me, but it flattered me instead. I bit my lower lip before working up enough courage to continue. "Actually I mean, everyone here says that they knew I was coming for a while. My birth was foretold or something. You mentioned that you, Mark, and Matt were on the plane escorting me here. So, how long before the plane ride from Boston did you actually know me?"

He shifted his heavy stare to the rustling leaves above us. Breathing deeply, his chest and shoulders expanded as if the weight of the universe was pushing down on him. "Forever," he mumbled.

"As in, 'forever' since I was born in Salem eighteen years ago or more like the super freaky 'forever' as in the beginning of time?"

His eyes snapped back piercing my soul. I felt naked like he could see into every inch of my mind, every thought I'd ever had, and every thought I had yet to dream.

"Forever, Angel. Forever," he spoke intently, his face solemn. His eyes confirmed everything I suspected or, at least, everything I wanted. I knew him the same way he knew me. Although, I wasn't clear on the details, but the feelings were the same.

I opened my mouth to say something. His angelic, god-like face was filled with hope waiting for me to speak.

Are you my soul mate, I wanted to ask. Somehow I knew he was, and would be more a part of my future than anyone else. The sentiment was totally irrational since I barely knew him. Saying this to him now would only increase the tension between us, as if we needed any more of that.

Without looking at him, I stepped toward the guys. He caught my hand forcing me to stop.

"What were you going to say?" he asked, his face filled with even more hope now than five seconds ago.

I should've just kept my big mouth shut. "Nothing, let's go." I couldn't say it. I wanted to, but I had to force myself to stop. I wondered what would hurt more: an angel's dagger piercing my heart or not having CJ in my life in less than three weeks. And this was about more than just hurting me. I had to stop hurting CJ.

He wouldn't release my hand from his grip. "Please, tell me," he begged. "Please…"

"For the sake of our friendship, it's best that I not say anything." From the disappointed look on his face he would rather have faced a thousand daggers than me at the moment.

Solemnly and hesitantly, he released my hand and I walked back to the others alone.

Cynan was demonstrating the cumberjung for Mark and Matt. His hands moved so quickly that we could barely see the flail with two spiked balls slicing through the air.

"Can we have a turn now?" Mark whined.

"Sure, but I'm not fixing you if you gouge holes in each other," Cynan warned with a chuckle.

Mark swiped a gladiator sword and cumberjung with razor blades around its spheres, which hung from chains at each end. He tossed a hoplite sword and a double bladed sickle to Matt. I winced not wanting to see if Matt caught the blades or handles. Of course, I should've known better. In an instant, he assumed an attack position and waited for Mark to lunge at him.

Swinging the cumberjung around himself, Mark's barbaric stance stood in terrifying contrast to Matt's calm air. On his last swing, Mark jumped toward Matt—the balls' blades speeding toward Matt's head.

Blindingly fast, Matt blocked the chains with the sickle's blade, yanking the flail from Mark's grip as he plunged the sword at his chest. Mark lurched to the side avoiding the stab by a few centimeters.

Kicking both feet off of the ground, Mark back flipped through the air landing beside the weapons' table. Grabbing a Bellatori dagger, he bounded toward Matt brandishing the gladiator sword in his other hand. Lunging, turning, weaving, ducking, their massive strength and speed could not be denied.

A cold breeze hit my neck shooting a lightning bolt of shivers through my frame. Impulsively, I spun around. Rustling leaves and a bright flash of color darted through the trees. The faint sound of voices echoed from deep within the dark forest.

"Guys, shhhh," I commanded.

Before I talked myself out of it, my feet ran after the sound, trailing after the white and shiny object.

As the voices got louder, I hid behind a large tree and peered around its frame.

Amidst the trees and relatively well hidden by the dense foliage, two figures faced off against each other. One was covered in a dark brown cloak; his face obscured by a hood. The other looked like a wild man wearing a long cloak of white pelts which matched his shoulder length white hair. His feet were covered in makeshift leather shoes extending up to his knees secured by red leather straps which wrapped from his ankles up his calves.

"Who sent thou?" the white-haired mad man asked.

"The High One, Excellency," the dark figure hissed, bowing deeply.

"Whilst thou provide protection?" the white-haired man continued.

The dark figure nodded once slowly. "First, the key," he commanded threateningly.

The white figure glanced at their surroundings, clearly suspicious of the other man. The dark figure waited.

"The one who flieth across the sky
And sleepeth beneath the moon
In her lieth the beginning and end

Tis our salvation to be won soon."

The dark figure nodded once deeply in approval. "The plans?"

The white figure stepped toward the dark one hesitantly. He whispered, "'Neath the altar in the Church of St. James, thou will find a passageway. Follow the ascending path but beware the enchantments cast upon it by the ancient ones. Enter only through the door of the three moons. Within she awaits."

The dark figure bowed slowly, stepping backwards.

"Payment, sir!" the white one demanded, drawing his sword.

Blindingly fast, the dark one pounced on the white one, biting into his neck so strongly that a gush of blood squirted around them painting the white pelt coat in a red river. I froze, completely unable to help the victim or run away.

Paralyzed in terror, the white one's eyes remained transfixed until his face drained of all color and one-by-one his eyes rolled to the back of his head.

"Huh!" I gasped horrified.

Dropping his victim and raising his hood to cover his head, the dark one turned to face me. Completely obscured by his outfit, only one thing was certain—his crimson eyes caught me.

Tilting his face toward the tree canopy, he howled at the sun in a strange deep, guttural voice, "Artemis!" He raced like a bullet straight at me. His red eyes locked on mine. Too petrified to move, my mind blanked.

Only a few yards from my frozen body, he vanished into thin air. A gust of wind swooshed through me knocking me to the ground.

I opened my eyes to find four bewildered sets staring at me. CJ and Mark extended their hands hoisting me to my feet.

"What was that?" I asked in utter disbelief.

"What was what, Ang?" Mark asked, looking at me like I had ten heads.

"That," I pointed over my shoulder. "The vampire who just rushed past here."

"What vampire?" Cynan asked. His eyes narrowed in concern.

"You didn't see the thing that knocked me down?"

Four heads shook in dissent.

"Follow me," I barked in aggravation. I made my way into the clearing to show them the evidence. The body was gone and there was no blood anywhere.

"But it was here just a minute ago. How could a dead body vanish in the middle of nowhere?" I asked of no one in particular.

"What did you see?" Matt worried.

"A vampire attacked a guy."

Four sets of eyes stared at me in open disbelief.

"I think you've had enough excitement for one day," CJ surmised, his eyes wide with concern until he exchanged a miniscule yet unmistakably omniscient glance with Cynan.

"What?" I barked. I hated being left in the dark when the unspoken conversation was about me.

Cynan sighed, debating whether or not to tell me. CJ looked at me darkly, his thoughts fighting over what he thought was best for me, no doubt. He exhaled in frustration at whatever played out in his head and nodded to Cynan.

Procrastinating, Cynan scratched his forehead while he figured out the best way to break the news. He grabbed my hand, dragged me into the center of the clearing, and turned me to face north before stepping a good ten feet away from me.

"Close your eyes. What do you feel and see?" he asked.

Highly speculative of this stupid exercise and still irritated that they didn't believe me, I forced my eyes shut indignantly.

"Breathe deeply," Cynan ordered. "Focus!"

"Shut up," I muttered under my breath, which began to slow automatically. As I slipped into a self-imposed meditative state, the temperature dropped significantly. The hair on my arms, head, and neck stood on end and my body shivered from the cold wind that suddenly began whirling around me.

"F...F...Freezing..." my teeth chattered. Scared, I opened one eye to find a blurry, spinning ring of black cloaked ghosts with red eyes closing in on me.

Cynan stepped through the figments of my overactive imagination. "What did you see?" he asked cautiously.

"Vampires," I whispered, trying to catch my breath as the temperature crept up to a balmy warmth. "Lots of 'em. Coming closer to me."

"How close?" Matt asked.

"Within an arm's length," I replied, wondering what this meant.

"That's what I thought," Cynan said simply, looking to CJ for assistance.

CJ stepped toward me cautiously. My nose and forehead creased in confusion.

CJ explained. "They're physically getting closer to finding you, Angel."

"I don't get it. Did I or didn't I see these vampires just now? Are they in my head or were they really here? If they're in my head, how did they get in there? Can't I block them out?" I screeched, terrified that my enemies would find another, easier way of getting to me. Everyone knew my mind wasn't fully functional.

"Where's your gypsy costume, Ang," Mark smirked. "You're psychic!"

"Come on. How was that psychic?" I shouted.

"You're connecting with them too," Matt said, "otherwise you wouldn't be able to see any of these things."

"How can we get her to flip it so that we're spying on them instead of the other way around?" Cynan wondered aloud.

"Too dangerous," CJ replied calmly. "She needs to figure out how to block them defensively before learning to hunt them."

"How?" I prodded, anxious that vampires were probably spying on us right now.

"Don't think about them," CJ said.

"That's it?" I doubted.

My four protectors nodded. How was I supposed to stop thinking about the things that scared me most?

"One thing is certain," Cynan began determinedly. "It's time to accelerate your training."

Great! I thought sarcastically.

Vampires were on the loose, in my head, and hell bent on capturing me. How I was supposed to build my strength and knowledge about them without thinking of them in case I let them in through my weakest link—my over-abused, over-emotional brain?

Filled with conflicting feelings of fear, depression, and anxiety, I stared emptily and hopelessly at CJ's back as we snaked through the dense bramble and forest flora.

Above all, the endless yearning for the friend and man I wanted to make mine throbbed sickeningly in my dead heart. Life was a waking nightmare. It couldn't possibly get any worse.

28 ~ Resolve

The visions from Manorbier preyed on my thoughts into Saturday. My basic conclusion—the only one that made me feel comfortable any way, the others were too scary—was that the first was an event from long ago. The men's language and clothes told me that much. The only part that didn't fit was that the vampire seemed to sense me in his time. Maybe I traveled back in time. Maybe the whole thing was sheer coincidence. The only thing of which I was absolutely certain was that the men were involved in Artemis' mystery somehow.

The second vision horrified me. What did the vampires want from me? No doubt they already knew where to find me. Why were they biding their time? Waiting was driving me crazy.

In a poor attempt to distract my thoughts, I emailed my mom. Although she had been more of a child than mother to me over the past year, she was still my mom and I loved her. We were always very close. She still embarrassed me and did mom things, but I accepted that because she was impossible not to like. When my friends would visit, they'd spend more time with her than me.

She missed me now partly because I wasn't there to watch my siblings and partly because she had to resume her role as mom. My trip was really opportune. She needed to be kicked back into the driver's seat. My siblings needed her and so did I.

From the time I was a little girl—no more than three or four—I sped through life so fast I often found it difficult to stop and appreciate the people and things around me. I was a kid on a serious mission—to grow up as soon as possible. Childhood was just a pothole in the road of life.

My parents always told me to slow down. "You're only a kid once," my mom used to say. I found it mildly amusing that since my dad died, I was forced to become 'mom' overnight as my mother struggled to cope with his loss.

When she finally emerged from her self-imposed confinement, she rivaled the zombies from "Night of the Living Dead." I guess that's why my added responsibilities didn't bother me. She needed my help and, while I was grieving for my dad too, I had to take care of the family since she couldn't.

I worried that if I heard her voice and spoke with her now, I'd feel so guilty that I'd jump on the next plane home. I missed my family— their familiar faces, jokes, and everyday activities. I tried not to think of what their lives would be like without me. My mom would surely be devastated and my sixteen-year-old brother would be forced to take care of our two younger siblings. I couldn't allow that to happen.

I knew I had to fight here. More than that though, I knew we had to win. Our side had to win for my family, for my friends, for everyone who deserved a chance at life. If we could do something to keep life as pure and peaceful as possible, then I would do my best to make it happen, even if I didn't quite know what I needed to do.

My thoughts drifted back to CJ. Knowing someone for a matter of days just wasn't enough time to determine whether or not we were destined for each other. Though I always thought Zach was my soul mate, my feelings for CJ were much stronger, much clearer.

No matter how I felt about him however, CJ was going to vanish in a few weeks never to be seen or heard from again. If I survived the battle, what would I do without him? If I grew more attached to him, the pain of our separation would certainly be too much to take.

I couldn't go through another Zach-like mourning period. Losing Zach was hard enough. I had to protect myself now. I'd surely die if I allowed myself to fall madly in love with CJ and then, POOF, he was gone one day.

Despite the CJ situation, my mind was making peace with the other issues revolving around me. This event was going to happen with or without me. With me, my side stood a winning chance; without me, they were on equal footing with the others.

It was time to accept the responsibilities given to me even though they didn't feel like mine. It seemed more like I won the jackpot in the lottery from hell.

Regardless, the job was in my hands now and I wanted to do my best. Failure was not an option even if the situation terrified me. I hoped that my secret, coveted power would reveal itself too, if I had one at all. I'd be more confident going into battle if I knew how to use a weapon so powerful that both sides wanted me.

I kept replaying the last line of my mom's email in my head:

Keep safe, Angel. Lots of hugs and kisses ~ Mom

Her words were both a comfort and a warning.

29 ~ The Good Guys

Feeling refreshed from my introspective Saturday, Sunday began early. Though I was still scared of the evil chasing me, I found my purpose for the next two and a half weeks. I had to devote myself to the task at hand. Content in my resolve, I nearly skipped downstairs.

This new outlook forced me to put my feelings for CJ on the back burner. My wants were secondary to my job. So many people counted on me. I couldn't let my petty, selfish desires get the best of me. Unfortunately, this split-second thought of him stabbed my heart painfully.

Edwin excused himself from breakfast. Other than his brief appearances at mealtimes, we barely saw him anymore. It was hard to imagine he had a regular day job in addition to his full-time duties for the coven. The stress weighing on his mind seeped through his tough exterior every time we saw him.

CJ never emerged to join us. The idea of his emotional pain tormented me, but I was too chicken to do anything about it. I caused enough problems already. The slightly more disturbing dilemma involving CJ was how I saved him accidentally. Cynan's practice haunted my now waking nightmares.

After breakfast, I insisted on cleaning the bathrooms and washing the laundry. It was time to be a contributing member of society again. Plus chores kept me grounded in reality. Unfortunately, Morgan insisted on lessons first.

The fresh, dew-kissed morning breeze caressed my face. A light wind blew the low-hanging, foggy mist overhead making the temperature feel significantly colder than yesterday. The trees' usual bright yellow-greenness appeared more like a dark, black forest green hue today.

Matt sat across from me at the picnic table while we waited for Sam. His drooping eyes were still half asleep although the frigid air seemed to be a fairly good alarm clock. A gust of wind slapped his face and twirled his reddish-blonde, spiky, unkempt hair.

"What's bugging you?" he yawned, seeing straight through my mask of determination.

How could I keep secrets from anyone in this house when they knew me better than I knew myself? "I still can't figure out how I saved CJ. I'm afraid to ask Cynan to recreate the scene in case any of you would get hurt."

"Stop worrying about us. We'll gladly play again," he smirked. "Besides, we'd like to even up the score with Cynan."

"If you can convince him to play fair this time, I'm game. Just leave CJ out of it."

"Why?" Matt asked—his big, brown, honest eyes filled with concern.

"Cynan nearly killed him to get a response from me. I couldn't live with myself if something happened to him or any of you." The words caught in my throat as my thoughts replayed the scene of the dagger diving straight for CJ's heart.

"We can just have Cynan practice killing Mark instead," Matt suggested with a wink.

His silly expression and tempting idea made me burst with laughter. "Matt, you're the best big brother anyone could ever have. Your sister is very lucky."

"Yes, she is," he said proudly.

We practiced energy expansion most of the morning. I tried to familiarize myself with my own energy field and then worked with Sam and Matt individually to feel their energy radiate against mine.

The heat of the pulsating energy between us was undeniable. It felt like ocean waves washing through me.

By the end of practice, we were able to extend our palms about five feet away from each other. Our collective power raced through our arms as we stood in a triangle formation.

Completely awestruck at this accomplishment, I didn't realize Sam broke the chain to tackle Matt. I tried to pry her claws out of his hair, but she pushed me away with a small burst of negative energy, never having touched me with her actual hand.

"He had this coming, Angel," she blurted without pausing her attack.

Looking like he was in pain, Matt laughed and feebly lifted his arms to defend himself against her blows. His kind, brown eyes playfully turned black in concentration. He flipped Sam and pinned her in the grass.

From somewhere in the house, Mark hollered, "Get a room, dude!"

Sam struggled futilely to free herself. Strewn wildly across the grass, her black hair encircled her cherubic face in a dark halo.

Highly amused, Matt laughed. "I think you need practice, Sam. You're a little rusty."

Her frustration melted into a wicked smirk. She wiggled free and punched both of her palms into his chest knocking him clear on his back. His stupefied eyes tried to focus.

Sam's expression softened while she extended her tiny hand to help him to his feet. "You were saying?"

"Clearly I underestimated you. Please forgive me," he begged sarcastically. "But," he continued, grinning ear-to-ear. If only he knew what was good for him, he'd keep his mouth shut. I winced at the provocation that was coming. "I think this shows just how much of a bitchy witchy you really are."

This was not going to end well.

Sam spun around glaring at him, her full black eyes seething with anger. She threw her arms toward him and knocked him a dozen feet through the air before he crashed into the picnic table.

Ignoring their playful interchange, I turned to Sam. "That's what I want to learn. How did you do that?"

Paying no attention to Matt's moaning amidst the table's splintered remnants, she replied, "It's the same principle we practiced just now. Your strongest emotions—anger and love—help project your energy. Feel the energy around you and use it to your advantage."

"Can we practice that?"

"Tomorrow," she glanced up at CJ as he approached quietly with a picnic basket. He eyed Matt suspiciously as he lay motionless in the wooden mess.

"I guess it's CJ's turn to teach. Do you want me to stay?" she whispered.

"No, we'll be fine. I'll see you afterwards." *If I'm not a blubbering mess or we haven't killed each other...*

"All right." She turned to Matt, "Come on you big baby. Let's go inside."

He groaned and she rolled her eyes. "Considering a 'bitchy witchy' just kicked your arse, I think you're the one in need of more practice."

Mark's laughter reverberated from the house and echoed through the forest. Matt's grunt satisfied Sam. Pleased, she yanked him up by the hand and dragged him inside.

"Hi," I managed to say as calmly as humanly possible to CJ, considering my heart wanted to explode through my chest.

"Morgan thought you might be hungry, so she made lunch," he said, offering the basket to me and successfully avoiding my gaze.

I looked at the broken picnic table. "Well, I guess a picnic in the backyard is out of the question." The basket dangled awkwardly from my fingertips.

With the uncomfortable tension mounting between us, I didn't know what to say. I feared anything I said would be misconstrued or might hurt him even more.

"We could sit by the brook," he suggested ruefully. "If you want to, that is."

The pain in his voice twisted in my heart. I hated how the flame, which burned brightly within us, had been squashed thanks to me. *It's for the best,* I kept trying to convince myself. Unfortunately, my heart didn't agree.

We walked along the path in complete silence. He followed my lead keeping a safe ten feet between us until we made it to the clearing.

I sat on a huge rock and opened the basket.

"Wow, are you sure Morgan didn't intend for all of us to eat?" An assortment of sandwiches, vegetables, cookies, and drinks nearly burst through the basket's seams.

"Do you want to join me?" I patted the boulder where there was easily enough room for three other people.

"No thanks," he muttered, leaning against one of the trees.

My stomach's hungry grumbling stopped instantly. I pushed the basket away and glared at him. How could we get passed this? The strain seemed insurmountable and it burned through my chest and stomach like acid.

The pain on his face was too much to bear. Tears welled in my eyes. I was caught in a losing battle with CJ. I'd hurt him whether or not I was with him.

His silence was more painful than if he would've yelled at me. I couldn't take it anymore. Hopping from my seat, I sprinted along the stream. I didn't know where I was going, but I was sure Mark and Matt would catch up with me when they realized I wasn't with CJ.

I didn't get very far before CJ appeared out of thin air in front of me.

"Get out of my way," I growled.

"You know I can't." He was very careful not to touch me. *Why? Touch me! Be with me!*

"I can't take this back-and-forth thing between us!" I screamed. "Either leave me alone completely or be with me. Your cold shoulder is driving me crazy!"

His eyes flickered between passion and confusion, but he remained mute, unsure of how to answer.

"Why don't you just leave and let someone else do your job. This way we won't have to see each other ever again."

His face contorted in anger—the anger I saw in his livid eyes the night the vampires and werewolves attacked us. "Is that what you want? To leave you alone forever?"

Angry tears blinded me, blocking the fuming CJ from my line of vision. "What I want forever is *you*. I'll even settle for the couple weeks we have left if it means I can have the CJ who has been in my every thought since I woke up next to you on the plane. But since we can't be together, the best thing is for *you* to go away!" I shouted, streams rushing down my cheeks.

Hysteria gripped me at the thought of never seeing CJ again. My body convulsed with the pain of love lost or, in our case, never found. The thought of life without CJ unfurled an endless agony churning deep inside me.

He reached for my hand, but I spun around and leapt onto the stepping stones protruding from the stream. I didn't exactly know where I was going. All I knew was that I had to get away from CJ, from the pain.

I made it halfway across the stream, which was about twenty-feet wide, when my damn ballet slipper slipped on the slick stone. Losing my balance, I plunged into the babbling brook. Thankfully, it was deeper than it looked; my whole body disappeared beneath the bubbling waves.

In half a second, CJ's arm wrapped around my waist and pulled me from the icy spring water. He held me close to his body so my feet couldn't reach the rocky floor.

I couldn't look in his eyes. Humiliation burned my cheeks.

"Put me down!" I demanded. "Now!"

He didn't budge. I still couldn't bring myself to look at him. I kicked and punched him as hard as I could but to no avail. Whatever he was, a human stood no chance against him.

I gave up. Hypnotized by the water, I muttered, "Please just put me down. I don't want to be near you." *No, don't let me go. I want you. I need you.*

He didn't move and didn't speak. I was locked in the vise grip of a stone statue. My embarrassment and anger gave way to a broken heart, which crumbled to pieces again. A hundred little trolls jumped gleefully on the parts, breaking them into miniscule dust particles.

The angry tears turned into sorrowful, tormented waterworks, which surged in a torrent passed my palms covering my eyes.

CJ let me slide gently to the stream's bed. Still holding me close, his right hand caressed my cheek and lifted my chin to face him. My severed heart throbbed excruciatingly. Reluctantly, I glimpsed at his face which was taut with an anguish that echoed my own.

In that same instant, his soft, perfect lips pressed against mine, gently at first and then with the force of a tornado. He wrapped both his arms around me and pulled me up. His mouth parted my lips, unleashing a surge of passionate intensity. I didn't care if I'd regret this in the morning. Every millisecond of this ecstasy was worth the pain.

My dying heart thudded, fluttered and stopped. A swift rush of electricity jump started it, forcing it to beat with more energy and speed than ever before. Being inhuman, surely CJ would've noticed the effect he had on me, but he wasn't backing down and I wasn't about to abandon the moment I'd dreamt of since I met him.

With a mind of their own, my arms curled around his neck and squeezed him closer to me as if that was even possible. My left hand weaved through his silky, golden hair. I didn't remember falling asleep, but this had to be a dream.

CJ's energy pulsated like an electrical current through my body, surging and ebbing making me want more. His tenacity sparked a fire of emotions setting my body ablaze.

This wasn't an ordinary kiss. It was celestial. I was in the midst of an out of body experience reflecting on the moment. We were hungry, starving for the love we both craved, starving for the passion we missed, starving for each other. In this moment my soul felt more complete than in all of my years till now. Even Zach didn't compare to this. I felt guilty immediately for thinking this, but it was true.

It had been so long since I felt this kind of love. I missed it.

CJ's hands urgently pulled my waist closer against his chiseled body and I melted into his embrace, forgetting to breathe. After an eternal second, the needy force of the kiss slowed as our lips gradually parted.

Our hurried breaths only increased my desire to attack him again. His god-like face was filled with excitement, love, and frustration. I had nothing to be sorry about and yet I felt guilty for allowing myself to cave in the face of temptation.

Staring into his eyes, I didn't know what to say. My mind was still trying to catch up to what just happened while my soul was attempting to reenter my body.

"I can't resist you any longer, Angel. I know I'm the reason for your pain and I want to make it go away," he said softly, caressing the side of my face and hair.

"You're not the one causing me pain," I clarified. "Not being with you is causing me pain. I want to stay with you forever."

"You have no idea how much I've wanted to hear you say that," he whispered into my hair, kissing my head. "I've loved you since the beginning of time," he said quietly.

Despite my supernatural attachment to him, I still felt like eighteen-year-old Angel Kiss from Salem, Massachusetts—an utterly average, insane teenager who was just beginning life's journey. I needed to pinch myself. Was he for real?

"Please don't ever leave me," I whispered, snuggling into his amazing, ripped chest muscles.

His arms tensed. I met his pained gaze and read his thoughts… *less than three weeks.*

"I'd rather have this time with you than nothing at all, CJ."

His body relaxed ever so slightly as he drew me up to his lips again, kissing me as if he'd disappear that second. The stream rushed around his statuesque frame. We stared into each other, our eyes communicating silently: love, fear, loss, hope, lust.

Pulling me closer, he closed his eyes and leaned his forehead against mine.

"I never want to forget this moment." The whispered words caught in his throat.

I sighed in agreement and then, unfortunately, he loosened his grasp around my waist.

The ancient pain plaguing his thoughts incessantly returned to his gaze. He shook his head, battling his internal demons.

"What?" I asked cautiously, wishing our blissful, stolen moment could've lasted longer.

"I hate to bring us back to reality, but I want you to be prepared. Since we're speeding up your training, it's time to tell you about the good angels." He smiled the beautiful CJ smile which taunted my daydreams. "But let's go back to the house and change first."

"Why?"

His eyes dropped to my dripping wet outfit.

"Oh, I kind of forgot about that. Your kiss made me forget about… well, it made me forget about pretty much everything."

He grinned smugly. "Glad to hear I have that kind of effect on you, but I still think you should change so you don't get sick."

"Hold on. I think the picnic basket has something in it."

"I don't think there are enough sandwiches to place strategically around your body," he quipped sarcastically.

Cradling me in his arms, he waded to the embankment and set my drenched body down carefully.

"Ah ha!" I proclaimed triumphantly, pulling a red and white checkered cloth from the bottom of the basket.

CJ cocked one eyebrow at me. "And what exactly are you going to do with that?"

"Change."

"What?!"

"You said that you didn't want me to catch a cold from my wet clothes, so I'm going to put on something dry."

"It's a tablecloth," he reasoned.

"Yes, and it's dry," I argued. "This way I don't have to walk all the way back to the house."

"But it's a tablecloth."

"As I recall, you've seen in me in less," I said, thinking of the nearly translucent gossamer gown.

"Mmmm," he nodded in agreement, blushing.

"So hold this up for me and don't peek," I said, turning toward the stream and away from the house in case anyone happened to walk into the clearing to check on us.

CJ's expression shifted ever so slightly as if he was offended. "I respect you too much. I would *never* violate your privacy." His voice rang with the sincerity and honor of his words.

"Good looking and a gentleman too," I winked, making him blush to a deeper Bing cherry color.

Spreading his arms as far as they could reach, CJ held the tablecloth out to cover every inch of me just in case anyone was nearby. I slipped out of my now see-through wet white shirt, white bra, undies, and black Capri pants. I wound the tablecloth around my body four times and tucked the top end around my chest securing it in place.

"What do you think?" I asked, turning around so he could give me a good 360° appraisal.

"Hmmm," CJ thought momentarily, his smirk growing into a full-fledged lustful smile. "Looks good, but I prefer gossamer."

I hit him playfully before outright attacking him with an incredibly violent kiss that shocked even me.

He gently unwound my arms and put twelve inches between us.

"I can't help it," I apologized half-heartedly. "You're addicting."

Although from the looks of it, this time he was the one swooning.

"Angel, we do need to talk too."

"Sorry," I whispered, ashamed of my lack of self-control. Fiery heat rushed to my cheeks.

Grinning, he clearly preferred kissing to lessons too. "Are you sure you're comfortable?"

"Absolutely."

He sighed reluctantly, "If you insist."

"I do. So tell me about the good guys."

CJ took his rightful place beside me on the boulder. Leaning against his shoulder, I munched on a crunchy cucumber sandwich. He ran his fingers through my hair lost deeper in thought with each gentle swipe. It felt so good.

"Ahem," I fake coughed to get his attention.

"Sorry," he said unapologetically. "So the good guys' story isn't nearly as exciting as the bad guys."

He sighed deeply before jumping into the middle of the tale. "Once the fallen were banished to earth, the Creator needed to make sure that the people here were protected. He sent the warriors of God— the Bellatori Dei—an army of archangels, seraphim, and cherubim to keep an eye on things.

"The good guys hid for a while to watch the others. For a very long time, the fallen didn't do anything. The angels retreated. Of course, Aeterna Flamma was counting on this. They had an eternity to wait, so a few centuries were nothing in comparison.

"Have you ever heard of Shangri La?"

I shook my head.

"It's a city hidden in the highest mountain peaks of Tibet. It was actually created by the good angels as a sanctuary. They were so concealed that the fallen thought they returned home.

"As the bad angels began to wreak havoc on the humans again, the good ones attacked and drove them back to their underworld of sorts."

"How do the angels fight each other?" I asked curiously. "I mean, how can two immortals actually kill each other?"

"Remember Cynan's weapons?"

I nodded, shivering at the thought of the Aeterna Flamma angels' black daggers.

"An angel must be stabbed straight through the heart with its enemy's weapon."

I bit my lip at the disgusting imagery that popped into my imagination.

Seeing I was content for the time being, he continued, "After they were defeated, the remaining fallen came up with a plan for creating new soldiers."

"Vampires?" I asked quietly, trying not to picture them. In my thoughts I replaced them with obscure black blobs. Hopefully, they wouldn't be able to get into my head. I didn't want them getting any closer than they already were.

CJ nodded.

"The Bellatori knew they were plotting something. If they had any hope of winning, their army needed to be expanded too. They found the strongest humans and trained them to be protectors.

"Similar to foot soldiers, these people had amazing strength, speed, loyalty, and passion. Unfortunately, by the time the first battle happened, the vampires easily killed many of them, because they didn't know what to expect. Each time a battle is about to take place, these guardians are born with the sole purpose of protecting the Bellatori's interests. Thankfully, their experiences are like memories in their blood. Even with little training, they're virtually unstoppable now.

"The Concilius Patri, a small group of the most powerful Bellatori Dei angels, then focused on creating its own immortals. Of course unlike the other side, they refused to convert humans solely for fighting.

"Instead, they reached out to people who were equivalent to our Wiccan friends here. They wanted nothing more than to live in harmony with the natural world. These ancient humans never harmed others and rejected every bribe and trick from the evil angels. They willingly put themselves in harm's way if it meant they could protect others.

"The immortality they received from the Bellatori wasn't physical like the vampires. By teaching their traditions, each generation built on the strength of the one before. Their knowledge and purity lives forever.

"The expanded Bellatori fought together, but Aeterna Flamma's vampires still overpowered them. The evil angels didn't have to lift a finger since the good side couldn't get passed their bloodsuckers.

"Fortunately for us, some of the vampires realized they were being used. Shocking as it was—and still is—a few of them grew consciences by recalling their human memories. This breakaway group tracked the Bellatori Dei angels and begged to join."

"Wait a second," I interrupted. "Don't all vampires drink blood? How can the good vampires be 'good' if they're killing people? Isn't that a conflict of interest?"

Patient as ever, CJ replied, "Yes, that would violate the code, but they don't kill people."

"Then what do they eat?"

"Anything that has blood, minus people."

"Ewww!"

"What? You'd rather have them drink human blood?"

"No, it's just that that seems normal."

CJ shrugged. "That's the deal they made with the Bellatori. Besides, they only need blood to keep their strength. Since they're not alive, blood and food aren't necessary.

"Over the millennia the evil vampires infiltrated the Bellatori Dei as spies, but the Bellatori snuck into their side as well."

The vision from Manorbier flooded my thoughts. Could I have seen one of these rare encounters between Bellatori Dei and Aeterna Flamma double agents?

"Basically since the beginning of human existence on earth, the good and bad sides have been warring against each other."

"Is this really just about a power struggle?" I asked.

"It's more like the angels want revenge for their banishment and they'll do anything to get it."

"But they're ruining everything. Why won't God intervene?"

"Because everyone on earth has free will, which is the ultimate test for anyone's soul. Choosing to do the right thing is what matters most."

My heart sank into my feet leaving a sickening trail of guilt in its wake. I was CJ's temptress, Eve, beckoning him with the snake's apple. What had I done?

I sat up, feeling my face turn a sick shade of green.

"What's wrong?" he asked suddenly worried.

"I didn't choose the right thing. You warned me, but I didn't listen," I began, disgusted with myself. "And now it's too late."

"What are you talking about?" His eyes narrowed in concern.

Shaking my head, I stared into his innocent eyes. "If everything fails, if something happens to you, it'll be because of me. What's gonna happen now?"

"Free will," CJ spoke softly. "I chose my path and it belongs alongside yours." The anxiety-ridden frustration of his face made complete sense to me now. He was battling the same demons as me. Right or wrong, we both chose this outcome.

"But what about the battle? What about protecting me and the others?"

"I can't go back and undo what's been done."

"Is there no hope then?"

"There's always hope," he said emphatically, catching both of my hands and squeezing them tightly against his chest. "The choice I made today was for you and me. You are my life's sun—its energy—and without you," he dipped his head shyly before raising his gaze to meet mine, "I can't exist."

I threw my arms around his neck finally realizing the consequences of giving into temptation. "Will you be in trouble?"

"I don't know," he said solemnly.

"Why does this have to be an either/or choice? Why can't we be together *and* fight side-by-side?"

"Good question." His tightly pursed lips curled into an impish grin. "But since we're breaking rules today, this couldn't hurt…"

His gentle fingers caressed my cheek and guided my chin into his warm, tender kiss.

Epilogue

Wanting to keep our relationship a secret from everyone, I snuck downstairs after midnight and met CJ by the stream.

Set on the rocks around the reflective, sleeping brook, a hundred white votives illuminated the pitch-black forest. CJ waited for me, leaning against the big boulder. A loose white linen shirt hung open revealing his amazing, drool-worthy body. He literally glowed in the sparkling gold candlelight.

CJ extended his hand to me. "*My* angel," he whispered, encircling me with his strong, magnetic arms. The energy between us sparked an instant firestorm as he leaned in to kiss my eager, ecstatic lips. "I love you. No matter what happens, never forget that."

Feeling lightheaded from his inescapable embrace, I nodded loosely. His dreamy blue eyes were hypnotizing as my lips reached for his.

Springing from the candles encircling us, a flash of fire suddenly ignited a ten foot wall. CJ's arms squeezed me protectively. We spun around looking for an escape from the inferno.

Hundreds of red eyes pierced the hazy blaze.

A black cloaked figure stepped from the flames untouched.

"Surprise," the voice belonging to my tattoo artist hissed happily. Red, orange and yellow hues danced on the velvet sheen of his black shroud.

"Stay away from her!" CJ barked menacingly, hiding me behind him.

Crimson-neon eyes illuminated the empty black hole where the vampire's face should've been. The figure lifted a pale white finger at CJ. His body buckled instantly and fell limply to the ground.

My knees collapsed beside him and I wrapped my arms around him as if my pathetic weakness could somehow protect him. His eyes rolled to the back of his head, but he was still breathing.

I jumped to my feet seething in murderous anger and stalked toward the vampire with my palms outstretched. Sam taught me enough. If I touched him, I knew the burst of energy I could unleash right now would kill him.

Raising his pointed index finger, my feet abruptly felt like a ton of bricks rooted firmly in place. While I struggled futilely, another tall hooded figure entered the fire's perimeter. "Should I take him to the others?" he motioned beyond my burning prison.

I squinted, trying to focus on the movement in the distance.

My stomach dropped into my toes. Nauseous sweat broke out across my forehead and palms as the fire receded revealing an endless army of vampires that stretched into the distance. Dressed in black, their hungry, ravenous red eyes devoured me greedily.

"Stop!" Mark cried, distracting me from their eager stares. Edwin, Morgan, Cynan, Mark, Matt, and Sam struggled uselessly in the grasps of their captors.

It took me a second to realize that Mark's warning wasn't for the vampires. Matt broke free from their vise-like clutches and jumped through the flames, his black gape intent on rescuing me.

There was no warning, not even a millisecond of silence amid the crackling fire. One moment Matt was soaring through the air aiming for my captor's back and in the next, his neck was ripped to shreds with the vampire's mouth implanted firmly beneath the bloody remnants of his ear.

"Matt!" I shrieked.

"Angel," Matt whispered, his dying eyes meeting mine. "Believe…" was all he managed to mutter before the ruthless murderer's dagger-like fingernails ripped through his vocal chords.

I opened my mouth to scream only to find my voice had vanished. Mortified, my energy faded, blood drained, and heart sank. My Matt. Poor, innocent Matt. Of all the people I knew, he was the least deserving of this fate.

I glanced at the frozen, horrified expressions of my friends and protectors. They forfeited their futures and their lives because of me. My very existence was their death sentence.

The flames sizzled.

A handful of seconds had passed. The servant reached for CJ.

"No!" my blood curdling scream resonated infinitely.

The vampire in front of me lifted his hand, halting the other bloodsucker as he hovered over CJ. "I have another use for him."

Before I could say anything, CJ's unconscious body disappeared, leaving me at the mercy of evil incarnate.

"I've waited so long for this moment." His melodic words seemed oddly out of character. He reached for my face and slid a disgusting, ice-like finger along the length of my cheek. The trail burned like a branding iron had scraped me from my temple to chin.

"Whatever you want, I don't have it. I can't give it to you," I rushed to explain as terror squeezed my throat.

He scoffed. "You will in time," he insisted. "If you want them to live, that is."

"You'll never get away with this," I threatened. "The Bellatori will save us." However, as I said this, I wasn't entirely sure they would. If they didn't rescue my friends, how and why would they save me?

Waves of guilt dragged me into the painful sea of failure. Matt was dead. My friends were trapped. CJ was imprisoned because of me.

And, as if that wasn't enough, I seduced CJ in selfish desperation because I felt unloved and lonely. I distracted him from his sole duty. I deserved this fate.

Alone.

But CJ *was* out there somewhere and we were connected with an unbreakable bond. Now that we were together, I wasn't about to lose him. Somehow I'd find him. Somehow I'd save my friends. Even if I had to manipulate the vampires to get them to trust me, I wasn't going to let them get away with Matt's cold-blooded murder. And I definitely wouldn't let them use me to fulfill their plans.

On top of that, I couldn't allow my friends to sacrifice themselves for me when I wasn't worthy of their friendship and protection in the first place. Above all, Matt didn't die in vain.

This wasn't going to be our end.

In memory of Nagymama & Nagypapa Kohalmi,
Nagypapa Horvath, Keresztpapa,
Grandma Baker, Grandma Gyomber,
Mr. & Mrs. Thompson,
Robert K., Alexis S., Andrea B., & John P.

No matter who you are in life,
No matter where you are in death,
Once you have touched another's heart,
Your life and love lasts eternally.